William E. Henley, Charles Whibley

A Book of English Prose

William E. Henley, Charles Whibley

A Book of English Prose

ISBN/EAN: 9783337368579

Printed in Europe, USA, Canada, Australia, Japan

Cover: Foto ©Andreas Hilbeck / pixelio.de

More available books at **www.hansebooks.com**

A BOOK OF
ENGLISH PROSE

CHARACTER AND INCIDENT
1387-1649

SELECTED BY

WILLIAM   ERNEST   HENLEY

AND CHARLES WHIBLEY

METHUEN AND CO.

36 ESSEX STREET, W.C.

LONDON

1894

Edinburgh: T. and A. Constable, Printers to Her Majesty

PREFACE

It is not the object of this Book of Prose to illustrate the history of the English language, or to trace the development of the English sentence. Still less has it been our purpose to collect within two covers any such purple patches of diction as the taste and fashion of the past have marked out for admiration. Our bias is neither philological nor fantastical. Beyond the essential resolve to maintain a scrupulous standard of style, we have been guided in our selection by two definite principles: (1) that each passage should be complete in itself; (2) that each should relate a single incident or unfold a single character. It seemed that these principles, liberally interpreted, would at once give the book a concordant character, and ensure for every extract a separate and individual interest. Moreover, since our anthology is for young as well as for old, we have preferred before the prose of reflection and analysis the prose of adventure and romance— surely the best motives for sound and spirited English?

*In the matter of length, we have permitted ourselves the widest
latitude, and this for an obvious reason. The limits of a poem
are generally set by its maker. A passage of prose cannot
always be disengaged, and even where disengagement is possible,
you must follow the episode to its legitimate conclusion. Also,
if some writers are absent whose presence was anticipated, it
is not that they have been overlooked, but that they were found
inadmissable. On the other hand, many are present whose
names are not familiar to the readers of anthologies; and it is
believed that the consideration of these will strengthen an opinion
that the level of prose our distant fathers held is far higher
than our own.*

*It remains to add that the passages are quoted verbally;
that the spelling has been modernised or Anglicised; and that
the very few places where editing was found necessary are
distinguished by dots of omission.*

W. E. H.

C. W.

CONTENTS

vii

ENGLISH PROSE
1387-1649

ENGLISH PROSE

A CHARACTER OF IRISHMEN

SOLINUS saith that men of this land be strange of nation, Trevisa 1387
houseless, and great fighters, and account right and
wrong all for one, and be single of clothing, scarce of meat,
cruel of heart, and angry of speech, and drink first blood of
dead men that be slain, and then wash their face therewith;
and hold them appeased with flesh and fruit instead of
meat, and with milk instead of drink, and they use much
plays and idleness and hunting, and travail full little. In
their childhood they be hard nourished and hard fed, and they
be unseemly of manners and of clothing, and have breeches
and hosen all one of wool, and straight hoods that stretch
a cubit over the shoulders behind, and black faldings instead of
mantles and cloaks. Also saddles, boots, and spurs they use
none when they ride; but they drive their horses with a
chambered yard[1] in the over end, instead of barnacles and of
britels of reest[2]; and they use bridles that let not their horses
of their meat. They fight unarmed, naked in body; nevertheless with two darts and spears and with broad sparths.[3]
They fight with one hand, and when other weapons fail, they
have good pebble stones ready at hand. These men forsake
tilling of land and keep pasture for beasts: they use
long beards and long locks hanging down behind their nolls.
They use no craft of flax and wool, of metal, neither of merchandise; but give them all to idleness and to sloth, and
count rest for liking and freedom for riches. And though
Scotland, the daughter of Ireland, use harp, timbre, and

---

[1] Bent rod.   [2] Bits of arrest.   [3] Axes.

Trevisa
1387
tabor (and Wales uses harp and pipe and tabor), nevertheless Irishmen be cunning in two manner of instruments
of music, in the harp and timbre that is armed with wire
and with strings of brass. In the which instruments they
play hastily and swiftly; they make well merry harmony and
melody with well thick tunes, warbles, and notes; and they
begin from B moll, and play privily under the deep sound of
the great strings, and turn again into the same, so that the
greatest part of the craft hide the craft; as it would seem
as though the craft so hidden should be ashamed, an it
were i-take. These men be of evil manners and of living;
they pay no tithings, they wed lawfully no wives, they
spare not their allies,[1] but the brother weds his brother's
wife. They be busy for to betray their neighbours and
others. They bear sparths in their hands instead of staves,
and fight therewith against them that trust to them best.
The men be variable and unsteadfast, treacherous and guileful.
Who that deals with them needs more to beware of guile than
of craft, of peace than of burning brands, of honey than of gall,
of malice than of knighthood. They have such manners that
they be not strong in war and battle, neither true in peace.
They become gossips to them that they would falsely betray in
gosibrede [2] and holy kindred; each drinketh the other's blood
when it is shed. They love somdel [3] their nurses and their
playing feres,[4] which that suck the same milk that they suck
while they be children. And they pursue their brethren, their
cousins, and their other kin; and despise their kin, while they
be alive, and wreak their death, an they be slain. Among
them long usage and evil custom hath so long endured, that it
hath made the mastery, and turneth among themselves treason
into kynd [5] so far forth, that as they be traitors by kynd, so
aliens and men of strange lands that wone long among them
draw after the manner of their company, and scape well

[1] Relations.   [2] Fellowship.   [3] Sometimes.
[4] Companions.   [5] Nature.

unnethe,[1] but they be besmutted with the shrewdness and become traitors also. . . . There be many men in this land wonderful and evil shaped in limbs and in body. For in their limbs lacketh the benefice of kynd, so that nowhere be none better shaped, than they that be here well shaped, and nowhere none worse shaped, than they that be here evil shaped. And skilfully kynd, hurt and defouled by wickedness of living, bringeth forth such foul grooms and evil shaped of them that with unlawful wedding, with foul manners and evil living, so wickedly defoul kynd. In this land and in Wales, old wives and women were wont, and be yet (as me pleyneth) oft for to shape themselves in likeness to hares, for to milk their neighbour's kine, and so steal their milk, and oft greyhounds run after them and pursue them, and ween that they be hares. Also some by craft of necromancy make fat swine (that be red of colour) and none other, and sell them in cheping and in fairs; but anon as these swine pass any water they turn again into their own kynd, where it be straw, hay, grass, other turves. But these swine may not be kept by no manner of craft for to dure in likeness of swine over three days. Among these wonders and others take heed that in the uttermost ends of the world full oft new marvels and wonders, as though kynd played with larger leave privily and far in the ends than openly and nigh in the middle. Therefore in this island be many grisly marvels and wonders.

Trevisa 1387

John Trevisa.

THE COURT OF THE GREAT CHAN

NOW shall I tell you the governance of the Court of the Great Chan, when he maketh solemn feasts, which is principally four times in the year. The first feast is of his

Maunde- ville 1410

[1] Hardly.

Maunde-
ville
1410

birth; the second is of his presentation in their temple, such
as they clepe here Moseache, where they make a manner
of circumcision; and the other two feasts are of his idols.
The first feast of the idol is, when he is first put into their
temple and throned.　The other feast is, when the idol
beginneth first to speak or work miracles.　More there are
not of solemn feasts, but if he marry any of his children.
Now understand, that at each of these feasts, he hath great
multitude of people, well ordained and well arrayed, by
thousands by hundreds, and by tens.　And every man
knoweth well what service he shall do; and every man giveth
so good heed and so good attendance to his service, that no
man findeth any default.

And there be first ordained four thousand Barons, mighty
and rich, for to govern and make ordinance for the feast, and
for to serve the Emperor.　And these solemn feasts are made
without, in halls and tents made of cloths of gold and of
tartaries,[1] full nobly.　And all the Barons have crowns of
gold upon their heads, full noble and rich, full of precious
stones and great pearls orient.　And they are all clothed in
clothes of gold, or of tartaries, or of camokas,[2] so richly and
perfectly, that no man in the world can amend it, nor better
devise it.　And all these robes are orfrayed[3] all about, and
dubbed full of precious stones and of great orient pearls, full
richly.　And they may well do so, for cloths of gold and of
silk are cheaper there by much than are cloths of wool.

And these four thousand barons are divided in four companies : and every thousand is clothed in cloths all of one
colour, and so well arrayed and so richly, that it is marvel
to behold.　The first thousand, that is of Dukes, of Earls,
of Marquises, and of Admirals, all clothed in cloths of gold,
with tissues of green silk, and bordered with gold, full of
precious stones, in manner as I have said before.　The

[1] Eastern fabrics.　　　　　　　　　[2] A silk fabric.
[3] Embroidered with gold.

second thousand is all in cloths diapered of red silk, all
wrought with gold, and the orfrayes set full of great pearls
and precious stones, full nobly wrought. The third thousand
is clothed in cloths of silk, of purple, or of Inde. And the
fourth thousand is in clothes of yellow. And all their
clothes are so nobly and richly wrought with gold and
precious stones and rich pearls, that if a man of this country
had but only one of their robes, he might well say that he
should never be poor. For the gold and the precious stones,
and the great orient pearls are of greater value on this half
the sea than they are beyond the sea in those countries.

And when they are thus apparelled, they go two and two
together, full ordinately, before the Emperor, without speech
of any word, save only inclining to him. And every one of them
beareth a tablet of jasper, or of ivory, or of crystal; and the
minstrels go before them, sounding their instruments of
divers melody. And when the first thousand is thus passed,
and hath made its muster, it withdraws it on that one side ;
and then entereth that other second thousand, and doth right
so, in the same manner of array and countenance as did the
first; and after the third, and then the fourth, and none of
them saith not one word.

And at one side of the Emperor's table sit many Philosophers, who are proved for wise men in many divers sciences ;
as of astronomy, necromancy, geomancy, pyromancy, hydro-
mancy, of augury, and of many other sciences. And every
one of them hath before him astrolabes of gold, some spheres,
some the brain-pan of a dead man, some vessels of gold full
of gravel or sand, some vessels of gold full of coals burning,
some vessels of gold full of water and of wine and of oil, and
some horologes of gold, made full nobly and richly wrought,
and many other manner of instruments after their sciences.
And at certain hours, when they think time, they say to
certain Officers who stand before them, ordained for the time
to fulfil their commandments : 'Make peace.' And then say

the Officers : 'Now peace, listen.' And after that, saitn another
of the Philosophers: ' Every man do reverence, and incline
to the Emperor, who is God's son and Sovereign Lord of all
the World ; for now is time.' And then every man boweth
his head towards the earth. And then commandeth the same
Philosopher again : ' Stand up.' And they do so. And at
another hour saith another Philosopher: ' Put your little finger
in your ears.' And anon they do so. And at another hour
saith another Philosopher: ' Put your hand before your mouth.'
And anon they do so. And at another hour saith another
Philosopher : ' Put your hand upon your head.' And after
that he biddeth them to do their hand away ; and they do so.

And so, from hour to hour, they command certain things.
And they say that those things have divers significations.
And I asked them privily what those things betokened. And
one of the Masters told me that the bowing of the head at
that hour betokened this, that all those that bowed their
heads should evermore after be obeissant and true to the
Emperor, and never for gifts, nor for promise in no kind be
false nor traitor unto him for good nor evil. And the
putting of the little finger in the ear betokeneth, as they say,
that none of them shall not hear spoken no contrarious
thing to the Emperor, but that he shall tell it anon to his
council, or discover it to some men that will make relation
to the Emperor, though he were his father or brother or son.
And so forth of all other things that are done by the Philosophers, they told me the causes of many divers things. And
trust right well in certain that no man doth no thing to the
Emperor that belongeth to him, neither clothing, nor bread,
nor wine, nor bath, nor other thing that belongeth to him,
but at certain hours, as his Philosophers will devise.

And if there fall war in any side to the Emperor, anon
the Philosophers come and say their advice after their cal-
culations, and counsel the Emperor of their advice by their
sciences; so that the Emperor doth nothing without their

counsel. And when the Philosophers have done and per- Maunde-
formed their commandments, then the Minstrels begin to ville
do their minstrelsy, every one on their instruments, each 1410
after the other, with all the melody that they can devise.
And when they have done a good while, one of the
Officers of the Emperor goeth up on a high stage, wrought
full curiously, and crieth and saith with a loud voice : ' Make
peace.' And then every man is still. And then, anon after,
all the Lords that are of the Emperor's lineage, nobly arrayed
in rich clothes of gold, and royally apparelled on white steeds,
as many as may well sue[1] him at that time, are ready to
make their presents to the Emperor. And then saith the
steward of the court to the Lords, by name, ' N. of N.,' and
nameth first the most noble and the worthiest by name, and
saith : ' Be ye ready with such a number of white horses for to
serve the Emperor your Sovereign Lord.' And, to another
lord, he saith : ' N. of N., be ye ready with such a number to
serve your Sovereign Lord.' And to another, right so. And
to all the Lords of the Emperor's lineage, one after the other,
as they are of estate.

And when they are all cleped, they enter each after the
other, and present the white horses to the Emperor, and
then go their way. And then after, all the other Barons,
every one of them, give him presents, or jewels, or some
other thing, after that they are of estate. And then, after
them, all the Prelates of their law, and religious men and
others ; and every man giveth him something. And when all
men have thus presented the Emperor, the greatest of dignity
of the Prelates giveth him a blessing, saying an orison of their
law. And then begin the Minstrels to make their minstrelsy
on divers instruments, with all the melody that they can
devise.

And when they have done their craft, then they bring
before the Emperor lions, leopards, and other divers beasts,

---

[1] Follow.

Maunde-
ville
1410

and eagles, and vultures, and other divers fowls, and fishes, and serpents, for to do him reverence. And then come jugglers and enchanters that do many marvels; for they make to come in the air the sun and the moon, beseeming, to every man's sight. And after they make the night so dark that no man may see no thing. And after they make the day to come again, fair and pleasant, with bright sun, to every man's sight. And then they bring in dances of the fairest damsels of the world, and richest arrayed.

And after they make to come in other damsels bringing cups of gold, full of milk of divers beasts, and give drink to Lords and to Ladies. And then they make knights to joust in arms full lustily; and they run together a great random and frush[1] together full fiercely; and they break their spears so rudely that the tronchouns[2] fly in sprotes[3] and pieces all about the hall. And then they make to come in hunting, for the hart and for the boar, with hounds running with open mouth. And many other things they do by craft of their enchantments, that it is marvel for to see. And such plays of disport they make, until the taking up of the boards.

This Great Chan hath full great people for to serve him, as I have told you before. For he hath of Minstrels the number of thirteen cumants,[4] but they abide not always with him. For all the Minstrels that come before him, of what nation they be of, they be witholden with him, as of his household, and entered in his books, as for his own men. And after that, where that ever they go, evermore they claim for Minstrels of the Great Chan; and, under that title, all Kings and Lords cherish them the more with gifts and all things. And therefore he hath so great multitude of them. And he hath of certain men, as though they were yeomen, that keep birds, as ostriches, gerfaucons, sparrow-hawks, falcons,

[1] Crash.   [2] Staves.   [3] Splinters.
[4] Ten-thousands.

gentles, lanyers,[1] sacres,[2] sacrettes,[3] popinjays well speaking, and birds singing. And also of wild beasts, as of elephants, tame and other, baboons, apes, marmozets, and other divers beasts; the mountance[4] of fifteen cumants of Yeomen.

Maunde-ville 1410

And of Physicians Christian he hath two hundred. And of Leeches that are Christians he hath two hundred and ten. And of Leeches and Physicians that are Saracens, twenty; but he trusteth more in the Christian Leeches than in the Saracens. And his other common household is without number; and they all have all necessaries and all that they need of the Emperor's court. And he has in his court many Barons, as servitors, that are Christians and converted to good faith by the preaching of religious Christian men that dwell with him, but there be many more that will not have it known that they are Christians.

This Emperor may dispend as much as he will, without estimation. For he dispendeth not nor maketh any money but of leather imprinted, or of paper. And of that money is some of greater price and some of less price, after the diversity of his statutes. And when that money has run so long that it beginneth to waste, then men bear it to the Emperor's treasury, and then they take new money for the old. And that money goeth throughout all the country and throughout all his provinces. For there, and beyond them, they make no money neither of gold nor of silver. And therefore, he may dispend enough, and outrageously. And of gold and silver that men bear in his country, he maketh ceilings, pillars and pavements in his palace, and other divers things that he liketh. This Emperor hath in his chamber, in one of the pillars of gold, a ruby and a carbuncle of half a foot long, which in the night giveth so great clearness and shining, that it is as light as day. And he hath many other precious stones, and many other rubies and carbuncles, but those are the greatest and the most precious.

[1] Hawks. [2] A falcon (female). [3] A falcon (male). [4] Amount.

Maunde-
ville
1410

This Emperor dwelleth in summer in a city that is toward the north, that is called Saduz, and there is cold enough. And in winter he dwelleth in a city that is called Camaaleche, and that is a hot country. But the country where he dwelleth in most commonly is in Gaydo, or in Jong, that is a good country and a temperate, after that the country is there; but to men of this country, it were passing hot. And when this Emperor will ride from one country to another, he ordaineth four hosts of his folk, of the which the first host goeth before him a day's journey. For that host shall be lodged the night where the emperor shall lie upon the morrow. And there shall every man have all manner of victuals and necessaries that are needful at the Emperor's costages.

And in this first host is the number of people fifty cumants; what of horse, what of foot, of the which every cumant amounteth to ten thousand, as I have told you before. And another host goeth on the right side of the Emperor, nigh half a journey from him. And another goeth on the left side of him in the same wise. And in every host is as much multitude of people as in the first host. And then after cometh the fourth host, that is much more than any of the other, and that goeth behind him, the mountance of a bow's draught. And every host hath its day's journey ordained in certain places, where they shall be lodged at night, and there they shall have all that they need. And if it befall that one of the host die, anon they put another in his place, so that the number shall ever be whole.

And you shall understand that the Emperor, in his proper person, rideth not as other great lords do beyond, but if he list to go privily with few men, for to be unknown. And else he rideth in a chariot with four wheels, upon the which is made a fair chamber; and it is made of a certain wood that comes out of Paradise Terrestrial, which they call *lignum aloes*, that the floods of Paradise bring out at diverse seasons, as I have told you here before. And this chamber is full

well smelling, because of the wood that it is made of. And Maunde-
all this chamber is covered within of plates of fine gold, ville
dubbed with precious stones and great pearls. And four 1410
elephants and four great destrercs,[1] all white and covered with
rich covertures, leading the chariot. And four, or five, or six
of the greatest Lords ride about this chariot, full richly arrayed
and full nobly, so that no man shall nigh the chariot but only
those lords, but if the Emperor call any man to him that he
lists to speak withal. And above the chamber of this chariot
the Emperor sitteth in, are set upon a perch four, five, or six
gerfaucons, to that intent, that when the Emperor seeth any
wild fowl, he may take it at his own list, and have the disport
and the play of the flight, first with one and after with
another ; and so he taketh his sport passing by the country.

And no man rideth before him of his company, but all after
him. And no man dare not come nigh the chariot by a bow-
draught, but those Lords only that are about him ; and all
the host come fairly after him, in great multitude. And also
such another chariot, with such hosts, ordained and arrayed,
go with the Empress upon another side, each by itself, with
four hosts, right as the Emperor did, but not with so great
multitude of people. And his eldest son goeth by another
way in another chariot, in the same manner. So that there
is between them so great multitude of folk, that it is marvel to tell it. And no man should trow the number, but
he had seen it. And sometimes it happens that when he
will not go far, and that it liketh him to have the Empress and
his children with him, then they go all together ; and here
folk are meddled [2] in one company, and divided in four parts
only.

And you shall understand that the empire of this Great
Chan is divided into twelve provinces ; and every province
hath more than two thousand cities, and towns without
number. This country is full great. For it hath twelve

1 Horses.   2 Mixed.

Maunde-
ville
1410 principal Kings in twelve provinces; and each of those Kings hath many Kings under him; and all they are obeissant to the Great Chan. And his land and his lordship dureth so far that a man may not go from ahead, neither by sea nor land, the space of seven years. And through the deserts of his lordship, there, as men may find no towns, there are inns ordained at every journey, to receive both man and horse, in the which they shall find plenty of victuals and of all things that they need for to go by the country.

And there is a marvellous custom in that country (but is profitable), that if there happen any contrarious thing that should be prejudice or grievance to the Emperor, in any kind, anon the Emperor hath tidings thereof and full knowledge in a day, though it be three or four journeys from him or more. For his ambassadors take their dromedaries, or their horses, and they prick in all that ever they may toward one of the inns; and when they come there, anon they blow a horn, and anon they of the inn know well enough that there are tidings to warn the Emperor of some rebellion against him. And then anon they make other men ready, in all haste that they may, to bear letters, and prick in all that ever they may, till they come to the other inns with their letters; and then they make fresh men ready, to prick forth with the letters towards the Emperor, while the last bringer resteth him, and baiteth his dromedary or his horse; and so from inn to inn, till it come to the Emperor. And thus anon he hath hasty tidings of anything that beareth charge by his couriers, that run so hastily throughout all the country.

And, also, when the Emperor sendeth his couriers hastily throughout his land, each of them hath a large thong full of small bells; and when they nigh near the inns of other couriers that are also ordained by the journeys, they ring their bells; and anon the other couriers make them ready, and run their way unto another inn; and thus runneth one to another, full speedily and swiftly, till the Emperor's intent be

served, in all haste.   And these couriers are called *Chydydo*,
Also when the Emperor goeth from one country to another,
as I have told you here before, and he passeth through cities
and towns, every man makes a fire before his door, and putteth
therein powder of good gums, that are sweet smelling, for to
make good savour to the Emperor.   And all the people kneel
down against him, and do him great reverence.   And there,
where religious Christian men dwell, as they do in many cities
in the land, they go before him with procession, with cross
and holy water ; and they sing, *Veni Creator, Spiritus*, with a
high voice, and go towards him.   And when he heareth them,
he commandeth to his lords to ride beside him, that the
religious men may come to him.

And when they are nigh him with the cross, then
he doth adown his galiot, which sitteth upon his head in
the manner of a chaplet, that is made of gold, and precious
stones, and great pearls.   And it is so rich that men
prize it to the value of a realm, in that country.   And then
he kneeleth to the cross.   And then the Prelate of the
religious men saith before him certain orisons, and giveth
him a blessing with the cross; and he inclineth to the blessing
full devoutly.   And then the Prelate giveth him some manner
of fruit, to the number of nine, in a platter of silver, with pears
or apples or other manner fruit.   And he taketh one; and then
men give to the other lords that are about him.   For the
custom is such that no stranger shall come before him but if
he give him some manner thing, after the old law, that
says, *Nemo accedat in conspectu meo vacuus*.   And then the
Emperor saith to the religious men that they withdraw them
again, that they be not hurt nor harmed of the great multitude of horse that come behind him.   And also in the same
manner do the monks that dwell there to the Empresses that
pass by them, and to his eldest son ; and to every one of
them they present fruit.

Maunde-
ville
1410

And you shall understand that the people that he hath so many hosts of about him, and about his wives and his sons, they dwell not continually with him, but always, when it liketh him, they are sent for ; and after, when they have done, they return to their own households, save only those that are dwelling with him in household for to serve him, and his wives, and sons for to govern his household. And albeit, that the others are departed from him after they have performed their service, yet there abideth continually with him in court fifty thousand men at horse, and twenty thousand men a foot, without Minstrels and those that keep wild beasts and diverse birds, of the which I have told you the number before. Under the firmament, is not so great a lord, nor so mighty, nor so rich, as the Great Chan ; neither Prester John, that is Emperor of the High Inde, nor the Sultan of Babylon, nor the Emperor of Persia.

All these are not in comparison to the Great Chan, neither of might, nor of nobleness, nor of royalty, nor of riches ; for in all these he passeth all earthly princes. Wherefore it is great harm that he believeth not faithfully in God. And, nevertheless, he will gladly hear speak of God ; and he suffereth well that Christian men dwell in his lordship, and that men of his faith be made Christian men, if they will, throughout all his country. For he defendeth no man to hold any law other than he liketh.

Sir John Maundeville.

THE BATTLE OF ST. ALBANS

Paston
1455

BE it known and had in mind that the 21st day of May the 33rd year of the reign of King Henry the Sixth, our sovereign Lord King took his journey from Westminster toward St. Albans, and rested at Watford all night ; and on the morrow betimes he came to St. Albans, and with him on

his party assembled under his banner the Duke of Buckingham, the Duke of Somerset, the Earl of Penbroke, the
Earl of Northumberland, the Earl of Devonshire, the Earl of
Stafford, the Earl of Dorset, the Earl of Wiltshire, the Lord
Clifford, the Lord Dudley, the Lord Burnys, the Lord Rose,
with other divers knights, squires, and other gentlemen
and yeomen to the number of 2000 and more. And upon
the 22d day of the said month above rehearsed assembled
the Duke of York, and with him came in company the Earl
of Salisbury, the Earl of Warwick, with divers knights and
squires unto their party into the field, called the Key Field,
beside St. Albans. Furthermore, our said sovereign Lord the
King, hearing and knowing of the said Duke's coming with
other Lords aforesaid, pitcheth his banner at the place called
Boslaw in St. Petrus Street, which place was called aforetime
past Sandeford, and commandeth the ward and barriers to be
kept in strong wise; for the said Duke of York abiding in
the field aforesaid from seven of the clock in the morn till it
was almost ten, without any stroke smitten on either party.

The said Duke sent to the King our sovereign Lord,
by the advice of his council, praying and beseeching him
to take him as his true man and humble subject; and
to consider and to tender at the reverence of Almighty
God, and in way of charity the true intent of his coming
—to be good and gracious sovereign Lord to his liegemen, which, with all their power and might, will be
ready at all times to live and die with him in his right.
And to what thing it should like his Majesty Royal to
command him, if it be his worship, keeping right of the
Crown and welfare of the land: 'Moreover, gracious Lord,
please it your Majesty Royal of your great goodness and
righteousness to incline your will to hear and feel the
righteous part of us your subjects and liegemen; first,
praying and beseeching to our Lord Jesus of His high and
mighty power to give unto you virtue and prudence, and

that through the mediation of the glorious martyr St. Alban
to give you very knowledge to know the intent of our
assembling at this time; for God that is in heaven knoweth
that our intent is rightful and true. And therefore we pray
unto Almighty Lord Jesus these words—*Domine sis clipeus
defensionis nostrae.* Wherefore, gracious Lord, please it your
high Majesty to deliver such as we will accuse, and they
to have like, as they have deserved and done, and ye to be
honourabled and worshipped as most rightful King and our
governor. For and we shall now at this time be promised,
as afore this time is not unknown, of promise broken which
full faith fully hath been promised, and thereupon great
oaths made, we will not now cease for none such promise,
surety, nor other, till we have him which have deserved
death, or else we to die therefore.'

And to that answered the King our sovereign Lord, and
said : ' I, King Henry, charge and command that no manner
person, of what degree, or state, or condition that ever he
be, abide not, but void the field, and not be so hardy to
make any resistance against me in mine own realm ; for I
shall know what traitor dare be so bold to raise a people in
mine own land, wherethrough I am in great disease and
heaviness. And by the faith that I owe to St. Edward and
to the Crown of England, I shall destroy them every mother
son, and they be hanged, and drawn, and quartered, that
may be taken afterward, of them to have ensample to all such
traitors to beware to make any such rising of people within
my land, and so traitorly to abide her King and governor.
And, for a conclusion, rather than they shall have any Lord
here with me at this time, I shall this day, for her sake. and
in this quarrel myself live or die.'

Which answer came to the Duke of York, the which
Duke, by the advice of the Lords of his Council, said unto
him these words : ' The King our sovereign Lord will not be
reformed at our beseeching nor prayer, nor will not under-

stand the intent that we be come hither and assembled for and gathered at this time; but only is full purpose, and there none other way but that he will with all his power pursue us, and if we be taken, to give us a shameful death, losing our liveload[1] and goods, and our hairs shamed for ever. And therefore, sith it will be none otherwise but that we shall utterly die, better it is for us to die in the field than cowardly to be put to a great rebuke and a shameful death ; moreover, considering in what peril England stands in at this hour, therefore every man help to help power for the right thereof, to redress the mischief that now reigneth, and to quit us like men in this quarrel; praying to that Lord that is King of Glory, that reigneth in the kingdom celestial, to keep us and save us this day in our right, and through the help of His holy grace we may be made strong to withstand the great abominable and cruel malice of them that purpose fully to destroy us with shameful death. We therefore, Lord, pray to Thee to be our comfort and defender, saying the words aforesaid, *Domine sis clipeus defensionis nostrae.*'

And when this was said, the said Duke of York, and the said Earl of Salisbury, and the Earl of Warwick, between eleven and twelve of the clock at noon, they broke into the town in three divers places and several places of the foresaid street. The King being then in the place of Edmond Westley, hunderdere[2] of the said town of St. Albans, commandeth to slay all manner men of lords, knights, and squires, and yeomen that might be taken of the foresaid Duke's of York. This done, the foresaid Lord Clifford kept strongly the barriers that the said Duke of York might not in any wise, with all the power that he had, enter nor break into the town. The Earl of Warwick, knowing thereof, took and gathered his men together, and furiously brake in by the

---

[1] Lands from which an income was derived.
[2] Headman of an hundred.

Paston   garden sides between the sign of the Key and the sign of
1455   the Chequer in Holwell Street; and anon as they were
within the town, suddenly they blew up trumpets, and set
a cry with a shout and a great voice, 'A Warwick! A
Warwick! A Warwick!' and into that time the Duke of York
might never have entry into the town; and they with
strong hand kept it, and mightily fought together, and anon,
forthwith after the breaking in, they set on them manfully.
And as of Lords of name were slain the Lord Clifford, the
Duke of Somerset, the Earl of Northumberland, Sir Bertram
Entuwysselle, Knight; and of men of court, William Zouch,
John Batryaux, Raaff of Bapthorp, and his son, William
Corbyn, squires; William Cotton, receiver of the Duchy of
Lancaster; Gilbert Starbrok, squire; Malmer Pagentoun,
William Botclore, yeomen; Roger Mercroft, the King's
messenger; Halyn, the King's porter; Raufe Wyllerby; and
25 more, which their names be not yet known. And of
them that be slain be buried in St. Albans 48. And
at this same time were hurt Lords of name—the King, our
sovereign Lord, in the neck with an arrow; the Duke of
Buckingham, with an arrow in the visage; the Lord of
Stafford in the hand, with an arrow; the Lord of Dorset,
sore hurt that he might not go, but he was carried home in
a cart; and Wenlok, knight, in likewise in a cart sore hurt;
and other divers knights and squires sore hurt. The Earl
of Wiltshire, Thorp, and many others fled, and left their
harness behind them cowardly, and the substance of the
King's party were despoiled of horse and harness. This
done, the said Lords, that is to wot, the Duke of York, the
Earl of Salisbury, the Earl of Warwick, came to the King,
our sovereign Lord, and on their knees besought him of
grace and forgiveness of that they had done in his presence,
and besought him of his highness to take them as his true
liegemen, saying that they never intended hurt to his own
person, and therefore the King our sovereign Lord took

them to grace, and so desired them to cease their people, Paston
and that there should no more harm be done; and they 1455
obeyed his commandment, and let make a cry on the King's
name that all manner of people should cease and not so
hardy to strike any stroke more after the proclamation of
the cry; and so ceased the said battle, *Deo gratias.*

And on the morrow the King and the said Duke, with
other certain Lords, came in to the Bishop's of London, and
there kept residence with joy and solemnity, concluding to
hold the Parliament at London, the 9th day of July next
coming.

The Paston Letters.

THE DOLOROUS SHIRT

WHEN Hercules had read this letter, he understood Caxton
well what it contained, and was smitten with re- 1474
morse of conscience. By this remorse he understood that
virtue was fouled in him; he was then all pensive, and so
much prived from pleasance that none durst come to him in
a great while and space, save only they that brought to him
meat and drink; neither Yole durst not go to him. Lycas
that had brought this letter was there awaiting and attending the answer long; no man could know whereof proceeded
the solitude of Hercules, nor the cause why he withdrew
him from the people. In the end, when Hercules had been
long pensive, and had thought upon all his affairs, and that
he had to do for to withdraw him and to eslonge[1] him from
Yole, he departed from his chamber on a day, saying that he
would go and make sacrifice to the god Apollo upon the
mount named Oethea, and commanded and defended upon
pain of death that no man should follow him, reserved
Philotes. Of adventure as he issued out of his palace,

---

[1] Estrange.

accompanied only of Philotes, for to go upon the mount, he
met Lycas. Lycas made to him reverence and demanded
him if it pleased him anything to send to Deyanira.
Hercules answered to Lycas that he would go make his
sacrifice to the god Apollo, and that at his return and coming again he would go unto her or else he would send
unto her.

With this word Hercules and Philotes passed forth and
went on their pilgrimage, and Lycas returned unto Deyanira
and told to her the joyous tidings that he had received of
Hercules, and also what life that Hercules had led since the
day and the hour that he had presented to him her letter.
Deyanira, all comforted of these good tidings, went into her
chamber and thanked the gods and fortune. Anon, after
she began to think on her estate, and thus thinking she
remembered her on the poison that Nessus had given her in
the article of his death, and how she had shut it in one of her
coffers, and forthwith incontinent she opened the coffer and
took the cursed poison and one of the shirts of Hercules,
and as she that imagined by the virtue of the poison to draw
again to her the love of Hercules, like as Nessus had said
unto her, she made the shirt to be boiled with the poison,
and gave the charge thereof to one of her women. When
the shirt was boiled enough the woman took off the vessel
and set it to cool ; after she took out the shirt appertly [1] and
wrung it, but she could not so soon have wrung it but the
fire sprang in her hands so anguishously, that as she cast it
upon a perch to dry she fell down dead.

In process of time Deyanira desiring to have the shirt,
and seeing that the woman that had charge thereof brought
it not, she went into the chamber where the shirt had been
boiled and found the woman dead, whereof she had great
marvel. Nevertheless, she passed the death lightly, and by
one of her damoiselles she made take the shirt that hung on

[1] Briskly.

the perch and was dry, and commanded her that she should
fold it and wind it in a kerchief. At the commandment of
Deyanira the damoiselle folded and enveloped the shirt, but
so doing she was served of the poison in such wise that she
lost her speech and died anon after. This notwithstanding,
Deyanira that thought on nothing but for to come to her
intention, took the shirt and delivered it to Lycas and
charged him that he should bear it to Hercules, praying him
in her name that he would wear it. Lycas, that was ready
to accomplish the will of his mistress, took the charge of the
dolorous shirt and departed from thence and went unto the
mountain whereas Hercules was, and there he found him in
a forest whereas was the temple of Diana. Hercules had no
man with him but Philotes, which made ready for him a
great fire for to sacrifice an hart that Hercules had taken
running at a course. Lycas then finding Hercules in the
temple, he kneeled down low to him and said : ‘ Sire, here is
a shirt that your ancille [1] and servant Deyanira sendeth unto
you, she recommendeth her humbly unto your good grace,
and prayeth you that ye will receive this present in gree [2] as
from your wife.’ Hercules was joyous of these words, and
anon unclothed him for to do on this cursed shirt, saying
that verily she was his wife and that he would for her sake
wear this shirt. In doing on this shirt, he felt a right great
dolour and pain in his body ; this notwithstanding, he did
on his other clothes above as he that thought none evil.
When he was clothed and the shirt was chauffed, [3] his pain
and sorrow grew more and more. Then he began to think,
and knew anon that his malady came off his shirt ; and feeling the pricking of the venom, without long tarrying he took
off his robe, and supposed to have taken off his shirt from his
back, and to have rent it and diffete it. [4] But he was not strong
enough for to do so, for the shirt held so sore and cleaved so
fast and terribly to his flesh, and was so fasted to his skin

[1] Handmaiden.   [2] Grace.   [3] Warmed.   [4] Undone.

by the vigour of the aspre poison, in such wise that he tare out his flesh and bare away certain pieces thereof when he would have taken off his shirt.

Hercules knew then that he was hurt and wounded to the death; the death began to fight against him. He began to resist by drawing off his shirt from his body by pieces of his flesh and of his blood. All might not avail; he all to-rent and dischaired[1] his back, his thighs, his body unto his entrails and guts, his arms, his shoulders unto the bones; his dolour and pain grew and enlarged to the utterance. Thus as he returned by the force of his great dolorous pain, he beheld Lycas and another fellow that he had brought with him that were all abashed of this adventure; then he went to them and said unto Lycas: 'Thou cursed and unhappy man! what thing has moved thee to come hither under the privy habitude of Deyanira to bring me into the chance of fortune? What weenest thou that thou hast done? Thou hast served me with a shirt intoxicate of mortal venom; who hath introduced thee to do this? Thou must needs receive thy desert.' And saying these words, Hercules caught by the head poor Lycas, that wist never what to say, and threw him against a rock so fiercely that he to-frushed[2] and to-brake his bones and so slew him. The fellow of Lycas fled and hid him in a bush; Philotes was so afraid that he wist not what to do. At the hour that Hercules was in this point, much people came into the temple. The entrails of Hercules broiled, his blood boiled in all his veins, the poison pierced unto his heart, his sinews shrunk and withdrew them; when he felt him in this misery, and that the death hasted him by terrible battle, as he that could not take away the repugnance of his virtuous force striving against the malice of venom, he began to run over hill and over valley, up and down in the forest, and pulled up the great trees and overthrew them. After he began to rend off his shirt with the

---

[1] Disfleshed.   [2] Crushed.

flesh then sodden and broiled. When he had long led this Caxton
life he returned into the temple all ascertained of the death, 1474
and lifted up his hands and his eyes unto the heaven and said :
    'Alas ! alas ! must it be that fortune laugh at me for this
miserable destiny, coming of the accusation of wood[1] jealousy
and sorcery of that woman that in the world I held and
reputed most wise and most virtuous.   O Deyanira, disnatural woman, without wit, without shame, and without
honour, with an heart of a tyrant, all affamed[2] of jealousy !
How hast thou might to contrive against me this furor and
treason envenomed, false feminine will disnatural, out of rule
and out of order.   Thou haddest never so much honour and
worship as thou now hast deserved blame, not only for thee
alone but for all the women that be or shall be ever in
the world ; for if it happen that the kings or princes acquaint
them with ladies or damoiselles for the human multipliance,
they shall never have credence nor affiance in their proper
wives.   O Deyanira, what hast thou done ?   The women
present and they that be in the wombs of their mothers, all
shall crach[3] thee in the face, and shall curse thee without
end, for the reproach by the turning upon them is infinite,
and the men shall have dread for to be served of the shirt.
Alas ! Deyanira, what shall Calcedonie now do that glorified
her in thy glory, and put and set thee in the front of
their honour as a carbuncle for the parement[4] of her precious
things ?   Instead to set thee in the front, they shall cast
thee under feet ; and instead to have glory of, they shall
have shame.   Hereof they may not fail, for by impiety and
diverse engines and by conspired and swollen cruelty, thou
hast conspired my death, and hast desloyed[5] and unbounden
one not recoverable infortune for thee and me and for our
friends and kinsmen.   O Deyanira, right remaudit,[6] unhappy,
and most cursed serpent, too malicious and reproachable

[1] Mad.   [2] An-hungered.   [3] Spit.
[4] Adornment.   [5] Set loose.   [6] Accursed.

Caxton
1474 murderer, thy false jealousy hath more power to extermine my life than have had all the monsters of the world; by thine offence and by thy machination hid and covert, wherefrom I could not keep me, I must die and pass out of this world. Since it is so, I thank fortune, and ask of the gods no vengeance of thee; but certes, to the end that it be not said that the vanquisher of men be vanquished by a woman, I shall not pass the bitter passage of death by thy mortal sorceries full of abomination, but by the fire that is neat and clear, and the most excellent of the elements.'

These dolorous and sorrowful words accomplished, Hercules took his club and cast it in the fire that was made ready for to make his sacrifice; after he gave to Philotes his bow and his arrows, and sin he prayed him that he would recommend him to Yole and his friends. And then, feeling that his life had no more for to sojourn, he took leave of Philotes and then as all burnt and sodden he laid him down in the fire, lifting his hands and his eyes unto the heaven, and there consumed the course of his glorious life. When Philotes saw the end of his master Hercules, he burnt his body into ashes and kept these ashes in intention to bear them to the temple that the King Evander had to make. After he departed from thence, and returned into Lycye greatly discomforted, and with great source of tears he recounted to Yole and to his friends the piteous death of Hercules. No man could recount the great sorrow that Yole made and they of Lycye, as well the students as the rural people; all the world fell in tears, in sighs, and in bewailings for his death. So much abounded Yole in tears and weepings that her heart was drowned and departed her soul from the body by the bitter water of her weeping.

Each body cursed and spake shame of Deyanira; finably Deyanira, advertised by the fellow of Lycas of the mischief that was come by the shirt, she fell in despair and made many piteous bewailings, and among all other she said:

'What have I done, alas, what have I done? The most solemn man of men, shining among the clerks, he that traversed the strong marches, the fundaments terrestrial, that bodily conversed among the men, and spiritually among the sun, the moon, and the stars, and that sustained the circumference of the heavens, is dead by my cause and by my culpe and without my culpe! He is dead by my culpe, for I have sent to him the shirt that gave to him the bite of death; but this is without my culpe, for I knew nothing of the poison. O mortal poison! By me is he prived of his life, of whom I loved the life as much as I did mine own; he that bodily dwelled among the men here in earth, and spiritually above with the sun, the moon, and celestial secrets; he that was fountain of science, by whom the Athenians aroused and bedewed their wits and engines; he that made the monsters of the sea to tremble in their abysms and swallows, and destroyed the monsters of Hell. He confounded the monsters of the earth; the tyrants he corrected; the orguillous and proud he humbled and meaked, the humble and meak he enhanced and exalted; he that made no treasure but of virtue; he that all the nations of the world subjuged and subdued with his club; and he that if he had willed by ambition of seignourie, might have attained to be King of the East, of the West, of the South, and of the North, of the Seas and of the Mountains, of all these he might have named him King and Lord by good right, if he had willed. Alas, alas! what am I, born in an unhappy time, when so high and so mighty a Prince is dead by my simplesse? He was the glory of the men; there was never to him none like, nor never shall be. Ought I to live after him? Nay, certes that shall I never do; for to the end that among the ladies I be not showed nor pointed with the finger, and that I fall not into strange hand for to be punished as much as I have of culpe and blame in this death, I shall do the vengeance to myself.' And with that she took a knife, and saying: 'I feel myself and

Caxton
1474

know that I am innocent of the death of my lord Hercules!'
And with the point of the knife she ended her despaired life.
Whereof Philotes was all abashed, and so were all they of
Greece that long bewept and bewailed Hercules and his
death ; and they of Athens bewailed him strongly, some for
his science, and other for his virtues.

William Caxton.

HOW THE MONK SAW HEAVEN

De Mach-
linia
1482

NOW when we were past all these places and sights
aforesaid, and had gone a good space more inward,
and ever grew to us more and more joy and fairness of
places: also at the last we saw afar a full glorious wall
of crystal, whose height no man might see, and length no
man might consider: and when we came thither I saw
withinforth a full fair bright shining gate, and stood open,
save it was signed and laid over with a cross.   Truly
thither came flockmeal the multitude of those blessed souls
that were next to it, and would come in at that fair gate.
The cross was set in the midst of that gate, and now she
was lift up on high, and so gave to them that came thither an
open and a free entering, and afterward she was let down
again, and so sparred[1] other out that would have come in. But
how joyful they were that went in, and how reverently they
tarried that stood without, abiding the lifting up of the cross
again, I cannot tell by no words.

Soothly here Saint Nicholas and I stood still together, and
the liftings up of the cross and the lettings down again,
whereby some went in and some tarried without, I beheld
long time with great wonder. And at the last Saint Nicholas
and I came thither to the same gate hand in hand. And when
we came thither the cross was lift up. And so they that were

[1] Barred, staked.

there went in. Soothly then my fellow, Saint Nicholas, freely De Mach-
went in and I followed, but suddenly and unavised[1] the cross   linia
of the gate came down upon our hands and departed me from   1482
my fellow Saint Nicholas, and when I saw this full sore afraid
I was.   Then said Saint Nicholas to me : ' Be not afraid, but
have only full certain faith in our Lord Jesus Christ, and
doubtless thou shalt come in.'   And after this my hope and
trust came again, and the cross was lift up, and so I came in ;
but what brightness and clearness of light was there withinforth all about no man ask nor seek of me, for I can not only
[not] tell it by word, but also I cannot remember it in mind.
That glorious shining light was bright and smooth, and so
ravished a man that beheld it, that it bare a man above himself by the great brightness of light, in so mickle that whatsoever I saw before, it was as nothing, methought, in comparison of it.   That brightness, though it were inestimable,
nevertheless it dulled not a man's sight; it rather sharpened
it.   Soothly it shone full marvellously, but more inestimably
it delighted a man that beheld it, and wonderfully coupled
a man's sight to see it.   And withinforth nothing I might
see but light and the wall of crystal through the which we
came in.   And also from the ground up to top of that wall
were gryces[2] ordained and disposed fair and marvellously, by
the which the joyful company that was come in at the foresaid gate gladly ascended up.   There was no labour, there
was no difficulty, there was no tarrying in their ascending,
and the higher they went the gladder they were.

Soothly I stood beneath on the ground, and long time I saw
and beheld how they that came in at the gate ascended up by
the same gryces.   And at the last, as I looked up higher, I
saw in a throne of joy sitting our blessed Lord and Saviour
Jesus Christ, in likeness of man; and about Him, as it seemed
to me, were a five hundred souls, the which late had stied[3] up
to that glorious throne ; and so they came to our Lord and

[1] Without warning.   [2] Steps.   [3] Gone.

De Mach-
linia
1482

worshipped Him, and thanked Him for His great mercy and grace showed and done to them : and some were seen on the upper parts of the wall as they had walked hither and thither. Truly I knew for certain that this place, where I saw our Lord sitting in a throne, was not the high Heaven of Heavens where the blessed spirits of angels and the holy souls of righteous men joy in the sight of God, seeing Him in His majesty as He is : where also innumerable thousands of holy spirits and angels serve him and assist him But then from thence, without any hardness or tarrying, they ascend up to the high heaven, the which is blessed of the sight of the everlasting Godhead, whereas only the holy angels, and the souls of righteous men that be of angels' perfection, see the invisible and immortal King of all worlds face to face, the which hath only immortality and dwelleth in light that is inaccessible: for no man may come to it, the which no mortal man seeth, neither may see. Soothly He is seen only of holy spirits that be pure and clean, the which be not grieved by no corruption of body, neither of soul. And in this vision that I saw, so mickle I conceived in my soul of joy and gladness, that whatsoever may be said of it by man's mouth, full little it is, and insufficient to express the joy of my heart that I had there.

Therefore when I had seen all these sights above said, and many other innumerable, my lord Saint Nicholas, that held me by the hand, said shortly this to me : ' Lo, son,' he said, ' now a part after thy petition and great desire thou hast seen and beholden the state of the world that is to come as it might be to possible. Also the perils of them that offend and err, the pains of sinners, the rest also of them that have done their purgation, the desires of them that be going to heavenward, and the joys of them that now be come to the Court of Heaven, and also the joy of Christ's reigning. And now thou must go again to thyself and to thine [own], and to the world's fighting. Truly thou shalt have

and perceive the joys that thou hast seen, and mickle more, De Mach-
if thou continue and persevere in the dread of God.' And linia 1482
when he had said this to me he brought me forth through
the same gate that we came in: wherefore full heavy and
sorry was I, and more than a man may suppose: for well I
knew that I must turn again from that heavenly bliss to this
world's wretchedness. And greatly he exhorted me how I
should dispose me to abide the day of my calling out of my
body in cleanness of heart and of body and meekness of
spirit, with diligent keeping of my religion. 'Diligently,' he
said to me, 'keep the commandments of God, and dispose thy
living after the example of righteous men. And truly so it
shall be, that after the term of thy bodily living thou shalt
be admitted blessedly to their fellowship everlastingly.'

And while the holy confessor, Saint Nicholas, this wise
spake yet with me, suddenly I heard there a solemn peal
and a ringing of a marvellous sweetness, and as all the bells
in the world, or whatsoever is of sounding, had been rung
together at once. Truly in this peal and ringing brake
out also a marvellous sweetness, and a variant meddling of
melody sounded withal. And I wot not whether the greatness of melody or the sweetness of sounding of bells was
more to be wondered [at]. And to so great a noise I took good
heed, and full greatly my mind was suspended to hear it.
Soothly, anon as that great and marvellous sounding and
noise was ceased, suddenly I saw myself departed from the
sweet fellowship of my duke and leader, Saint Nicholas.
Then was I returned to myself again, and anon I heard the
voices of my brethren that stood about our bed.

William De Machlinia.

THE ADVENTURE OF THE CHARIOT

Malory
1485

THEN by the Queen's commandment they left battle, and dressed the wounded knights on horseback, some sitting, some overthwart their horses, that it was pity to behold them. And then Sir Meliagrance charged the Queen and all her knights that none of all her fellowship should depart from her; for full sore he drad Sir Launcelot du Lake, lest he should have any knowledging. All this espied the Queen, and privily she called unto her a child of her chamber, that was swiftly horsed, to whom she said : 'Go thou, when thou seest thy time, and bear this ring unto Sir Launcelot du Lake, and pray him as he loveth me, that he will see me, and rescue me if ever he will have joy of me; and spare thou not thy horse,' (said the Queen), 'neither for water, neither for land.' So the child espied his time, and lightly he took his horse with the spurs, and departed as fast as he might. And when Sir Meliagrance saw him so flee, he understood that it was by the Queen's commandment for to warn Sir Launcelot. Then they that were best horsed chased him, and shot at him, but from them all the child went suddenly; and then Sir Meliagrance said unto the Queen: 'Madam, ye are about to betray me, but I shall ordain for Sir Launcelot that he shall not come lightly at you.' And then he rode with her and they all to his castle in all the haste that he might. And by the way Sir Meliagrance laid in an enbushment the best archers that he might get in his country, to the number of a thirty, to await upon Sir Launcelot, charging them that if they saw such a manner of knight come by the way upon a white horse, that in any wise they slay his horse, but in no manner of wise have not ado with him bodily, for he is over hard to be overcome. So this was done, and they were come to his castle, but in no wise the Queen would never let none of the ten knights and

her ladies out of her sight, but always they were in her
presence, for the book saith Sir Meliagrance durst make no masteries for dread of Sir Launcelot, in so much he deemed that he had warning.

So when the child was departed from the fellowship of Sir Meliagrance, within a while he came to Westminster. And anon he found Sir Launcelot. And when he had told his message, and delivered him the Queen's ring, 'Alas,' said Sir Launcelot, 'now am I shamed for ever, unless that I may rescue that noble lady from dishonour.' Then eagerly he asked his armour, and ever the child told Sir Launcelot how the ten knights fought marvellously, and how Sir Pelleas, and Sir Ironside, and Sir Brandiles, and Sir Persant of Inde, fought strongly, but namely Sir Pelleas, there might none withstand him, and how they all fought till at the last they were laid to the earth, and then the Queen made appointment for to save their lives, and go with Sir Meliagrance. 'Alas,' said Sir Launcelot, 'that most noble lady, that she should be so destroyed! I had lever (said Sir Launcelot) than all France that I had been there well armed.' So when Sir Launcelot was armed and upon his horse, he prayed the child of the Queen's chamber to warn Sir Lavaine how suddenly he was departed, and for what cause: 'And pray him, as he loveth me, that he will hie him after me, and that he stint not until he come to the castle where Sir Meliagrance abideth,' or dwelleth, for there (said Sir Launcelot) 'shall he hear of me and I am a man living, and rescue the Queen and the ten knights the which he traitorously hath taken, and that shall I prove upon his head, and all them that hold with him.'

Then Sir Launcelot rode as fast as he might, and the book saith he took the water at Westminster Bridge, and made his horse to swim over Thames to Lambeth. And then within a while he came to the place there as the ten knights had fought with Sir Meliagrance, and then Sir

Malory
1485 Launcelot followed that track until that he came to a wood, and there was a strait way, and there the thirty archers bade Sir Launcelot turn again, and follow no longer that track. 'What commandment have ye thereto,' said Sir Launcelot, 'to cause me, that am a knight of the Round Table, to leave my right way?' 'This way shalt thou leave, or else thou shalt go it on thy foot, for wit thou well thy horse shall be slain.' 'That is little mastery,' said Sir Launcelot, 'to slay my horse: but as for myself, when my horse is slain, I give right nought for you, not and ye were five hundred more.' So then they shot Sir Launcelot's horse, and smote him with many arrows. And then Sir Launcelot avoided his horse, and went on foot: but there were so many ditches and hedges betwixt them and him, that he might not meddle with none of them. 'Alas, for shame,' said Launcelot, 'that ever one knight should betray another knight, but it is an old saw, "A good man is never in danger but when he is in the danger of a coward."'

Then Sir Launcelot went a while, and then he was foul cumbered of his armour, his shield, and his spear, and all that longed unto him. Wit ye well he was full sore annoyed, and full loth he was to leave anything that longed unto him, for he dreaded sore the treason of Sir Meliagrance. And then by fortune there came by a chariot, that came thither for to fetch wood. 'Say me, carter,' said Sir Launcelot, 'what shall I give thee for to suffer me to leap into thy chariot, and that thou bring me unto a castle within this two mile?' 'Thou shalt not come within my chariot,' said the carter, 'for I am sent for to fetch wood for my lord Sir Meliagrance.'— 'With him would I speak.' 'Thou shalt not go with me,' said the carter. Then Sir Launcelot leapt to him, and gave him such a buffet that he fell to the earth stark dead. Then the other carter, his fellow, was afraid, and weened to have gone the same way, and then he cried, 'Fair lord, save my life, and I shall bring you where you will.' 'Then I charge

thee,' said Sir Launcelot, 'that thou drive me and this chariot, Malory
even unto Sir Meliagrance's gate.' 'Leap up into the chariot,' 1485
said the carter, 'and ye shall be there anon.'

So the carter drove on a great wallop,[1] and Sir Launcelot's
horse followed the chariot, with more than a forty arrows broad
and rough in him : and more than an hour and an half Dame
Guenever was in a bay window with her ladies, and espied an
armed knight standing in a chariot. 'See, madam,' said a lady,
'where rideth in a chariot a goodly armed knight: I suppose
he rideth unto hanging.' 'Where?' said the Queen. Then
she espied by his shield that he was there himself Sir
Launcelot du Lake. And then she was ware where came
his horse ever after that chariot, and ever he trod his entrails
and his paunch under his feet. 'Alas,' said the Queen, 'now
I see well and prove that well is him that hath a trusty
friend. Ha, hey, most noble knight! I see well thou art
hard bested when thou ridest in a chariot.' Then she
rebuked that lady that likened Sir Launcelot to ride in a
chariot to hanging. 'It was foul-mouthed,' said the Queen,
'and evil likened, so for to liken the most noble knight
of the world unto such a shameful death. O Jesu, defend
him and keep him,' said the Queen, 'from all mischievous
end!'

By this was Sir Launcelot come to the gates of that castle,
and there he descended down, and cried, that all the castle
rang of it: 'Where art thou, false traitor Sir Meliagrance,
and knight of the Table Round? Now come forth here, thou
traitor knight, thou and thy fellowship with thee : for here
I am, Sir Launcelot du Lake, that shall fight with you.'
And therewithal he bare the gate wide open upon the
porter, and smote him under his ear with his gauntlet that
his neck burst in sunder. When Sir Meliagrance heard that
Sir Launcelot was there, he ran unto Queen Guenever, and
fell upon his knee, and said, 'Mercy, madam, now I put me

[1] Gallop.

wholly into your grace. 'What aileth you now?' said Queen
Guenever. 'Forsooth I might well wit some good knight
would revenge me, though my lord Arthur wist not of this
your work.' 'Madam,' said Sir Meliagrance, 'all this that is
amiss on my part shall be amended right as yourself will
devise, and wholly I put me in your grace.' 'What would
ye that I did?' said the Queen. 'I would no more,' said
Meliagrance, 'but that ye would take all in your own hands,
and that ye will rule my lord Sir Launcelot: and such cheer
as may be made him in this poor castle ye and he shall
have until to-morn, and then may ye and all they return
unto Westminster, and my body and all that I have I shall
put in your rule.' 'Ye say well,' said the Queen, 'and better
is peace than ever war, and the less noise the more is my
worship.'

Then the Queen and her ladies went down unto the
knight Sir Launcelot, that stood wroth out of measure in
the inner court, to abide battle; and ever he bade 'Thou
traitor knight, come forth!' Then the Queen came to him
and said, 'Sir Launcelot, why be ye so moved?' 'Ha, madam,'
said Sir Launcelot, 'why ask ye me that question? Me-
seemeth' (said Sir Launcelot) 'ye ought to be more wroth
than I am, for ye have the hurt and the dishonour. For wit
ye well, madam, my hurt is but little, for the killing of a
mare's son; but the despite grieveth me much more than
all my hurt.' 'Truly,' said the Queen, 'ye say truth, but
heartily I thank you' (said the Queen) 'but ye must come in
with me peaccably, for all thing is put in my hand, and all
that is evil shall be for the best, for the knight full sore
repenteth him of the misadventure that is befallen him.'
'Madam,' said Sir Launcelot, 'sith it is so that ye are accorded
with him, as for me I may not be against it, howbeit Sir
Meliagrance hath done full shamefully to me, and cowardly.
Ah, madam, and I had wist ye would have been so soon
accorded with him, I would not have made such haste unto

you.' 'Why say ye so?' said the Queen, 'do ye forthink[1] Malory 1485
yourself of your good deeds? Wit you well' (said the
Queen), 'I accorded never unto him for favour nor love that I
had unto him, but for to lay down every shameful noise.'
'Madam,' said Sir Launcelot, ' ye understand full well I was
never willing nor glad of shameful slander, nor noise ; and
there is neither king, queen, nor knight, that beareth the
life, except my lord King Arthur, and you, madam, that
should let me, but I should make Sir Meliagrance's heart
full cold or ever I departed from hence.' 'That I wot well,'
said the Queen, 'but what will ye more? ye shall have all
thing ruled as ye list to have it.' 'Madam,' said Sir Launcelot,
'so ye be pleased I care not, as for my part ye shall soon
please.'

Right so the Queen took Sir Launcelot by the bare hand,
for he had put off his gauntlet, and so she went with him
till her chamber; and then she commanded him to be
unarmed, and then Sir Launcelot asked where the ten
knights were that were wounded sore. So she showed
them unto Sir Launcelot, and there they made great joy
of the coming of him, and Sir Launcelot made great dole[2] of
their hurts, and bewailed them greatly; and there Sir
Launcelot told them how cowardly and traitorly Meliagrance
set archers to slay his horse, and how he was fain to put
himself in a chariot. Thus they complained every each to
other, and full fain they would have been revenged, but
they peaced themselves because of the Queen. Then, as
the French book saith, Sir Launcelot was called many a day
after, Le Chevaler du Chariot, and did many deeds, and
great adventures he had.

Sir Thomas Malory.

---

[1] Repent.   [2] Sorrow.

A MOURNING REMEMBRANCE

Fisher
1505 SHE came of noble blood, lineally descending of King
Edward the Third, within the fourth degree of the
same.   Her father was John, Duke of Somerset; her mother
was called Margaret, right noble as well in manners as in
blood, to whom she was a very daughter in all noble
manners, for she was bounteous and liberal to every person
of her knowledge or acquaintance. Avarice and covetousness she most hated, and sorrowed it full much in all
persons, but specially in any that belonged unto her.
She was also of singular easiness to be spoken unto, and
full courteous answer she would make to all that came
unto her.   Of marvellous gentleness she was unto all
folks, but specially unto her own, whom she trusted and
loved right tenderly.   Unkind she would not be unto no
creature, nor forgetful of any kindness or service done
to her before, which is no little part of very nobleness.
She was not vengeable, nor cruel, but ready anon to forget
and to forgive injuries done unto her at the least desire
or motion made unto her for the same.   Merciful also and
piteous she was unto such as were grieved and wrongfully
troubled, and to them that were in poverty or sickness or
any other misery.

To God and to the Church full obedient and tractable,
searching His honour and pleasure full busily. A wariness
of herself she had alway to eschew everything that might
dishonest any noble woman, or distain her honour in any
condition.   Frivolous things, that were little to be regarded,
she would let pass by, but the other, that were of weight
and substance, wherein she might profit, she would not
let for any pain or labour to take upon hand. These and
many other such noble conditions, left unto her by her

ancestors, she kept and increased therein with a great
diligence. . . .

Also she wanted not the nobleness of Nature. She had
in manner all that was praiseable in a woman, either in
soul or in body. First, she was of singular wisdom, far
passing the common rate of women. She was good in
remembrance, and of holding memory; a ready wit she
had also to conceive all things, albeit they were right
dark. Right studious she was in books, which she had in
great number, both in English and in French, and for her
exercise and for the profits of others, she did translate divers
matters of devotion out of the French into English. Full
often she complained that in her youth she had not given
her to the understanding of Latin, wherein she had a little
perceiving, specially of the rubric of the ordinal, for the
saying of her service, which she did well understand. Here-
unto in favour, in words, in gesture, in every demeanour of
herself, so great nobleness did appear, that what she spake
or did it marvellously became her. . . .

A nobleness gotten or increased, she had also. For
albeit she of her lineage was right noble, yet, nevertheless, by marriage and adjoining of other blood, it took
some increasement. For in her tender age, she being
endued with so great towardness of nature, and likelihood
of inheritance, many sued to have had her to marriage. The
Duke of Suffolk, which then was a man of great experience,
most diligently procured to have had her for his son and
heir. Of the contrary part, King Henry the Sixth did make
means for Edmond, his brother, then the Earl of Richmond.
She, which as then was not fully nine years old, doubtful in
her mind, what she were best to do, asked counsel of an old
gentlewoman, whom she much loved and trusted, which did
advise her to commend herself to St. Nicholas, the patron
and helper of all true maidens; and to beseech him to put
in her mind what she were best to do. This counsel she

followed, and made her prayer so full often, but specially that night, when she should the morrow after make answer of her mind determinately. A marvellous thing! the same night, as I have heard her tell many a time, as she lay in prayer, calling upon St. Nicholas, whether sleeping or waking she could not assure, but about four of the clock in the morning, one appeared unto her arrayed like a bishop, and naming unto her Edmond, bade take him unto her husband. And so by this mean she did incline her mind unto Edmond, the King's brother, and Earl of Richmond, by whom she was made mother of the King that dead is (whose soul God pardon) and grandam to our sovereign lord, King Henry the Eighth; which now, by the grace of God, governeth the realm. So, what by lineage, what by affinity, she had thirty Kings and Queens within the fourth degree of marriage unto her, beside Earls, Marquises, Dukes, and Princes. And thus much we have spoken of her nobleness. . . .

Her sober temperance in meats and drinks was known to all them that were conversant with her, wherein she lay in as great weight of herself as any person might, keeping alway her straight measure, and offending as little as any creature might: eschewing banquets, rere-suppers,[1] joueries[2] betwixt meals. As for fasting, for age and feebleness, albeit she were not bound, yet those days, that by the Church were appointed, she kept them diligently and seriously, and in especial the holy Lent, throughout that she restrained her appetite till one meal and till one fish on the day; besides her other peculiar fasts of devotion, as St. Anthony, St. Mary Magdalene, St. Catherine, with other; and throughout all the year, the Friday and Saturday she full truly observed. As to hard clothes' wearing, she had her shirts and girdles of hair, which, when she was in health, every week she failed not certain days to wear, sometime the one, sometime the

---

[1] Late suppers.   [2] Sweetmeats.

other, that full often her skin, as I heard her say, was
pierced therewith. . . .

Her own household, with marvellous diligence and wisdom,
this noble Princess ordered, providing reasonable statutes
and ordinances for them, which by her officers she commanded to be read four times a year. And oftentimes
by herself she would so lovingly courage every of them
to do well, and sometime by other mean persons.[1] If any
factions or bonds were made secretly amongst her head
officers, she with great policy did bolt it out, and likewise if any strife or controversy, she would with great discretion study the reformation thereof. For the strangers, O
marvellous God! what pain, what labour she of her very
gentleness would take with them, to bear them manner and
company and entreat every person, and entertain them,
according to their degree and honour, and provide by her
own commandment, that nothing should lack that might be
convenient for them, wherein she had a wonderful ready
remembrance and perfect knowledge.

For the suitors, it is not unknown how studiously she procured justice to be administered by a long season, so long as
she was suffered, and of her own charges provided men
learned for the same purpose, evenly and indifferently to hear
all causes, and administer right and justice to every party,
which was in no small number; and yet meat and drink was
denied to none of them. . . .

But specially, when they saw the death so haste upon her,
and that she must needs depart from them, and that they
should forego so gentle a mistress, so tender a lady; then
wept they marvellously, wept her ladies and kinswomen, to
whom she was full kind; wept her poor gentlewomen, whom
she had loved so tenderly before; wept her chamberers,[2] to
whom she was full dear; wept her chaplains and priests, wept
her true and faithful servants. And who would not have

---

[1] Go-betweens.   [2] Gentlemen of the Household.

Fisher
1505

wept that there had been present. All Englana for her death had cause of weeping. The poor creatures that were wont to receive her alms, to whom she was alway piteous and merciful; the students of both the universities, to whom she was a mother; all the learned men of England, to whom she was a very patroness; all the virtuous and devout persons, to whom she was as a loving sister; all the good religious men and women, whom she so often was wont to visit and comfort; all good priests and clerks to whom she was a true defendress; all the noblemen and women, to whom she was a mirror and exemplar of honour; all the common people of this realm, for whom she was in their causes a common mediatress, and took right great displeasure for them, and generally the whole realm hath cause to complain and to mourn her death. And all we, considering her gracious and charitable mind, so universally, and considering the readiness of mercy and pity in our Saviour Jesus, may say, by lamentable complaint of our unwisdom unto Him: *Ah, domine, si fuisses hic*—Ah, my Lord! if thou had been present and had heard these sorrowful cries of her thy Servant, with the other lamentable mournings of her friends and servants, thou, for thy goodness would not have suffered her to die: but thou wouldst have taken pity and compassion upon her. . . .

Dare I say of her, she never yet was in that prosperity, but the greater it was, the more alway she dreaded the adversity. For when the King, her son, was crowned, in all that great triumph and glory, she wept marvellously; and likewise at the great triumph of the marriage of Prince Arthur, and at the last coronation, wherein she had full great joy, she let not to say that some adversity would follow; so that either she was in sorrow by reason of the present adversities, or else when she was in prosperity, she was in dread of the adversity for to come. I pass over the perils and dangers innumerable, which daily and hourly might have happed unto her, whereof this life is full, and therefore St. Gregory saith: *Vita haec terrena, aeternae vitae comparata, mors est potius dicenda, quam vita,* and for that cause, who that once hath tasted the pleasures of that life, this is unto them a very death for ever after. . . . Now, therefore, would I ask you this one question : Were it, suppose ye, at this considered, a meetly thing for us to desire, to have this noble princess here amongst us again? To forego the joyous life above, to want the presence of the glorious Trinity whom she so long hath sought and honoured, to leave that most noble kingdom, to be absent from the most blessed company of Saints and Saintesses, and hither to come again to be wrapped and endangered with the miseries of this wretched world, with the painful diseases of her age, with the other encumbrances that daily happeth in this miserable life. Were this a reasonable request of our party ?[1] Were this a kind desire ? Were this a gentle wish ? that where she hath been so kind and loving a mistress unto us, all we should more regard our own profits than her more singular weal and comfort ? The mother that hath so great affection unto her son, that she will not suffer him to depart from her to his promotion and furtherance, but alway keep him at home, more regarding her own pleasure than his weal, were not she an unkind and ungentle mother? Yes, verily. Let us, therefore, think our most loving mistress is gone hence for her promotion, for her great furtherance, for her most weal and profit, and herein comfort us, herein rejoice ourself, and thank Almighty God, which of His infinite mercy so graciously hath disposed for her.

John Fisher, Bishop of Rochester.

[1] On our part.

Marginal note: Fisher 1505

A PAGEANT

Makefyrr
1506
R IGHT worshipful masters, I recommend me unto you, certifying you that the King's Grace and the King of Castile met this day at three of the clock, upon Cleworth Green, two mile out of Windsor, and there the King received him in the goodliest manner that ever I saw, and each of them embraced other in arms.

To show you the King's apparel of England, thus it was: his horse of bay, trapped with needlework; a gown of purple velvet, a chain with a George[1] of diamonds, and a hood of purple velvet, which he put not off at the meeting of the said King of Castile; his hat and his bonnet he availed,[2] and the King of Castile in case like. And the King of Castile rode upon a sorrelled hobby, which the King gave unto him; his apparel was all black, a gown of black velvet, a black hood, a black hat, and his horse's harness of black velvet.

To show you of the King's company: my Lord Harry of Stafford rode in a gown of cloth of tusser,[3] tucked, furred with sables, a hat of goldsmith work, and full of stones, diamonds, and rubies, riding upon a sorrelled courser barded with a bard[4] of goldsmith's work, with roses and dragons red.

And my Lord Marquis riding upon a bald sorrelled horse, with a deep trapper full of long tassels of gold of Venice, and upon the crupper of his horse a white feather, with a coat upon his back, the body goldsmith's work, the sleeves of crimson velvet, with letters of gold.

My Lord of Kent upon a sorrelled horse, bald, the harness of Venice gold, with a deep fringe of half yard of length. My Lord of Kent's coat was one bar of cloth of gold, another

---

[1] Ensign of the Garter.   [2] Took off.   [3] Silk.
[4] Caparisoned with a horse-armour.

of crimson velvet, pyrled[1] with a demy manche[2] cut off by Makefyrr the elbow.   These be the lords that bear the bruit.

Sir Hew Waghan upon a bay horse trapped with crimson velvet full of gilt bells, a gown of black velvet, and a chain of gold, baldric-wise, worth five hundred pound.

These be the spears : Master St. John upon a black horse, with harness of cloth of gold with tassels of plunket[3] and white, a coat of plunket and white, the body of goldsmith's work ; the sleeves full of spangles.

John Carr and William Parr coats like, the horses grey, of Parr trapped with crimson velvet with tassels of gold, and bells gilt.   Carr, horse bay, with an Almain harness of silver, an inch broad of beaten silver, both the coats of goldsmith's work the bodies, the sleeves one strip of silver, the other gilt.

Edward Neville upon a gray horse trapped with black velvet full of small bells, his coat the one half of green velvet, the other of white cloth of gold ; these to the rutters[4] of the spears, with other divers well appointed.

On the King of Castile's party : the Lord Chamberlain chief, I cannot tell his name as yet ; his apparel was sad, and so was all the residue of his company, with cloaks of sad tawny black, guarded, some with velvet, and some with sarcenet, not passing a dozen in number.   It is said there is many behind, which comes with the Queen of Castile, which shall come upon Tuesday.

When the King rode forth from Windsor Castle, the King rode upon the right hand the King's of Castile ; howbeit, the King's Grace offered him to take him upon the right hand, the which he refused.   And at the alighting the King of Castile was off his horse a good space or our King was alight ; and then the King's Grace offered to take him by the arm, the which he would not, but took the King by the

---

[1] Fringed.　　　　[2] Sleeve.　　　　[3] Light blue.
[4] Troopers.

Makefyrr
1506 the arm, and so went to the King of Castile's chamber, which is the richestly hanged that ever I saw; seven chambers together hanged with cloth of arras, wrought with gold as thick as could be; and as for three beds of state, no King christened can show such three.

This is as far as I can show you of this day, and when I can know more, ye shall have knowledge.

The Paston Letters.

THE KILLING OF LORD HASTINGS

More
1513 WHEREUPON soon after, that is to wit, on the Friday the — day of — many Lords assembled in the Tower, and there sat in council, devising the honourable solemnity of the King's coronation, of which the time appointed then so near approached, that the pageants and subtleties were in making day and night at Westminster, and much victual killed therefore, that afterwards was cast away. These Lords so sitting together commoning of this matter, the Protector came in among them, first about nine of the clock, saluting them courteously, and excusing himself that he had been from them so long, saying merely that he had been asleep that day. And after a little talking with them, he said unto the Bishop of Ely : ' My lord, you have very good strawberries at your garden in Holborn, I require you let us have a mess of them.' 'Gladly, my lord,' quoth he, ' would God I had some better thing as ready to your pleasure as that.' And therewith in all the haste he sent his servant for a mess of strawberries. The Protector set the Lords fast in commoning, and thereupon praying them to spare him for a little while, departed thence. And soon, after one hour, between ten and eleven he returned into the chamber among them, all changed, with a wonderful sour

angry countenance, knitting the brows, frowning and froth-
ing and knawing on his lips, and so sat him down in his
place ; all the Lords much dismayed and sore marvelling of
this manner of sudden change, and what thing should him
ail.   Then when he had sitten still a while, thus he began :
' What were they worthy to have, that compass and imagine
the destruction of me, being so near of blood unto the King
and Protector of his royal person and his realm ? '   At this
question, all the Lords sat sore astonished, musing much by
whom this question should be meant, of which every man
wist himself clear.   Then the Lord Chamberlain, as he
that for the love between them thought he might be boldest
with him, answered and said, that they were worthy to be
punished as heinous traitors, whatsoever they were.   And
all the other affirmed the same.   ' That is ' (quoth he) ' yonder
sorceress, my brother's wife and other with her,' meaning the
Queen.   At these words many of the other Lords were
greatly abashed that favoured her.   But the Lord Hastings
was in his mind better content, that it was moved by her,
than by any other whom he loved better.   Albeit his heart
somewhat grudged, that he was not afore made of counsel in
this matter, as he was of the taking of her kindred, and of
their putting to death, which were by his assent before devised to be beheaded at Pomfret, this self same day, in
which he was not ware that it was by other devised, that
himself should the same day be beheaded at London.   Then
said the Protector: 'Ye shall all see in what wise that sorceress
and that other witch of her counsel, Shore's wife, with their
affinity, have by their sorcery and witchcraft wasted my body.'
And therewith he plucked up his doublet sleeve to his elbow
upon his left arm, where he shewed a werish [1] withered arm
and small, as it was never other.   And thereupon every
man's mind sore misgave them, well perceiving that this
matter was but a quarrel.   For well they wist, that the Queen

[1] Ill-shapen.

was too wise to go about any such folly. And also if she would, yet would she of all folk least make Shore's wife of counsel, whom of all women she most hated, as that concubine whom the King her husband had most loved. And also no man was there present, but well knew that his arm was ever such since his birth. Natheles the Lord Chamberlain answered and said: 'Certainly, my Lord, if they have so heinously done, they be worthy heinous punishment.' 'What,' quoth the Protector, 'thou servest me, I wene, with ifs and with ands, I tell thee they have so done, and that I will make good on thy body, traitor.' And, therewith, as in great anger, he clapped his fist upon the board a great rap. At which token given, one cried treason without the chamber. Therewith a door clapped, and in come there rushing men in harness, as many as the chamber might hold. And anon the Protector said to the Lord Hastings: 'I arrest thee, traitor.' 'What, me, my Lord?' quoth he. 'Yea thee, traitor,' quoth the Protector. And another let fly at the Lord Stanley, which shrank at the stroke and fell under the table, or else his head had been cleft to the teeth: for as shortly as he shrank, yet ran the blood about his ears. Then were they all quickly bestowed in diverse chambers, except the Lord Chamberlain, whom the Protector bade speed and shrive him apace, 'for by Saint Paul' (quoth he) 'I will not to dinner till I see thy head off.' It boded him not to ask why, but heavily he took a priest at adventure, and made a short shrift, for a longer would not be suffered, the Protector made so much haste to dinner; which he might not go to till this were done for saving of his oath. So was he brought forth into the green beside the chapel within the Tower, and his head laid down upon a long log of timber, and there stricken off, and afterward his body with the head interred at Windsor beside the body of King Edward, whose both souls our Lord pardon.

Sir Thomas More.

WAT TYLER'S ENDING

THE Saturday the King departed from the Wardrobe in Bourchier the Royal, and went to Westminster and heard mass 1523 in the church there, and all his lords with him; and beside the church there was a little chapel, with an image of Our Lady, which did great miracles, and in whom the Kings of England had ever great trust and confidence. The King made his orisons before this image, and did there his offering; and then he leapt on his horse, and all his lords, and so the King rode toward London; and when he had ridden a little way on the left hand, there was a way to pass without London.

The same proper morning, Wat Tyler, Jack Straw, and John Ball had assembled their company to common together, in a place called Smithfield, whereas every Friday there is a market of horses; and there were together all of affinity more than twenty thousand, and yet there were many still in the town, drinking and making merry in the taverns, and paid nothing, for they were happy that made them best cheer. And these people in Smithfield had with them the King's banners, the which were delivered them the day before; and all these gluttons were in mind to overrun and to rob London the same day, for their captains said how they had done nothing as yet: 'These liberties that the King hath given us is to us but a small profit; therefore let us be all of one accord, and let us overrun this rich and puissant city, or they of Essex, of Sussex, of Cambridge, of Bedford, of Arundel, of Warwick, of Reading, of Oxford, of Guildford, of Linne, of Stafford, of Germany, of Lincoln, of York, and of Durham do come hither; for all these will come hither. Wallyor and Lyster will bring them hither; and if we be first lords of London, and have the possession of the riches that is therein

Bourchier we shall not repent us; for if we leave it, they that come
1523   after will have it from us.' To this counsel they all agreed.
And therewith the King came the same way unaware of
them, for he had thought to have passed that way without
London, and with him a forty horse; and when he came
before the abbey of St. Bartilmeus, and beheld all these
people, then the King rested and said how he would go no
farther till he knew what these people ailed, saying, if they
were in any trouble, how he would repease[1] them again. The
lords that were with him tarried also, as reason was when
they saw the King tarry. And when Wat Tyler saw the
King tarry, he said to his people : 'Sirs, yonder is the King,
I will go and speak with him; stir not from hence without I
make you a sign, and when I make you that sign, come on,
and slay all them, except the King; but do the King no
hurt; he is young, we shall do with him as we list, and
shall lead him with us all about England, and so shall we be
lords of all the realm without doubt.'

And there was a doublet maker of London called John
Tycle, and he had brought to these gluttons a sixty doublets,
the which they wore; then he demanded of these captains who
should pay him for his doublets ; he demanded thirty marks.
Wat Tyler answered him and said : ' Friend, appease yourself,
thou shalt be well payed ere this day be ended ; keep thee
near me, I shall be thy creditor.' And therewith he spurred
his horse and departed from his company, and came to the
King, so near him that his horse's head touched the croup
of the King's horse. And the first word that he said was
this : ' Sir King, seest thou all yonder people ?' ' Yea, truly,˙
said the King ; 'wherefore sayest thou?' ' Because,' said
he, ' they be all at my commandment, and have sworn to me
faith and truth to do all that I will have them.' ' In a good
time,' said the King, ' I will well it be so.' Then Wat Tyler
said, as he that nothing demanded but riot : ' What, believest

---

[1] Appease.

thou, King, that these people, and as many more as be in London at my commandment, that they will depart from thee thus, without having thy letters?' 'No,' said the King; 'ye shall have them, they be ordained for you, and shall be delivered every one each after other; wherefore, good fellows, withdraw fair and easily to your people, and cause them to depart out of London, for it is our intent that each of you by villages and townships shall have letters patent, as I have promised you.'

With those words Wat Tyler cast his eyes on a squire that was there with the King, bearing the King's sword. And Wat Tyler hated greatly the same squire, for the same squire had displeased him before for words between them. 'What,' said Tyler, 'art thou there? Give me thy dagger.' 'Nay,' said the squire, 'that will I not do. Wherefore should I give it thee?' The King beheld the squire, and said: 'Give it him, let him have it.' And so the squire took it him sore against his will. And when this Wat Tyler had it he began to play therewith, and turned it in his hand, and said again to the squire: 'Give me also that sword.' 'Nay,' said the squire, 'it is the King's sword; thou art not worthy to have it, for thou art but a knave; and if there were no more here but thou and I, thou durst not speak those words for as much gold in quantity as all yonder Abbey.' 'By my faith,' said Wat Tyler, 'I shall never eat meat till I have thy head.' And with those words the Mayor of London came to the King with a twelve horses, well armed under their coats, and so he brake the press, and saw and heard how Wat Tyler demeaned himself, and said to him: 'Ha! thou knave, how art thou so hardy in the King's presence to speak such words? It is too much for thee so to do.' Then the King began to chafe, and said to the Mayor: 'Set hands on him.' And while the King said so, Tyler said to the Mayor: 'A God's name, what have I said to displease thee?' 'Yes, truly,' quoth the Mayor, 'thou false stinking knave, shalt thou speak thus in the presence

Bourchier
1523

Bourchier of the King, my natural lord? I commit[1] never to live
1523 without thou shalt dearly abye[2] it.' And with those words
the Mayor drew out his sword and struck Tyler so great a
stroke on the head, that he fell down at the feet of his horse;
and as soon as he was fallen, they environed him all about,
whereby he was not seen of his company. Then a squire
of the King's alighted, called John Standish, and he drew
out his sword and put it into Wat Tyler's belly, and so he
died.

Then the ungracious people there assembled, perceiving
their captain slain, began to murmur among themselves and
said: 'Ah! our captain is slain; let us go and slay them all;'
and therewith they arranged themselves on the place in
manner of battle, and their bows before them. Thus the
King began a great outrage; howbeit, all turned to the
best, for as soon as Tyler was on the earth the King departed
from all his company, and all alone he rode to these people,
and said to his own men: 'Sirs, none of you follow me; let
me alone.' And so when he came before these ungracious
people, who put themselves in ordinance to revenge their
captain, then the King said to them: 'Sirs, what aileth you?
ye shall have no captain but me: I am your King; be all in
rest and peace.' And so the most part of the people that
heard the King speak and saw him among them were
shamefast, and began to wax peaceable and to depart; but
some, such as were malicious and evil, would not depart, but
made semblant[3] as though they would do somewhat. Then
the King returned to his own company and demanded ot
them what was best to be done. Then he was counselled te
draw into the field, for to fly away was no boot. Then said
the Mayor: 'It is good that we do so, for I think surely we
shall have shortly some comfort of them of London, and of
such good men as be of our part, who are purveyed,[4] and
have their friends and men ready armed in their houses.'

---

[1] Promise.   [2] Repay.   [3] Made as they would.   [4] Provided.

And in this meantime voice and bruit ran through London,
how these unhappy people were likely to slay the King and
the Mayor in Smithfield; through the which noise all manner
of good men of the King's party issued out of their houses and
lodgings, well armed, and so came all to Smithfield and to
the field where the King was; and they were anon to the
number of seven or eight thousand men well armed. And
first thither came Sir Robert Knolles and Sir Perducas
Dalbret, well accompanied, and divers of the Aldermen of
London, and with them a six hundred men in harness, and a
puissant man of the city, who was the King's draper, called
Nicholas Bramber, and he brought with him a great company;
and ever as they came they ranged them afoot in order of
battle. And on the other part these unhappy people were
ready ranged, making semblance to give battle; and they
had with them divers of the King's banners. There the King
made three knights: the one the Mayor of London, Sir
Nicholas Walworth, Sir John Standish, and Sir Nicholas
Braule.

Then the lords said among themselves: 'What shall we
do? We see here our enemies, who would gladly slay
us, if they might have the better hand of us.' Sir Robert
Knolles counselled to go and fight with them and slay them
all; yet the King would not consent thereto, but said:
'Nay, I will not so; I will send to them, commanding them
to send me again my banners, and thereby we shall see what
they will do; howbeit, either by fairness or otherwise, I
will have them.' 'That is well said, sir,' quoth the Earl of
Salisbury. Then these new knights were sent to them, and
these knights made token to them not to shoot at them.
And when they came so near them that their speech might
be heard, they said: 'Sirs, the King commandeth you to
send to him again his banners, and we think he will have
mercy of you.' And incontinent they delivered again the
banners, and sent them to the King: also they were com-

Bourchier
1523
manded, on pain of their heads, that all such as had letters
of the King to bring them forth, and to send them again to
the King.   And so, many of them delivered their letters, but
not all: then the King made them to be all torn in their
presence.   And as soon as the King's banners were delivered
again, these unhappy people kept none array, but the most
part of them did cast down their bows, and so break their
array, and returned into London.   Sir Robert Knolles was
sore displeased in that he might not go to slay them all; but
the King would not consent thereto, but said he would be
revenged of them well enough, and so he was after.

John Bourchier, Lord Berners.

THE CONQUEST OF BRITAIN

Tiptoft
1530
THE horsemen of the Britons and their essedaries fought
sharply with the horsemen of the Romans as they were
on their journey: but the Romans were victors, and chased
them into the woods and mountains.   But after that the
Romans had slain many of their enemies, and followed them
farther for covetousness, they lost many of their men.   And
after that a little time, the Romans, being negligent and
nothing doubting, were about to fortify their camp, the
Britons suddenly leapt out of the wood, and began to assail
fiercely, and set on them which kept the watch of the
camp, the which withstood them strongly.   Then Caesar
sent for succours, two companies, and with them the first
legion of the two next legions, between which legions and
their first fighters was a little space.   But the Romans were
abashed because of the new manner and fashion that they
of Britain used in fighting, the which struck courageously
in the midst of the Romans and departed again at their
pleasure, without any hurt or wounds.   That same day was

Quintus Laberius Durus, captain of the horsemen, slain.
But after that Caesar had sent in aid certain company with
all things necessary, the Britons were soon discomfited. Now,
for so much as this was open in the sight of all men, because
it was fought before the camp where the whole host lay, it
was well perceived that the Romans, for weight of their
heavy armour, were not able to follow quickly, nor chase
their enemies, nor also they durst not depart from their
standards. Wherefore they were not meet to fight with
their enemies, which used such manner of battle. They
perceived also the horsemen could not fight without great
peril, because their enemies would oftentimes flee for the
nonce. And when they had moved by fraud the Romans a
good distance from the legions, then they leapt out of their
chariots and began a new battle on foot, after another
fashion than the Romans used. And the manner of fight
of the horsemen was very perilous, whether they assailed
their enemies or whether they followed them. Their
enemies also fought not all together, but some here and
some there, and great spaces between them when they
fought. And some stood still to see the array kept, and to
furnish the field ever with fresh men when the other were
weary or hurt.

The next day after this battle the Britons were lodged
on the mountains not far from the host of the Romans,
and showed themselves in a small company, and began
to assail the horsemen of the Romans, but not so fiercely
as they had done the day before. But about the hour
of noon, when Caesar had sent on foraging three legions
and all his horsemen, under the conduct of Caius Tre-
bonius, his lieutenant, their enemies leapt suddenly out
of all parts on them that went a-foraging, insomuch as
they came and assailed them that bare the banners and
the legions. But after that the Romans had made a strong
assault against them, they put them to flight, and ceased

not to follow them : for the horsemen had much confidence to have succours, because they perceived the legions following after them : they chased their enemies, and slew a great number of them, and followed them so near that they had neither space to gather themselves together in array, nor to arrest themselves, nor yet to leap out of their chariots. After this flight, all the aliens which were come out of all parts to succour the Britons departed, and after this time never made any plain field with their power against the Romans. When this battle was thus finished, Caesar having knowledge of the counsel of all his enemies, caused his host to march toward the country of Cassevelan by the river of the Thames, over which flood a man can pass afoot, and that very hardily, but at one place. And when he came thither, he perceived on the other side of the river a great army of enemies ready in good ordinance.

Now, the side of the river where his enemies stood was pitched full of sharp piles : and beside it, at the brink of the river, were other piles which were covered with water. Of the which things, when Caesar was advertised by the report of the prisoners, and by them which had left the Britons and were come to Caesar, he sent first his men of arms, and commanded the legions should follow them immediately without delay. And the army went so hastily and with such great violence together, notwithstanding that they had their heads all only above the water, that the Britons, which were not able to resist the strength of the legions and of the horsemen, were compelled to leave the banks and to flee away. Then Cassevelanus, as before, showed when he had lost all his hope that he had to make war, and also had put from him his great army, and kept all only with him four thousand essedaries: he espied all that he might what way the Romans held, and ever kept himself aloof a little out of the way, and lurked in woods and other places that were not easy to journey in. And in all countries where he knew the Romans should come, he caused both the people and the beasts out of the towns and fields to be chased into the forests. And when the horsemen of the Romans would boldly go into the fields on foraging, or else in destroying the country, he would send his essedaries by privy ways and by-paths that he knew out of the woods against the Romans to fight with them, to the great hurt and damage of the horsemen. And by reason of the fear that they put the Romans in, they letted them to stray any more abroad, wherefore it came to this point, that Caesar would suffer his people to go no further on foraging than the host of the legions extended, and ordained that in burning of houses and destroying the land of their enemies, there should be done as much hurt as the men of arms of the legions with all their power might do in riding by the way. In this season the Trinobantes (which men suppose to be them of London), the which is almost the strongest and surest city of all the country of Britain, sent ambassadors to Caesar, and offered themselves to be at his commandment. Of which city a certain young man called Mandubracius, taking part with Caesar, came to him into the stablished land, whose father, Imanuencius, before that time had borne great rule and authority in the said city, and was slain by Cassevelan ; and his son, fearing death, fled out of the city. Which ambassadors required Caesar that he would defend and help Mandubracius to avenge the wrongs that Cassevelan did to him, and that he would send to them Mandubracius to have the rule and governing of the city. Then Caesar commanded to the ambassadors that they should send him eleven hostages and corn sufficient for his host, and so he sent to them Mandubracius. When the ambassadors were returned, the Trinobantes with all diligence did that which Caesar had commanded, and sent to him the number of hostages and the corn which he did command. When the

Tiptoft
1530

Trinobantes were thus assured because that Caesar had commanded that no man of war should do them any hurt or damage, the Cenimagnies, the Segontiaces, the Ancalytes, the Bibroces and Cassiens (which be inhabiting near the sea), sent their ambassadors to Caesar, and yielded them to him. Of them Caesar had perfect knowledge that the fortress where Cassevelan held himself was not far from thence. The which fortress was fortified with forests and marshes, and there was assembled together a great number of men and also of beasts. Note that the Britons call a fortress or a walled town when they have fortified a strong wood with ditches and pales, there where they may assemble together to eschew the danger of their enemies. Then Caesar marched toward this fortress, and found the place marvellous strong, both by situation of nature and by labour of men's hands. Yet notwithstanding he enforced to assault it at two sides. The enemies after that they had tarried a little, perceiving that they were not able to resist the assault, fled out by another part. When the fortress was taken, there was found a great number of bestial, and many men were slain and taken in the flight. While these things were adoing in these parts, Cassevelan sent his messengers into the country of Kent, the which country, as is showed before, doth stand on the sea coast.

In the which country were four Kings reigning, that is to say, Cingetorix, Carvilius, Taximagulus, and Segonax, whom he commanded to assemble together all their armies and suddenly to assail and destroy all the navy (which Caesar had left at the sea coast). When those four Kings were arrived where the navy was, the Romans made out and slew many of them, and took prisoner the noble captain Cingetorix, and brought home all their people safe unhurt. After that the losing of this battle was showed to Cassevelan, and that he considered the great misfortunes and damages that he had sustained, and perceived his country so robbed, pilled,[1] and exiled, and the most of all troubled him that so many cities and towns had forsaken him and were yielded to Caesar: he therefore sent ambassadors to Caesar, which, by the means of Attribatus Comius, should intreat that he might yield him to ransom. Now, because Caesar before intended to lie the winter time in continent land, because of the sudden movings in France, and because that little of the summer remained, and the rest would be soon spent, he commanded Cassevelan to send him hostages, and ordained what tribute Britain should pay yearly to the Romans. He also forbade and commanded Cassevelan that he should do no prejudice neither to Mandubracius nor to the Trinobantes. And when he had received the hostages, he drew with his host toward the seaside, where he found his navy repaired. And insomuch as Caesar had great number of prisoners, and because one part of his navy was perished by the tempest, he purposed to make his navy to repass at two several times. But it happened so that of all the number of ships, and for all the passages that were made, neither this year nor the last year, yet there lacked no ships to recarry over the host. But as for all the ships that should have been sent from the other part, and the ships in which the first men of war passed and should have come again, and also such ships as Labienus had in charge to see made to the number of forty, few or none of them came to the even port. Wherefore it was necessary to make again the remnant which were broken. The which navy, when Caesar had long tarried for in vain, lest he should be hindered or let to pass because of the late season that the nights and days were of one length; he was compelled by necessity to shift his men together more straightly in such ships as he had. And as soon as the weather was fair and convenient to sail, he parted about the second hour

---

[1] Pillaged.

Tiptoft
1530

of the night, and at the point of day he took land, and all his navy safe and sound, which he caused to be drawn up on land.

John Tiptoft, Earl of Worcester.

THE IMAGE OF DETRACTION

Elyot
1531

THERE is much conversant among men in authority a vice very ugly and monstruous, who under the pleasant habit of friendship and good counsel with a breath pestilential infecteth the wits of them that nothing mistrusteth. This monster is called in English Detraction, in Latin *Calumnia*, whose property I will now declare. If a man, being determined to equity, having the eyes and ears of his mind set only on the truth and the public weal of his country, will have no regard to any request or desire, but proceedeth directly in the administration of justice, then either he which by justice is offended, or some his fautours, abettors, or adherents, if he himself or any of them be in service or familiarity with him that is in authority, as soon as by any occasion mention happeneth to be made of him who hath executed justice exactly, forthwith they imagine some vice or default, be it never so little, whereby they may minish his credence, and craftly omitting to speak anything of his rigour in justice, they will note and touch something of his manners, wherein shall either seem to be lightness or lack of gravity, or too much sourness, or lack of civility, or that he is not benevolent to him in authority, or that he is not sufficient to receive any dignity, or to dispatch matters of weighty importance, or that he is superfluous in words, or else too scarce. Also if he live temperately and delighteth much in study, they embraid[1] him with nigardship, or in

[1] Upbraid.

derision do call him a clerk or a poet, unmete for any other
purpose. And this do they covertly and with a more gravity
than any other thing that they enterprise.

This evil report is called Detraction, who was wonderfully
well expressed in figures by the most noble painter Apelles,
after that he was discharged of the crime whereof he was
falsely accused to Ptholomee, King of Egypt, having for his
amends of the said king twelve thousand pounds sterling and
his accuser to his bondman perpetually. The table wherein
Detraction was expressed was painted in this form: at the right
hand was made sitting a man having long ears, putting forth
his hand to Detraction, who far off came towards him ; about
this man stood two women, that is to say, Ignorance and Suspicion. On the other side came Detraction, a woman above
measure well trimmed, all chafed and angry, having her aspect
or look like to the fire, in showing a manner of rage or fury.
In her left hand she held a burning torch or brand, and with
her other hand she drew by the hair of his head a young
man who held up his hands toward heaven, calling God and
the Saints for witness. With her came a man, pale and evil
favoured, beholding the young man intentively, like unto one
that had been with long sickness consumed, whom ye might
lightly conject to be Envy. Also there followed two other
women, that trimmed and apparelled Detraction ; the one
was Treason, the other Fraud. After followed a woman in
a mourning weed, black and ragged, and she was called
Repentance, who turning her back weeping and sore ashamed
beheld Verity, who then approached. In this wise Apelles
described Detraction, by whom he himself was in peril.
Which, in mine opinion, is a right necessary matter to be in
tables or hangings set in every man's house that is in
authority, considering what damage and loss hath ensued,
and may hereafter ensue, by this horrible pestilence, false
Detraction.

To the avoiding whereof, Luciane, who writeth of this

Elyot
1531

picture, giveth a notable counsel, saying, that a wise man, when he doubteth of the honesty and virtue of the person accused, he should keep close his ears and not open them hastily to them which be with this sickness infected, and put reason for a diligent porter and watch, which ought to examine and let in the reports that be good, and exclude and prohibit them that be contrary. For it is a thing to laugh at and very unfitting to ordain for thy house a keeper or porter, and thine ears and mind to leave to all men wide open. Wherefore, when any person cometh to us to tell us any report or complaint, first, it shall behove us throughly and evenly to consider the thing, not having respect to the ears of him that reporteth, or to his form of living or wisdom in speaking. For the more vehement the reporter is in persuading, so much more diligent and exact trial and examination ought to be used. Therefore trust is not to be given to another man's judgment, much less to the malice of an accuser. But every man shall retain to himself the power to ensearch out the truth, and leaving the envy or displeasure to the detractor, he shall ponder or weigh the matter indifferently, that everything in such wise being curiously ensearched and proved, he may at his pleasure either love or hate him whom he hath so substantially tried. For in good faith to give place to Detraction at the beginning, it is a thing childish and base, and to be esteemed among the most great inconveniences and mischiefs. These be well nigh the words of Luciane; whether the counsel be good I remit it to the wise readers. Of one thing am I sure, that by Detraction as well many good wits have been drowned, as also virtue, and painful study have been unrewarded, and many zelatours or favourers of the public weal have been discouraged.

Sir Thomas Elyot.

THE CROWNING OF ANN BOLEYN

T HE Thursday next before the feast of Pentecost, the Cranmer
King and the Queen being at Greenwich, all the   1533
crafts of London thereunto well appointed, in several barges
decked after the most gorgeous and sumptuous manner,
with divers pageants thereunto belonging, repaired and
waited all together upon the Mayor of London ; and so well
furnished came all unto Greenwich, where they tarried and
waited for the Queen's coming to her barge : which so done,
they brought her unto the Tower, trumpets, shawms, and
other divers instruments all the ways playing and making
great melody, which, as is reported, was so comely done as
never was like in any time nigh to our remembrance.

And so her Grace came to the Tower on Thursday at
night, about five of the clock, where also was such a peal of
guns as hath not been heard like a great while before.
And the same night, and Friday all day, the King and Queen
tarried there ; and on Friday at night the King's Grace made
eighteen Knights of the Bath, whose creation was not alonely
so strange to hear of, as also their garments stranger to behold or look on ; which said Knights the next day, which
was Saturday, rid before the Queen's Grace throughout the
city of London towards Westminster Palace, over and
besides the most part of the nobles of the realm, which
like accompanied her Grace throughout the said City ; she
sitting in her hair upon a horse litter, richly apparelled, and
four Knights of the five ports bearing a canopy over her
head. And after her came four rich chariots, one of them
empty, and three other furnished with divers ancient old
ladies ; and after them came a great train of other ladies
and gentlewomen ; which said progress, from the beginning
to the ending, extended half a mile in length by estimation,
or thereabout. To whom also, as she came along the City,

Cranmer was shewed many costly pageants, with divers other
1533 encomies spoken of children to her. Wine also running at
certain conduits plentifully. And so proceeding throughout
the streets, [she] passed forth unto Westminster Hall, where
was a certain banquet prepared for her; which done, she
was conveyed out of the backside of the palace into a
barge, and so unto York Place, where the King's Grace was
before her coming: for this you must ever presuppose, that
his Grace came always before her secretly in a barge, as well
from Greenwich to the Tower as from the Tower to York
Place.

Now, then, on Sunday was the Coronation, which also was
of such a manner. In the morning there assembled with
me at Westminster Church the Bishop of York, the Bishop
of London, the Bishop of Winchester, the Bishop of Lincoln,
the Bishop of Bath, and the Bishop of St. Asse, the Abbot
of Westminster, with ten or twelve more abbots, which all
revestred ourselves in our pontificalibus, and so furnished,
with our crosses and crosiers, proceeded out of the abbey in
a procession unto Westminster Hall, where we received the
Queen apparelled in a robe of purple velvet, and all the
ladies and gentlewomen in robes and gowns of scarlet, according to the manner used before time in such business:
and so her Grace, sustained of each side with two Bishops,
the Bishop of London and the Bishop of Winchester, came
forth in procession unto the Church of Westminster, she in
her hair, my Lord of Suffolk bearing before her the Crown,
and two other lords bearing also before her a Sceptre and
a white rod, and so entered up into the high altar, where
divers ceremonies used about her, I did set the Crown on
her head, and then was sung *Te Deum*, etc. And after that
was sung a solemn mass: all which while her Grace sat
crowned upon a scaffold, which was made between the high
altar and the choir in Westminster Church; which mass and
ceremonies done and finished, all the assembly of noblemen

brought her into Westminster Hall again, where was kept
a great solemn feast all that day; the good order thereof
were too long to write at this time to you.   But now, Sir,
you may not imagine that this Coronation was before her
marriage; for she was married much about St. Paul's day
last, as the condition thereof doth well appear, by reason
she is now somewhat big with child.   Notwithstanding it
hath been reported throughout a great part of the realm
that I married her; which was plainly false, for I myself
knew not thereof a fortnight after it was done.   And many
other things be also reported of me which be mere lies and
tales.

Thomas Cranmer, Archbishop of Canterbury.

Cranmer
1533

A ROMAN VICTORY

MAXIMUS, in the year following, was so ithandly [1]
occupied with this trouble of Britain's, afore rehearsed, that he might not return to the wars of Scots.
Nevertheless, many frequent incursions continued all the said
time betwixt his wageours [2] and the Scots.   At last, when the
Scots had assayed long time, howbeit it was in vain, to recover the strengths of Galloway, they passed through Men-
teith, Stirling, and Fife, and sundry other bounds of Picts,
invading the same with such cruelty, that they were left
desert.   Maximus appeared right heavy at their offences;
howbeit nothing was more pleasing to him than to hear the
Scots and Picts invading other, to both their mischiefs.
Finally, he came in Galloway, with purpose to pass through
all the remanent bounds of Scots.

Then was Eugenius not far from the Romans, abiding the
coming of his people : to whom compeared great confluence
of fencible [3] men and women, to the number of fifty thousand

Bellenden
1536

---

[1] Continually.   [2] Mercenaries.   [3] Able-bodied.

people, right desirous to fight, and crying at once with huge noise, either to die, or else to have victory; for they were cruelly slain in all parts where they might be apprehended by Romans, but[1] any mercy or ransom. And, notwithstanding their great courage, they were some part astonist, hearing the Romans coming in their lands, with more multitude and puissance of people than ever was seen in any of their bounds afore. Yet others, having the Roman tyranny at despite, were raised in most fury, regarding nothing their life in defence of their liberty. Then Eugenius, with great courage, dissimuled his countenance, as he were affrighted of nothing less than of the Romans; and divided his army in three battles: the right wing was given to his brother Ethodius; the left wing to Doalus, captain of Argyll; and in the middleward was himself. These battles were arrayed in such craft, that in the place where the battle was set, he believed not only to have the river of Munda, deep but[1] any ford, on the backs of his army, that they should fight but refuge, but also to have the sun going to suchlike on their backs, that their enemies might not hold up their een for reflection of contrary beams in their sight.

Such things done, Eugenius went to a high mound, and called his army to the standard, and said in this manner: 'Our elders that began this realm with continual labour, and brought the same with honour to our days, forcy[2] champions, commanded their posterity to defend their realm and liberty, which is most dulce and heavenly treasure in the earth, against all invaders; having esperance of victory, when time was to fight against their enemies, in nothing more than in their hands: and to be obedient to the wise and noble captains of this realm; whose authority and prudence be sicker targe,[3] both to their goods, lands, and lives, against all press and danger of enemies. All our elders, that are passed afore us, were aye obedient to the

---

[1] Without.   [2] Strong.   [3] A sure shield.

command of their nobles; and though they have fought Bellenden
oftimes, with sundry chances of battle, against the dantours[1] 1536
of the world, yet they were finally victors.   Now maun
we fight, most valiant champions, with such manhood and
courage as our elders fought afore us; or else maun we tine[2]
our realm and liberty, and be thirled[3] to most vile servitude,
at the will of our enemies.   Now approaches Maximus, our
cruel and unmerciful enemy, to reif[4] both our lands and goods,
if we support not ourself by grace of God and our manhood.
He is so full of false ingine[5] and slights, that he is now confed-
erate with Picts, as well in perdition of them as of us; intending
therethrough to bring the whole empire of Albion, howbeit the
same was never heard afore, under Roman obedience.   The
Picts, by mischant[6] folly, pass to battle in support of their
professed enemies, which are right desirous to reif from them
their kingdom and honours.   They come against us, which were
aye their protectors, since first their realm began.   It is uncertain by what mischief these Picts be abused, not knowing
the irrecoverable damage that is to fall on them, in eversion
of their common weal and liberty : and though they know
the same, they give no attendance thereto.   Yet, so far as
pertains to our action, consider that our enemies are to
fight against us, whom we never offended with injuries :
through which, their works shall be the more unchancy, and
more odious to God.   By contrary, remember ye are to
resist their invasion, and in your pure defence, are to fight
for your realm and liberty : and are the posterity of those
forcy champions that sometime most gloriously chased the
Romans out of these bounds.   Now it is come to such point,
that we maun either be vanquished, and suffer extreme misery
and servitude, or else to be victors, and stable[7] our lands
to us with glory, honour, and permanent ease.   I beseech
you, my good companions, for the unvincible manhood, faith,

---

[1] Tamers.   [2] Lose.   [3] Bound.   [4] Take by violence.
[5] Cunning (*ingenium*).   [6] Wicked.   [7] Stablish.

VOL. I.   E

Bellenden and virtue of your elders, and for their pale ghosts, which
1536 defended this your realm in liberty to these days; to suffer
not you, their sons, to be reft and spoilt of your realm,
liberties, and goods; nor yet to be taken, as caitiffs, to
underlie their tyrannies. And if it happens you by adverse
chance, which God defend, to die, then do, so far as in you,
to acquit your death; and think, better is to die honestly,
than to live in shame. Know yourself dotat[1] with incredible
manhood and virtue; and heritors, by ancient lineage, as
well to your noble fathers in wisdom and chivalry as in their
lands; not gathered of divers nations, but of one people
under one mind: and servants to the eternal God, that
gives victory to just people in reward of their virtue; and
to false and wrongous people shame, discomfiture, and
slaughter. Belt you, therefore, lusty gallants, with manhood and wisdom, to have victory: which shall not fail to
succeed,[2] if ye, with constant courage, have nothing but
shameful fleeing in dread; and invade your enemies with
suchlike cruelty as they intend to invade you.'

Scarcely had Eugenius raised the spright of his army by
this hortation, when Maximus appeared in sight, with all his
army, and came forthward with more diligence than was
believed: for he came soon after the sun rising. The Scots
were astonished by huge multitude of enemies: nonetheless,
seeing no refuge, they determined to assay the extreme
jeopardy of arms. Soon after, they arrayed them, with
their backs to the sun, that the glance and beams thereof
should not be impediment to their fighting: and scarcely
were they well arrayed, when they rushed forward on their
enemies. This fierce running was impediment to Maximus to
do his devoir: nonetheless, seeing the time so short, he exhorted his army to remember the Roman virtue, and to be
not afraid of barbarous people, whom they recently discomfist.
Incontinent, both the armies, by sound of trumpet, joined,

1 Endowed.   2 Follow.

Bellenden
1536

with huge noise and clamour on all sides. At the first coun-
tering, it was so cruelly fought, that it was uncertain to what
party most danger succeeded : then followed sundry chances
of fortune. For the Scots that fought in the right wing under
Ethodius, to win no less honour than glory, set on the Picts
forenence[1] them, and chased them through the water of Dune;
where many of them, overset with slik and glar[2] thereof,
were slain : then, by proud and insolent glory, as they had
been sicker of victory, they straggled from their fellows,
cassin[3] to spoil ; through which many of them were slain after,
by a Roman legion that was sent by Maximus in support
of the said Picts. In the last wing, where Doalus fought,
the Scots met with Frenchmen, Britons, and Almains :
where they were slain, fighting with persevering manhood to
the death, for defence of their realm. Then all the Roman
army, by command of Maximus, rushed on the middle ward,
where Eugenius fought with his nobles, weary, and near
vanquished by multitude of their enemies : howbeit, many of
them, fiercely repugnant while they might, failed nothing
that pertained to forcy champions. The nobles that fought
in Eugenius's army, seeing the victory incline to Romans,
desired Eugenius to save him by flight to better fortune ;
and incontinent they raif[4] off his coat armour perforce, to
make him unknown : nonetheless, he abode, fighting with
persevering malice against the Romans ; and was slain the
third year of his reign.

While such terrible murder was made in the army of
Scots, all their carriage men, that were left to keep their
bestial and victuals, having no armour but swords to defend
them, and seeing so many noblemen slain ; by piteous com-
miseration rushed on their enemies, and were all slain,
fighting to the death.

While the Romans were following in the chase, by great
ire and hatred, on this manner, they fell in an uncouth

---

[1] In front of.   [2] Slime and mud.   [3] Broken up.   [4] Tore.

Bellenden manner of bergane[1]; for the aged and feeble persons, that
1536   were left at home as unfencible bodies, right desirous to hear
what chance was fallen to their sons, came to the place
where the battle was: but when they saw so piteous and
lamentable slaughter made on their sons and friends, they
rushed on their enemies like furious creatures, regarding
neither life, reason, nor age.   The women came after, with
terrible noise, rummishing[2] as wood,[3] raging beasts, and set
on the Romans.   Nonetheless, both the aged men and
women were finally slain.   The Romans passed the night
following with so huge fear and dread, that no trenches nor
watching might be sufficient munition to their army; for the
hills, valleys, and lesures[4] resounded all the night with most
terrible spraichs[5] of yammering[6] people in the deaththrow: for
nought was heard but horrible mourning of sobbing and dying
people, crying a vengeance on Romans and Picts, by whose
treasonable slights this huge murder was made on them.
On the morrow, Maximus parted the spoil of the field among
his army, and made the dead bodies to be buried: and to
show him nothing degenerate from Roman mercy, he made
them that were left on life, and sore wounded, to be cured
with most crafty surgeons: among whom was Ethodius,
brother to Eugenius, taken, and cured, by ruth of Maximus,
of all his wounds.

John Bellenden, Archdean of Moray.

SEEING THE WIND

Ascham   TO see the wind, with a man his eyes, it is impossible,
1545   the nature of it is so fine, and subtile; yet this experience of the wind had I once myself, and that was in the
great snow that fell four years ago: I rode in the highway

| 1 Skirmish. | 2 Roaring. | 3 Mad. |
| 4 Meadow-lands. | 5 Shrieks. | 6 Lamenting. |

betwixt Topcliff-upon-Swale, and Borowe Bridge, the way
being somewhat trodden afore, by wayfaring men. The
fields on both sides were plain and lay almost yard deep
with snow, the night afore had been a little frost, so that
the snow was hard and crusted above. That morning the
sun shone bright and clear, the wind was whistling aloft,
and sharp according to the time of the year. The snow in
the highway lay loose and trodden with horse feet: so as the
wind blew, it took the loose snow with it, and made it so
slide upon the snow in the field which was hard and crusted
by reason of the frost overnight, that thereby I might see
very well the whole nature of the wind as it blew that day.
And I had a great delight and pleasure to mark it, which
maketh me now far better to remember it. Sometime the
wind would be not past two yards broad, and so it would carry
the snow as far as I could see. Another time the snow would
blow over half the field at once. Sometime the snow would
tumble softly, by and by it would fly wonderful fast. And
this I perceived also, that the wind goeth by streams and
not whole together. For I should see one stream within a
score on me, then the space of two score no snow would stir,
but after so much quantity of ground, another stream of
snow at the same very time should be carried likewise, but
not equally. For the one would stand still when the other
flew apace, and so continue sometime swiftlier, sometime
slowlier, sometime broader, sometime narrower, as far as I
could see. Nor it flew not straight, but sometime it crooked
this way, sometime that way, and sometime it ran round
about in a compass. And sometime the snow would be lift
clean from the ground up into the air, and by and by it
would be all clapped to the ground as though there had
been no wind at all, straightway it would rise and fly
again.

And that which was the most marvel of all, at one time two
drifts of snow flew, the one out of the West into the East,

Ascham the other out of the North into the East: and I saw two
1545   winds by reason of the snow the one cross over the other, as
it had been two highways. And again I should hear the
wind blow in the air, when nothing was stirred at the ground.
And when all was still where I rode, not very far from me
the snow should be lifted wonderfully. This experience
made me more marvel at the nature of the wind, than it
made me cunning in the knowledge of the wind: but yet
thereby I learned perfectly that it is no marvel at all though
men in a wind lease their length in shooting, seeing so many
ways the wind is so variable in blowing.

Roger Ascham.

A CHARACTER OF LONDON

Latimer NOW what shall we say of these rich citizens of London?
1548   What shall I say of them? Shall I call them proud
men of London, malicious men of London, merciless men of
London? No, no, I may not say so; they will be offended
with me then. Yet must I speak. For is there not reigning
in London as much pride, as much covetousness, as much
cruelty, as much oppression, and as much superstition, as
was in Nebo? Yes, I think, and much more too. Therefore
I say, repent, O London; repent, repent. Thou hearest
thy faults told thee, amend them, amend them. I think, if
Nebo had had the preaching that thou hast, they would
have converted. And, you rulers and officers, be wise and
circumspect, look to your charge, and see you do your duties;
and rather be glad to amend your ill living than to be angry
when you are warned or told of your fault. What ado was
there made in London at a certain man, because he said

(and indeed at that time on a just cause), 'Burgesses!' quoth he, 'nay, Butterflies.' Lord, what ado there was for that word. And yet would God they were no worse than butterflies! Butterflies do but their nature; the butterfly is not covetous, is not greedy of other men's goods; is not full of envy and hatred, is not malicious, is not cruel, is not merciless. The butterfly glorieth not in her own deeds, nor preferreth the traditions of men before God's word; it committeth not idolotry, nor worshippeth false gods. But London cannot abide to be rebuked; such is the nature of man. If they be pricked, they will kick; if they be rubbed on the gall, they will wince; but yet they will not amend their faults, they will not be ill spoken of. But how shall I speak well of them? If you could be content to receive and follow the word of God, and favour good preachers, if you could bear to be told of your faults, if you could amend when you hear of them, if you would be glad to reform that is amiss: If I might see any such inclination in you, that you would leave to be merciless, and begin to be charitable, I would then hope well of you, I would then speak well of you. But London was never so ill as it is now. In times past men were full of pity and compassion, but now there is no pity; for in London their brother shall die in the streets for cold, he shall lie sick at the door between stock and stock, I cannot tell what to call it, and perish there for hunger: Was there ever more unmercifulness in Nebo? I think not. In times past, when any rich man died in London, they were wont to help the poor scholars of the Universities with exhibition. When any man died, they would bequeath great sums of money towards the relief of the poor. When I was a scholar in Cambridge myself, I heard very good report of London, and knew many that had relief of the rich men of London; but now I can hear no such good report, and yet I inquire of it, and hearken for it; but now charity is waxen cold, none helpeth the scholar,

Latimer nor yet the poor. And in those days, what did they when
1548   they helped the scholars? Marry, they maintained and
         gave them livings that were very papists, and professed the
         Pope's doctrine : and now that the knowledge of God's
         word is brought to light, and many earnestly study and
         labour to set it forth, now almost no man helpeth to main-
         tain them.

         O London, London! repent, repent; for I think God is
         more displeased with London than ever he was with the
         city of Nebo. Repent therefore, repent, London, and re-
         member that the same God liveth now that punished Nebo,
         even the same God, and none other; and he will punish sin
         as well now as he did then : and he will punish the iniquity
         of London, as well as he did then of Nebo. Amend therefore.

         Hugh Latimer.

RALPH HYTHLODAYE

Robinson **W**HILE I was there abiding, oftentimes among other,
1551   but which to me was more welcome than any
          other, did visit me one Peter Giles, a citizen of Antwerp, a
          man there in his country of honest reputation, and also pre-
          ferred to high promotions, worthy truly of the highest. For
          it is hard to say whether the young man be in learning or
          in honesty more excellent. For he is both of wonderful
          virtuous conditions, and also singularly well learned, and
          towards all sorts of people exceeding gentle : but towards
          his friends so kind-hearted, so loving, so faithful, so trusty, and
          of so earnest affection, that it were very hard in any place
          to find a man, that with him in all points of friendship may
          be compared. No man can be more lowly or courteous.
          No man useth less simulation or dissimulation, in no man is
          more prudent simplicity. Besides this, he is in his talk and

communication so merry and pleasant, yea and that without Robinson 1551
harm, that through his gentle entertainment, and his sweet
and delectable communication, in me was greatly abated
and diminished the fervent desire that I had to see my
native country, my wife, and my children, whom then I did
much long and covet to see, because that at that time I had
been more than four months from them. Upon a certain
day when I had heard the divine service in our Lady's
Church, which is the fairest, the most gorgeous and curious
Church of building in all the city, and also most frequented
of people, and the service being done, was ready to go home
to my lodging, I chanced to espy this foresaid Peter talking
with a certain stranger, a man well stricken in age, with a
black sunburned face, a long beard, and a cloak cast homely
about his shoulders, whom, by his favour and apparel forthwith I judged to be a mariner. But the said Peter seeing
me, came unto me and saluted me.

And as I was about to answer him : 'See you this man,'
saith he (and therewith he pointed to the man, that I saw
him talking with before), ' I was minded,' quoth he, ' to bring
him straight home to you.' 'He should have been very
welcome to me,' said I, 'for your sake.' ' Nay ' (quoth he)
' for his own sake, if you knew him : for there is no man this
day living that can tell you of so many strange and unknown
peoples, and countries, as this man can. And I know well
that you be very desirous to hear of such news.'

'Then I conjectured not far amiss ' (quoth I), 'for even at
the first sight I judged him to be a mariner.'

' Nay ' (quoth he), 'there ye were greatly deceived : he hath
sailed indeed, not as the mariner Palinure, but as the expert and prudent prince Ulysses : Yea, rather as the ancient
and sage philosopher Plato. For this same Raphael Hyth-
lodaye (for this is his name) is very well learned in the Latin
tongue, but profound and excellent in the Greek language.
Wherein he ever bestowed more study than in the Latin,

Robinson because he had given himself wholly to the study of Philo-
1551 sophy. Whereof, he knew that there is nothing extant in
Latin, that is to any purpose, saving a few of Seneca's and
Cicero's doings. His patrimony that he was born unto, he
left to his brethren (for he is a Portugal born), and for the
desire that he had to see and know the far countries of the
world, he joined himself in company with Amerike Vespuce,
and in the three last voyages of those four that be now in
print and abroad in every man's hands, he continued still
in his company, saving that in the last voyage he came not
home again with him. For he made such means and shift,
what by intreatance, and what by importune suit, that he
got licence of Master Amerike (though it were sore against
his will) to be one of the twenty-four, which in the end of
the last voyage were left in the country of Gulike. He
was therefore left behind for his mind sake, as one that
took more thought and care for travelling than dying:
having customably in his mouth these sayings: He that
hath no grave is covered with the sky; and, The way to
heaven out of all places is of like length and distance.
Which fantasy of his (if God had not been his better friend)
he had surely bought full dear. But after the departing of
of Master Vespuce, when he had travelled through and about
many countries with five of his companions, Gulikians, at the
last by marvellous chance he arrived in Taprobane, from
whence he went to Caliquit, where he chanced to find
certain of his country ships, wherein he returned again into
his country, nothing less than looked for.'

    All this when Peter had told me, I thanked him for his
gentle kindness, that he had vouchsafed to bring me to the
speech of that man, whose communication he thought should
be to me pleasant and acceptable. And therewith I turned
me to Raphael. And when we had halsed [1] each other, and
had spoken these common words that be customably

---

[1] Embraced.

spoken at the first meeting and acquaintance of strangers,
we went thence to my house, and there in my garden, upon
a bench covered with green turves, we sat down talking together. There he told us, how that after the departing of
Vespuce, he and his fellows, that tarried behind in Gulike,
began by little and little, through fair and gentle speech, to
win the love and favour of the people of that country, insomuch that within short space they did dwell amongst them,
not only harmless, but also occupying with them very fami-
iarly. He told us also, that they were in high reputation and
favour with a certain great man (whose name and country is
now quite out of my remembrance), which of his mere liberality did bear the costs and charges of him and his five companions. And besides that gave them a trusty guide to
conduct them in their journey (which by water was in boats,
and by land in wagons) and to bring them to other princes
with very friendly commendations. Thus after many days'
journeys, he said, they found towns, and cities, and weal
publics, full of people, governed by good and wholesome laws.
For under the line equinoctial, and on both sides of the
same, as far as the sun doth extend his course, lieth (quoth
he) great and wide deserts and wildernesses, parched,
burned, and dried up with continual and intolerable heat.
All things be hideous, terrible, loathsome, and unpleasant
to behold : all things out of fashion and comeliness, inhabited with wild beasts and serpents, or at the leastwise,
with people that be no less savage, wild, and noisome than
the very beasts themselves be. But a little farther beyond
that, all things begin by little and little to wax pleasant.
The air soft, temperate, and gentle. The ground covered
with green grass. Less wildness in the beasts. 'At the last
shall ye come again to people, cities, and towns, wherein is
continual intercourse and occupying of merchandise and
chaffer, not only among themselves and with their bor-
derers, but also with merchants of far countries, both by land

Robinson
1551
and water. There I had occasion' (said he) 'to go to many countries on every side. For there was no ship ready to any voyage or journey but I and my fellows were into it very gladly received.' The ships that they found first were made plain, flat, and broad in the bottom, troughwise. The sails were made of great rushes, or of wickers, and in some places of leather. Afterward they found ships with ridged keels, and sails of canvas: 'yea, and shortly after having all things like ours. The shipmen also very expert and cunning both in the sea and in the weather.' But he said, that he found great favour and friendship among them, for teaching them the feat and the use of the loadstone, which to them before that time was unknown. And therefore they were wont to be very timorous and fearful upon the sea, nor to venture upon it but only in the summer time. But now they have such a confidence in that stone, that they fear not stormy winter: in so doing farther from care than danger, insomuch that it is greatly to be doubted, lest that thing, through their own foolish hardiness, shall turn them to evil and harm, which at the first was supposed should be to them good and commodious.

Ralph Robinson.

WOLSEY'S ARREST

Cavendish
1557
MY lord sitting at dinner upon All-Halloween day in Cawood Castle, having at his board's end divers of his most worthiest chaplains sitting at dinner to keep him company, for lack of strangers, ye shall understand that my lord's great cross of silver accustomably stood in the corner, at the table's end, leaning against the tappet or hanging of the chamber. And when the table's end was taken up, and a convenient time for them to arise; in arising

from the table, one Doctor Augustine, physician, being a Cavendish 1557 Venetian born, having a boisterous gown of black velvet upon him ; as he would have come out at the table's end, his gown overthrew the cross that stood there in the corner, and the cross trailing down along the tappet, it chanced to fall upon Doctor Bonner's head, who stood among others by the tappet, making of curtsy to my lord, and with one of the points of the cross razed his head a little, that the blood ran down. The company standing there were greatly astonished with the chance. My lord sitting in his chair, looking upon them, perceived the chance, demanded of me, being next him, what the matter meant of their sudden abashment. I showed him how the cross fell upon Doctor Bonner's head. 'Hath it,' quoth he, 'drawn any blood?' 'Yea, forsooth, my lord,' quoth I, 'as it seemeth me.' With that he cast down his head, looking very soberly upon me a good while without any word speaking; at the last, quoth he, shaking of his head : '*Malum omen*' ; and therewith said grace, and rose from the table, and went into his bedchamber, there lamenting, making his prayers. Now mark the signification, how my lord expounded this matter unto me afterward at Pomfret Abbey. First, ye shall understand, that the cross, which belonged to the dignity of York, he understood to be himself; and Augustine, he understood, that overthrew the cross, to be he that should accuse him, by means whereof he should be overthrown. The falling upon Master Bonner's head, who was master of my lord's faculties and spiritual jurisdictions, which was damnified by the overthrowing of the cross by the physician, and the drawing of blood betokened death, which shortly after came to pass. About the very same time of the day of this mischance, Master Walshe took his horse at the Court Gate, as nigh as it could be judged. And thus my lord took it for a very sign or token of that which after ensued, if the circumstance be equally considered and noted, although no man was there

Cavendish present at that time that had any knowledge of Master
1557 Walshe's coming down, or what should follow. Wherefore,
as it was supposed that God showed him more secret knowledge of his latter days and end of his trouble than all men
supposed; which appeared right well by divers talks that
he had with me at divers times, of his last end. And now
that I have declared unto you the effect of this prodigy and
sign, I will return again to my matter.

The time drawing nigh of his stallation; sitting at dinner,
upon the Friday next before Monday on the which he intended to be stalled at York, the Earl of Northumberland
and Master Walshe, with a great company of gentlemen, as
well of the Earl's servants as of the country, which he had
gathered together to accompany him in the King's name, not
knowing to what purpose or to what intent, came into the hall
at Cawood, the officers sitting at dinner, and my lord not
fully dined, but being at his fruits, nothing knowing of the
Earl's being in his hall. The first thing that the Earl did,
after he came into the castle, commanded the porter to
deliver him the keys of the gates, who would in no wise deliver him the keys, although he were very roughly commanded in the King's name to deliver them to one of the
Earl's servants; saying unto the Earl: 'Sir, ye do intend to
deliver them to one of your servants to keep them and the
gates, and to plant another in my room; I know no cause
why ye should so do, and this I assure you, that you have
no one servant, but that I am as able to keep them as he,
to what purpose soever it be; and also, the keys were delivered me by my lord, my master, with a charge both by
oath and by other precepts and commandments; therefore
I beseech your lordship to pardon me, though I refuse your
commandment. For whatsoever ye shall command me to
do that belongeth to my office, I shall do it with a right good
will, as justly as any other of your servants.' With that
quoth the gentlemen there present unto the Earl, hearing

him speak so stoutly, like a man, and with so good reason : Cavendish
'Sir,' quoth they, 'he is a good fellow, and speaketh like a 1557
faithful servant to his master; and like an honest man :
therefore give him your charge, and let him keep still the
gates; who, we doubt not, will be obedient to your lordship's
commandment.' 'Well then,' quoth the Earl, 'hold him a
book,' and commanded him to lay his hand upon the book,
whereat the porter made some doubt, but being persuaded
by the gentlemen there present, was contented, and laid his
hand upon the book, to whom, quoth the Earl : 'Thou shalt
swear, to keep well and truly these gates to the king our
sovereign lord's use, and to do all such things as we shall
command thee in the king's name, being his highness's commissioners, and as it shall seem to us at all times good, as
long as we shall be here in this castle; and that ye shall
not let in nor out at these gates, but such as ye shall be
commanded by us, from time to time.' And upon this oath
he received the keys at the Earl's and Master Walshe's
hands.

Of all these doings knew my lord nothing; for they
stopped the stairs that went up into my lord's chamber where
he sat, so that no man could pass up again that was come
down. At the last, one of my lord's servants chanced to look
down into the hall at a loop that was upon the stairs, and
returned to my lord, and showed him that my Lord of
Northumberland was in the hall; whereat my lord marvelled,
and would not believe him at the first; but commanded a
gentleman, being his gentleman-usher, to go down and bring
him perfect word. Who going down the stairs, looking
down at the loop, where he saw the Earl, who then returned
to my lord, and showed him that it was very he. 'Then,'
quoth my lord, 'I am sorry that we have dined, for I fear that
our officers be not stored of any plenty of good fish, to make
him such honourable cheer as to his estate is convenient.
Notwithstanding, he shall have such as we have, with a right

Cavendish good will, and loving heart. Let the table be standing still,
1557 and we will go down and meet him, and bring him up; and
then he shall see how far forth we be at our dinner.' With
that he put the table from him and rose up; going down, he
encountered the Earl upon the midst of the stairs, coming
up, with all his men about him. nd as soon as my lord
espied the Earl, he put off his cap, and said to him : ' My
lord, ye be most heartily welcome,' and therewith they embraced each other. 'Although, my lord,' quoth he, ' that I
have often desired and wished in my heart to see you in my
house, yet if ye had loved me as I do you, ye would have
sent me word before of your coming, to the intent that I
might have received you according to your honour and mine.
Notwithstanding, ye shall have such cheer as I am able to
make you, with a right good will; trusting that ye will
accept the same of me as of your very old and loving friend,
hoping hereafter to see you oftener, when I shall be more
able, and better provided to receive you with better fare.'
And then my lord took the Earl of Northumberland by the
hand, and led him up into the chamber; whom followed all
the Earl's servants ; where the table stood in the state that
my lord left it when he rose, saying unto the Earl : ' Sir, now
ye may perceive how far forth we were at our dinner.' Then
my lord led the Earl to the fire, saying : ' My lord, ye shall
go into my bedchamber, where is a good fire made for you,
and there ye may shift your apparel until your chamber be
made ready. Therefore, let your male be brought up: and
or ever I go, I pray you give me leave to take these gentlemen, your servants, by the hands.' And when he had taken
them all by the hands, he returned to the Earl, and said :
' Ah ! my lord, I perceive well that ye have observed my old
precepts and instructions which I gave you, when you were
abiding with me in your youth, which was, to cherish your
father's old servants, whereof I see here present with you a
great number. Surely, my lord, ye do therein very well and

Cavendish
1557

nobly, and like a wise gentleman; for these be they that
will not only serve and love you, but they will also live and
die with you, and be true and faithful servants to you, and
glad to see you prosper in honour; the which I beseech
God to send you, with long life.' This said, he took the
Earl by the hand, and led him into his bedchamber. And
they being there all alone, save only I, that kept the door,
according to my duty, being gentleman usher, these two
lords standing at a window by the chimney, in my lord's
bedchamber, the Earl trembling said, with a very faint and
soft voice, unto my lord (laying his hand upon his arm):
'My lord, I arrest you of high treason.' With which words
my lord was marvellously astonied, standing both still a
long space without any further words. But at the last,
quoth my lord: 'What moveth you, or by what authority do
you this?' 'Forsooth, my lord,' quoth the Earl, 'I have a
commission to warrant me and my doings.' 'Where is your
commission?' quoth my lord, 'let me see it.' 'Nay, sir,
that you may not,' quoth the Earl. 'Well, then,' quoth my
lord, 'I will not obey your arrest; for there hath been between some of your predecessors and mine great contentions
and debate grown upon an ancient grudge, which may succeed in you, with like inconvenience, as it hath done heretofore. Therefore, unless I see your authority and commission,
I will not obey you.' Even as they were debating this
matter between them in the chamber, so busily was Master
Walshe arresting of Doctor Augustine, the physician, at
the door within the portal, whom I heard say unto him: 'Go
in then, traitor, or I shall make thee'; and with that, I
opened the portal door, and the same being opened, Master
Walshe thrust Doctor Augustine in before him with violence.
These matters on both the sides astonied me very sore,
musing what all this should mean; until at the last, Master
Walshe, being entered the chamber, began to pluck off his
hood, the which he had made him with a coat of the same

Cavendish
1557

cloth, of cotton, to the intent he would not be known.   And
after he had plucked it off, he kneeled down to my lord, to
whom he spake first, commanding him to stand up, saying
thus : 'Sir, here my Lord of Northumberland hath arrested
me of treason, but by what authority or commission he
showeth me not; but saith he hath one.   If ye be privy
thereto, or be joined with him therein, I pray you show me.'
'Indeed, my lord,' quoth Master Walshe, 'if it please your
Grace, it is true that he hath one.'   'Well, then,' said my
lord, 'I pray you let me see it.'   'Sir, I beseech your Grace
hold us excused,' quoth Master Walshe, 'there is annexed
unto our commission a schedule with certain instructions
which ye may in no wise be privy unto.'   'Why,' quoth my
lord, 'be your instructions such that I may not see them?
Peradventure, if I might be privy to them, I could the better
help you to perform them.   It is not unknown unto you
both, I am assured, but I have been privy and of counsel in
as weighty matters as this is, for I doubt not for my part
but I shall prove and clear myself to be a true man against
the expectation of all my cruel enemies.   I have an understanding whereupon all this matter groweth.   Well, there is
no more to do.   I trow, gentlemen, ye be one of the King's
Privy Chamber; your name, I suppose, is Walshe; I am content to yield unto you, but not to my Lord of Northumberland, without I see his commission.   And also you are a
sufficient commissioner yourself in that behalf, inasmuch as
ye be one of the King's Privy Chamber; for the worst person
there is a sufficient warrant to arrest the greatest peer of
this realm, by the King's only commandment, without any
commission.   Therefore I am ready to be ordered and disposed at your will.   Put therefore the King's commission and
your authority in execution, a' God's name, and spare not,
and I will obey the King's will and pleasure; for I fear
more the cruelty of my unnatural enemies than I do my
truth and allegiance; wherein, I take God to witness, I

never offended the King's Majesty in word or deed; and Cavendish
therein I dare stand face to face with any man alive, having   1557
indifferency without partiality.'

Then came my Lord of Northumberland unto me, standing at the portal door, and commanded me to avoid the
chamber : and being loth to depart from my master, I stood
still, and would not remove ; to whom he spake again, and
said : 'There is no remedy, ye must needs depart.' With
that I looked upon my lord, as who sayeth, shall I go ? Upon
whom my lord looked very heavily, and shook at me his
head. Perceiving by his countenance it booted me not to
abide, and so I departed the chamber, and went into the
next chamber, where abode many gentlemen of my fellows
and other, to learn of me some news of the matter within ;
to whom I made report what I saw and heard ; which was
to them great heaviness to hear.

George Cavendish.

TWO BISHOPS

I

A MONG many other worthy and sundry histories and   Foxe
notable acts of such as of late days have been tur-   1563
moiled, murdered, and martyred for the true gospel of Christ
in Queen Mary's reign, the tragical story and life of Dr.
Ridley I thought good to commend to chronicle and leave
to perpetual memory ; beseeching thee (gentle reader) with
care and study well to peruse, diligently to consider, and
deeply to print the same in thy breast, seeing him to be a
man beautified with such excellent qualities, so ghostly
inspired and godly learned, and now written doubtless in the
book of life, with the blessed saints of the Almighty, crowned
and throned amongst the glorious company of martyrs. First,
descending of a stock right worshipful, he was born in

Northumberlandshire, who, being a child, learned his grammar with great dexterity in Newcastle, and was removed from thence to the University of Cambridge, where he in short time became so famous, that for his singular aptness, he was called to higher functions and offices of the University, by degree attaining thereunto, and was called to be head of Pembroke Hall, and there made doctor of divinity. After this, departing from thence, he travelled to Paris, who, at his return, was made chaplain to King Henry the Eighth, and promoted afterwards by him to the bishopric of Rochester; and so from thence translated to the see and bishopric of London in King Edward's days.

In which calling and offices he so travailed and occupied himself by preaching and teaching the true and wholesome doctrine of Christ, that never good child was more singularly loved of his dear parents than he of his flock and diocese. Every holiday and Sunday he lightly preached in some one place or other, except he were otherwise letted by weighty affairs and business, to whose sermons the people resorted, swarming about him like bees, and coveting the sweet flowers and wholesome juice of the fruitful doctrine, which he did not only preach, but showed the same by his life, as a glittering lanthorn to the eyes and senses of the blind, in such pure order and chastity of life (declining from all evil desires and concupiscences) that even his very enemies could not reprove him in any one jot thereof.

Besides this, he was passingly well learned, his memory was great, and he of such reading withal, that of right he deserved to be comparable to the best of this our age, as can testify as well divers his notable works, pithy sermons, and sundry his disputations in both the Universities, as also his very adversaries, all which will say no less themselves.

Besides all this, wise he was of counsel, deep of wit, and very politic in all his doings. How merciful and careful he was to reduce the obstinate papists from their erroneous

opinions, and by gentleness to win them to the truth, his
gentle ordering and courteous handling of Dr. Heath, late
Archbishop of York, being prisoner with him in King
Edward's time in his house one year, sufficiently declareth.
In fine, he was such a prelate, and in all points so good,
godly, and ghostly a man, that England may justly rue the
loss of so worthy a treasure. And thus hitherto concerning
these public matters.

Now will I speak something further, particularly of his
person and conditions. He was a man right comely and well
proportioned in all points, both in complexion and lineaments
of the body. He took all things in good part, bearing no
malice nor rancour in his heart, but straightways forgetting
all injuries and offences done against him. He was very
kind and natural to his kinsfolk, and yet not bearing with
them anything otherwise than right would require, giving
them always for a general rule, yea to his own brother and
sister, that they, doing evil, should seek or look for nothing
at his hand, but should be as strangers and aliens unto him ;
and they to be his brother and sister, which used honesty
and a godly trade of life.

He, using all kinds of ways to mortify himself, was given
to much prayer and contemplation ; for duly every morning,
so soon as his apparel was done upon him, he went forthwith
to his bedchamber, and there upon his knees prayed the
space of half an hour ; which being done, immediately he
went to his study, if there came no other business to
interrupt him, where he continued till ten of the clock, and
then came to the common prayer, daily used in his house.
The prayers being done, he went to dinner, where he used
little talk, except otherwise occasion by some had been
ministered, and then was it sober, discreet, and wise, and
sometimes merry, as cause required.

The dinner done, which was not very long, he used to sit
an hour or thereabouts, talking, or playing at the chess : that

done, he returned to his study, and there would continue, except suitors or business abroad were occasion of the contrary, until five of the clock at night, and then would come to common prayer, as in the forenoon : which being finished, he went to supper, behaving himself there as at his dinner before. After supper recreating himself in playing at chess the space of an hour, he would then return again to his study, continuing there till eleven of the clock at night, which was his common hour to go to bed, then saying his prayers upon his knees, as in the morning when he rose. Being at his manor of Fulham, as divers times he used to be, he read daily a lecture to his family at the common prayer, beginning at the Acts of the Apostles, and so going through all the Epistles of St. Paul, giving, to every man that could read, a New Testament, hiring them besides with money to learn by heart certain principal chapters, but especially Acts xiii., reading also unto his household oftentimes Psalm ci., being marvellous careful over his family, that they might be a spectacle of all virtue and honesty to others. To be short, as he was godly and virtuous himself, so nothing but virtue and godliness reigned in his house, feeding them with the food of our Saviour Jesus Christ.

Now remaineth a word or two to be declared of his gentle nature and kindly pity in the usage of an old woman called Mrs. Bonner, mother to Dr. Bonner, sometime Bishop of London, which I thought good to touch, as well for the rare clemency of Dr. Ridley, as the unworthy inhumanity and ungrateful disposition again of Dr. Bonner. Bishop Ridley, being at his manor of Fulham, always sent for this said Mrs. Bonner, dwelling in a house adjoining to his house, to dinner and supper, with one Mrs. Mungey, Bonner's sister, saying, ' Go for my mother Bonner '; who, coming, was ever placed in the chair at the table's end, being so gently entreated, welcomed, and taken, as though he had been born of her own body, being never displaced of her seat, although the

King's Council had been present; saying, when any of them were there, as divers times they were: 'By your Lordship's favour, this place of right and custom is for my mother Bonner.' But how well he was recompensed for this his singular gentleness and pitiful piety after, at the hands of the said Dr. Bonner, almost the least child that goeth by the ground can declare. For who afterward was more enemy to Ridley than Bonner and his? Who more went about to seek his destruction than he? Recompensing this his gentleness with his extreme cruelty; as well appeared by the strait handling of Ridley's own natural sister, and George Shipside her husband, from time to time: whereas the gentleness of the other did suffer Bonner's mother, sister, and other of his kindred, not only quietly to enjoy all that which they had of Bonner, but also entertained them in his house, showing much courtesy and friendship daily unto them: whereas on the other side, Bishop Bonner, being restored again, would not suffer the brother and natural sister of Bishop Ridley, and other his friends, not only not to enjoy that which they had by the said their brother Bishop Ridley, but also currishly, without all order of law or honesty, by extort power wrested from them all the livings they had.

And yet, being not therewith satisfied, he sought all the means he could to work the death of the foresaid Shipside, saying, that he would make twelve godfathers to go upon him; which had been brought to pass indeed, at what time he was prisoner at Oxford, had not God otherwise wrought his deliverance by means of Dr. Heath, then the Bishop of Worcester.

Hereby all good indifferent readers notoriously have to understand what great diversity was in the disposition of these two natures, whereof as the one excelled in mercy and pity, so the other again as much or more excelled in churlish ingratitude and despiteful disdain. But of this matter enough.

II

THE next month after the burning of Dr. Ridley and
Master Latimer, which was the month of November, Stephen
Gardiner, Bishop and Chancellor, a man hated of God and
all good men, ended his wretched life: concerning the
qualities, nature, and disposition of which man, forsomuch as
somewhat hath been declared before in the story of King
Edward's reign, I shall need therefore the less now to stand
greatly upon the same. First, this viper's bird, crept out of
the town of Bury in Suffolk, was brought up most part of his
youth in Cambridge; his wit, capacity, memory, and other
endowments of nature were not to be complained of, if he
had well used and rightly applied the same; wherein there
was no great want of God's part in him, if he had not rather
himself wanted to the goodness of his gifts. Through this
promptness, activity, and towardness of his, he profited not a
little in such studies as he gave his head unto, as first in the
civil law, then in languages and such other like, especially in
those arts and faculties which had any prospect to dignity
and preferment to be hoped for. Besides other ornaments or
helps of nature, memory chiefly seemed in him very beneficial, rather than diligence of study.

To these gifts and qualities were joined again as great or
greater vices, which not so much followed him, as overtook
him; not so much burdened him, as made him burdenous to
the whole realm. He was of a proud stomach and high-
minded, in his own opinion and conceit flattering himself too
much; in wit, crafty and subtle; towards his superiors
flattering and fair spoken; to his inferiors fierce; against his
equal stout and envious, namely, if in judgment and sentence
he anything withstood him, as appeared between the good
Lord Cromwell and him in the reign of King Henry, being
of like haughtiness of stomach as the poets write of Pelides,

cedere nescius : who, although he would give no place to men, yet notwithstanding I wish he would have given place to truth, according as he seemed not altogether ignorant of that truth. What his knowledge was therein, it is evidently partly to understand as well by his book *De Verâ Obedientiâ*, as also by his sermon before King Edward. Also by his answers to the council the same time, and moreover by his own words it may be gathered in sundry places, as more plainly may appear by that which hereafter followeth.

F o x e
1563

Upon his estimation and fame he stood too much, more than was meet for a man of his coat and calling, whose profession was to be crucified unto the world, which thing made him so stiff in maintaining that he had once begun to take upon him. I will not here speak of that which hath been constantly reported to me touching the monstrous making and misshaped fashion of his feet and toes, the nails whereof were said not to be like to other men's, but to crook downward, and to be sharp like the claws of ravening beasts. What his learning was in the civil and canon law I have not to say. What it was in other liberal sciences and arts, this I suppose, that neither his continuance in study, nor diligence of reading was such (by reason of his too much intermeddling in prince's matters) as could truly well merit unto him the title of a deep learned man. But what learning or cunning soever it was he had, so it fared in him, as it doth in butchers, which used to blow up their flesh : even so he with boldness and stoutness, and specially with authority, made those gifts that he had to appear much greater than they were in very deed. Whereunto, peradventure, use also, and experience abroad, brought no little helps, rather than either quickness of wit or happiness of education.

And as touching divinity, he was so variable, wavering with time, that no constant censure can be given what to make of him. If his doings and writings were according to his conscience, no man can rightly say whether he was a right protestant or papist. If he wrote otherwise than he thought, for fear or to bear with time, then was he a double deep dissembler before God and man, to say and unsay, to write and unwrite, to swear and forswear, so as he did. For first in the beginning of Queen Anne's time, who was so forward or so busy in the matter of the King's divorce as Stephen Gardiner, who was first sent to Rome, and then to the Emperor with Edmund Foxe, as chief agent in the behalf of the Lady Anne? by whom also he was preferred to the bishopric of Winchester, as Edward Bonner was preferred to the bishopric of London. Again, at the abolishing of the Pope, who so ready to swear or so vehement to write against the Pope as he, as not only by his sermons, but also by his book *De Obedientiâ* may appear? in which book *De Obedientiâ*, lest any should think him drawn thereunto otherwise than by his own consent, he plainly declareth how, not rashly nor upon a sudden, but upon a long deliberation and advertisement in himself about the matter, he at length uttered his judgment; whereof read before. And moreover, so he uttered his judgment in writing against the usurped supremacy of the Pope, that, coming to Louvain afterward, he was there accounted for a person excommunicate and a schismatic, insomuch that he was not permitted in their church to say mass; and moreover in their public sermons they openly cried out against him. Whereof read hereafter following.

And thus long continued he firm and forward, so that who but Winchester, during all the time and reign of Queen Anne? After her decease that time by little and little carried him away, till at length the emulation of Cromwell's estate, and especially (as it seemeth) for his so much favouring of Bonner, whom Winchester at that time in no case could abide, made him an utter enemy both against him, and also his religion: till again, in King Edward's days, he began a little to rebate from certain points of popery, and

somewhat to smell of the gospel, as both by his sermon Foxe 1563
before King Edward, as also by his subscribing to certain
articles, may appear. And this was a half turn of Stephen
Gardiner from popery again to the gospel, and, no doubt, he
would have further turned, had not the unlucky decay of
the Duke of Somerset clean turned him away from true
divinity to plain popery, wherein he continued a cruel
persecutor to his dying day.

And thus much concerning the trade and profession of
Stephen Gardiner's popish divinity. In which his popish
trade, whether he followed more true judgment, or else time,
or rather the spirit of ambition and vainglory, it is doubtful
to say; and so much the more doubtful, because in his
doings and writings a man may see him not only contrary to
himself, but also in some points contrary to other papists.
And furthermore, where he agreeth with them, he seemeth
therein not so much to follow his own sense, as the mind
and meaning of Perescus; out of whose book the greatest
part of Winchester's divinity seemeth to be borrowed.

And therefore as in the true knowledge of God's holy word
and scripture he appeareth nobody; so in his pen and style of
writing no less far is he from commendation, than he is from
all plainness and perspicuity : in whose obscure and perplex
kind of writing, although peradventure some sense may be
found with some searching, yet shall no reader find any
sweetness in his reading.

John Foxe.

A PRETTY THEFT

THEN by and by Bahulus and I devised a pretty sport : Adlington 1566
we drew one of the greatest of the bears to our lodging, as though we would prepare to eat thereof, where we

flayed off his skin, and kept his ungles[1] whole, but we meddled not with the head, but cut it off by the neck, and so let it hang to the skin. Then we rased off the flesh from the neck, and cast dust thereon, and set it in the sun to dry.

When the skin was a drying we made merry with the flesh, and then we devised with ourselves, that one of us being more valiant than the rest both in body and courage (so that he would consent thereto) should put on the skin, and feigning that he were a bear, should be led to Demochares' house in the night, by which means we thought to be received and let in. Many were desirous to play the bear, but especially one Thrasileon of a courageous mind would take this enterprise in hand. Then we put him into the bear's skin, which fitted him finely in every point, we buckled it fast under his belly, and covered the seam with the hair, that it might not be seen. After this we made little holes through the bear's head, and through his nostrils and eyes, for Thrasileon to see out and take wind at, in such sort that he seemed a very lively and natural beast: when this was done we went into a cave which we hired for the purpose, and he crept in after like a bear with a good courage. Thus we began our subtility, and then we imagined thus: we feigned letters as though they came from one Nicanor, which dwelt in the country of Thracia, which was of great acquaintance with this Demochares, wherein we wrote, that he had sent him being his friend, the first fruits of his coursing and hunting. When night was come, which was a meet time for our purpose, we brought Thrasileon and our forged letters and presented them to Demochares. When Demochares beheld this mighty bear, and saw the liberality of Nicanor his friend, he commanded his servants to deliver unto us ten crowns, having great store in his coffers. Then (as the novelty of a thing doth accustom to stir men's minds to behold the same) many persons came on every side

---

[1] Claws.

to see this bear: but Thrasileon, lest they should by curious
viewing and prying perceive the truth, ran upon them to
put them in fear that they durst not come nigh. The people
said: 'Verily Demochares is right happy, in that after the
death of so many beasts, he hath gotten, maugre fortune's
head, so goodly a bear.' Then Demochares commanded
him with all care to be put into the park among the other
beasts: but immediately I spake unto him and said: 'Sir,
I pray you take heed how you put a beast tired with
the heat of the sun and with long travel among others
which, as I hear say, have divers maladies and diseases; let
him rather lie in some open place of your house nigh some
water, where he may take air and ease himself, for do not
you know that such kind of beasts do greatly delight to
couch under the shadow of trees and hillocks near pleasant
wells and waters?' Hereby Demochares admonished, and
remembering how many he had before that perished, was contented we should put the bear where we would. Moreover
we said unto him, that we ourselves were determined to lie
all night near the bear, to look unto him, and to give him
meat and drink at his due hour.

Then he answered: 'Verily, masters, you need not put
yourselves to such pains, for I have men that serve for
nothing but for that purpose.' So we took leave of him and
departed: and when we were come without the gates of the
town, we perceived before us a great sepulchre standing out
of the highway in a privy and secret place, and thither we
went and opened the mouth thereof, whereas we found the
sides covered with the corruption of man, and the ashes and
dust of his long-buried body, wherein we got ourselves to
bring our purpose to pass, and having respect to the dark
time of night, according to our custom, when we thought
that every one was asleep, we went with our weapons and
besieged the house of Demochares round about. Then
Thrasileon was ready at hand, and leaped out of the cavern,

and went to kill all such as he found asleep: but when he
came to the porter, he opened the gates and let us all in, and
then he showed us a large counter, wherein we saw put the
night before a great abundance of treasure: which when
by violence we had broken open, I bade every one of my
fellows take as much gold and silver as they could carry
away, and bear it to the sepulchre, and still as they carried
I stood at the gate, watching diligently when they should
return.   The bear runned about the house, to make such
of the family afeared as fortuned to wake and come out.   For
who is he that is so puissant and courageous, that at the
ugly sight of so great a monster will not quail and keep
his chamber, especially in the night?   But when we had
brought this matter to so good a point, there chanced a
pitiful case, for as I looked for my companions that should
come from the sepulchre, behold there was a boy of the
house that fortuned to look out of a window, and espied the
bear running about, and he went and told all the servants
of the house.   Whereupon incontinently they came forth
with torches, lanthorns, and other lights, that they might
see all the yard over: they came with clubs, spears, naked
swords, greyhounds, and mastiffs to slay the poor beast.
Then I during this broyle thought to run away, but because
I would see Thrasileon fight with the dogs, I lay behind the
gate to behold him.   And although I might perceive that
he was well nigh dead, yet remembered he his own faithful-
ness and ours, and valiantly resisted the gaping and ravenous
mouths of the hell hounds, so took he in gree the pageant
which willingly he took in hand himself, and with much ado
tumbled at length out of the house: but when he was at
liberty abroad yet could he not save himself, for all the dogs
of the street joined themselves to the greyhounds and
mastiffs of the house, and came upon him.

Alas, what a pitiful sight it was to see our poor Thrasileon
thus environed and compassed with so many dogs that tare

and rent him miserably. Then I, impatient of so great a Adlington misery, ran in amongst the press of the people, and aiding 1566 him with my words as much as I might, exhorted them all in this manner: ' O great and extreme mischance, what a precious and excellent beast have we lost.'   But my words did nothing prevail, for there came out a tall man with a spear in his hand, that thrust him clean through, and afterwards many that stood by drew out their swords, and so they killed him.   But verily our good Captain Thrasileon, the honour of our comfort, received his death so patiently, that he would not betray the league between us, either by crying, howling, or any other means, but being torn with dogs and wounded with weapons, did yield forth a doleful cry, more like unto a beast than a man.   And taking his present fortune in good part, with courage and glory enough did finish his life, with such a terror unto the assembly, that no person was so hardy until it was day, as to touch him, though he were stark dead : but at last there came a butcher more valiant than the rest, who, opening the paunch of the beast, slit out an hardy and venturous thief.

In this manner we lost our Captain Thrasileon, but he lost not his fame and honour.

William Adlington.

AN OLD MAN'S MISADVENTURE

I HAD of late years an old man to my tenant, who cus-   Harman tomably a great time went twice in the week to   1567 London, either with fruit or with peascods, when time served therefor.   And as he was coming homeward on Black-heath, at the end thereof next to Shooters' Hill, he overtook two rufflers,[1] the one mannerly waiting on the other, as one had been the master, and the other the man or servant,

---

[1] Part foot-pad, part cheat, part beggar.

Harman
1567

carrying his master's cloak.   This old man was very glad that he might have their company over the Hill, because that day he had made a good market; for he had seven shillings in his purse, and an old angel, which this poor man had thought had not been in his purse, for he willed his wife over night to take out the same angel, and lay it up until his coming home again.   And he verily thought that his wife had so done, which indeed forgot to do it.   Thus after salutations had, this master ruffler entered into communication with this simple old man, who, riding softly beside them, communed of many matters.   Thus feeding this old man with pleasant talk, until they were on the top of the Hill, where these rufflers might well behold the coast about them clear, quickly steps unto this poor man, and taketh hold of his horse-bridle, and leadeth him into the wood, and demandeth of him what and how much money he had in his purse.   'Now, by my troth,' quoth this old man; 'you are a merry gentleman.   I know you mean not to take away anything from me, but rather to give me some if I should ask it of you.'   By and by, this servant thief casteth the cloak that he carried on his arm about this poor man's face, that he should not mark or view them, with sharp words to deliver quickly that he had, and to confess truly what was in his purse.   This poor man, then all abashed, yielded, and confessed that he had but just seven shillings in his purse; and the truth is he knew of no more.   This old angel was fallen out of a little purse into the bottom of a great purse.   Now, this seven shillings in white money they quickly found, thinking indeed that there had been no more; yet farther groping and searching, found this old angel.   And with great admiration this gentleman thief began to bless him, saying: 'Good Lord, what a world is this!   How may' (quoth he) 'a man believe or trust in the same?   See you not' (quoth he) 'this old knave told me that he had but seven shillings, and here is more by an angel: what an old knave and a false knave have we here!' quoth this ruffler; 'Our Lord have mercy on us, will this world never be better?'—and therewith went their way.   And left the old man in the wood, doing him no more harm.   But sorrowfully sighing, this old man, returning home, declared his misadventure, with all the words and circumstances above showed.   Whereat for the time was great laughing, and this poor man for his losses among his loving neighbours well considered in the end.

Harman
1567

Thomas Harman.

AN ESCAPE

AFTER this a long time there was peace and rest in the realm, and that through the court and counsel of the Duke of Albany, who soon thereafter married the Earl of Orkney's daughter, and begat upon her a son, called Alexander, who was thereafter Bishop of Moray, but not long after he parted with her, and passed in France, and was married upon the Duchess of Boulogne.   But this Alexander, Duke of Albany, had the great indignation of many of the nobles in Scotland, for fortifying and maintaining the King in his private affairs, and gave him the wyte that so many Lords were in captivity at that time, and for rendering of Berwick, according to the King's promise, who gave him commission to render the same for his relief.   And the Lords could not be content therewith, but alleged it to be treason; and were very desirous to have had some crime to accuse the Duke of Albany, and to have put a new suspicion betwixt him and his brother the King, thinking well they could [not] anyways get their will of the King except they had his brother put off.   And for that effect they caused certain flatterers and evil speakers show the King that the Duke of Albany

Lindsay
1570

Lindsay intended to have the Crown, for he was likelier to be king
1570 nor the King himself as he proceeded; for he disponed all
things pertaining to the liberty of the Crown, and caused
the King to understand that he would fulfil the prophecy of
the witch who prophesied to the King that the nearest of
his kin should destroy him. These words, and sic like
other feigned tales, made the King so afeard of the Duke of
Albany, that he could have been content to have been quit of
him, notwithstanding of all the travails he had made for the
King's weal, and for the delivering of him out of captivity.
All his good service was forgot with this flattery, and the
fear that the King took of him by the persuasion of wicked
counsellors caused him to summon his brother before the
Council for such points of treason as after follows. That is
to say : for rendering the town of Berwick in Englishmen's
hands but counsel or commission of the Lords of Scotland. So the Duke of Albany compeared pertly[1] before the
King and Council, and produced the King's commission, under
his Great Seal, to render the same, to the effect that support
might come to the King for his deliverance. But the Lords
alleged that commission was of no effect at that time, because
he was in captivity, and did the same without the advice of
the Lords and Council. Wherefore the Lords of Council for
the time convicted the said Duke, and sent him to the Castle
to be imprisoned.

In this meantime, the Earl of Angus got the whole lords
that was in ward relieved,[2] upon caution to enter again when
the King pleased, under the pain of ten thousand pounds
each man, etc. Soon after this they counselled the King to
justify[3] his brother, the Duke of Albany, thinking if they
were quit of him they should do with the King what they
pleased. For they stood in sic awe of the Duke that they
durst never meddle with the King, nor put hands on him,
he being alive. Wherefore these conspirators insisted and

[1] Readily.   [2] Released.   [3] Execute.

were very desirous to have this noble and famous man put Lindsay
to death, and continued in this ungodly and unleisum [1] suit, 1570
till it was known in France by sic as favoured the Duke
of Albany; and therefore there came a French ship out of
France hastily in Scotland, with secret writings to the Duke
of Albany, who was then in prison in the Castle of Edinburgh, to advertise him that it was concluded by the King
and Council that he should be justified upon a certain day,
which was the day after the ship came to the town of Leith,
beside Newhaven, and gave herself forth as a passenger with
wine. When he had heard of these news, he desired leave of
the Captain to send for two bottles of wine, who gave him
leave gladly, and provided the bosses [2] himself: and then the
Duke of Albany sent one of his familiar servants to the
Frenchman, and desired him to bring him of the finest and
starkest wine, who was obeyed thankfully, and sent him two
bosses of Malvesie; and in the one end of the bottle put a
roll of wax, wherein was enclosed a secret writing, which
showed the Duke of Albany sic news as he was not content
therewith; and in the other boss there was a long tow [3] to
support him in his need. So the messenger hasted him back
to the Castle, and showed his master certain things by tongue
which the Frenchman had told him; and that night the
Duke called the Captain to supper, and promised him a
drink of good wine. So the Captain came to him gladly,
and supped with him. The Duke gave his chamber-child
command that he should drink no wine that night, but hold
himself temperate, for he knew not what he would have to
do, and if there arose any dissention betwixt him and the
Captain, he prayed him to stand by him, as he should be a
good master to him thereafter. When the supper was done,
the Captain passed to the King's chamber to see what was
doing, who was then lodged in the Castle: and when he had
visited all, he caused them close the gates and set the watch-

___

[1] Hateful.   [2] Bottles.   [3] Rope.

men; and thereafter came to the Duke's chamber to the collation. And after they had drunken their collation, and all men in their beds, the Duke and the Captain passed to the tables and played for the wine. The fire was hot and the wine was strong, and the Captain and his men became merry, till at the last the Duke perceived his time, and saw them merry, and made a sign to his chamber-child to be ready as he had instructed him, for the Duke was fully resolved either to do or to die; for he was surely informed by the French ship that he was to be beheaded on the morrow. So he thought best to prevein[1] the time, and leaped from the board and struck the Captain with a whinger and slew him, and also sticked other two with his own hand. And in the meantime his chamber-child was very busy; and so they two overthrew five: that is, the Captain and four of his men: and when they had done, cast them in the fire; and afterwards took out their tows and passed to the wall-head, at a quiet place where the watchmen might have no sight of them, and then stretched their cords over the wall-head, and the chamber-boy passed first; but the tows were short, and he fell and broke his thigh-bone. Then he cried to his master to make the tow longer, for he was gone. Then the Duke rived the sheets off his bed and lengthened the tow, and passed safely himself. And when he was come down and perceived his servant in point of death, he took him upon his back and carried him away as far as he might, and left him in a quiet place where he trowed he might be safe, and syne went to the Newhaven beside Leith, and made him a sign to the ship, who sent a boat to the land and received him in. But no man knew whether his servant went with him or not; but surely many gentlemen of Scotland wished themselves to have been with him, and, amongst the rest, Sir Alexander Jardine of Applegarth, knight, passed with him, and sundry other gentlemen.

[1] Anticipate.

But on the morn, when the watchmen perceived that Lindsay
the tows were hanging over the walls, then ran they to seek 1570
the Captain to show him the matter and manner, but he was
not in his own chamber. Then they passed to the Duke's
chamber and found the door open, and a dead man lying in
the chamber door, and the Captain and the rest burning in the
fire, which was very dolorous to them ; and when they missed
the Duke of Albany and his chamber-child, they ran speedily
and showed the King how the matter had happened. But
he would not give it credence till he passed himself and saw
the matter. Then he considered the whole cause how it
stood, and caused the gates to be holden close, that no word
should pass to the town, till he had searched all the place,
to see whether the Duke of Albany was within or not. But
when he could not find him, he caused horsemen to be sent
forth in all parts to see if they could apprehend him in any
place, and bring him to him again, and they should have
great rewards therefor. But yet they could get no kind of
trial[1] of him, until at the last there came a man out of Leith
and showed the King that there came a boat from the French
ship and took in certain men, and thereafter pulled up her
sails, and travished[2] up and down the Firth, whom they judged
to be the Duke of Albany, as it was true; for he passed
to France incontinent, and got in marriage the Duchess of
Boulogne.   *Robert Lindsay of Pitscottie.*

THE KILLING OF DAVID BEATON

AFTER the death of this blessed martyr of God [George Knox
Wishart] began the people, in plain speaking, to damn 1572
and detest the cruelty that was used. Yea, men of great birth,
estimation, and honour, at open tables avowed, that the blood
of the said Master George should be revenged, or else they

---

[1] Sign, news.   [2] Sailed back and forward.

should cost life for life. Amongst whom John Lesley, brother to the Earl of Rothes, was the chief; for he, in all companies, spared not to say, 'That same whinger (showing forth his dagger), and that same hand, should be priests to the Cardinal.' These bruits came to the Cardinal's ears; but he thought himself stout enough for all Scotland; for in Babylon, that is, in his new block-house, he was sure, as he thought; and upon the fields he was able to match all his enemies. And to write the truth, the most part of the nobility of Scotland had either given unto him their bonds of manrent,[1] or else were in confederacy and promised amity with him. He only feared them in whose hands God did deliver him, and for them had he laid his nets so secretly (as that he made a full compt), that their feet could not escape, as we shall after hear; and something of his former practices we maun reaccompt.

After the Pasche he came to Edinburgh to hold the scinzie[2] (as the Papists term their unhappy assembly of Baal's shaven sort). It was bruited that something was purposed against him at that time by the Earl of Angus and his friends, whom he mortally hated, and whose destruction he sought. But it failed, and so returned he to his strength[3]; yea, to his God and only comfort, as well in heaven as in earth. And there he remained without all fear of death, promising unto himself no less pleasure nor did the rich man, of whom mention is made by our Master in the Evangel; for he did not only rejoice and say, 'Eat and be glad, my soul, for thou hast great riches laid up in store for many days;' but also he said: 'Tush, a fig for the fead,[4] and a button for the bragging of all the heretics and their assistance in Scotland! Is not my Lord Governor mine? Witness his eldest son, their pledge at my table? Have I not the Queen at my own devotion? (He meant of the mother to Mary that now mischievously reigns.) Is not France my friend, and I friend to France? What danger should I fear?'

---

[1] Allegiance.   [2] Synod.   [3] Stronghold.   [4] Feud. (?)

And thus in vanity the carnal Cardinal delighted himself a little before his death. But yet he had devised to have cut off such as he thought might cumber him; for he had appointed the whole gentlemen of Fife to have met him at Falkland the Monday after that he was slain upon the Saturday. His treasonable purpose was not understanded but by his secret Council; and it was this: That Norman Lesley, Sheriff of Fife, and appearing heir to his father, the Earl of Rothes; the said John Lesley, father-brother to Norman; the Lairds of Grange, elder and younger; Sir James Leirmonth of Dairsye, and Provost of St. Andrews; and the faithful Laird of Raith; should either have been slain, or else taken, and after to have been used at his pleasure. This enterprise was disclosed after his slaughter, partly by letters and memorials found in his chamber, but plainly affirmed by such as were of the Council. Many purposes were devised how that wicked man might have been taken away. But all failed till Friday, the 28th of May, Anno 1546, when the foresaid Norman came at night to St. Andrews; William Kirkcaldy of Grange, younger, was in the town before, awaiting upon the purpose; last came John Lesley foresaid, who was most suspected. What conclusion they took that night it was not known but by the issue which followed.

But early upon the Saturday, in the morning, the 29th of May, were they in sundry companies in the Abbey kirkyard, not far distant from the Castle. First, the gates being open, and the drawbridge letten down, for receiving of lime and stones, and other things necessary for building (for Babylon was almost finished)—first, we say, assayed William Kirkcaldy of Grange, younger, and with him six persons, and getting entrance, held purpose with the porter: 'If my Lord was waking?' who answered, 'No.' (And so it was indeed; for he had been busy at his compts with Mistress Marion Ogilvy that night, who was espyed to depart from him by the privy postern that morning; and therefore quietness,

after the rules of physic, and a morning sleep was requisite
for My Lord.) While the said William and the porter talked,
and his servants made them to look the work and the workmen, approached Norman Lesley with his company; and
because they were in no great number, they easily got
entrance. They address them to the midst of the close,
and immediately came John Lesley, somewhat rudely, and
four persons with him. The porter, fearing, would have
drawn the bridge; but the said John, being entered thereon,
stayed, and leapt in. And while the porter made him for
defence, his head was broken, the keys taken from him, and
he castin in the fosse; and so the place was seized. The
shout arises: the workmen, to the number of more than a
hundred, ran off the walls, and were without hurt put forth
at the wicket gate. The first thing that ever was done,
William Kirkcaldy took the guard of the privy postern, fearing that the fox should have escaped. Then go the rest to
the gentlemen's chambers, and without violence done to any
man, they put more than fifty persons to the gate. The
number that enterprised and did this was but sixteen persons.
The Cardinal, awakened with the shouts, asked from his
window, What meant that noise? It was answered that
Norman Lesley had taken his Castle. Which understand, he
ran to the postern; but perceiving the passage to be kept
without, he returned quickly to his chamber, took his two-
handed sword, and gart[1] his chamber-child cast chests and
other impediments to the door. In this meantime came John
Lesley unto it and bids open. The cardinal asking, 'Who
calls?' he answers, 'My name is Lesley.' He redemands,
'Is that Norman?' The other says, 'Nay; my name is
John.' 'I will have Norman,' says the cardinal; 'for he is
my friend.' 'Content yourself with such as are here; for
other shall ye get none.' There were with the said John,
James Melvin, a man familiarly acquainted with Master

[1] Made.

George Wishart, and Peter Carmichael, a stout gentleman. Knox 1572
In this meantime, while they force at the door, the Cardinal
hides a box of gold under coals that were laid in a secret
corner.   At length he asked : ' Will ye save my life ? '   The
said John answered : ' It may be that we will.'   ' Nay,' says
the Cardinal ; ' swear unto me by God's wounds, and I will
open unto you.'   Then answered the said John : ' It that
was said is unsaid ; ' and so cried, ' Fire, fire ' (for the door
was very stark) ; and so was brought a chimleyful of
burning coals.   Which perceived, the Cardinal or his chamber-child (it is uncertain) opened the door, and the Cardinal
sat down in a chair, and cried : ' I am a priest ; I am a priest :
ye will not slay me.'   The said John Lesley (according to his
former vows) struck him first once or twice, and so did the
said Peter.   But James Melvin (a man of nature most gentle
and most modest) perceiving them both in choler, withdrew
them, and said : ' This work and judgment of God (although
it be secret) ought to be done with greater gravity ; ' and
presenting unto him the point of the sword, said : ' Repent
thee of thy former wicked life, but especially of the shedding
of the blood of that notable instrument of God, Master
George Wishart, which albeit the flame of fire consumed
before men, yet cries it a vengeance upon thee, and we
from God are sent to revenge it.   For here, before my God,
I protest that neither the hetterent [1] of thy person, the love
of thy riches, nor the fear of any trouble thou could have
done to me in particular, moved, nor moves me to strike
thee ; but only because thou hast been, and remains, an
obstinate enemy against Christ Jesus and his holy Evangel.'
And so he struck him twice or thrice through with a stog [2]
sword ; and so he fell, never word heard out of his mouth,
but ' I am a priest, I am a priest : fie, fie : all is gone.'

While they were thus occupied with the Cardinal, the fray [3]
rises in the town.   The Provost assembles the community,

---

[1] Hatred (?)   [2] Stabbing.   [3] Panic.

Knox
1572

and comes to the fosse's side, crying: 'What have ye done with my Lord Cardinal? Where is my Lord Cardinal? Have ye slain my Lord Cardinal? Let us see my Lord Cardinal!' They that were within answered gently: 'Best it were unto you to return to your own houses; for the man ye call the Cardinal has received his reward, and in his own person will trouble the world no more.' But then, more enragedly, they cry: 'We shall never depart till that we see him.' And so was he brought to the east blockhouse head, and shown dead over the wall to the faithless multitude, which would not believe before it saw how miserably lay David Beaton, careful Cardinal. And so they departed, without *Requiem æternam*, and *Requiescat in pace*, sung for his soul. Now, because the weather was hot (for it was in May, as ye have heard), and his funerals could not suddenly be prepared, it was thought best, to keep him from stinking, to give him great salt enough, a cope of lead, and a nook in the bottom of the Sea-Tower (a place where many of God's children had been imprisoned before) to await what exequies his brethren the bishops would prepare for him.

These things we write merrily. But we would that the reader should observe God's just judgments, and how that he can deprehend the worldly wise in their own wisdom, make their table to be a snare to trap their own feet, and their own presupposed strength to be their own destruction. These are the works of our God, whereby He would admonish the tyrants of this earth, that in the end He will be revenged of their cruelty, what strength soever they make in the contrary. But such is the blindness of man (as David speaks), 'That the posterity does ever follow the footsteps of their wicked fathers, and principally in their impiety.' For how little differs the cruelty of that bastard, that yet is called Bishop of St. Andrews, from the cruelty of the former, we will after hear.   *John Knox.*

A SCOT ABROAD

Melvill
1574

BECAUSE I said before that Scotland received never a greater benefit at the hands of God nor this man, I will shortly set down, first, a little discourse of his life before his coming home, and syne what he brought with him.   He was born in Baldowy, a place pleasant, fertile, and well aired, lying within a mile to the town of Montrose, upon the south-west, hard by the *Æstuarium fluminis Æskae meridionalis*, in the year of Christ's birth 1545, the first day of the month August, begotten of gentle and honest parents, Richard Melvill of Baldowy, brother-german of John Melvill of Dysart, and Gills Abercrombie, daughter to Thomas Abercrombie, burgess of Montrose, of the house of Murthley. He was the youngest of nine brothers, all left alive when their father was slain with the greatest part of the gentlemen of Angus, in the vanguard of the field of Pinkie.   His mother lived an honourable widow till he was twelve years of age, trained up in letters in the school of Montrose, under Mr. Thomas Anderson, esteemed the best master in his time, howbeit not the most learned.   She left six of her sons in honest rooms; all, even then or shortly thereafter, bearing office in Kirk or commonweal, and with the best esteemed in their rank and above.   They were, Richard Melvill of Baldowy, and minister of Christ's Evangel soon after, the eldest: Mr. Thomas, a fine scholar, well travelled in France and Italy, Secretary-Depute of Scotland: Walter, burgess, and oft bailie of Montrose, a wise and stout man: Roger, burgess of Dundee, a man of singular gifts of nature and God's grace, but was not trained up in letters (I heard that faithful pastor of Dundee, William Christison, a little after his death, with tears say, 'Alas! when God took this Roger Melvill, he took from me my father, and the care-

Melvill fullest father that ever Dundee had.   His name will be
1574 remembered so long as Dundee is a town '): Mr. James,
minister of Christ's Evangel : John, then guidman and ruler
of his mother's affairs, and after a minister in the Kirk : the
rest were Robert, David, and Andrew ; whereof the first two
were kept at the school till they tired, and were put to
crafts ; the last was a sickly, tender boy, and took pleasure
in nothing so mickle as his book.   So, with the portion
that was left him, he spent a year or two in Montrose,
namely, hiring a France man, called Petrus de Marsiliers,
teach the Greek grammar, and something of that language,
honestly conduced to the same as a rare thing in the country,
not heard of before, by that notable instrument in the Kirk,
John Erskine of Done, of most honourable and happy
memory ; wherein he profited so, that, entering thereafter in
the course of Philosophy within the University of St. Andrews,
all that was teached of Aristotle he learned and studied it
out of the Greek text, which his masters understood not.
He passed his course in the New College, tenderly beloved
of Mr. John Douglas, Provost of that College and Rector of
the University ; who would take him betwixt his legs at the
fire in winter, and warm his hands and cheeks, and, blessing
him, say, ' My silly fatherless and motherless child, it 's ill
to wit what God may make of thee yet !'

So, ending his course of philosophy, he left the University
of St. Andrews with the commendation of the best philosopher, poet, and Grecian of any young master in the land ;
and with all possible diligence made his preparation and
past to France.   By the way he was extremely tormented
with sea-sickness and storm of weather, so that ofttimes,
whiles by danger of shipwreck, whiles by infirmity and
sickness, he looked for death.   He arrived first in England,
and again embarking came to Bordeaux, where he tarried
not long, but embarking from that came to Dieppe ; from
that to Paris, where he remained in the University two

years at his own studies, hearing the lights of the most shining Melvill age in all good letters, the king's public professors, Andreas **1574** Tornebus in Greek and Latin Humanity; Petrus Ramus in Philosophy and Eloquence; Johannes Mercerus in the Hebrew language, whereupon he was specially set. In the last year of they two, he grew so expert in the Greek, that he declaimed and teached lessons, uttering never a word but Greek, with such readiness and plenty, as was marvellous to the hearers. From Paris he passed to Poitiers, where he regented [1] in the College of St. Marcian three years. There he had the best lawyers, and studied so mickle thereof as might serve for his purpose, which was Theology, whereto he was dedicate from his mother's womb. And when the Colleges were given up, because of the siege laid to the town, which was long and fearful, he was employed by an honourable Councillor to instruct his only son. The bairn profited exceeding well, and was of a sweet inclination, taken away from him and his parents by a shot out of the camp, which parted the wall of his chamber, and wounded him deadly in the thigh. He called incontinent for his master, whom how soon he saw, he caught him in his arms, and uttered the words of the apostle in Greek, διδάσκαλε, τὸν δρόμον μοῦ τετέληκα, 'Master, I have perfected my course!' and so, with many other godly and sweet words, he died. That bairn gaed never out of his heart; but in teaching of me, he often remembered him with tender compassion of mind. He tarried in that house, which was well furnished, during the time of the siege. There was a corporal with a few suddarts [2] put to keep the house, who espied him in his prayers and speeches to be holy and devout; and one day (being a Papist and man of war), with a great oath he challenged Mr. Andrew that he was a Huguenot, and would help to betray the town; therefore, because the alarm was stricken, he could not trust him in

[1] Acted as regent or professor.   [2] Soldiers.

Melvill
1574

that house. Mr. Andrew answers incontinent, 'I am as honest a man to my God, and magistrate, and estate of the town, and master of this family, as thou art; and so shall prove this day—do thy best!' And with that starts to the next armour, and on with it; and all in arms to the stable, and takes the best horse by the head. This when the corporal saw, he comes with felon fair [1] terms, and intreats him to leave off and forgive him. 'O no, no!' says he, 'I shall prove as honest and stout as thyself.' 'O Monsieur,' says the other, 'my captain and the master of this house will rebuke me and put me from it, if ye be thus troubled; therefore, I pray you, take me oblesit [2] to my uttermost, and tarry and forgive me.' So he took ease in good part, and was never troubled thereafter. If it had come to the worst, he was resolved, being well horsed, to have gotten him to the camp of the Admiral, who was in person besieging the town.

The siege of the town being raised, he left Poitiers, and accompanied with a Frenchman, he took journey to Geneva, leaving books and all there, and carried nothing with him but a little Hebrew Bible in his belt. So he came to Geneva all upon his feet, as he had done before from Dieppe to Paris, and from that to Poitiers; for he was small and light of body, but full of sprights, vigorous and courageous. His companions of the way, when they came to the inn, would lie down like tired tykes, but he would out and sight the towns and villages whithersoever they came. The ports of Geneva were tentily [3] kept, because of the troubles of France, and multitude of strangers that came. Being therefore inquired what they were, the Frenchman, his companion, answered, 'We are poor scholars.' But Mr. Andrew, perceiving that they had no will of poor folks, being already overlaid therewith, said, 'No, no, we are not poor! We have as mickle as will pay for all we take, so

---

[1] Very smooth.   [2] Bound.   [3] Carefully.

long as we tarry. We have letters from his acquaintance to Monsieur de Beza; let us deliver those, we crave no farther.' And so, being convoyed to Beza, and then to their lodging, Beza, perceiving him a scholar, and they having need of a Professor of Humanity in the College, put him within a two or three days to trial in Virgil and Homer; which he could acquit so well, that but farther [1] he is placed in that room of profession; and at his first entry, a quarter's fee paid him in hand. So that, howbeit there was but a crown to the fore betwixt them both, and the Frenchman weak-spirited, and wist not what to do, yet he found God's providence to relieve both himself and help his marrow [2] till he was provided.

In Geneva he abode five years; during the which time his chief study was Divinity, whereanent he heard Beza his daily lessons and preachings; Cornelius Bonaventura, Professor of the Hebrew, Chaldaic, and Syriac languages; Portus, a Greek born, Professor of the Greek tongue, with whom he would reason about the right pronunciation thereof; for the Greek pronounced it after the common form, keeping the accents; the which Mr. Andrew controlled by precepts and reason, till the Greek would grow angry, and cry out: *Vos Scoti, vos barbari! docebitis nos Graecos pronunciationem linguae nostrae, scilicet?* He heard there also Francis Ottoman, the renowndest lawyer in his time. There he was well acquainted with my eame,[3] Mr. Henry Scrymgeour, who, by his learning in the laws and policy and service of many noble princes, had attained to great riches, conquaced [4] a pretty room within a league to Geneva, and biggit [5] thereon a trim house called 'The Vilet,' and a fair lodging within the town, which all, with a daughter, his only bairn, he left to the Syndiques of the town.

About the end of five years, the Bishop of Brechin, and Mr. Andrew Polwart with him, came there; and, tarrying a

[1] Without more ado.   [2] Companion.   [3] Uncle.   [4] Purchased.   [5] Builded.

while, purposed homeward ; with whom Mr. Andrew Melvill, after the receiving of letters from his brethren and me, with great difficulty purchased leave of the Kirk and Magistrates of Geneva (who would on no ways have contented to part with him, if his conscience had suffered him to reserve his gifts any longer unoffered to his country, and employed for the benefit of his friends. Beza, in his letter to the General Kirk of Scotland, alleges, that as the greatest token of affection the Kirk of Geneva could show to Scotland, that they had suffered themselves to be spoiled of Mr. Andrew Melvill, whereby the Kirk of Scotland might be enriched, and taking journey came homeward. From Lyons they traversed the Franche-Compté to the head of the river of Loire, and came down the same by water to Orleans, having in company, seven or eight days, a captain, a mediciner, and a priest, superstitious papists at their meeting, kythed[1] in their speech and meats, but by merry and solid reasoning withal, became flesh-eaters on Friday, and the captain not far from the kingdom of heaven or they parted. The ports of Orleans were strait kept (being but a year and half after the horrible massacres). Brechin and Mr. Andrew Polwart was on foot, and Mr. Andrew well mounted on horse, because he had wrested his leg, they past the two footmen, and, detaining the horseman, the soldiers inquires what he was. He answered, 'A Scotsman.' 'O! ye Scotsmen are all Huguenots,' says the guard. 'Huguenots!' says he, 'what's that? we ken none such.' 'O!' says the soldier, 'ye have not mess?' 'Forsooth,' says he merrily, 'our bairns in Scotland go daily to mess!' 'Good companion,' says the other, laughing, 'go thy way.' Coming to their lodging, he tells his neighbours, and gars them laugh : 'But surely,' say they, 'we were very fleyed[2] our passport should have been loked,[3] and finding us come from Geneva, should have been troubled.' 'Yea,' says their host, 'take

---

1 Open, *i.e.* conforming.　　2 Frightened.　　3 Inspected.

it for a special providence of God, for within this twelve month many thousands for less have lost their lives.' Going out of the town again, at the turn of a rew,[1] they met the procession; Brechin and his pedagogue were before, Mr. Andrew a little after. Brechin turns back and says, 'What shall I do?' 'Forward!' quoth he, and so he does. Mr. Andrew holds out his side cloak with his arms as though he had been bearing something under his oxters, and so passes by. But his heart beat him thereafter oft and sore, that he should have so stoutly counselled the other, and used a piece of dissimulation himself. Coming to Paris, there they remained divers days; where Mr. Andrew, meeting with the Lord Ogilvy, his countryman, is requested by him to go to the Jesuits' College, where he reasoned with Father Tyrie sundry days; but the time being so dangerous, and [because] of some menacing speeches of the Bishop of Glasgow, he was counselled to haste [out] of the town. So they came from Dieppe over to Rye in England, from thence to London, where they remained a space; and buying horses, came home London-way, by Berwick, to Edinburgh. And this for a short recital of his life till his coming home.

Melvill
1574

Rev. James Melvill.

AGINCOURT

THE King the same day found a shallow, between Corbie and Peron, which never was espied before, at which he with his army and carriages the night ensuing passed the water of Some without let or danger, and therewith determined to make haste towards Calis, and not to seek for battle, except he were thereto constrained, because that his army by sickness was sore diminished, insomuch that he had but only two thousand horsemen and thirteen thousand archers, billmen, and of all sorts of other footmen.

Holinshed
1577

[1] Street.

The Englishmen were brought into some distress in this journey, by reason of their victuals in manner spent, and no hope to get more; for the enemies had destroyed all the corn before they came. Rest could they none take, for their enemies with alarms did ever so infest them; daily it rained and nightly it freezed; of fuel there was great scarcity, of fluxes plenty; money enough, but wares for their relief to bestow it on had they none. Yet in this great necessity, the poor people of the country were not spoiled, nor anything taken of them without payment, nor any outrage or offence done by the Englishmen, except one, which was, that a soldier took a pyx out of a church, for which he was apprehended, and the King not once removed till the box was restored and the offender strangled. The people of the countries thereabout, hearing of such zeal in him to the maintenance of justice, ministered to his army victuals and other necessaries, although by open proclamation so to do they were prohibited.

The French King being at Rone, and hearing that King Henry was passed the river of Some, was much displeased therewith, and assembling his Council to the number of five and thirty, asked their advice what was to be done. There were amongst these five and thirty his son the Dolphin, calling himself King of Sicille; the Dukes of Berre and Brittaine, the Earl of Pontieu, the King's youngest son, and other high estates. At length thirty of them agreed that the Englishmen should not depart unfought withal, and five were of a contrary opinion, but the greater number ruled the matter: and so Montjoy, King-at-Arms, was sent to the King of England to defy him as the enemy of France, and to tell him that he should shortly have battle. King Henry advisedly answered: 'Mine intent is to do as it pleaseth God, I will not seek your master at this time; but if he or his seek me, I will meet with them, God willing. If any of your nation attempt once to stop me in my journey now towards Calis, at their jeopardy

be it; and yet I wish not any of you so unadvised as to be the Holinshed
occasion that I dye your tawny ground with your red blood.'   1577

When he had thus answered the herald, he gave him a
princely reward, and licence to depart. Upon whose return,
with this answer, it was incontinently on the French side
proclaimed, that all men of war should resort to the Constable
to fight with the King of England. Whereupon, all men apt
for armour and desirous of honour drew them toward the
field. The Dolphin sore desired to have been at the battle,
but he was prohibited by his father: likewise Philip, Earl of
Charolois, would gladly have been there, if his father the
Duke of Burgognie would have suffered him: many of his
men stole away, and went to the Frenchmen. The King of
England hearing that the Frenchmen approached, and that
there was another river for him to pass with his army by a
bridge, and doubting lest if the same bridge should be broken
it would be greatly to his hindrance, appointed certain captains with their bands to go thither with all speed before
him, and to take possession thereof, and so to keep it till his
coming thither.

Those that were sent, finding the Frenchmen busy to break
down their bridge, assailed them so vigourously, that they
discomfited them, and took and slew them; and so the bridge
was preserved till the King came, and passed the river by the
same with his whole army. This was on the two and twentieth
day of October. The Duke of York that led the vanguard
(after the army was passed the river) mounted up to the
height of an hill with his people, and sent out scouts to discover the country, the which upon their return advertised
him that a great army of Frenchmen was at hand, approaching towards them. The Duke declared to the King what he
had heard, and the King thereupon, without all fear or trouble
of mind, caused the battle which he led himself to stay, and
incontinently rode forth to view his adversaries, and that
done, returned to his people, and with cheerful countenance

Holinshed caused them to be put in order of battle, assigning to every
1577 captain such room and place as he thought convenient, and
so kept them still in that order till night was come, and then
determined to seek a place to encamp and lodge his army in
for that night.

There was not one amongst them that knew any certain
place whither to go, in that unknown country: but by chance
they happened upon a beaten way, white in sight; by the
which they were brought unto a little village, where they
were refreshed with meat and drink somewhat more plen-
teously than they had been divers days before.   Order was
taken by commandment from the King after the army was
first set in battle array, that no noise or clamour should be
made in the host; so that in marching forth to this village
every man kept himself quiet: but at their coming into the
village, fires were made to give light on every side, as there
likewise were in the French host, which was encamped not
past two hundred and fifty paces distant from the English.
The chief leaders of the French host were these: the Constable of France, the Marshal, the Admiral, the Lord Ram-
bures, Master of the Crossbows, and other of the French
nobility, which came and pitched down their standards and
banners in the county of St. Paul, within the territory of
Agincourt, having in their army (as some write) to the number
of threescore thousand horsemen, besides footmen, waggoners,
and other.

They were lodged even in the way by the which the
Englishmen must needs pass towards Calis, and all that night
after their coming thither, made great cheer, and were very
merry, pleasant, and full of game.   The Englishmen also for
their parts were of good comfort and nothing abashed of the
matter, and yet they were both hungry, weary, sore travelled,
and vexed with many cold diseases.   Howbeit reconciling
themselves with God by housel[1] and shrift, requiring assis-

[1] Confession.

tance at His hands that is the only giver of victory, they Holinshed
determined rather to die than to yield or flee. The day 1577
following was the five and twentieth of October in the year
1415, being then Friday, and the feast of Crispin and
Crispinian, a day fair and fortunate to the English, but most
sorrowful and unlucky to the French.

In the morning, the French captains made three battles,
in the vaward were eight thousand helmes of knights and
esquires, four thousand archers, and fifteen hundred crossbows, which were guided by the Lord de la Breth, Constable
of France, having with him the Dukes of Orleance and Bur-
bon, the Earls of Ewe and Richmond, the Marshal Bouci-
quault, and the Master of the Crossbows, the Lord Dampier,
Admiral of France, and other captains. The Earl of Van-
dosme, with sixteen hundred men of arms, were ordered for a
wing to that battle ; and the other wing was guided by Sir
Guichard Dolphine, Sir Clugnet of Brabant, and Sir Lewis
Bourdon, with eight hundred men of arms, of elect chosen
persons. And to break the shot of the Englishmen were
appointed Sir Guilliam de Saveuses, with Hector and Philip,
his brethren, Ferric de Maillie, and Allen de Gaspanes, with
other eight hundred of arms.

In the middle ward were assigned as many persons, or
more, as were in the foremost battle, and the charge thereof
was committed to the Dukes of Barr and Alanson, the Earls
of Nevers, Vaudemont, Blamont, Salinges, Grant Préc, and
of Russie. And in the rearward were all the other men of
arms guided by the Earls of Marle, Dampmartine, Fauconberg, and the Lord of Lourreie, Captain of Arde, who had
with him the men of the frontiers of Bolonois. Thus the
Frenchmen, being ordered under their standards and banners,
made a great show : for surely they were esteemed in number
six times as many or more than was the whole company of
the Englishmen, with waggoners, pages, and all. They rested
themselves, waiting for the bloody blast of the terrible

trumpet, till the hour between nine and ten of the clock of
the same day, during which season the Constable made unto
the captains and other men of war a pithy oration, exhorting
and encouraging them to do valiantly, with many comfortable
words and sensible reasons. King Henry also like a leader
and not as one led, like a sovereign and not an inferior,
perceiving a plot of ground very strong and meet for his purpose, which on the back half was fenced with the village,
wherein he had lodged the night before, and on both sides
defended with hedges and bushes, thought good there to em-
battle his host, and so ordered his men in the same place, as
he saw occasion, and as stood for his most advantage.

First he sent privily two hundred archers into a low
meadow, which was near to the vanguard of his enemies, but
separated with a great ditch; commanding them there to
keep themselves close till they had a token to them given, to
let drive at their adversaries: beside this, he appointed a
vaward, of the which he made captain Edward, Duke of
York, who of an haughty courage had desired that office, and
with him were the Lords Beaumont, Willoughby, and Fan-
hope, and this battle was all of archers. The middle ward
was governed by the King himself, with his brother the
Duke of Glocester, and the Earls of Marshall, Oxenford, and
Suffolk, in the which were all the strong billmen. The Duke
of Excester, uncle to the King, led the rearward, which was
mixed both with billmen and archers. The horsemen like
wings went on every side of the battle.

Thus the King, having ordered his battles, feared not the
puissance of his enemies, but yet to provide that they should
not with the multitude of horsemen break the order of his
archers, in whom the force of his army consisted (for in those
days the yeomen had their limbs at liberty, sith their hosen
were then fastened with one point, and their jacks long
and easy to shoot in; so that they might draw bows of great
strength, and shoot arrows of a yard long, beside the head),

he caused stakes bound with iron, sharp at both ends, of the Holinshed
length of five or six feet to be pitched before the archers, 1577
and of each side the footmen like an hedge, to the intent
that if the barded horses ran rashly upon them, they might
shortly be gored and destroyed. Certain persons also were
appointed to remove the stakes, as by the moving of the
archers occasion and time should require, so that the footmen
were hedged about with stakes, and the horsemen stood like
a bulwark between them and their enemies, without the
stakes. This device of fortifying an army was at this time
first invented.; but since that time they have devised cal-
trops, harrows, and other new engines against the force of
horsemen; so that if the enemies run hastily upon the
same, either ere their horses wounded with the stakes, or
their feet hurt with the other engines, so as thereby the
beasts are gored, or else made unable to maintain their
course.

King Henry, by reason of his small number of people to
fill up his battles, placed his vanguard so on the right hand
of the main battle, which himself led, that the distance
betwixt them might scarce be perceived, and so in like case
was the rearward joined on the left hand, that the one might
the more readily succour another in time of need. When he
had thus ordered his battles, he left a small company to keep
his camp and carriage, which remained still in the village,
and then calling his captains and soldiers about him, he made
to them a right grave oration, moving them to play the men,
whereby to obtain a glorious victory, as there was hope
certain they should, the rather if they would but remember
the just cause for which they fought, and whom they should
encounter, such faint-hearted people as their ancestors had
so often overcome. To conclude, many words of courage he
uttered, to stir them to do manfully, assuring them that
England should never be charged with his ransom, nor any
Frenchman triumph over him as a captive; for either by

famous death or glorious victory would he (by God's grace) win honour and fame.

It is said that as he heard one of the host utter his wish to another thus: 'I would to God there were with us now so many good soldiers as are at this hour within England!' the King answered: 'I would not wish a man more here than I have: we are indeed in comparison to the enemies but a few, but, if God of His clemency do favour us and our just cause (as I trust He will), we shall speed well enough. But let no man ascribe victory to our own strength and might, but only to God's assistance, to whom I have no doubt we shall worthily have cause to give thanks therefor. And if so be that for our offences' sakes we shall be delivered into the hands of our enemies, the less number we be, the less damage shall the realm of England sustain; but if we should fight in trust of multitude of men, and so get the victory (our minds being prone to pride), we should thereupon peradventure ascribe the victory not so much to the gift of God as to our own puissance, and thereby provoke his high indignation and displeasure against us: and if the enemy get the upper hand, then should our realm and country suffer more damage and stand in further danger. But be you of good comfort, and show yourselves valiant, God and our just quarrel shall defend us, and deliver these our proud adversaries with all the multitude of them which you see (or at the least the most of them) into our hands.' Whilst the King was yet thus in speech, either army so maligned the other, being as then in open sight, that every man cried, 'Forward, forward.' The Dukes of Clarence, Glocester, and York were of the same opinion, yet the King stayed a while, lest any jeopardy were not foreseen, or any hazard not prevented. The Frenchmen in the meanwhile, as though they had been sure of victory, made great triumph, for the captains had determined before how to divide the spoil, and the soldiers the night before had played the Englishmen at dice. The noblemen had devised

a chariot, wherein they might triumphantly convey the King
captive to the city of Paris, crying to their soldiers: 'Haste
you to the spoil, glory, and honour'; little weening (God
wot) how soon their brags should be blown away.

Here we may not forget how the French thus in their
jollity sent an herald to King Henry, to inquire what ransom
he would offer. Whereunto he answered, that within two or
three hours he hoped it would so happen that the Frenchmen should be glad to commune rather with the Englishmen
for their ransoms, than the English to take thought for their
deliverance, promising, for his own part, that his dead carcass
should rather be a prize to the Frenchmen, than that his
living body should pay any ransom. When the messenger
was come back to the French host, the men of war put on
their helmets and caused their trumpets to blow to the
battle. They thought themselves so sure of victory, that
divers of the noblemen made such haste towards the battle,
that they left many of their servants and men of war behind
them, and some of them would not once stay for their standards: as amongst other the Duke of Brabant, when his
standard was not come, caused a banner to be taken from a
trumpet and fastened to a spear, the which he commanded
to be borne before him instead of his standard.

But when both these armies coming within danger either
of other, set in full order of battle on both sides, they stood
still at the first, beholding either other's demeanour, being
not distant in sunder past three bow shoots. And when they
had on both parts thus stayed a good while without doing anything (except that certain of the French horsemen advancing
forwards, betwixt both the hosts, were by the English archers
constrained to return back) advice was taken amongst the
Englishmen what was best for them to do. Thereupon all
things considered, it was determined, that sith the Frenchmen would not come forward, the King with his army em-
battled (as ye have heard) should march towards them, and

so leaving their truss and baggage in the village where they lodged the night before, only with their weapons, armour, and stakes prepared for the purpose, as ye have heard.

These made somewhat forward, before whom there went an old knight, Sir Thomas Erpingham (a man of great experience in the war) with a warder in his hand; and when he cast up his warder, all the army shouted, but that was a sign to the archers in the meadow, which therewith shot wholly altogether at the vaward of the Frenchmen, who when they perceived the archers in the meadow, and saw they could not come at them for a ditch that was betwixt them, with all haste set upon the fore ward of King Henry; but ere they could join, the archers in the forefront and the archers on that side which stood in the meadow so wounded the footmen, galled the horses, and cumbered the men of arms, that the footmen durst not go forward, the horsemen ran together upon plumps without order, some overthrew such as were next them, and the horses overthrew their masters, and so at the first joining, the Frenchmen were foully discomforted and the Englishmen highly encouraged.

When the French vaward was thus brought to confusion, the English archers cast away their bows, and took into their hands axes, malls,[1] swords, bills, and other hand-weapons, and with the same slew the Frenchmen, until they came to the middle ward. Then approached the King, and so encouraged his people, that shortly the second battle of the Frenchmen was overthrown and dispersed, not without great slaughter of men; howbeit, divers were relieved by their varlets and conveyed out of the field. The Englishmen were so busied in fighting, and taking of the prisoners at hand, that they followed not in chase of their enemies, nor would once break out of their array of battle. Yet

[1] Maces.

sundry of the Frenchmen strongly withstood the fierceness
of the English, when they came to handy strokes, so that
the fight sometime was doubtful and perilous. Yet as part
of the French horsemen set their course to have entered
upon the King's battle, with the stakes overthrown, they were
either taken or slain. Thus this battle continued three long
hours.

The King that day showed himself a valiant knight,
albeit almost felled by the Duke of Alanson; yet with plain
strength he slew two of the Duke's company, and felled the
Duke himself; whom when he would have yielded, the
King's guard (contrary to his mind) slew out of hand. In
conclusion, the King, minding to make an end of that day's
journey, caused his horsemen to fetch a compass about, and
to join with him against the rearward of the Frenchmen, in
the which was the greatest number of people. When the
Frenchmen perceived his intent, they were suddenly amazed
and ran away like sheep, without order or array. Which
when the King perceived, he encouraged his men, and
followed so quickly upon the enemies, that they ran hither
and thither, casting away their armour: many on their knees
desired to have their lives saved.

In the mean season, while the battle thus continued, and
that the Englishmen had taken a great number of prisoners,
certain Frenchmen on horseback, whereof were Captains
Robinet of Borneville, Rifflart of Clamas, Isambert of Agincourt, and other men of arms, to the number of six hundred
horsemen, which were the first that fled, hearing that the
English tents and pavilions were a good way distant from
the army, without any sufficient guard to defend the same,
either upon a covetous meaning to gain by the spoil, or
upon a desire to be revenged, entered upon the King's camp,
and there spoiled the hails,[1] robbed the tents, broke up
chests, and carried away caskets, and slew such servants as

[1] Mails?

they found to make any resistance. For which treason and
haskardie[1] in thus leaving their camp at the very point
of fight, for winning of spoil where none to defend it, very
many were after committed to prison, and had lost their
lives if the Dolphin had longer lived.

But when the outcry of the lackeys and boys, which ran
away for fear of the Frenchmen thus spoiling the camp,
came to the King's ears, he doubting lest his enemies should
gather together again, and begin a new field, and mistrusting further that the prisoners would be an aid to his enemies,
or the very enemies to their takers in deed if they were
suffered to live, contrary to his accustomed gentleness,
commanded, by sound of trumpet, that every man (upon pain
of death) should incontinently slay his prisoner. When this
dolorous decree and pitiful proclamation was pronounced,
pity it was to see how some Frenchmen were suddenly
sticked with daggers, some were brained with poleaxes, some
slain with malls, other had their throats cut, and some their
bellies panched,[2] so that in effect, having respect to the great
number, few prisoners were saved.

When this lamentable slaughter was ended, the Englishmen disposed themselves in order of battle, ready to abide
a new field, and also to invade, and newly set on their
enemies. With great force they assailed the Earls of Marle
and Fauconberg, and the Lords of Lourreie and of Thine,
with six hundred men of arms, who had all that day kept
together, but now slain and beaten down out of hand. Some
write, that the King perceiving his enemies in one part to
assemble together, as though they meant to give a new
battle for preservation of the prisoners, sent to them an
herald, commanding them either to depart out of his sight,
or else to come forward at once and give battle: promising
herewith, that if they did offer to fight again, not only
those prisoners which his people already had taken, but also

---

[1] Savagery.   [2] Ripped.

so many of them as in this new conflict which they thus attempted should fall into his hands, should die the death without redemption.

The Frenchmen fearing the sentence of so terrible a decree, without further delay parted out of the field. And so about four of the clock in the afternoon, the King, when he saw no appearance of enemies, caused the retreat to be blown; and gathering his army together, gave thanks to Almighty God for so happy a victory, causing his prelates and chaplains to sing this psalm: *In exitu Israel de Ægypto*, and commanded every man to kneel down on the ground at this verse: *Non nobis Domine, non nobis, sed nomini tuo da gloriam*. Which done, he caused *Te Deum*, with certain anthems, to be sung, giving laud and praise to God, without boasting of his own force or any human power. That night he and his people took rest, and refreshed themselves with such victuals as they found in the French camp, but lodged in the same village where he lay the night before.

In the morning, Montjoy King-at-Arms and four other French heralds came to the King to know the number of prisoners, and to desire burial for the dead. Before he made them answer (to understand what they would say) he demanded of them why they made to him that request, considering that he knew not whether the victory was his or theirs? When Montjoy by true and just confession had cleared that doubt to the high praise of the King, he desired of Montjoy to understand the name of the castle near adjoining. When they had told him that it was called Agincourt, he said, 'Then shall this conflict be called the Battle of Agincourt.' He feasted the French officers of arms that day and granted them their request, which busily sought through the field for such as were slain. But the Englishmen suffered them not to go alone, for they searched with them, and found many hurt, but not in jeopardy of their lives, whom they took prisoners, and brought them to their tents. When the

Holinshed
1577 King of England had well refreshed himself and his soldiers, that had taken the spoil of such as were slain, he with his prisoners in good order returned to his town of Calis.

When tidings of this great victory was blown into England, solemn processions and other praisings to Almighty God, with bonfires and joyful triumphs, were ordained in every town, city, and burgh, and the mayor and citizens of London went the morrow after the day of St. Simon and Jude from the church of St. Paul to the church of St. Peter at Westminster in devout manner, rendering to God hearty thanks for such fortunate luck sent to the king and his army. The same Sunday that the King removed from the camp at Agincourt towards Calis, divers Frenchmen came to the field to view again the dead bodies; and the peasants of the country spoiled the carcases of all such apparel and other things as the Englishmen had left, who took nothing but gold and silver, jewels, rich apparel, and costly armour. But the ploughmen and peasants left nothing behind, neither shirt nor clout, so that the bodies lay stark naked until Wednesday. On the which day divers of the noblemen were conveyed into their countries, and the remnant were by Philip, Earl Charolois (sore lamenting the chance, and moved with pity) at his costs and charges buried in a square plot of ground of fifteen hundred yards; in the which he caused to be made three pits, wherein were buried by account five thousand and eight hundred persons, beside them that were carried away by their friends and servants, and others, which being wounded died in hospitals and other places.

Raphael Holinshed.

THE YOUNG ALEXANDER

T HE ambition and desire he had of honour shewed a North 1579
certain greatness of mind and noble courage, passing
his years. For he was not (as his Father Philip) desirous of
all kind of glory : who, like a rhetorician, had a delight to
utter his eloquence, and stamped in his coins the victories
he had won at the Olympian games, by the swift running of
his horse and coaches. For when he was asked one day
(because he was swift of foot) whether he would assay to
run for victory at the Olympian games, ' I could be content '
(said he) ' so I might run with Kings.' And yet, to speak
generally, he misliked all such contention for games. For
it seemeth that he utterly misliked all wrestling and other
exercise for prize, where men did use all their strength : but
otherwise, he himself made certain festival days and games
of prize for common Stage-players, Musicians, and Singers,
and for the very Poets also. He delighted also in hunting of
divers kinds of beasts, and playing at the staff. Ambassadors
being sent on a time from the King of Persia, whilst his
Father was in some journey out of his realm, Alexander
familiarly entertaining of them, so won them with his
courteous entertainment (for that he used no childish
questions unto them, nor asked them trifling matters, but
what distance it was from one place to another, and which
way they went into the high countries of Asia, and of the
King of Persia himself, how he was towards his Enemies, and
what power he had), that he did ravish them with delight
to hear him, insomuch that they made no more account of
Philip's eloquence and sharp wit, in respect of his Son's
courage and noble mind to attempt great enterprises. For
when they brought him news that his Father had taken some
famous city, or had won some great battle, he was nothing
glad to hear it, but would say to his playfellows : ' Sirs, my

Father will have all, I shall have nothing left me to conquer with you that shall be ought worth.' For he delighting neither in pleasure nor riches, but only in valiantness and honour, thought that the greater conquests and realms his Father should leave him the less he should have to do for himself. And therefore, seeing that his Father's dominions and empire increased daily more and more, perceiving all occasion taken from him to do any great attempt, he desired no riches nor pleasure, but wars and battles, and aspired to a seigniory where he might win honour.

He had divers men appointed him (as it is to be supposed) to bring him up: as Schoolmasters, Governors, and Grooms of his chamber to attend upon him: and among those, Leonidas was the chiefest man that had the government and charge of him, a man of a severe disposition, and a kinsman, also, unto the Queen Olympias. He misliked to be called a Master or Tutor, though it be an office of good charge; whereupon others called him Alexander's Governor, because he was a Nobleman, and allied to the Prince. But he that bare the name of his Schoolmaster was Lysimachus, an Acarnanian born, who had no other manner of civility in him, saving that he called himself Phœnix, Alexander Achilles, and Philip Peleus: and therefore he was well thought of, and was the second person next unto Leonidas. At what time Philonicus, Thessalian, had brought Bucephall, the horse, to sell unto King Philip, asking thirteen talents, they went into the field to ride him. The horse was found so rough and churlish that the riders said he would never do service; for he would let no man get upon his back, nor abide any of the gentlemen's voices about King Philip, but would jerk out at them. Thereupon Philip, being afraid, commanded them to carry him away as a wild beast, and altogether unprofitable: the which they had done, had not Alexander that stood by said: 'O gods, what a horse do they turn away for lack of skill and heart to handle him?' Philip

heard what he said, but held his peace. Alexander, oft North
repeating his words, seeming to be sorry that they should   1579
send the horse back again : ' Why,' said Philip, ' dost thou
control them that have more experience than thou, and
that know better than thou how to handle a horse ?'
Alexander answered, 'And yet methinks I should handle
him better than all they have done.' ' But if thou canst not,
no more than they,' replied Philip, ' what wilt thou forfeit
for thy folly ?' ' I am content,' quoth Alexander, ' to
jeopard the price of the horse.' Every man laughed to hear
his answer, and the wager was laid between them. Then
ran Alexander to the horse, and took him by the bridle : and
turned him towards the Sun. It seemed that he had marked
(as I suppose) how mad the horse was to see his own shadow,
which was ever before him in his eye, as he stirred too and
fro.   Then Alexander, speaking gently to the horse, and
clapping him on the back with his hand, till he had left his
fury and snorting, softly let fall his cloak from him, and
lightly leaping on his back, got up without any danger, and
holding the reins of the bridle hard, without striking or
stirring the horse, made him to be gentle enough. Then
when he saw that the fury of the horse was past, and that
he began to gallop, he put him to his full career, and laid
on spurs and voice a good.   Philip at the first with fear
beholding his Son's agility, lest he should take some hurt,
said never a word : but when he saw him readily turn the
horse at the end of his career, in a bravery for that he had
done, all the lookers-on gave a shout for joy. The Father on
the other side (as they say) fell a-weeping for joy. And
when Alexander was lighted from the horse, he said unto
him, kissing his head : ' O son, thou must needs have a
realm that is meet for thee, for Macedon will not hold thee.'
Furthermore, considering that of nature he was not to be
won by extremity, and that by gentle means and persuasion
he could make him do what he would, he ever sought

rather to persuade than command him in anything he had
to do.

Now Philip, putting no great affiance in his Schoolmasters
of music and humanity, for the instruction and education of
his Son, whom he had appointed to teach him, but thinking
rather that he needed men of greater learning than their
capacities would reach unto : and that, as Sophocles saith,

'He needed many reins and many bits at once,'

he sent for Aristotle (the greatest Philosopher in his time
and best learned) to teach his Son, unto whom he gave
honourable stipend.   For Philip having won and taken
before the City of Stagira, where Aristotle was born, for his
sake he built it again, and replenished it with inhabitants
which fled away, or otherwise were in bondage.   He
appointed them for a schoolhouse and dwelling-place the
pleasant house that is by the City of Mieza.   In that place
are yet seen seats of stone which Aristotle caused to be
made, and close walks to walk in the shadow.   It is thought
also, that Alexander did not only learn of Aristotle moral
philosophy and humanity, but also he heard of him other
more secret, hard, and grave doctrine, which Aristotle's
Scholars do properly call Acroamata, or Epoptica, meaning
things speculative, which requireth the master's teaching to
understand them, or else are kept from common knowledge:
which sciences they did not commonly teach.   Alexander
being passed into Asia, and hearing that Aristotle had put
out certain books of that matter, for the honour's sake of
philosophy, he wrote a letter unto him, somewhat too plain,
and of this effect: 'Alexander unto Aristotle, greeting:
Thou hast not done well to put forth the Acroamatical
sciences.   For wherein shall we excel other if those things
which thou hast secretly taught us be made common to all?
I do thee to understand that I had rather excel others in
excellency of knowledge than in greatness of power.

Farewell.' Aristotle, to pacify this his ambitious humour,
wrote unto him again, that these books were published,
and not published. For, to say truly, in all his treatises,
which he called μετὰ τὰ φυσικὰ, there is no plain instruction profitable for any man, neither to pick out by himself, nor yet to be taught by any other than Aristotle
himself, or his Scholars. So that it is written as a memorial
for them that have been entered and brought up in the
peripatetic sect and doctrine.

It seemeth, also, that it was Aristotle above all other that
made Alexander take delight to study physic. For Alexander
did not only like the knowledge of speculation, but would
exercise practice also, and help his friends when they were
sick : and made, besides, certain remedies and rules to live
by : as appeareth by his letters he wrote, that of his own
nature he was much given to his book and desired to read
much. He learned, also, the *Iliads* of Homer of Aristotle's
correction, which they call τὴν ἐκ τοῦ νάρθηκος, the corrected,
as having passed under the rule : and laid it every night
under his bed's head with his dagger, calling it (as Onesi-
critus writeth) the institution of martial discipline. And when
he was in the high countries of Asia, where he could not
readily come by other books, he wrote unto Harpalus to
send them to him. Harpalus sent him the histories of
Philistus, with divers tragedies of Euripides, Sophocles, and
Æschylus, and certain hymns of Telestus and Philoxenus.
Alexander did reverence Aristotle at the first as his Father,
and so he termed him : because from his natural Father he
had life, but from him the knowledge to live. But afterwards he suspected him somewhat ; yet he did him no hurt,
neither was he so friendly to him as he had been : whereby
men perceived that he did not bear him the good-will he
was wont to do. This notwithstanding, he left not that zeal
and desire he had to the study of philosophy, which he had
learned from his youth, and still continued with him. For

North
1579
he shewed divers testimonies thereof: as the honour he did
unto Anaxarchus, the Philosopher; the fifty talents which
he sent unto Xenocrates, Damdamis, and Calanus, of whom
he made great account.

When King Philip made war with the Bizantines, Alexander, being but sixteen years old, was left his lieutenant
in Macedon, with the custody and charge of his great seal:
at what time he also subdued the Medarians which had
rebelled against him: and having won their city by assault,
he drave out the barbarous people, and made a colony of it
of sundry nations, and called it Alexandropolis, to say, the
City of Alexander.   He was with his father at the battle of
Chæronea against the Grecians, where it was reported that
it was he that gave charge first of all upon the holy band of
the Thebans.   Furthermore, there was an old oak seen in
my time, which the countrymen commonly call Alexander's
Oak, because his tent or pavilion was fastened to it; and
not far from thence is the charnel house where those
Macedonians were buried that were slain at the battle.
For these causes his Father Philip loved him very dearly,
and was glad to hear the Macedonians call Alexander King
and himself their Captain.

Sir Thomas North.

THE BANISHING OF CORIOLANUS

North
1579
WHEN they came to tell the voices of the Tribes, there
were three voices odd which condemned him to be
banished for ever.   After declaration of the sentence, the
People made such joy, as they never rejoiced more for any
battle they had won upon their enemies, they were so brave
and lively, and went home so jocundly from the Assembly,
for triumph of this sentence.   The Senate again, in contrary
manner, were as sad and heavy, repenting themselves

beyond measure that they had not rather determined to have North 1579
done and suffered anything whatsoever, before the common
People should so arrogantly and outrageously have abused
their authority.   There needed no difference of garments, I
warrant you, nor outward shows to know a Plebeian from a
Patrician, for they were easily discerned by their looks.
For he that was on the People's side looked cheerfully on
the matter: but he that was sad, and hung down his head,
he was sure of the Noblemen's side.   Saving Martius alone,
who neither in his countenance nor in his gait did ever
show himself abashed, or once let fall his great courage: but
he only of all other Gentlemen that were angry at his fortune, did outwardly show no manner of passion, nor care at
all of himself.   Not that he did patiently bear and temper
his evil hap, in respect of any reason he had, or by his quiet
condition: but because he was so carried away with the
vehemency of anger and desire of revenge, that he had no
sense nor feeling of the hard state he was in, which the
common People judge not to be sorrow, although indeed it
be the very same.   For when sorrow (as you would say) is
set on fire, then it is converted into spite and malice, and
driveth away for that time all faintness of heart and natural
fear.   And this is the cause why the choleric man is so
altered and mad in his actions, as a man set on fire with a
burning ague: for when a man's heart is troubled within, his
pulse will beat marvellous strongly.

Now that Martius was even in that taking, it appeared
true soon after by his doings.   For when he was come
home to his house again, and had taken his leave of
his mother and wife, finding them weeping and shrieking
out for sorrow, and had also comforted and persuaded
them to be content with his chance: he went immediately to the gate of the city, accompanied with a great
number of Patricians, that brought him thither, from
whence he went on his way with three or four of his friends

only, taking nothing with him, nor requesting anything of any man. So he remained a few days in the country at his houses, turmoiled with sundry sorts and kinds of thoughts, such as the fire of his choler did stir up. In the end, seeing he could resolve no way to take a profitable or honourable course, but only was pricked forward still to be revenged of the Romans : he thought to raise up some great wars against them by their nearest neighbours. Whereupon he thought it his best way first to stir up the Volsces against them, knowing they were yet able enough in strength and riches to encounter them, notwithstanding their former losses they had received not long before, and that their power was not so much impaired as their malice and desire was increased to be revenged of the Romans. Now in the City of Antium there was one called Tullus Aufidius, who for his riches, as also for his nobility and valiantness was honoured among the Volsces as a King. Martius knew very well that Tullus did more malice and envy him than he did all the Romans besides : because that many times in battles where they met, they were ever at the encounter one against another, like lusty courageous youths, striving in all emulation of honour, and had encountered many times together. Insomuch as besides the common quarrel between them, there was bred a marvellous private hate one against another. Yet notwithstanding, considering that Tullus Aufidius was a man of a great mind, and that he above all other of the Volsces most desired revenge of the Romans, for the injuries they had done unto them, he did an act that confirmed the words of an ancient Poet to be true, who said :

> It is a thing full hard, man's anger to withstand,
>   If it be stifly bent to take an enterprise in hand.
> For then most men will have the thing that they desire,
>   Although it cost their lives therefor, such force hath
>   wicked ire.

And so did he. For he disguised himself in such array and

attire as he thought no man could ever have known him for   North
the person he was, seeing him in that apparel he had upon   1579
his back : and as Homer said of Ulysses :

> So did he enter into the enemies' town.

It was even twilight when he entered the city of Antium,
and many people met him in the streets, but no man knew
him. So he went directly to Tullus Aufidius house, and
when he came thither, he got him up straight to the chimney
hearth, and sate him down, and spake not a word to any man,
his face all muffled over. They of the house spying him,
wondered what he should be, and yet they durst not bid
him rise. For ill-favouredly muffled and disguised as he
was, yet there appeared a certain majesty in his countenance
and in his silence : whereupon they went to Tullus, who was
at supper, to tell him of the strange disguising of this man.
Tullus rose presently from the board, and coming towards
him, asked him what he was, and wherefore he came. Then
Martius unmuffled himself, and after he had paused awhile,
making no answer, he said unto him : ' If thou knowest me
not yet, Tullus, and seeing me, dost not perhaps believe me
to be the man I am indeed, I must of necessity bewray myself to be that I am. I am Caius Martius, who hath done to
thyself particularly, and to all the Volsces generally, great
hurt and mischief, which I cannot deny for my surname of
Coriolanus that I bare. For I never had other benefit nor recompence of the true and painful service I have done, and
the extreme dangers I have been in, but this only surname :
a good memory and witness of the malice and displeasure
thou shouldest bear me. Indeed the name only remaineth
with me ; for the rest, the envy and cruelty of the People
of Rome have taken from me, by the sufferance of the
dastardly Nobility and Magistrates, who have forsaken me,
and let me be banished by the People. This extremity
hath now driven me to come as a poor suitor, to take thy

North chimney hearth, not of any hope I have to save my life thereby.
1579 For if I had feared death, I would not have come hither to
have put myself in hazard : but pricked forward with desire
to be revenged of them that thus have banished me, which
now I do begin, in putting my person into the hands of their
enemies.   Wherefore, if thou hast any heart to be recked
of the injuries thy Enemies have done thee, speed thee now,
and let my misery serve thy turn, and so use it, as my service
may be a benefit to the Volsces : promising thee that I will
fight with better good will for all you than I did when I was
against you, knowing that they fight more valiantly who
know the force of the Enemy than such as have never proved
it.   And if it be so that thou dare not, and that thou art
weary to prove fortune any more, then am I also weary to
live any longer.   And it were no wisdom in thee to save
the life of him who hath been heretofore thy mortal Enemy,
and whose service now can nothing help nor pleasure thee.'
Tullus hearing what he said, was a marvellous glad man,
and taking him by the hand, he said unto him : 'Stand up,
O Martius, and be of good cheer, for in proffering thyself
unto us, thou dost us great honour : and by this means
thou mayest hope also of greater things at all the Volsces'
hands.'   So he feasted him for that time, and entertained
him in the honourablest manner he could, talking with him
of no other matter at that present.

                                                    Sir Thomas North.

ENGLAND

Lyly   THERE is an Isle lying in the Ocean Sea, directly against
1579   that part of France which containeth Picardy and
Normandy, called now England, heretofore named Britain.
It hath Ireland upon the West side, on the North the main

sea, on the East side, the Germany Ocean. This island is in
circuit 1720 miles, in form like unto a triangle, being
broadest in the South part, and gathering narrower and
narrower till it come to the farthest point of Caithness,
Northward, where it is narrowest, and there endeth in manner
of a promontory. To repeat the ancient manner of this
island, or what sundry nations have inhabited there, to set
down the Giants, which in bigness of bone have passed the
common size, and almost common credit, to rehearse what
diversities of languages have been used, into how many
kingdoms it hath been divided, what religions have been
followed before the coming of Christ, although it would
breed great delight to your eyes, yet might it happily seem
tedious: for that honey taken excessively cloyeth the stomach
though it be honey.

But my mind is briefly to touch such things as at my
being there I gathered by mine own study and enquiry, not
meaning to write a Chronicle, but to set down in a word
what I heard by conference.

It hath in it twenty and six cities, of the which the chiefest
is named London, a place both for the beauty of building,
infinite riches, variety of all things, that excelleth all the cities
in the world : insomuch that it may be called the storehouse
and mart of all Europe. Close by this city runneth the
famous river called the Thames, which from the head where
it riseth, named Isis, unto the full midway, it is thought to be
an hundred and fourscore miles. What can there be in any
place under the heavens that is not in this noble city either
to be bought or borrowed ?

It hath divers Hospitals for the relieving of the poor, six-
score fair Churches for divine service, a glorious Burse which
they call the Royal Exchange, for the meeting of merchants
of all countries where any traffic is to be had. And among
all the strange and beautiful shows, methinketh there is none
so notable as the Bridge which crosseth the Thames, which

Lyly
1579

is in manner of a continual street, well replenished with large and stately houses on both sides, and situate upon twenty arches, whereof each one is made of excellent freestone squared, every one of them being threescore foot in height, and full twenty in distance one from another.

To this place the whole Realm hath his recourse, whereby it seemeth so populous, that one would scarce think so many people to be in the whole island, as he shall see sometimes in London.

This maketh Gentlemen brave, and Merchants rich, Citizens to purchase, and sojourners to mortgage, so that it is to be thought, that the greatest wealth and substance of the whole realm is couched within the walls of London, where they that be rich keep it from those that be riotous, not detaining it from the lusty youths of England by rigour, but increasing it until young men shall savour of reason, wherein they show themselves treasurers for others, not hoarders for themselves: yet although it be sure enough, would they had it [not]: in my opinion, it were better to be in the Gentleman's purse than in the Merchant's hands.

There are in this Isle two and twenty Bishops, which are as it were superintendents over the Church, men of great zeal and deep knowledge, diligent preachers of the word, earnest followers of their doctrine, careful watchmen that the Wolf devour not the Sheep, in civil government politic, in ruling the spiritual sword (as far as in them under their Prince appertaineth) just, cutting off those members from the Church by rigour that are obstinate in their heresies, and instructing those that are ignorant, appointing godly and learned Ministers in every of their sees, that in their absence may be lights to such as are in darkness, salt to those that are unsavoury, leaven to such as are not seasoned.

Visitations are holden oftentimes, whereby abuses and disorders, either in the laity for negligence, or in the clergy for superstition, or in all for wicked living, there are punish-

ments, by due execution whereof the divine service of God Lyly
is honoured with more purity, and followed with greater 1579
sincerity.

There are also in this Island two famous Universities, the
one Oxford, the other Cambridge, both for the profession of
all sciences, for Divinity, Physic, Law, and all kind of learning,
excelling all the Universities in Christendom.

I was myself in either of them, and like them both so
well, that I mean not in the way of controversy to prefer
any for the better in England, but both for the best in the
world : saving this, that colleges in Oxford are much more
stately for the building, and Cambridge much more sumptuous
for the houses in the town ; but the learning neither lieth in
the freestones of the one, nor the fine streets of the other,
for out of them both do daily proceed men of great wisdom,
to rule in the commonwealth, of learning to instruct the
common people, of all singular kind of professions to do
good to all. And let this suffice, not to enquire which of
them is the superior, but that neither of them have their
equal; neither to ask which of them is the most ancient,
but whether any other be so famous.

But to proceed : in England their buildings are not very
stately, unless it be the houses of noble men, and here and
there the place of a Gentleman, but much amended, as they
report that have told me. For their munition they have
not only great store, but also great cunning to use them,
and courage to practise them: their armour is not unlike unto
that which in other countries they use, as corselets, Almain
rivets, shirts of mail, jacks quilted and covered over with
leather, fustian, or canvas, over thick plates of iron that are
sowed into the same.

The Ordnance they have is great, and thereof great store.
Their Navy is divided as it were into three sorts, of the
which the one serveth for wars, the other for burthen, the
third for fishermen. And some vessels there be (I know not

by experience, and yet I believe by circumstance) that will
sail nine hundred miles in a week, when I should scarce
think that a bird could fly four hundred.

Touching other commodities, they have four baths, the
first called St. Vincent's; the second, Holywell; the third,
Buxton; the fourth (as in old time they read) Cair Bledud,
but now taking his name of a town near adjoining, it is
called the Bath.

Besides this many wonders there are to be found in this
Island, which I will not repeat, because I myself never saw
them, and you have heard of greater.

Concerning their diet, in number of dishes and change of
meat, the Nobility of England do exceed most, having all
things that either may be bought for money or gotten for
the season.   Gentlemen and Merchants feed very finely, and
a poor man it is that dineth with one dish, and yet so content
with a little, that having half dined, they say as it were in a
proverb, that they are as well satisfied as the Lord Mayor of
London, whom they think to fare best, though he eat not
most.

In their meals there is great silence and gravity, using
wine rather to ease the stomach than to load it; not like
unto other nations, who never think that they have dined
till they be drunken.

The attire they use is rather led by the imitation of
others than their own invention, so that there is nothing in
England more constant than the inconstancy of attire: now
using the French fashion, now the Spanish, then the Morisco
gowns, then one thing, then another: insomuch that in
drawing of an Englishman the painter setteth him down
naked, having in the one hand a pair of shears, in the other
a piece of cloth, who having cut his collar after the French
guise is ready to make his sleeve after the Barbarian manner.
And although this were the greatest enormity that I could
see in England, yet is it to be excused, for they that cannot

maintain this pride must leave of necessity, and they that be
able will leave when they see the vanity.

The laws they use are different from ours, for although
the Common and Civil Law be not abolished, yet are they
not had in so great reputation as their own common laws,
which they term the laws of the Crown.

The regiment that they have dependeth upon statute law,
and that is by Parliament which is the highest court, consisting of three several sorts of people, the Nobility, Clergy,
and Commons of the Realm, so as whatsoever be among them
enacted, the Queen striketh the stroke, allowing such things
as to Her Majesty seemeth best.   Then upon Common Law,
which standeth upon maxims and principles, years and
terms ; the cases in this law are called pleas or actions, and
they are either criminal or civil ; the mean to determine are
writs, some original, some judicial. Their trials and recoveries
are either by verdict or demur, confession or default, wherein
if any fault have been committed, either in process or
form, matter or judgment, the party grieved may have a
writ of error.

Then upon Customable Law, which consisteth upon laudable
customs used in some private country.

Last of all upon Prescription, which is a certain custom
continued time out of mind, but it is more particular than
their Customary Law.

Murtherers and thieves are hanged, witches burnt, all
other villainies that deserve death punished with death, insomuch that there are very few heinous offences practised in
respect of those that in other countries are commonly used.

Of savage beasts and vermin they have no great store, nor
any that are noisome. · The cattle they keep for profit are
oxen, horses, sheep, goats, and swine, and such like, whereof
they have abundance ; wildfowl and fish they want none,
nor anything that either may serve for pleasure or profit.

They have more store of pasture than tillage, their

Lyly meadows better than their corn fields, which maketh more
1579 graziers than cornmongers, yet sufficient store of both.

They excel for one thing, their dogs of all sorts: spaniels,
hounds, mastiffs, and divers such: the one they keep for
hunting and hawking, the other for necessary uses about
their houses, as to draw water, to watch thieves, etc., and
thereof they derive the word mastiff of *Mase* and *Thief*.

There is in that Isle salt made, and saffron; there are
great quarries of stones for building, sundry minerals of
quicksilver, antimony, sulphur, black-lead, and orpiment red
and yellow. Also there groweth the finest alum that is, ver-
milion, bittament, chrisocolla, coperus, the mineral stone
whereof petroleum is made, and that which is most strange,
the mineral pearl, which as they are for greatness and colour
most excellent, so are they digged out of the mainland, in
places far distant from the shore.

Besides these, though not strange, yet necessary, they
have coal mines, saltpetre for Ordnance, salt sode for glass.
They want no tin nor lead, there groweth iron, steel, and
copper, and what not: so hath God blessed that country, as it
should seem not only to have sufficient to serve their own turns,
but also others' necessities; whereof there was an old saying,
all countries stand in need of Britain, and Britain of none.

Their air is very wholesome and pleasant, their civility
not inferior to those that deserve best, their wits very sharp
and quick, although I have heard that the Italian and the
Frenchman have accompted them but gross and dull-pated,
which I think came not to pass by the proof they made of
their wits, but by the Englishman's report.

For this is strange (and yet how true it is, there is none
that ever travelled thither but can report) that it is always
incident to an Englishman to think worst of his own nation,
either in learning, experience, common reason, or wit,
preferring always a stranger rather for the name than
the wisdom. I for mine own part think, that in all Europe

Lyly
1579

there are not Lawyers more learned, Divines more profound, Physicians more expert, than are in England.

But that which most allureth a stranger is their courtesy, their civility, and good entertainment. I speak this by experience, that I found more courtesy in England among those I never knew, in one year, than I have done in Athens or Italy among those I ever loved, in twenty.

But having entreated sufficiently of the country and their conditions, let me come to the Glass I promised, being the Court, where although I should as order requireth begin with the chiefest, yet I am enforced with the painter to reserve my best colours to end Venus, and to lay the ground with the basest.

First then I must tell you of the grave and wise Councillors, whose foresight in peace warranteth safety in war, whose provision in plenty maketh sufficient in dearth, whose care in health is as it were a preparative against sickness, how great their wisdom hath been in all things, the twenty-two years' peace doth both show and prove. For what subtilty hath there been wrought so closely, what privy attempts so craftily, what rebellions stirred up so disorderly, but they have by policy bewrayed, prevented by wisdom, repressed by justice? What conspiracies abroad, what confederacies at home, what injuries in any place hath there been contrived, the which they have not either foreseen before they could kindle, or quenched before they could flame?

If any wily Ulysses should feign madness, there was among them always some Palamedes to reveal him: if any Thetis went about to keep her son from the doing of his country service, there was also a wise Ulysses in the court to bewray it: if Sinon came with a smooth tale to bring in the horse into Troy, there hath been always some courageous Lacaon to throw his spear against the bowels, which being not bewitched with Lacaon, has unfolded that which Lacaon suspected.

If Argus with his hundred eyes went prying to undermine Jupiter, yet met he with Mercury, who whistled all his eyes out; insomuch as there could never yet any craft prevail against their policy, or any challenge against their courage. There hath always been Achilles at home to buckle with Hector abroad, Nestor's gravity to countervail Priam's counsel, Ulysses' subtilties to match with Antenor's policies. England hath all those that can and have wrestled with all others, whereof we can require no greater proof than experience.

Besides they have all a zealous care for the increasing of true religion, whose faiths for the most part hath been tried through the fire, which they had felt had not they fled over the water. Moreover the great study they bend towards schools of learning, doth sufficiently declare that they are not only furtherers of learning, but fathers of the learned. O thrice happy England where such counsellors are, where such people live, where such virtue springeth!

Among these shall you find Zopirus that will mangle himself to do his country good, Achates that will never start an inch from his Prince Æneas, Nausicla that never wanted a shift in extremity, Cato that ever counselled to the best, Ptolomeus Philadelphus that always maintained learning. Among the number of all which noble and wise Councillors (I cannot but for his honour's sake remember) the most prudent and right honourable the Lord Burleigh, High Treasurer of that realm, no less reverenced for his wisdom than renowned for his office, more loved at home than feared abroad, and yet more feared for his counsel among other nations than sword or fire, in whom the saying of Agamemnon may be verified: who rather wished for one such as Nestor, than many such as Ajax.

This noble man I found so ready, being but a stranger, to do me good, that neither I ought to forget him, neither cease to pray for him, that as he hath the wisdom of Nestor, so he may have the age; that having the policies of Ulysses, **Lyly** he may have his honour; worthy to live long, by whom so **1579** many live in quiet, and not unworthy to be advanced, by whose care so many have been preferred.

Is not this a Glass, fair Ladies, for all other countries to behold, where there is not only an agreement in faith, religion, and counsel, but in friendship, brotherhood, and living? By whose good endeavours vice is punished, virtue rewarded, peace established, foreign broils repressed, domestical cares appeased? What nation can of councillors desire more? what dominion, that excepted, hath so much? when neither courage can prevail against their chivalry, nor craft take place against their counsel, nor both joined in one be of force to undermine their country. When you have dazzled your eyes with this Glass, behold here another. It was my fortune to be acquainted with certain English gentlemen, which brought me to the Court, where when I came I was driven into a maze to behold the lusty and brave gallants, the beautiful and chaste ladies, the rare and godly orders, so as I could not tell whether I should most commend virtue or bravery.

John Lyly.

HOW WE CAME TO THE TOWN OF HOCHELAGA

SO soon as we were come near the town, a great number **Florio** of the inhabitors thereof came to present themselves **1580** before us after their fashion, making very much of us: we were by our guides brought into the midst of the town. They have in the middlemost part of their houses a large square place, being from side to side a good stone's cast, where we were brought, and there with signs were commanded to stay. Then suddenly all the women and maidens of the town gathered themselves together, part of which had their arms full of young children, and as many as could

Florio
1580

came to rub our faces, our arms, and what part of the body soever they could touch, weeping for very joy that they saw us, showing us the best countenance that possible was, desiring us with their signs that it would please us to touch their children. That done, the men caused the women to withdraw themselves back, then they every one sate down on the ground round about us, as if they would have shown and rehearsed some comedy or other show.

Then presently came the women again, every one bringing a four-square mat in manner of carpets, and spreading them abroad on the ground in that place ; then they caused us to sit upon them. That done, the Lord and King of the country was brought upon nine or ten men's shoulders (whom in their tongue they call Agouhanna), sitting upon a great stag's skin, and they laid him down upon the foresaid mats near to our Captain, every one beckoning unto us that he was their Lord and King. This Agouhanna was a man about fifty years old ; he was no whit better apparelled than any of the rest, only excepted, that he had a certain thing made of beasts' skins (called *Ricci*) like a red towel, and that was instead of his crown. He was full of the palsy, and his members shrunk together. After he had with certain signs and becks saluted our Captain and all his company, and by manifest tokens bid us all welcome, he showed his legs and arms to our Captain, and with signs desired him to touch them, and so he did, rubbing them with his own hands. Then did Agouhanna take the wreath or crown he had about his head, and gave it unto our Captain.

That done, they brought before him divers diseased men, some blind, some cripple, some lame and impotent, and some so old that the hair of their eyelids came down and covered their cheeks, and laid them all along before our Captain, to the end they might of him be touched, for it seemed unto them that God had been descended and come down from heaven to heal them. Our Captain, Florio 1580 seeing the misery and devotion of this poor people, recited the Gospel of St. John, that is to say, In the beginning was the word: touching every one that was diseased, praying to God that it would please Him to open the hearts of this poor people, and to make them know His holy Word, and that they might receive baptism and Christendom. That done, he took a book in his hand, and with a loud voice read all the Passion of Christ, word by word, that all the bystanders might hear him, all which while this poor people kept silence, and were marvellously attentive, looking up to heaven, and imitating us in gestures.

Then he caused the men all orderly to be set on one side, the women on another, and likewise the children on another, and to the chiefest of them he gave hatchets, to the other knives, and to the women beads, and such other small trifles. Then where the children were, he cast rings, counters, and branches made of tin, whereat they seemed to be very glad. That done, our Captain commanded shawms and other musical instruments to be sounded, which, when they heard, they were very merry. Then we took our leave and went to our boat. The women seeing that, put themselves before to stay us, and brought us out of their meats that they had made ready for us, as fish, pottage, beans, and such other things, thinking to make us eat and dine in that place; but because the meats had no savour at all of salt, we liked them not, but thanked them, and with signs gave them to understand that we had no need to eat. When we were out of the town, divers of the men and women followed us, and brought us to the top of the foresaid mountain, which we named Mount Royal: it is about a league from the town. When as we were on the top of it, we might discern and plainly see thirty leagues off.

On the north side of it there are many hills to be seen, running west and east, and as many more on the south, amongst

Florio
1580
and between the which the country is as fair and as pleasant
as possibly can be seen, being level, smooth, and very plain,
fit to be husbanded and tilled: and in the midst of those
fields we might see further a great way than where we had
left our boats, where was the greatest and the swiftest fall
of water that anywhere hath been seen, as great, wide, and
large as our sight might discern, going south-west along
three fair and round mountains that we saw, as we judged
about fifteen leagues from us. Those which brought us
thither told and showed us, that in the said river there
were three such falls of water more, as it was where we had
left our boats, but because we could not understand their
language, we could not know how far they were from
another. Moreover, they showed us with signs, that the
said three falls being past, a man might sail the space of
three months more alongst that river, and that along the
hills that are on the north side, there is a great river, which,
even as the other cometh from the east, we thought it to be
the river that runneth through the country of Saguenay;
and without any sign or question moved or asked of them,
they took the chain of our Captain's whistle, which was of
silver, and the dagger haft of one of our fellow mariners,
hanging on his side, being of yellow copper gilt, and showed
us that such stuff came from the said river, and that there
be *Agouionda*, that is as much as to say, as evil people, who
go all armed, even to their finger ends.

Also, they showed us the manner and making of their
armour: they are made of cords and wood, finely and cunningly wrought together. They gave us also to understand
that those *Agouionda* do continually war against them: but
because we did not understand them well, we could not perceive how far it was to that country. Our Captain showed
them red copper, which in their language they call *Caignet-
adze*, and, looking toward that country with signs, asked them
if any came from thence, they, shaking their heads, answered

no : but they showed us that it came from Saguenay, and that Florio 1580 lieth clean contrary to the other. After we had heard and seen these things of them, we drew to our boats, accompanied with great multitude of those people. Some of them, whenas they saw any of our fellows weary, they would take them upon their shoulders, and carry them as on horseback. So soon as we came to our boats, we hoisted sail to go toward our galleon, doubting of some mischance. Our departure grieved and displeased them very much, for they followed us along the river as far as they could. We went so fast that on Monday, being the fourth of October, we came where our galleon was. The Tuesday following, being the fifth of the month, we hoisted sail, and with our galleon and boats, departed from thence toward the province of Canada, to the port of the Holy Cross, where we had left our ships. The seventh day we came against a river that cometh from the north, and entered into that river, at the entrance whereof are four little islands, full of fair and goodly trees. We named that river the River of Fouetz. But because one of those islands stretcheth himself a great way into the river, our Captain at the point of it caused a goodly great cross to be set up, and commanded the boats to be made ready, that with the next tide he might go up to the said river, and consider the quality of it, which we did, and that day went up as far as we could ; but because we found it to be of no importance, and that we could sound no bottom, we returned down and back again.

John Florio.

A CORONATION

THE time of mourning after their use being expired, Horsey 1584 called Sorachyn, or forty orderly days, the day of the solemnising of this coronation, with great preparations, was come, being upon the 10th day of June 1584 ; and that day then Sunday, he being of the age of twenty-five years, at which time, Master Jerome Horsey was orderly sent for, and placed in a fit room to see all the solemnity. The Emperor coming out of his Palace, there went before him the Metropolitan, Archbishops, Bishops, and chiefest Monks, and Clergymen, with very rich copes and priests' garments upon them, carrying pictures of our Lady, etc., with the Emperor's angel, banners, censers, and many other such ceremonious things, singing all the way. The Emperor with his nobility in order entered the church named Blaueshina, or Blessedness, where prayers and service were used, according to the manner of their Church: that done, they went thence to the Church called Michael the Archangel, and there also used the like prayers and service: and from thence to our Lady Church, Prechista, being their Cathedral Church. In the midst thereof was a chair of majesty placed, wherein his Ancestors used to sit at such extraordinary times: his robes were then changed, and most rich and invaluable garments put on him. Being placed in this princely seat, his Nobility standing round about him in their degrees, his imperial crown was set upon his head by the Metropolitan, his sceptre globe in his right hand, his sword of justice in his left of great riches; his six crowns also, by which he holdeth his kingdoms, were set before him, and the Lord Boris Pheodorowich was placed at his right hand. Then the Metropolitan read openly a book of a small volume, with exhortations to the Emperor to minister true justice, to enjoy with tranquillity the crown of his Ancestors, which God had given him, and used these words following:

'Through the will of the Almighty and without beginning God, Which was before this world, Whom we glorify in the Trinity, one only God, the Father, the Son, and the Holy Ghost, maker of all things, worker of all in all everywhere, fulfiller of all things, by which will and working He both liveth and giveth life to man: that our only God Which inspireth

every one of us, His only children, with His word to discern
God through our Lord Jesus Christ, and the holy quickening
spirit of life, now in these perilous times establish us to keep
the right sceptre, and suffer us to reign of ourselves to the
good profit of the land, to the subduing of the people, together with the enemies, and the maintenance of virtue.'
And so the Metropolitan blessed and laid his cross upon
him. After this, he was taken out of his chair of majesty,
having upon him an upper robe adorned with precious stones
of all sorts, orient pearls of great quantity, but always augmented in riches : it was in weight two hundred pounds, the
train and parts thereof borne up by six Dukes, his chief
imperial crown upon his head very precious : his staff imperial in his right hand of an unicorn's horn of three foot
and a half in length, beset with rich stones, bought of
merchants of Augsburg by the old Emperor in Anno 1581,
and cost him 7000 marks sterling. This jewel Master Horsey
kept sometimes, before the Emperor had it. His sceptre
globe was carried before him by the Prince Boris Pheodorowich, his rich cap, beset with rich stones and pearls, was
carried before him by a Duke : his six crowns also were
carried by Demetrius Ivanowich Godonova, the Emperor's
uncle, Mekita Romanowich, the Emperor's uncle, Stephan
Vasiliwich, Gregory Vasiliwich, Ivan Vasiliwich, brothers
of the blood royal. Thus at last the Emperor came to
the great Church door, and the people cried : ' God save
our Emperor Pheodor Ivanowich of all Russia.' His horse
was there ready most richly adorned, with a covering of embroidered pearl and precious stones, saddle, and all furniture
agreeable to it, reported to be worth 300,000 marks sterling.

There was a bridge made of 150 fathom in length, three
manner of ways, three foot above ground and two fathom
broad, for him to go from one Church to the other with his
princes and nobles from the press of the people, which were
in number infinite, and some at that time pressed to death with

the throng.   As the Emperor returned out of the Churches,
they were spread under foot with cloth of gold, the porches
of the Churches with red velvet, the bridges with scarlet,
and stammell cloth [1] from one church to another: and as
soon as the Emperor was passed by, the cloth of gold, velvet,
and scarlet was cut, and taken of those that could come by
it, every man desirous to have a piece, to reserve it for a
monument: silver and gold coin, then minted of purpose,
was cast among the people in great quantity.   The Lord
Boris Pheodorowich was sumptuously and richly attired,
with his garments decked with great orient pearl, beset
with all sorts of precious stones.   In like rich manner were
apparelled all the family of the Godonovaes in their degrees, with the rest of the princes and nobility, whereof one
named Knez Ivan Michalowich Glynsky, whose robe, horse,
and furniture was in register found worth 100,000 marks
sterling, being of great antiquity.   The Empress being in her
palace, was placed in her chair of Majesty also before a great
open window : most precious and rich were her robes, and
shining to behold, with rich stones and orient pearl beset ;
her crown was placed upon her head, accompanied with her
Princesses and Ladies of Estate.   Then cried out the people :
' God preserve our noble Empress Irenia.'   After all this the
Emperor came into the Parliament House, which was richly
decked : there he was placed in his royal seat adorned as
before : his six crowns were set before him upon a table : the
basin and ewer royal of gold held by his Knight of Guard
with his men standing two on each side in white apparel of
cloth of silver, called Kindry, with sceptres and battleaxes
of gold in their hands : the princes and nobility were all
placed according to their degrees all in their rich robes.

The Emperor after a short oration permitted every man
in order to kiss his hand, which being done, he removed to
a princely seat prepared for him at the table : where he was

---

[1] A coarse woollen.

served by his nobles in very princely order. The three out- Horsey
rooms being very great and large, were beset with plate of 1584
gold and silver round, from the ground up to the vaults one
upon the other : among which plate were many barrels of
silver and gold. This solemnity and triumph lasted a whole
week, wherein many royal pastimes were showed and used,
after which the chiefest men of the nobility were elected to
their places of office and dignity, as the Prince Boris Pheodorowich was made Chief Counsellor to the Emperor, Master
of the Horse, had the charge of his person, Lieutenant of
the Empire and warlike engines, Governor or Lieutenant
of the Empire of Cazan and Astrakan and others. To this
dignity were by Parliament and gift of the Emperor given
him many revenues and rich lands, as there was given him
and his for ever to inherit a province called Vaga, of 300
English miles in length and 250 in breadth, with many towns
and great villages populous and wealthy : his yearly revenue
out of that province is 35,000 marks sterling, being not the
fifth part of his yearly revenue. Further, he and his house be
of such authority and power, that in forty days' warning they
are able to bring into the field 100,000 soldiers well furnished.

The conclusion of the Emperor's Coronation was a peal of
ordnance, called a peal royal, two miles without the city, being
170 great pieces of brass of all sorts, as fair as any can be
made. These pieces were all discharged with shot against bul-
warks made of purpose: 20,000 harquebusers standing in eight
ranks two miles in length, apparelled all in velvet, coloured
silk, and stammels, discharged their shot also twice over
in good order : and so the Emperor, accompanied with all
his Princes and Nobles, at the least 50,000 horse, departed
through the city to his palace. This royal coronation would
ask much time, and many leaves of paper to be described
particularly as it was performed : it shall suffice to understand that the like magnificence was never seen in Russia.

Hakluyt : Navigations.

A FALSE WITCH

Scot
1584

MILDRED, the base daughter of Alice Norrington, and now servant to William Sponer of West-well in the county of Kent, being of the age of seventeen years, was possessed with Satan in the night and day afore-said. About two of the clock in the afternoon of the same day, there came to the same Sponer's house, Roger New-man, minister of Westwell, John Brainford, minister of Kenington, with others whose names are underwritten, who made their prayers unto God, to assist them in that needful case; and then commanded Satan in the name of the eternal God, and of His Son Jesus Christ, to speak with such a voice as they might understand, and to declare from whence he came. But he would not speak, but roared and cried mightily. And though we did command him many times in the name of God, and of His Son Jesus Christ, and in His mighty power to speak, yet he would not: until he had gone through all his delays, as roaring, crying, striving, and gnashing of teeth; and otherwhile with mowing, and other terrible countenances, and was so strong in the maid, that four men could scarce hold her down. And this con-tinued by the space almost of two hours. So sometimes we charged him earnestly to speak, and again praying unto God that He would assist us. At the last he spake, but very strangely, and that was thus: 'He comes, He comes;' and that oftimes he repeated; and, 'He goes, He goes.' And then we charged him to tell us who sent him. And he said: 'I lay in her way like a log, and I made her run like fire, but I could not hurt her.' 'And why so?' said we. 'Because God kept her,' said he. 'When camest thou to her?' said we. 'To-night in her bed,' said he. Then we charged him, as before, to tell what he was, and who sent him, and what his name was. At first he said, 'The devil, the devil.' Then we charged him as before. Then he roared and cried as before, and spake terrible words: 'I will kill her, I will kill her, I will tear her in pieces, I will tear her in pieces.' We said, 'Thou shalt not hurt her.' He said, 'I will kill you all.' We said, 'Thou shalt hurt none of us all.' Then we charged him as before. Then he said, 'You will give me no rest.' We said, 'Thou shalt have none here, for thou must have no rest within the servants of God: but tell us in the name of God what thou art, and who sent thee.' Then he said, he would tear her in pieces. We said, 'Thou shalt not hurt her.' Then he said again, he would kill us all. We said again, 'Thou shalt hurt none of us all, for we are the servants of God.' And we charged him as before. And he said again, 'Will you give me no rest?' We said, 'Thou shalt have none here, neither shalt thou rest in her, for thou hast no right in her, since Jesus Christ hath redeemed her with His blood, and she belongeth to Him, and therefore tell us thy name, and who sent thee?' He said his name was Satan. We said, 'Who sent thee?' He said, 'Old Alice, Old Alice.' 'Which Old Alice?' said we. 'Old Alice,' said he. 'Where dwelleth she?' said we. 'In Westwell Street,' said he. We said, 'How long hast thou been with her?' 'These twenty years,' said he. We asked him where she did keep him? 'In two bottles,' said he. 'Where be they?' said we. 'In the backside of her house,' said he. 'In what place?' said we. 'Under the wall,' said he. 'Where is the other?' 'In Kenington.' 'In what place?' said we. 'In the ground,' said he. Then we asked him, what she did give him. He said, 'Her will, her will.' 'What did she bid thee do?' said we. He said, 'Kill her maid.' 'Wherefore did she bid thee kill her?' said we. 'Because she did not love her,' said he. We said, 'How long is it ago since she sent thee to her?' 'More than a year,' said he. 'Where was that?' said we. 'At her master's,' said he. 'Which master's?' said we. 'At

her Master Brainford's, at Kenington,' said he. 'How oft
wert thou there?' said we. 'Many times,' said he. 'Where
first?' said we. 'In the garden,' said he. 'Where the
second time?' 'In the hall.' 'Where the third time?'
'In her bed.' 'Where the fourth time?' 'In the field.'
'Where the fifth time?' 'In the court.' 'Where the sixth
time?' 'In the water, where I cast her into the moat.'
'Where the seventh time?' 'In her bed.' We asked him
again, 'Where else?' He said, 'In Westwell.' 'Where
there?' said we. 'In the Vicarage,' said he. 'Where
there?' 'In the loft.' 'How camest thou to her?' said
we. 'In the likeness of two birds,' said he.' 'Who sent
thee to that place?' said we. 'Old Alice,' said he. 'What
other spirits were with thee there?' said we. 'My servant,'
said he. 'What is his name?' said we. He said 'Little Devil.'
'What is thy name?' said we. 'Satan,' said he. 'What doth
Old Alice call thee?' said we. 'Partner,' said he. 'What
doth she give thee?' said we. 'Her will,' said he. 'How
many hast thou killed for her?' said we. 'Three,' said he.
'Who are they?' said we. 'A man and his child,' said he.
'What were their names?' said we. 'The child's name was
Edward,' said he. 'What more than Edward?' said we.
'Edward Ager,' said he. 'What was the man's name?' said
we. 'Richard,' said he. 'What more?' said we. 'Richard
Ager,' said he. 'Where dwelt the man and the child?' said
we. 'At Dig, at Dig,' said he. This Richard Ager of Dig
was a gentleman of forty pounds land by the year, a very
honest man, but would often say he was bewitched, and
languished long before he died. 'Whom else hast thou
killed for her?' said we. 'Wolton's wife,' said he. 'Where
did she dwell?' 'In Westwell,' said he. 'What else hast
thou done for her?' said we. 'What she would have me,'
said he. 'What is that?' said we. 'To fetch her meat,
drink, and corn,' said he. 'Where hadst thou it?' said we.
'In every house,' said he. 'Name the houses,' said we.

' At Petman's, at Farme's, at Millen's, at Fuller's, and in every
house.' After this, we commanded Satan in the name of
Jesus Christ to depart from her, and never to trouble her
any more, nor any man else. Then he said, he would go,
he would go : but he went not. Then we commanded him
as before, with some more words. Then he said, ' I go, I
go ;' and so he departed. Then said the maid : ' He
is gone, Lord have mercy upon me, for he would have
killed me.' Then we kneeled down and gave God thanks,
with the maiden, praying that God would keep her from
Satan's power, and assist her with His grace. And noting
this in a piece of paper, we departed. Satan's voice did
differ much from the maid's voice, and all that he spake was
in his own name. . . .

But to make short work with the confutation of this
bastardly quean's enterprise and cosenage ; you shall understand that upon the bruit of her divinity and miraculous
trances, she was convented before Master Thomas Wotton of
Bocton Malherbe, a man of great worship and wisdom, and
for deciding and ordering of matters in this commonwealth
of rare and singular dexterity; through whose discreet
handling of the matter, with the assistance and aid of Master
George Darrel, Esq.; being also a right good and discreet
Justice of the same limit, the fraud was found, and the
cosenage confessed, and she received condign punishment.
Neither was her confession won according to the form of
the Spanish Inquisition, to wit, through extremity of tortures,
nor yet by guile or flattery, nor by presumptions ; but through
wise and perfect trial of every circumstance the illusion was
manifestly disclosed. Not so (I say) as witches are commonly
convinced and condemned ; to wit, through malicious accusations, by guesses, presumptions, and extorted confessions
contrary to sense and possibility, and for such actions as they
can show no trial nor example before the wise, either by
direct or indirect means ; but after due trial she showed her

Scot
1584

feats, illusions, and trances, with the residue of all her miraculous works, in the presence of divers gentlemen and gentlewomen of great worship and credit, at Bocton Malherbe, in the house of the said Mr. Wotton. Now compare this wench with the Witch of Endor, and you shall see that both the cosenages may be done by one art.

Reginald Scot.

THE FIRST LANDING IN VIRGINIA

Barlow
1584

THE second of July we found shoal water, where we smelt so sweet and so strong a smell, as if we had been in the midst of some delicate garden abounding with all kind of odoriferous flowers, by which we were assured that the land could not be far distant; and keeping good watch, and bearing but slack sail, the fourth of the same month we arrived upon the coast, which we supposed to be a continent and firm land, and we sailed along the same 120 English miles before we could find any entrance, or river issuing into the sea. The first that appeared unto us we entered, though not without some difficulty, and cast anchor about three harquebus-shot within the haven's mouth, on the left hand of the same; and after thanks given to God for our safe arrival thither, we manned our boats and went to view the land next adjoining, and 'to take possession of the same, in the right of the Queen's most excellent Majesty, as rightful Queen and Princess of the same, and after delivered the same over to your use, according to her Majesty's grant and letters patent, under her Highness's great seal.' Which being performed, according to the ceremonies used in such enterprises, we viewed the land about us, being, whereas we first landed, very sandy and low towards the water's side, but so full of grapes, as the very beating and surge of the sea overflowed them, of which we found such plenty, as well there as in all places else, both on the sand and on the green soil on the hills, as in the plains, as well on every little shrub, as also climbing towards the tops of high cedars, that I think in all the world the like abundance is not to be found: and myself having seen those parts of Europe that most abound, find such difference as were incredible to be written.

We passed from the sea side towards the tops of those hills next adjoining, being but of mean height, and from thence we beheld the sea on both sides to the North and to the South, finding no end any of both ways. This land lay stretching itself to the West, which after we found to be but an island of twenty miles long, and not above six miles broad. Under the bank or hill whereon we stood, we beheld the valleys replenished with goodly cedar trees, and having discharged our harquebus-shot, such a flock of cranes (the most part white) arose under us, with such a cry redoubled by many echoes, as if an army of men had shouted all together.

This island had many goodly woods full of deer, conies, hares, and fowl, even in the midst of summer in incredible abundance. The woods are not such as you find in Bohemia, Moscovia, or Hercynia, barren and fruitless, but the highest and reddest cedars of the world, far bettering the cedars of the Açores, of the Indies, or Lybanus, pines, cypresses, sassafras, the lentisk, or the tree that beareth the mastic, the tree that beareth the rine of black cinnamon, of which Mr. Winter brought from the Straits of Magellan, and many other of excellent smell and quality. We remained by the side of this island two whole days before we saw any people of the country: the third day we espied one small boat rowing towards us having in it three persons: this boat came to the island side, four harquebus-shot from our ships, and there two of the people remaining, the third came along the shoreside towards us, and we being then all within board, he walked up and down upon the point of the land

Barlow
1584

next unto us. Then the Master and the Pilot of the admiral, Simon Ferdinando, and the Captain Philip Amadas, myself, and others rowed to the land, whose coming this fellow attended, never making any show of fear or doubt. And after he had spoken of many things not understood by us, we brought him with his own good liking aboard the ships, and gave him a shirt, a hat, and some other things, and made him taste of our wine and our meat, which he liked very well: and after having viewed both barques, he departed and went to his own boat again, which he had left in a little cove or creek adjoining: as soon as he was two bow-shoot into the water, he fell to fishing, and in less than half-an-hour he had laden his boat as deep as it could swim, with which he came again to the point of the land, and there he divided his fish into two parts, pointing one part to the ship, and the other to the pinnace ; which, after he had (as much as he might) requited the former benefits received, departed out of our sight.

The next day there came unto us divers boats, and in one of them the King's brother, accompanied with forty or fifty men, very handsome and goodly people, and in their behaviour as mannerly and civil as any of Europe. His name was Granganimeo, and the King is called Wingina, the country Wingandacoa, and now by her Majesty Virginia. The manner of his coming was in this sort: he left his boats altogether as the first man did a little from the ships by the shore, and came along to the place over against the ships, followed with forty men. When he came to the place, his servants spread a long mat upon the ground, on which he sate down, and at the other end of the mat four others of his company did the like, the rest of his men stood round about him, somewhat afar off: when we came to the shore to him with our weapons, he never moved from his place, nor any of the other four, nor never mistrusted any harm to be offered from us, but sitting still he beckoned us to come

and sit by him, which we performed : and being set, he
made all signs of joy and welcome, striking on his head and
his breast and afterwards on ours, to show we were all one,
smiling and making show the best he could of all love and
familiarity. After he had made a long speech unto us, we
presented him with divers things, which he received very
joyfully and thankfully. None of the company durst speak
one word all the time : only the four which were at the
other end spake one in the other's ears very softly.

The King is greatly obeyed, and his brothers and children
reverenced : the King himself in person was at our being
there sore wounded in a fight which he had with the King
of the next country, called Wingina, and was shot in two
places through the body, and once clean through the thigh,
but yet he recovered : by reason whereof and for that he
lay at the chief town of the country, being six days' journey
off, we saw him not at all.

After we had presented this his brother with such things
as we thought he liked, we likewise gave somewhat to the
other that sat with him on the mat : but presently he arose
and took all from them and put it into his own basket,
making signs and tokens that all things ought to be delivered
unto him, and the rest were but his servants and followers.
A day or two after this, we fell to trading with them,
exchanging some things that we had for chamois, buff,
and deer skins : when we showed him all our packet of
merchandise, of all things that he saw, a bright tin dish
most pleased him, which he presently took up and clapt it
before his breast, and after made a hole in the brim thereof
and hung it about his neck, making signs that it would
defend him against his enemies' arrows : for those people
maintain a deadly and terrible war with the people and
King adjoining. We exchanged our tin dish for twenty
skins, worth twenty crowns, or twenty nobles : and a copper
kettle for fifty skins worth fifty crowns. They offered us

good exchange for our hatchets and axes, and for knives, and would have given anything for swords: but we would not depart with any. After two or three days the King's brother came aboard the ships, and drank wine, and ate of our meat and of our bread, and liked exceedingly thereof: and after a few days overpassed, he brought his wife with him to the ships, his daughter and two or three children: his wife was very well favoured, of mean stature, and very bashful: she had on her back a long cloak of leather, with the fur side next to her body, and before her a piece of the same: about her forehead she had a band of white coral, and so had her husband many times: in her ears she had bracelets of pearls hanging down to her middle (whereof we delivered your worship a little bracelet), and those were of the bigness of good peas. The rest of her women of the better sort had pendants of copper hanging in either ear, and some of the children of the King's brother and other noblemen have five or six in either ear: he himself had upon his head a broad plate of gold or copper, for being unpolished we knew not what metal it should be, neither would he by any means suffer us to take it off his head, but feeling it, it would bow very easily. His apparel was as his wife's, only the women wear their hair long on both sides, and the men but on one. They are of colour yellowish, and their hair black for the most part, and yet we saw children that had very fine auburn and chestnut-coloured hair.

After that these women had been there, there came down from all parts great store of people, bringing with them leather, coral, divers kinds of dyes, very excellent, and exchanged with us; but when Granganimeo, the King's brother, was present, none durst trade but himself, except such as wear red pieces of copper on their heads like himself: for that is the difference between the noblemen and the governors of countries, and the meaner sort. And we both noted there, and you have understood since by these men, which we brought home, that no people in the world carry more respect to their King, Nobility, and Governors, than these do. The King's brother's wife, when she came to us (as she did many times), was followed with forty or fifty women always ; and when she came into the ship, she left them all on land, saving her two daughters, her nurse, and one or two more. The King's brother always kept this order : as many boats as he would come withal to the ships, so many fires would he make on the shore afar off, to the end we might understand with what strength and company he approached. Their boats are made of one tree, either of pine or of pitch trees : a wood not commonly known to our people, nor found growing in England. They have no edge-tools to make them withal : if they have any they are very few, and those it seems they had twenty years since, which, as those two men declared, was out of a wreck which happened upon their coast of some Christian ship being beaten that way by some storm and outrageous weather, whereof none of the people were saved, but only the ship, or some part of her being cast upon the sand, out of whose sides they drew the nails and the spikes, and with those they made their best instruments. The manner of making their boats is thus : they burn down some great tree, or take such as are windfallen, and putting gum and rosin upon one side thereof, they set fire into it, and when it hath burnt it hollow, they cut out the coal with their shells, and ever where they would burn it deeper or wider they lay on gums, which burn away the timber, and by this means they fashion very fine boats, and such as will transport twenty men. Their oars are like scoops, and many times they set with long poles, as the depth serveth.

The King's brother had great liking of our armour, a sword, and divers other things which we had, and offered to lay a great box of pearl in gage for them, but we refused it for this time, because we would not make them know that

Barlow
1584

we esteemed thereof, until we had understood in what places of the country the pearl grew : which now your worship doth very well understand.

He was very just of his promise : for many times we delivered him merchandise upon his word, but ever he came within the day and performed his promise.   He sent us every day a brace or two of fat bucks, conies, hares, fish, the best of the world.   He sent us divers kinds of fruits, melons, walnuts, cucumbers, gourds, peas, and divers roots, and fruits very excellent good, and of their country corn, which is very white, fair and well tasted, and groweth three times in five months : in May they sow, in July they reap : in June they sow, in August they reap : in July they sow, in September they reap; only they cast the corn into the ground, breaking a little of the soft turf with a wooden mattock or pickaxe : ourselves proved the soil, and put some of our peas in the ground, and in ten days they were of fourteen inches high : they have also beans very fair of divers colours and wonderful plenty : some growing naturally and some in their gardens, and so have they both wheat and oats.

The soil is the most plentiful, sweet, fruitful, and whole-some of all the world : there are above fourteen several sweet-smelling timber trees, and the most part of their underwoods are bays and such like : they have those oaks that we have, but far greater and better.   After they had been divers times aboard our ships, myself, with seven more, went twenty mile into the river that runneth toward the City of Skicoak, which river they call Occam, and the evening following we came to an island which they call Raonoak, distant from the harbour by which we entered seven leagues : and at the North end thereof was a village of nine houses, built of cedar, and fortified round about with sharp trees, to keep out their enemies, and the entrance into it made like a turnpike very artificially; when we

came towards it, standing near unto the water's side, the
wife of Granganimeo, the King's brother, came running out to
meet us very cheerfully and friendly, her husband was not
then in the village; some of her people she commanded to
draw our boat on shore for the beating of the billow: others
she appointed to carry us on their backs to the dry ground,
and others to bring our oars into the house for fear of
stealing. When we were come into the outer room, having
five rooms in her house, she caused us to sit down by a great
fire, and after took off our clothes and washed them, and
dried them again: some of the women plucked off our
stockings and washed them, some washed our feet in warm
water, and she herself took great pains to see all things
ordered in the best manner she could, making great haste
to dress some meat for us to eat.

After we had thus dried ourselves, she brought us into
the inner room, where she set on the board standing along
the house some wheat like furmenty, sodden venison and
roasted, fish sodden, boiled, and roasted, melons raw and
sodden, roots of divers kinds and divers fruits: their drink
is commonly water, but while the grape lasteth, they drink
wine, and for want of casks to keep it all the year after
they drink water, but it is sodden with ginger in it, and
black cinnamon, and sometimes sassafras, and divers other
wholesome and medicinable herbs and trees. We were
entertained with all love and kindness, and with as much
bounty (after their manner) as they could possibly devise.
We found the people most gentle, loving, and faithful, void
of all guile and treason, and such as live after the manner of
the golden age. The people only care how to defend
themselves from the cold in their short winter, and to feed
themselves with such meat as the soil affordeth: their
meat is very well sodden, and they make broth very sweet
and savoury: their vessels are earthen pots, very large,
white, and sweet; their dishes are wooden platters of

Barlow
1584 sweet timber: within the place where they feed was their
lodging, and within that their Idol, which they worship, of
whom they speak incredible things.   While we were at
meat, there came in at the gates two or three men with
their bows and arrows from hunting, whom when we espied,
we began to look one towards another, and offered to reach
our weapons, but as soon as she espied our mistrust, she
was very much moved, and caused some of her men to run
out, and take away their bows and arrows and break them,
and withal beat the poor fellows out of the gate again.
When we departed in the evening and would not tarry all
night she was very sorry, and gave us into our boat our
supper half dressed, pots and all, and brought us to our
boat side, in which we lay all night, removing the same a
pretty distance from the shore : she perceiving our jealousy,
was much grieved, and sent divers men and thirty women to
sit all night on the bank side by us, and sent us into our
boats five mats to cover us from the rain, using very many
words to intreat us to rest in their houses : but because we
were few men, and if we had miscarried, the voyage had
been in very great danger, we durst not adventure anything,
although there was no cause of doubt, for a more kind and
loving people there cannot be found in the world, as far as
we have hitherto had trial.

Hakluyt : Navigations.

AN AFFAIR OF HONOUR

Greville
1586 AND in this freedom of heart being one day at tennis, a
Peer of this Realm, born great, greater by alliance,
and superlatively in the Prince's favour, abruptly came into
the tennis-court ; and speaking out of these three paramount
authorities, he forgot to entreat that which he could not

legally command. When by the encounter of a steady object, finding unrespectiveness in himself (though a great Lord) not respected by this princely spirit, he grew to expostulate more roughly. The returns of which style coming still from an understanding heart, that knew what was due to itself, and what it ought to others, seemed (through the mists of my Lord's passions, swollen with the wind of his faction then reigning) to provoke in yielding. Whereby, the less amazement or confusion of thoughts he stirred up in Sir Philip, the more shadows this great Lord's own mind was possessed with : till at last with rage (which is ever ill-disciplined) he commands them to depart the court. To this Sir Philip temperately answers : that if his Lordship had been pleased to express desire in milder characters, perchance he might have led out those, that he should now find would not be driven out with any scourge of fury. This answer (like a bellows) blowing up the sparks of excess already kindled, made my Lord scornfully call Sir Philip by the name of Puppy. In which progress of heat, as the tempest grew more and more vehement within, so did their hearts breathe out their perturbations in a more loud and shrill accent. The French Commissioners unfortunately had that day audience in those private galleries whose windows look into the tennis-court. They instantly drew all to this tumult : every sort of quarrels sorting well with their humours, especially this. Which Sir Philip perceiving, and rising with inward strength, by the prospect of a mighty faction against him, asked my Lord, with a loud voice, that which he heard clearly enough before. Who (like an echo, that still multiplies by reflections) repeated this epithet of Puppy the second time. Sir Philip, resolving in one answer to conclude both the attentive hearers and passionate actor, gave my Lord a lie, impossible (as he averred) to be retorted ; in respect all the world knows puppies are gotten by dogs, and children by men.

Hereupon those glorious inequalities of Fortune in his Lordship were put to a kind of pause, by a precious inequality of nature in this gentleman. So that they both stood silent a while, like a dumb show in a tragedy; till Sir Philip, sensible of his own wrong, the foreign and factious spirits that attended, and yet, even in this question between him and his superior, tender to his country's honour, with some words of sharp accent, led the way abruptly out of the tennis-court, as if so unexpected an accident were not fit to be decided any farther in that place. Whereof the great Lord making another sense, continues his play, without any advantage of reputation, as by the standard of humours in those times it was conceived.

A day Sir Philip remains in suspense, when hearing nothing of or from the Lord, he sends a Gentleman of worth to awake him out of his trance; wherein the French would assuredly think any pause, if not death, yet a lethargy of true honour in both. This stirred a resolution in his Lordship to send Sir Philip a challenge. Notwithstanding, these thoughts in the great Lord wandered so long between glory, anger, and inequality of state, as the Lords of her Majesty's Council took notice of the differences, commanded peace, and laboured a reconciliation between them. But needlessly in one respect, and bootlessly in another. The great Lord being (as it should seem) either not hasty to adventure many inequalities against one, or inwardly satisfied with the progress of his own acts: Sir Philip, on the other side, confident he neither had nor would lose, or let fall anything of his right. Which her Majesty's Council quickly perceiving, recommended this work to herself.

The Queen, who saw that by the loss or disgrace of either she would gain nothing, presently undertakes Sir Philip; and (like an excellent Monarch) lays before him the difference in degrees between Earls and Gentlemen; the respect inferiors ought to their superiors, and the necessity in

Princes to maintain their own creations, as degrees descend-   Greville
ing between the people's licentiousness and the anointed   1586
sovereignty of Crowns ; how the Gentleman's neglect of the
Nobility taught the Peasant to insult upon both.

Whereunto Sir Philip, with such reverence as became
him, replied : First, that place was never intended for privilege to wrong: witness herself, who how sovereign soever
she were by Throne, Birth, Education, and Nature, yet
was she content to cast her own affections into the same
moulds her subjects did, and govern all her rights by their
laws.   Again, he besought her Majesty to consider, that
although he were a great Lord by birth, alliance, and grace,
yet he was no lord over him ; and therefore the difference
of degrees between free men could not challenge any other
homage than precedency.   And by her father's act (to make
a princely wisdom become the more familiar) he did instance
the government of King Henry the Eighth, who gave the
gentry free and safe appeal to his feet, against the oppression of the grandees ; and found it wisdom, by the stronger
corporation in number, to keep down the greater in power :
inferring else, that if they should unite, the overgrown
might be tempted, by still coveting more, to fall (as the
Angels did) by affecting equality with their Maker.

Sir Fulk Greville, Lord Brooke.

THE LAST FIGHT OF THE *REVENGE*

THE Lord Thomas Howard, with six of Her Majesty's   Raleigh
ships, six victuallers of London, the barque *Ralegh*,   1591
and two or three pinnaces riding at anchor near unto
Flores, one of the westerly islands of the Azores, the
last of August in the afternoon, had intelligence by one
Captain Midleton, of the approach of the Spanish Armada.

Which Midleton being in a very good sailer, had kept them
company three days before, of good purpose, both to discover their forces the more, as also to give advice to my Lord
Thomas of their approach.   He had no sooner delivered the
news but the fleet was in sight: many of our ships' companies were on shore in the island ; some providing ballast
for their ships ; others filling of water and refreshing themselves from the land with such things as they could either
for money or by force recover.   By reason whereof our
ships being all pestered and rummaging everything out of
order, [were] very light for want of ballast.   And that which
was most to our disadvantage, the one half part of the men of
every ship sick, and utterly unserviceable.   For in the
Revenge there were ninety diseased : in the *Bonaventure*
not so many in health as could handle her mainsail.   For
had not twenty men been taken out of a barque of Sir George
Cary's, his being commanded to be sunk, and those appointed to her, she had hardly ever recovered England.
The rest for the most part were in little better state.   The
names of Her Majesty's ships were these as followeth : the
Defiance, which was admiral ; the *Revenge*, vice-admiral ; the
Bonaventure, commanded by Captain Cross ; the *Lion*, by George
Fenner ; the *Foresight*, by Master Thomas Vavisour ; and
the *Crane*, by Duffeild.   The *Foresight* and the *Crane* being
but small ships ; only the other were of the middle size ; the
rest, besides the barque *Ralegh*, commanded by Captain Thin,
were victuallers, and of small force or none.   The Spanish
fleet having shrouded their approach by reason of the island,
were now so soon at hand as our ships had scarce time to
weigh their anchors, but some of them were driven to let
slip their cables, and set sail.   Sir Richard Grinvile was the
last weighed, to recover the men that were upon the island,
which otherwise had been lost.   The Lord Thomas with the
rest very hardly recovered the wind, which Sir Richard
Grinvile not being able to do, was persuaded by the Master

and others to cut his mainsail and cast about, and to trust
to the sailing of his ship: for the squadron of Sivil were on
his weather-bow. But Sir Richard utterly refused to turn
from the enemy, alleging that he would rather choose to die
than to dishonour himself, his country, and her Majesty's
ship, persuading his company that he would pass through the
two squadrons, in despite of them, and enforce those of
Sivil to give him way. Which he performed upon divers of
the foremost, who, as the mariners term it, sprang their luff,
and fell under the lee of the *Revenge*. But the other course
had been the better, and might right well have been answered
in so great an impossibility of prevailing. Notwithstanding,
out of the greatness of his mind, he could not be persuaded.
In the meanwhile as he attended those which were nearest
him, the great *San Philip* being in the wind of him, and
coming towards him, becalmed his sails in such sort, as the
ship could neither weigh nor feel the helm: so huge and
high cargued was the Spanish ship, being of a thousand and
five hundred tons. Who after laid the *Revenge* aboard. When
he was thus bereft of his sails, the ships that were under his
lee luffing up, also laid him aboard: of which the next was
the Admiral of the *Biscaines*, a very mighty and puissant ship
commanded by Brittan Dona. The said *Philip* carried three
tier of ordnance on a side, and eleven pieces in every tier.
She shot eight forth right out of her chase, besides those of
her stern ports.

After the *Revenge* was intangled with this *Philip*, four
other boarded her: two on her larboard, and two on her
starboard. The fight, thus beginning at three of the clock in
the afternoon, continued very terrible all that evening. But
the great *San Philip* having received the lower tier of the
Revenge, discharged with crossbarshot, shifted herself with all
diligence from her sides, utterly misliking her first entertainment. Some say that the ship foundered, but we cannot
report it for truth, unless we were assured. The Spanish

ships were filled with companies of soldiers, in some two
hundred besides the mariners; in some five, in others eight
hundred.   In ours there were none at all, beside the mariners, but the servants of the commanders and some few
voluntary gentlemen only.   After many interchanged volleys
of great ordnance and small shot, the Spaniards deliberated
to enter the *Revenge*, and made divers attempts, hoping to
force her by the multitudes of their armed soldiers and
musketeers, but were still repulsed again and again, and at all
times beaten back, into their own ships, or into the seas.
In the beginning of the fight, the *George Noble* of London,
having received some shot through her by the Armadoes, fell
under the lee of the *Revenge*, and asked Sir Richard what he
would command him, being but one of the victuallers and of
small force : Sir Richard bid him save himself, and leave him
to his fortune.   After the fight had thus without intermission
continued while the day lasted and some hours of the night,
many of our men were slain and hurt, and one of the great
galleons of the Armada, and the admiral of the Hulks both
sunk, and in many other of the Spanish ships great slaughter
was made.   Some write that Sir Richard was very dangerously
hurt almost in the beginning of the fight, and lay speechless
for a time ere he recovered.   But two of the *Revenge's* own
company brought home in a ship of Lime from the Islands,
examined by some of the Lords and others, affirmed that
he was never so wounded as that he forsook the upper deck,
till an hour before midnight ; and then being shot into the
body with a musket as he was a-dressing, was again shot
into the head, and withal his Chirurgeon wounded to death.
This agreeth also with an examination taken by Sir Frances
Godolphin, of four other mariners of the same ship being
returned, which examination the said Sir Frances sent unto
Mr. William Killigrue, of her Majesty's Privy Chamber.

But to return to the fight : the Spanish ships which attempted to board the *Revenge*, as they were wounded and

beaten off, so always others came in their places, she having Raleigh
never less than two mighty galleons by her sides, and aboard 1591
her. So that ere the morning from three of the clock the
day before, there had fifteen several Armadoes assailed her;
and all so ill approved their entertainment, as they were by
the break of day far more willing to hearken to a composition
than hastily to make any more assaults or entries.   But as
the day increased, so our men decreased : and as the light
grew more and more, by so much more grew our discomforts.
For none appeared in sight but enemies, saving one small
ship called the *Pilgrim*, commanded by Jacob Whiddon, who
hovered all night to see the success : but, in the morning
bearing with the *Revenge*, was hunted like a hare amongst
many ravenous hounds, but escaped.

All the powder of the *Revenge* to the last barrel was now
spent, all her pikes broken, forty of her best men slain, and
the most part of the rest hurt. In the beginning of the
fight she had but one hundred free from sickness, and fourscore and ten sick, laid in hold upon the ballast. A small
troop to man such a ship, and a weak garrison to resist so
mighty an army.   By those hundred all was sustained, the
volleys, boardings, and enterings of fifteen ships of war, besides those which beat her at large.   On the contrary, the
Spanish were always supplied with soldiers brought from
every squadron : all manner of arms and powder at will.
Unto ours there remained no comfort at all, no hope, no
supply either of ships, men, or weapons ; the masts all beaten
overboard, all her tackle cut asunder, her upper work altogether rased, and in effect evened she was with the water,
but the very foundation or bottom of a ship, nothing being
left overhead either for flight or defence.   Sir Richard
finding himself in this distress, and unable any longer to make
resistance, having endured in this fifteen hours' fight the
assault of fifteen several Armadoes, all by turns aboard him,
and by estimation eight hundred shot of great artillery,

besides many assaults and entries ; and that himself and the
ship must needs be possessed by the enemy, who were now all
cast in a ring round about him ; the *Revenge* not able to move
one way or other, but as she was moved with the waves and
billow of the sea : commanded the Master-Gunner, whom he
knew to be a most resolute man, to split and sink the ship ;
that thereby nothing might remain of glory or victory to the
Spaniards, seeing in so many hours' fight, and with so great
a navy they were not able to take her, having had fifteen
hours' time, fifteen thousand men, and fifty and three sail of
men-of-war to perform it withal : and persuaded the company, or as many as he could induce, to yield themselves
unto God, and to the mercy of none else ; but as they had
like valiant resolute men repulsed so many enemies, they
should not now shorten the honour of their nation, by pro-
longing their own lives for a few hours, or a few days.   The
Master-Gunner readily condescended, and divers others ; but
the Captain and the Master were of another opinion, and
besought Sir Richard to have care of them : alleging that the
Spaniard would be as ready to entertain a composition as
they were willing to offer the same : and that there being
divers sufficient and valiant men yet living, and whose
wounds were not mortal, they might do their country and
prince acceptable service hereafter.   And (that where Sir
Richard had alleged that the Spaniards should never glory
to have taken one ship of Her Majesty's, seeing that they
had so long and so notably defended themselves) they answered, that the ship had six foot water in hold, three shot
under water, which were so weakly stopped as with the first
working of the sea she must need sink, and was besides so
crushed and bruised as she could never be removed out of
the place.

   And as the matter was thus in dispute, and Sir Richard
refusing to hearken to any of those reasons, the Master of
the *Revenge* (while the Captain wan unto him the greater

party) was convoyed aboard the General, Don Alonso Bassan.
Who finding none over hasty to enter the *Revenge* again,
doubting lest Sir Richard would have blown them up and
himself, and perceiving by the report of the Master of the
Revenge his dangerous disposition : yielded that all their
lives should be saved, the company sent for England, and
the better sort to pay such reasonable ransom as their estate
would bear, and in the mean season to be free from galley or
imprisonment.   To this he so much the rather condescended
as well, as I have said, for fear of further loss and mischief to
themselves, as also for the desire he had to recover Sir
Richard Grinvile ; whom for his notable valour he seemed
greatly to honour and admire.

When this answer was returned, and that safety of life was
promised, the common sort being now at the end of their
peril, the most drew back from Sir Richard and the Master-
Gunner, being no hard matter to dissuade men from death to
life.   The Master-Gunner finding himself and Sir Richard
thus prevented and mastered by the greater number, would
have slain himself with a sword, had he not been by force
withheld and locked into his cabin.   Then the General sent
many boats aboard the *Revenge*, and divers of our men fearing Sir Richard's disposition, stole away aboard the general
and other ships.   Sir Richard, thus overmatched, was sent
unto by Alonso Bassan to remove out of the *Revenge*, the
ship being marvellous unsavoury, filled with blood and bodies
of dead and wounded men like a slaughter house.   Sir
Richard answered that he might do with his body what he
list, for he esteemed it not, and as he was carried out of
the ship he swooned, and reviving again desired the company
to pray for him.   The General used Sir Richard with all
humanity, and left nothing unattempted that tended to his
recovery, highly commending his valour and worthiness, and
greatly bewailed the danger wherein he was, being unto
them a rare spectacle, and a resolution seldom approved, to

Raleigh
1591

see one ship turn towards so many enemies, to endure the charge and boarding of so many huge Armadoes, and to resist and repel the assaults and entries of so many soldiers. All which, and more, is confirmed by a Spanish Captain, of the same Armada, and a present actor in the fight, who being severed from the rest in a storm, was by the *Lyon* of London, a small ship, taken, and is now prisoner in London.

The general commander of the Armada was Don Alonso Bassan, brother to the Marquess of Santa Cruce. The Admiral of the *Biscaine* squadron was Brittan Dona. Of the squadron of Sivil, Marquess of Arumburch. The Hulks and Fly-boats were commanded by Luis Cutino. There were slain and drowned in this fight, well near two thousand of the enemies, and two especial commanders Don Luis de Sant John, and Don George de Prunaria de Mallaga, as the Spanish Captain confesses, besides divers others of special account, whereof as yet report is not made.

The admiral of the Hulks and the *Ascention* of Sivil were both sunk by the side of the *Revenge*; one other recovered the road of Saint Michels, and sunk also there; a fourth ran herself with the shore to save her men. Sir Richard died, as it is said, the second or third day aboard the general, and was by them greatly bewailed. What became of his body, whether it were buried in the sea or on the land we know not: the comfort that remaineth to his friends is, that he hath ended his life honourably in respect of the reputation won to his nation and country, and of the same to his posterity, and that being dead, he hath not outlived his own honour.

Sir Walter Raleigh.

GLORIANA

Melville
1593

IN the meantime I was favourably and familiarly used, for during nine days that I remained at that Court, her Majesty pleased to confer with me every day, and sometimes

thrice upon a day, to wit a forenoon, afternoon, and after
supper. Sometimes she would say, that since she could not
meet with the Queen, her good sister, herself, to confer familiarly with her, that she should open a good part of her inward mind unto me, that I might show it again unto the
Queen; and said that she was not so offended at the Queen's
angry letter, as for that she seemed to disdain so far the
marriage with my Lord of Leicester; which she had caused
Mr. Randolph propone unto her. I said that it might be he
had touched something thereof to my Lords of Murray and
Lethington, but that he had not proponed the matter directly
unto herself; and that as well her Majesty, as they that
were her most familiar counsellors, could conjecture nothing
thereupon but delays and drifting of time, anent the declaring of her to be second person; which would try at the
meeting of the Commissioners above specified. She said
again, that the trial and declaration thereof would be hasted
forward, according to the Queen's good behaviour, and apply-
ing to her pleasure and advice in her marriage; and seeing
the matter concerning the said declaration was so weighty,
she had ordained some of the best lawyers in England
diligently to search out who had the best right; which she
would wish should be her dear sister rather than any other.
I said I was assured that her Majesty was both out of doubt
thereof, and would rather she should be declared than any
other; but I lamented that even the wisest princes will
not skance[1] sufficiently upon the partialities and pretences of
some of their familiar counsellors and servants; except it
were such a notable and rare prince as King Harry the
Eighth, her Majesty's father, of good memory, who of his
own head was determined to declare his sister's son, King
James the Fifth (at what time her Majesty was not yet born,
but only her sister, Queen Mary), heir-apparent to the crown
of England, failing the heirs gotten of his own body, for the

[1] Consider with suspicion.

Melville
1593
earnest desire he had to unite this whole island. She said she was glad he did it not. I said that then he had but a daughter, and was in doubt to have any more children, and yet had not so many suspicions in his head ; and that her Majesty was out of all doubt ever to have any children, as being deliberate to die a virgin. She said that she was never minded to marry, except she were compelled by the Queen her sister's hard behaviour towards her, in doing by her counsel as said is. I said : ' Madam, ye need not to tell me that ; I know your stately stomach : ye think if ye were married, ye would be but Queen of England, and now ye are King and Queen both ; ye may not suffer a commander.'

She appeared to be so affectionate to the Queen, her good sister, that she had a great desire to see her ; and because their desired meeting could not be so hastily brought to pass, she delighted oft to look upon her picture, and took me into her bedchamber, and opened a little lettroun[1] wherein were divers little pictures wrapped within paper, and written upon the paper their names with her own hand. Upon the first that she took up was written, ' My lord's picture.' I held the candle and pressed to see my lord's picture. Albeit she was loath to let me see it, at length I by importunity obtained the sight thereof, and asked the same to carry home with me unto the Queen ; which she refused, alleging she had but that one of his. I said again that she had the principal ; for he was at the farthest part of the chamber speaking with the Secretary Cecil. Then she took out the Queen's picture and kissed it ; and I kissed her hand, for the great love I saw she bore to the Queen. She showed me also a fair ruby, great like a racket ball. Then I desired that she would either send it as a token unto the Queen, or else my Lord of Leicester's picture. She said, gin the Queen would follow her counsel, that she would get them both with time, and all that she had ; but should send her a diamond for a token

---

[1] Lectern, desk : also work-table.

with me. Now it was late after supper; she appointed me
to be at her the next morning by eight hours, at which time
she used to walk in her garden ; and inquired sundry things
at me of this country, or other countries wherein I had
lately travelled; and caused me to eat with her dame of
honour, my Lady Stafford, an honourable and godly lady,
who had been at Geneva, banished during the reign of
Queen Mary, that I might be always near her Majesty, that
she might confer with me ; and my Lady Stafford's daughter
was my mistress, for I was of their acquaintance when they
passed through France, and had good intelligence by her
and by my Lady Throgmorton.

At divers meetings there would be divers purposes; and
the Queen, my sovereign, had instructed me sometimes
to leave matters of gravity and cast in some purposes of
merriness, or else I would be tired upon, as being well informed of her sister's naturelle.[1] Therefore, in declaring the
customs of Dutchland, Polle, and Italy, the busking and
clothing of the dames and women was not forgot, and what
country weed was best setten[2] for gentlewomen to wear. The
Queen of England said she had of divers sorts; which
every day so long as I was there she changed ; one day the
English weed, one the French, and one the Italian, and so of
others; asking at me which of them set her best. I said
the Italian weed ; which pleased her well, for she delighted
to show her golden-coloured hair, wearing a kell[3] and bonnet
as they do in Italy. Her hair was redder than yellow, curled
apparently of nature. Then she entered to discern what
kind of colour of hair was reputed best ; and inquired whether
the queen's or hers was best, and which of them two was
fairest. I said the fairness of them both was not their worst
faults. But she was earnest with me to declare which of
them I thought fairest. I said she was the fairest Queen in
England, and ours the fairest Queen in Scotland. Yet she

[1] Disposition.   [2] Suited.   [3] Caul.

Melville was earnest. I said they were both the fairest ladies of their
1593 Courts, and that the Queen of England was whiter, but our
Queen was very lusome.[1] She inquired which of them was of
highest stature. I said, our Queen. Then she said the Queen
was over high, and that herself was neither over high nor
over low. Then she asked what kind of exercises she used.
I said that I was dispatched out of Scotland, that the Queen
was but new come back from the Highland hunting; and
when she had leisure from the affairs of her country, she read
upon good books the histories of divers countries, and sometimes would play upon lute and virginals. She speered gin
she played well. I said, reasonably for a queen.

That same day, after dinner, my Lord of Hunsdon drew
me up to a quiet gallery, that I might hear some music, but
he said he durst not avow it, where I might hear the Queen
play upon the virginals. But after I had hearkened a while,
I took by the tapestry that hung before the door of the
chamber, and seeing her back was toward the door, I
entered within the chamber and stood still at the door-cheek,
and heard her play excellently well; but she left off so soon
as she turned her about and saw me, and came forwards,
seeming to strike me with her left hand, and to think shame;
alleging that she used not to play before men, but when she
was solitary her allane,[2] to eschew melancholy; and asked
how I came there. I said, as I was walking with my Lord
of Hunsdon, as we passed by the chamber door I heard such
melody, which roused and drew me within the chamber I
wist not how; excusing my fault of homeliness as being
brought up in the Court of France, and was now willing to
suffer what kind of punishment would please her lay upon
me for my offence. Then she sat down low upon a cushion,
and I upon my knee beside her; but she gave me a cushion
with her own hand to lay under my knee, which I refused,
but she compelled me; and called for my Lady Stafford out

---

[1] Loveable.　　　　　　　　　　[2] By herself.

of the next chamber, for she was her allane there. Then she asked whether the Queen or she played best. In that I gave her the praise. She said my French was good; and speired if I could speak Italian, which she spake reasonably well. I said I tarried not above two months in Italy, and had brought with me some books to read upon; but had no leisure to learn the language perfectly. Then she spake to me in Dutch, but it was not good; and would wit what kind of books I liked best, whether of theology, history, or love matters. I said I liked well of all the sorts.

I was earnest to be dispatched; but she said that I tired sooner of her company nor she did of mine. I said, albeit I had no occasion to tire, that it was time to return; but I was stayed two days longer till I might see her dance, as I was informed; which being done, she inquired at me whether she or the Queen danced best. I said the Queen danced not so high and disposedly as she did. Then again she wished that she might see the Queen at some convenient place of meeting. I offered to convoy her secretly to Scotland by post, clothed like a page disguised, that she might see the Queen; as King James the Fifth passed in France disguised, with his own ambassador, to see the Duke of Vendome's sister that should have been his wife; and how that her chamber should be kept as though she were sick, in the meantime, and none to be privy thereto but my Lady Stafford and one of the grooms of her chamber. She said, Alas! gin she might do it; and seemed to like well of such kind of language, and used all the means she could to cause me persuade the Queen of the great love that she bore unto her, and was minded to put away all jealousies and suspicions, and in times coming a straiter friendship to stand between them than ever had been of before; and promised that my dispatch should be delivered unto me very shortly by Mr. Cecil at London.

Sir James Melville.

Melville 1593

JOHN DAVYS THE NAVIGATOR

Jane
1593

THE sixth of August we set sail and went to Penguin Isle, and the next day we salted twenty hogsheads of seals, which was as much as our salt could possibly do, and so we departed for The Straits [of Magellan] the poorest wretches that ever were created. The seventh of August, toward night, we departed from Penguin Isles, shaping our course for The Straits, where we had full confidence to meet with our General [Cavendish]. The ninth we had a sore storm, so that we were constrained to hull, for our sails were not to endure any force. The fourteenth we were driven in among certain Isles, never before discovered by any known relation, lying fifty leagues or better from the shore, East and Northerly from The Straits: in which place, unless it had pleased God of his wonderful mercy to have ceased the wind, we must of necessity have perished. But the wind shifting to the East, we directed our course for The Straits, and the eighteenth of August we fell with the Cape in a very thick fog; and the same night we anchored ten leagues within the Cape. The nineteenth day we passed the first and the second Straits. The twenty-first we doubled Cape Froward. The twenty-second we anchored in Savage Cove, so named because we found many savages there. Notwithstanding the extreme cold of this place, yet do all these wild people go naked, and live in the woods like satyrs, painted and disguised, and fly from you like wild deer. They are very strong, and threw stones at us of three or four pound weight an incredible distance. The twenty-fourth, in the morning, we departed from this cove, and the same day we came into the North-West reach, which is the last reach of The Straits. The twenty-fifth we anchored in a good cove, within fourteen leagues of the South Sea: in this place we purposed to stay for the

General, for the strait in this place is scarce three miles broad, so that he could not pass but we must see him. After we had stayed here a fortnight in the deep of winter, our victuals consuming (for our seals stunk most vilely, and our men died pitifully through cold and famine, for the greatest part of them had not clothes to defend the extremity of the winter's cold), being in this heavy distress, our Captain [John Davys] and Master thought it the best course to depart from The Straits into the South Sea, and to go for the Isle of Santa Maria, which is to the Northward of Baldivia in thirty-seven degrees and a quarter, where we might have relief, and be in a temperate clime, and there stay for the General, for of necessity he must come by that Isle.

So we departed the thirteenth of September, and came in sight of the South Sea. The fourteenth we were forced back again, and recovered a cove three leagues within The Straits from the South Sea. Again we put forth, and being eight or ten leagues free of the land, the wind rising furiously at West-North-West, we were enforced again into The Straits only for want of sails; for we never durst bear sail in any stress of weather, they were so weak. So again we recovered the cove three leagues within The Straits, where we endured most furious weather, so that one of our two cables brake, whereby we were hopeless of life. Yet it pleased God to calm the storm, and we unrived our sheets, tacks, halliers, and other ropes, and moored our ship to the trees close by the rocks. We laboured to recover our anchor again, but could not by any means, it lay so deep in the water, and, as we think, clean covered with ooze. Now had we but one anchor, which had but one whole fluke, a cable spliced in two places, and a piece of an old cable. In the midst of these our troubles it pleased God that the wind came fair the first of October; whereupon with all expedition we loosed our moorings and weighed our

Jane
1593
anchor, and so towed off into the channel; for we had
mended our boat in Port Desire, and had five oars of the
pinnace. When we had weighed our anchor, we found our
cable broken, only one strand held : then we praised God,
for we saw apparently His mercies in preserving us. Being in
the channel, we rived our ropes, and again rigged our ship;
no man's hand was idle, but all laboured even for the last
gasp of life. Here our company was divided ; some desired
to go again for Port Desire, and there to be set on shore,
where they might travel for their lives, and some stood with
the Captain and Master to proceed.

Whereupon the Captain said to the Master: 'Master,
you see the wonderful extremity of our estate, and the
great doubts among our company of the truth of your
reports, as touching relief to be had in the South Sea.
Some say in secret, as I am informed, that we undertake
these desperate attempts through blind affection that we
bear to the General. For mine own part, I plainly make
known unto you that the love which I bare to the General
caused me first to enter into this action, whereby I have
not only heaped upon my head this bitter calamity now
present, but also have in some sort procured the dislike of
my best friends in England, as it is not unknown to some in
this company. But now, being thus entangled by the providence of God for my former offences (no doubt), I desire
that it may please His Divine Majesty to show us such
merciful favour, that we may rather proceed than otherwise :
or if it be His will that our mortal being shall now take an
end, I rather desire that it may be in proceeding than in
returning. And because I see in reason that the limits of
our time are now drawing to an end, I do in Christian charity
entreat you all, first to forgive me in whatsoever I have been
grievous unto you ; secondly, that you will rather pray for
our General than use hard speeches of him ; and let us be
fully persuaded that not for his cause and negligence, but

for our own offences against the Divine Majesty, we are presently punished; lastly, let us forgive one another and be
reconciled as children in love and charity, and not think
upon the vanities of this life: so shall we in leaving this
life live with our glorious Redeemer, or abiding in this life
find favour with God.   And now (good Master), forasmuch as
you have been in this voyage once before with your master
the General, satisfy the company of such truths as are to you
best known; and you the rest of the General's men, which
likewise have been with him in his first voyage, if you hear
anything contrary to the truth, spare not to reprove it, I pray
you.   And so I beseech the Lord to bestow his mercy upon
us.'

Then the Master began in these speeches: 'Captain, your
request is very reasonable, and I refer to your judgment my
honest care and great pains taken in the General's service,
my love towards him, and in what sort I have discharged my
duty, from the first day to this hour.   I was commanded by
the General to follow your directions, which hitherto I have
performed.   You all know that when I was extremely sick the
General was lost in my mate's watch, as you have well examined: sithens which time, in what anguish and grief of mind
I have lived, God only knoweth, and you are in some part a
witness.   And now, if you think good to return, I will not
gainsay it: but this I assure you, if life may be preserved by
any means, it is in proceeding. For at the Isle of Santa Maria I
do assure you of wheat, pork, and roots enough.   Also I will
bring you to an Isle where pelicans be in great abundance,
and at Santos we shall have meal in great plenty, besides all
our possibility of intercepting some ships upon the coast of
Chili and Peru.   But if we return there is nothing but death
to be hoped for: therefore do as you like, I am ready, but
my desire is to proceed.' These his speeches being confirmed
by others that were in the former voyage, there was a
general consent of proceeding; and so the second of October

we put into the South Sea, and were free of all land. This
night the wind began to blow very much at West-North-West,
and still increased in fury, so that we were in great doubt
what course to take ; to put into the straits we durst not for
lack of ground tackle ; to bear sail we doubted, the tempest
was so furious, and our sails so bad. The pinnace came room
with us, and told us that she had received many grievous
seas, and that her ropes did every hour fail her, so as they
could not tell what shift to make : we, being unable in any
sort to help them, stood under our courses in view of the
lee-shore, still expecting our ruinous end.

The fourth of October the storm growing beyond all
reason furious, the pinnace being in the wind of us, struck
suddenly ahull, so that we thought she had received some
grievous sea, or sprung a leak, or that her sails failed her,
because she came not with us ; but we durst not hull in that
unmerciful storm, but sometimes tried under our main
course, sometime with a haddock off our sail, for our ship
was very leeward and most laboursome in the sea. This
night we lost the pinnace and never saw her again.

The fifth our foresail was split and all to torn ; then our
Master took the mizzen and brought it to the foremast, to
make our ship work, and with our spritsail we mended our
foresail, the storm continuing without all reason in fury, with
hail, snow, rain, and wind such and so mighty as that in
nature it could not possibly be more : the seas such and so
lofty with continual breach, that many times we were doubtful whether our ship did sink or swim.

The tenth of October, being by the accompt of our Captain
and Master very near the shore, the weather dark, the storm
furious, and most of our men having given over to travail, we
yielded ourselves to death, without further hope of succour.
Our Captain sitting in the gallery very pensive, I came and
brought him some rosa solis to comfort him ; for he was so
cold that he was scarce able to move a joint. After he had

drunk, and was comforted in heart, he began for the ease of
his conscience to make a large repetition of his forepassed
time, and with many grievous sighs he concluded in these
words: 'O most glorious God, with Whose power the
mightiest things among men are matters of no moment, I
most humbly beseech Thee that the intolerable burthen of
my sins may through the blood of Jesus Christ be taken from
me: and end our days with speed, or show us some merciful
sign of Thy love and our preservation.' Having thus ended,
he desired me not to make known to any of the company his
intolerable grief and anguish of mind, because they should
not thereby be dismayed. And so suddenly, before I went
from him, the sun shined clear; so that he and the Master
both observed the true elevation of the Pole, whereby they
knew by what course to recover The Straits. Wherewithal
our Captain and Master were so revived, and gave such comfortable speeches to the company, that every man rejoiced,
as though we had received a present deliverance.

The next day, being the eleventh of October, we saw Cabo
Deseado, being the cape on the South shore (the North shore
is nothing but a company of dangerous rocks, isles, and shoals).
This cape being within two leagues to leeward of us, our
Master greatly doubted that we could not double the same.
Whereupon the Captain told him: 'You see there is no
remedy, either we must double it, or before noon we must
die: therefore loose your sails, and let us put it to God's
mercy.' The Master, being a man of good spirit, resolutely
made quick dispatch and set sail. Our sails had not been half-
an-hour aboard, but the foot-rope of our foresail broke, so
that nothing held but the oylet holes. The seas continually
broke over the ship's poop, and flew into the sails with such
violence that we still expected the tearing of our sails
or oversetting of the ship, and withal to our utter discomfort we perceived that we fell still more and more to
leeward, so that we could not double the cape. We were

now come within half a mile of the cape, and so near the
shore that the counter-surf of the sea would rebound against
the ship's side, so that we were much dismayed with the
horror of our present end.   Being thus at the very pinch of
death, the wind and seas raging beyond measure, our Master
veered some of the main sheet; and whether it was by that
occasion, or by some current, or by the wonderful power of
God, as we verily think it was, the ship quickened her way,
and shot past that rock, where we thought she would have
shored.   Then between the cape and the point there was a
little bay; so that we were somewhat farther from the shore.
And when we were come so far as the cape, we yielded to
death.   Yet our good God, the Father of all mercies, delivered us, and we doubled the cape about the length of our
ship, or very little more.   Being shot past the cape, we presently took in our sails, which only God had preserved unto
us: and when we were shot in between the high lands, the
wind blowing trade, without any inch of sail, we spooned
before the sea, three men being not able to guide the helm,
and in six hours we were put five-and-twenty leagues within
The Straits, where we found a sea answerable to the Ocean.

In this time we freed our ship from water, and after we
had rested a little, our men were not able to move; their
sinews were stiff, and their flesh dead, and many of them
(which is most lamentable to be reported) were so eaten with
lice, as that in their flesh did lie clusters of lice as big as
peason, yea, and some as big as beans.   Being in this misery,
we were constrained to put into a cove for the refreshing
our men.   Our Master knowing the shore and every cove
very perfectly, put in with the shore and moored to the
trees, as beforetime we had done, laying our anchor to
the seaward.   Here we continued until the twentieth of
October; but not being able any longer to stay through
extremity of famine, the one-and-twentieth we put off into
the channel, the weather being reasonable calm: but before

night it blew most extremely at West-North-West. The storm growing outrageous, our men could scarcely stand by their labour; and The Straits being full of turning reaches, we were constrained by discretion of the Captain and Master in their accounts to guide the ship in the hell-dark night, when we could not see any shore, the channel being in some places scarce three miles broad. But our Captain, as we first passed through The Straits, drew such an exquisite plat [1] of the same, as I am assured it cannot in any sort be bettered; which plat he and the Master so often perused, and so carefully regarded, as that in memory they had every turning and creek, and in the deep dark night without any doubting they conveyed the ship through that crooked channel: so that I conclude the world hath not any so skilful pilots for that place as they are: for otherwise we could never have passed in such sort as we did.

The twenty-fifth we came to an Island in The Straits named Penguin Isle, whither we sent our boat to seek relief, for there were great abundance of birds, and the weather was very calm; so we came to an anchor by the Island in seven fathoms. While our boat was at shore, and we had great store of penguins, there arose a sudden storm, so that our ship did drive over a breach, and our boat sank at the shore. Captain Cotton and the Lieutenant, being on shore, leaped in the boat and freed the same, and threw away all the birds, and with great difficulty recovered the ship: myself also was in the boat the same time, where for my life I laboured to the best of my power. The ship all this while driving upon the lee shore, when we came aboard, we helped to set sail, and weighed the anchor; for before our coming they could scarce hoist up their yards, yet with much ado they set their fore-course. Thus in a mighty fret of weather the seven-and-twentieth day of October we were free of The Straits, and the thirtieth of October we came to Penguin Isle,

---

[1] Chart.

Jane
1593
being three leagues from Port Desire, the place where we purposed to seek for our relief.

When we were come to this Isle, we sent our boat on shore, which returned laden with birds and eggs; and our men said that the penguins were so thick upon the Isle, that ships might be laden with them, for they could not go without treading upon the birds, whereat we greatly rejoiced. Then the Captain appointed Charles Parker and Edward Smith, with twenty others, to go on shore, and to stay upon the Isle for the killing and drying of those penguins, and promised after the ship was in harbour to send the rest, not only for expedition, but also to save the small store of victuals in the ship. But Parker, Smith, and the rest of their faction suspected that this was a device of the Captain to leave his men on shore, that by these means there might be victuals for the rest to recover their country; and when they remembered that this was the place where they would have slain their Captain and Master, surely (thought they) for revenge hereof will they leave us on shore. Which, when our Captain understood, he used these speeches unto them : ' I understand that you are doubtful of your security through the perverseness of your own guilty consciences : it is an extreme grief unto me that you should judge me bloodthirsty, in whom you have seen nothing but kind conversation : if you have found otherwise, speak boldly, and accuse me of the wrongs that I have done ; if not, why do you then measure me by your own uncharitable consciences ? All the company knoweth indeed that in this place you practised to the utmost of your powers to murther me and the Master, causeless, as God knoweth, which evil in this place we did remit you : and now I may conceive without doing you wrong, that you again purpose some evil in bringing these matters to repetition : but God hath so shortened your confederacy, as that I nothing doubt you : it is for your master's sake that I have forborne you in your unchristian practices :

and here I protest before God that for his sake alone I will
yet endure this injury, and you shall in no sort be prejudiced,
or in anything be by me commanded ; but when we come
into England (if God so favour us), your master shall know
your honesties. In the mean space be void of these suspicions, for, God I call to witness, revenge is no part of my
thought.' They gave him thanks, desiring to go into the
harbour with the ship, which he granted. So there were
ten left upon the Isle, and the last of October we entered
the harbour.   Our Master at our last being here having
taken careful notice of every creek in the river, in a very
convenient place, upon sandy ooze, ran the ship on ground,
laying our anchor to seaward, and with our running ropes
moored her to stakes upon the shore, which he had fastened
for that purpose; where the ship remained till our departure.

The third of November our boat with water, wood, and as
many as she could carry, went for the Isle of Penguin ; but
being deep, she durst not proceed, but returned again the
same night. Then Parker, Smith, Townsend, Purpet, with
five others, desired that they might go by land, and that the
boat might fetch them when they were against the Isle, it
being scarce a mile from the shore. The Captain bade them
do what they thought best, advising them to take weapons
with them : ' For,' said he, ' although we have not at any
time seen people in this place, yet in the country there may
be savages.' They answered that here were great store of
deer and ostriches; but if they were savages, they would
devour them. Notwithstanding, the Captain caused them
to carry weapons, calivers, swords, and targets : so the
sixth of November they departed by land, and the boat by
sea ; but from that day to this day we never heard of our
men. The eleventh, while most of our men were at the
Isle, only the Captain and Master with six others being left
in the ship, there came a great multitude of savages to the

Jane
1593

ship, throwing dust in the air, leaping and running like brute beasts, having vizards on their faces like dogs' faces, or else their faces are dogs' faces indeed. We greatly feared lest they would set our ship on fire, for they would suddenly make fire, whereat we much marvelled: they came to windward of our ship, and set the bushes on fire, so that we were in a very stinking smoke: but as soon as they came within our shot, we shot at them, and striking one of them in the thigh, they all presently fled, so that we never heard nor saw more of them. Hereby we judged that these cannibals had slain our nine men. When we considered what they were that thus were slain, and found that they were the principal men that would have murdered our Captain and Master, with the rest of their friends, we saw the just judgment of God, and made supplication to His Divine Majesty to be merciful unto us. While we were in this harbour, our Captain and Master went with the boat, to discover how far this river did run, that if need should enforce us to leave our ship, we might know how far we might go by water. So they found that further than twenty miles they could not go with the boat. At their return they sent the boat to the Isle of Penguin; whereby we understood that the penguins dried to our heart's content, and that the multitude of them was infinite. This penguin hath the shape of a bird, but hath no wings, only two stumps in the place of wings, by which he swimmeth under water with as great swiftness as any fish. They live upon smelts, whereof there is great abundance upon this coast: in eating they be neither fish nor flesh: they lay great eggs, and the bird is of a reasonable bigness, very near twice so big as a duck. All the time that we were in this place we fared passing well with eggs, penguins, young seals, young gulls, besides other birds, such as I know not: of all which we had great abundance. In this place we found an herb called scurvy grass, which we fried with eggs, using train oil instead of butter. This herb did so purge the blood that it took away all kind of swellings, of which many died, and restored us to perfect health of body, so that we were in as good case as when we came first out of England. We stayed in this harbour until the twenty-second of December, in which time we had dried twenty thousand penguins; and the Captain, the Master, and myself had made some salt by laying salt water upon the rocks in holes, which in six days would be kerned.[1] Thus God did feed us even as it were with manna from heaven.

The twenty-second of December we departed with our ship for the Isle, where with great difficulty, by the skilful industry of our Master, we got fourteen thousand of our birds, and had almost lost our Captain in labouring to bring the birds aboard. And had not our Master been very expert in the set of those wicked tides, which run after many fashions, we had also lost our ship in the same place. But God of His goodness hath in all our extremities been our protector. So the twenty-second, at night, we departed with fourteen thousand dried penguins, not being able to fetch the rest, and shaped our course for Brazil. Now our Captain rated our victuals, and brought us to such allowance as that our victuals might last six months; for our hope was that within six months we might recover our country, though our sails were very bad. So the allowance was two ounces and a half of meal for a man a day, and to have so twice a week, so that five ounces did serve for a week. Three days a week we had oil, three spoonfuls for a man a day ; and two days in a week peason, a pint between four men a day ; and every day five penguins for four men, and six quarts of water for four men a day. This was our allowance; wherewith (we praise God) we lived, though weakly, and very feeble.

The thirtieth of January we arrived at the Isle of Placencia, in Brazil, the first place that outward bound we were at; and having made the shold,[2] our ship lying off at sea, the Captain,

---

[1] Hardened into lumps.   [2] Shoal.

with twenty-four of the company, went with the boat on shore, being a whole night before they could recover it. The last of January at sun-rising they suddenly landed, hoping to take the Portugals in their houses, and by that means to recover some Casavi-meal, or other victuals for our relief. But when they came to the houses they were all razed and burnt to the ground, so that we thought no man had remained on the Island. Then the Captain went to the gardens, and brought from thence fruits and roots for the company, and came aboard the ship, and brought her into a fine creek which he had found out, where we might moor her by the trees, and where there was water, and hoops to trim our cask. Our case being very desperate, we presently laboured for dispatch away; some cut hoops, which the coopers made, others laboured upon the sails and ship, every man travailing for his life, and still a guard was kept on shore to defend those that laboured, every man having his weapon likewise by him. The third of February our men, with twenty-three shot, went again to the gardens, being three miles from us upon the North shore, and fetched Casavi roots out of the ground, to relieve our company instead of bread; for we spent not of our meal while we stayed here. The fifth of February being Monday, our Captain and Master hasted the company to their labour; so some went with the coopers to gather hoops, and the rest laboured aboard. This night many of our men in the ship dreamed of murther and slaughter. In the morning they reported their dreams, one saying to another: 'This night I dreamt that thou wert slain'; another answered, 'And I dreamed that thou wert slain': and this was general through the ship. The Captain hearing this, who likewise had dreamed very strangely himself, gave very strict charge that those which went on shore should take weapons with them, and saw them himself delivered into the boat, and sent some of purpose to guard the labourers. All the forenoon they laboured in quietness,

and when it was ten of the clock, the heat being extreme,
they came to a rock near the wood side (for all this country
is nothing but thick woods), and there they boiled Casavi
roots and dined.   After dinner some slept, some washed
themselves in the sea, all being stripped to their shirts, and
no man keeping watch, no match lighted, not a piece
charged.   Suddenly, as they were thus sleeping and sport-
ing, having gotten themselves into a corner out of sight of
the ship, there came a multitude of Indians and Portugals
upon them, and slew them sleeping.   Only two escaped, one
very sore hurt, the other not touched, by whom we understood of this miserable massacre.   With all speed we manned
our boat, and landed to succour our men ; but we found them
slain, and laid naked on a rank, one by another, with their
faces upward, and a cross set by them.   And withal we saw
two very great pinnaces come from the river of Jenero very
full of men ; whom we mistrusted came from thence to take
us ; because there came from Jenero soldiers to Santos when
the General had taken the town, and was strong in it.

Of seventy-six persons which departed in our ship out of
England, we were now left but twenty-seven, having lost
thirteen in this place, with their chief furniture, as muskets,
calivers, powder, and shot.   Our cask was all in decay, so
that we could not take in more water than was in our ship,
for want of cask, and that which we had was marvellous ill-
conditioned.   And being there moored by trees for want of
cables and anchors, we still expected the cutting of our
moorings, to be beaten from our decks with our own
furniture, and to be assailed by them of Jenero : what
distress we were now driven into I am not able to express.
To depart with eight tons of water in such bad cask was to
starve at sea, and in staying our case was ruinous.   These
were hard choices ; but being thus perplexed, we made
choice rather to fall into the hands of the Lord than into the
hands of men : for His exceeding mercies we had tasted, and

of the others' cruelty we were not ignorant. So concluding
to depart, the sixth of February we were off in the channel,
with our ordnance and small shot in a readiness for any
assault that should come, and having a small gale of wind,
we recovered the sea in most deep distress. Then bemoaning our estate one to another, and recounting over all our
extremities, nothing grieved us more than the loss of our men
twice, first by the slaughter of the cannibals at Port Desire,
and at this Isle of Placencia by the Indians and Portugals.
And considering what they were that were lost, we found
that all those that conspired the murthering of our Captain and
Master were now slain by savages, the Gunner only excepted.
Being thus at sea, when we came to Cape Frio the wind was
contrary; so that three weeks we were grievously vexed
with cross winds, and our water consuming, our hope of life
was very small. Some desired to go to Baya, and to submit
themselves to the Portugals, rather than to die for thirst:
but the Captain with fair persuasions altered their purpose of
yielding to the Portugals.

In this distress it pleased God to send us rain in such
plenty, as that we were well watered, and in good comfort to return. But after we came near unto the sun our
dried penguins began to corrupt, and there bred in them
a most loathsome and ugly worm of an inch long. This
worm did so mightily increase, and devour our victuals,
that there was in reason no hope how we should avoid
famine, but be devoured of these wicked creatures. There
was nothing that they did not devour, only iron excepted:
our clothes, boots, shoes, hats, shirts, stockings: and for the
ship, they did so eat the timbers, as that we greatly feared
they would undo us by gnawing through the ship's side.
Great was the care and diligence of our Captain, Master, and
company to consume these vermin; but the more we
laboured to kill them, the more they increased; so that at
the last we could not sleep for them, but they would eat our

flesh and bite like mosquitoes. In this woful case, after
we had passed the equinoctial toward the North, our men
began to fall sick of such a monstrous disease as I think the
like was never heard of: for in their ankles it began to
swell; from thence in two days it would be in their breasts,
so that they could not draw their breath, and then . . . .
so that they could neither stand, lie, nor go. Whereupon
our men grew mad with grief. Our Captain, with extreme
anguish of his soul, was in such woful case that he desired
only a speedy end, and though he were scarce able to
speak for sorrow, yet he persuaded them to patience, and
to give God thanks, and like dutiful children to accept of
His chastisement. For all this divers grew raging mad,
and some died in most loathsome and furious pain. It
were incredible to write our misery as it was: there was
no man in perfect health but the Captain and one boy.
The Master, being a man of good spirit, with extreme
labour bore out his grief, so that it grew not upon him.
To be short, all our men died except sixteen, of which
there were but five able to move. The Captain was in good
health, the Master indifferent, Captain Cotton and myself
swollen and short winded, yet better than the rest that were
sick, and one boy in health : upon us five only the labour of
the ship did stand. The Captain and Master, as occasion
served, would take in and heave out the topsails, the
Master only attended on the spritsail, and all of us at the
capstan without sheets and tacks. In fine our misery and
weakness was so great that we could not take in nor heave
out a sail: so our topsail and spritsails were torn all in
pieces by the weather. The Master and Captain taking their
turns at the helm, were mightily distressed and monstrously
grieved with the most woful lamentation of our sick men.
Thus, as lost wanderers upon the sea, the eleventh of June
1593, it pleased God that we arrived at Bearhaven in Ireland, and there ran the ship on shore; where the Irishmen

Jane
1593

helped us to take in our sails and to moor our ship for floating: which slender pains of theirs cost the Captain some ten pounds before he could have the ship in safety. Thus without victuals, sails, men, or any furniture, God only guided us into Ireland, where the Captain left the Master and three or four of the company to keep the ship; and within five days after he and certain others had passage in an English fisher-boat to Padstow in Cornwall. In this manner our small remnant by God's only mercy were preserved and restored to our country, to whom be all honour and glory, world without end.

Hakluyt : Navigations.

THE DIVINE ARETINE

Nash
1594

BEFORE I go any further, let me speak a word or two of this Aretine. It was one of the wittiest knaves that ever God made. If out of so base a thing as ink there may be extracted a spirit, he writ with nought but the spirit of ink, and his style was the spirituality of art's, and nothing else, whereas all others of his age were but the lay temporality of inkhorn terms. For indeed they were mere temporisers, and no better. His pen was sharp pointed like [a] poniard. No leaf he wrote on but was like a burning glass to set on fire all his readers. With more than musket shot did he charge his quill, where he meant to inveigh. No one hour but he sent a whole legion of devils into some herd of swine or other. If Martiall had ten Muses (as he saith of himself) when he but tasted a cup of wine, he had ten score when he determined to tyrannise. Ne'er a line of his but was able to make a man drunken with admiration. His sight pierced like lightning into the entrails of all abuses. This I must needs say, that most of his learning he got by hearing the lectures at Florence. It is sufficient that learning he had, and a conceit exceeding all learning, to quintessence everything which he heard. He was no timorous servile flatterer of the commonwealth wherein he lived. His tongue and his invention were foreborne, what they thought they would confidently utter. Princes he spared not, that in the least point transgressed. His life he contemned in comparison of the liberty of speech.

Nash
1594

Thomas Nash.

DISCOVERING GUIANA

Raleigh
1596

AFTER we departed from the port of these Ciawani, we passed up the river with the flood, and anchored the ebb, and in this sort we went onward. The third day that we entered the river our galley came on ground, and stuck so fast as we thought that even there our discovery had ended, and that we must have left sixty of our men to have inhabited like rooks upon trees with those nations: but the next morning, after we had cast out all her ballast, with tugging and hauling to and fro, we got her afloat, and went on. At four days' end we fell into as goodly a river as ever I beheld, which was called the great Amana, which ran more directly without windings and turnings than the other. But soon after the flood of the sea left us, and we enforced either by main strength to row against a violent current, or to return as wise as we went out ; we had then no shift but to persuade the companies that it was but two or three days' work, and therefore desired them to take pains, every gentleman and others taking their turns to row, and to spell one the other at the hour's end. Every day we passed by goodly branches of rivers, some falling from the West, others from the East into Amana, but those I leave to the description in the chart of discovery, where every one shall be named, with his rising and descent. When three days more were over-gone, our companies began to despair, the weather being extremely hot, the river bordered with very high trees that kept away the air, and the current against us every day stronger than other. But we evermore commanded our pilots to promise an end the next day, and used it so long as we were driven to assure them from four reaches of the river to three, and so to two, and so to the next reach; but so long we laboured as many days were spent, and so driven to draw ourselves to harder allowance, our bread even at the last, and no drink at all; and our men and ourselves so wearied and scorched, and doubtful withal whether we should ever perform it or no, the heat increasing as we drew towards the Line : for we were now in five degrees.

The farther we went on (our victual decreasing and the air breeding great faintness) we grew weaker and weaker when we had most need of strength and ability, for hourly the river ran more violently than other against us, and the barge, wherries, and ship's boat of Captain Gifford and Captain Calfield had spent all their provisions, so as we were brought into despair and discomfort, had we not persuaded all the company that it was but only one day's work more to attain the land, where we should be relieved of all we wanted, and if we returned that we were sure to starve by the way, and that the world would also laugh us to scorn. On the banks of these rivers were divers sorts of fruits good to eat, flowers and trees of that variety as were sufficient to make ten volumes of herbals; we relieved ourselves many times with the fruits of the country, and sometimes with fowl and fish : we saw birds of all colours, some carnation, some crimson, orange-tawny, purple, green, watchet, and of all other sorts both simple and mixed, as it was unto us a great good passing of the time to behold them, besides the relief we found by killing some store of them with our fowling-pieces, without which, having little or no

bread and less drink, but only the thick and troubled water
of the river, we had been in a very hard case.

Our old pilot of the Ciawani (whom, as I said before, we
took to redeem Ferdinando) told us, that if we would enter
a branch of a river on the right hand with our barge and
wherries, and leave the galley at anchor the while in the
great river, he would bring us to a town of the Arwacas
where we should find store of bread, hens, fish, and of the
country wine, and persuaded us that departing from the
galley at noon, we might return ere night. I was very glad
to hear this speech, and presently took my barge, with eight
musketeers, Captain Gifford's wherry with himself and four
musketeers, and Captain Calfield with his wherry and as
many, and so we entered the mouth of this river, and
because we were persuaded that it was so near, we took no
victual with us at all. When we had rowed three hours we
marvelled we saw no sign of any dwelling, and asked the
pilot where the town was; he told us a little farther: after
three hours more, the sun being almost set, we began to
suspect that he led us that way to betray us, for he confessed
that those Spaniards which fled from Trinidad, and also
those that remained with Carapana in Emeria, were joined
together in some village upon that river. But when it grew
towards night, and we demanding where the place was, he
told us but four reaches more ; when we had rowed four
and four, we saw no sign, and our poor watermen, even
heartbroken and tired, were ready to give up the ghost; for
we had now come from the galley near forty miles.

At the last we determined to hang the pilot, and if we
had well known the way back again by night, he had surely
gone, but our own necessities pleaded sufficiently for his
safety; for it was as dark as pitch, and the river began so
to narrow itself, and the trees to hang over from side to
side, as we were driven with arming swords to cut a passage
through those branches that covered the water. We were

very desirous to find this town, hoping of a feast, because we made but a short breakfast aboard the galley in the morning, and it was now eight o'clock at night; and our stomachs began to gnaw apace; but whether it was best to return or go on, we began to doubt, suspecting treason in the pilot more and more: but the poor old Indian ever assured us that it was but a little farther, and but this one turning, and that turning, and at last about one o'clock after midnight we saw a light, and rowing towards it, we heard the dogs of the village. When we landed we found few people for the lord of that place was gone with divers canoas about 400 miles off, upon a journey towards the head of Orenoque to trade for gold, and to buy women of the cannibals, who afterwards unfortunately passed by us as we rode at an anchor in the port of Morequito in the dark of night, and yet came so near us, as his canoas grated against our barges: and [he] left one of his company at the port of Morequito, by whom we understood that he had brought thirty young women, divers plates of gold, and had great store of fine pieces of cotton cloth and cotton beds. In his house we had good store of bread, fish, hens, and Indian drink, and so rested that night; and in the morning, after we had traded with such of his people as came down, we returned towards our galley, and brought with us some quantity of bread, fish, and hens.

On both sides of this river we passed the most beautiful country that ever mine eyes beheld; and whereas all that we had seen before was nothing but woods, prickles, bushes, and thorns, here we beheld plains of twenty miles in length, the grass short and green, and in divers parts groves of trees by themselves, as if they had been by all the art and labour in the world so made of purpose: and still as we rowed, the deer came down feeding by the water-side, as if they had been used to a keeper's call. Upon this river there were great store of fowl, and of many sorts: we saw in it divers

sorts of strange fishes, and of marvellous bigness; but for Raleigh
lagartos[1] it exceeded, for there were thousands of those ugly 1596
serpents, and the people call it, for the abundance of them,
the River of Lagartos in their language. I had a negro, a
very proper young fellow, who leaping out of the galley to
swim in the mouth of this river, was in all our sights taken
and devoured by one of those lagartos.

In the meanwhile our companies in the galley thought
we had been all lost (for we promised to return before
night), and sent the *Lion's Whelp's* ship-boat with Captain
Whiddon to follow us up the river; but the next day after
we had rowed up and down some fourscore miles, we
returned, and went on our way up the great river: and
when we were even at the last cast for want of victuals,
Captain Gifford being before the galley and the rest of
the boats, seeking out some place to land upon the banks
to make fire, espied four canoas coming down the river,
and with no small joy caused his men to try the uttermost
of their strength, and after a while two of the four gave
over, and ran themselves ashore, every man betaking
himself to the fastness of the woods; the two other
lesser got away, while he landed to lay hold of these, and
so turned into some by-creek we knew not whither: those
canoas that were taken were loaden with bread, and were
bound for Marguerita in the West Indies, which those
Indians (called Arwacas) proposed to carry thither for exchange.   But in the lesser there were three Spaniards,
who having heard of the defeat of their Governor in
Trinidado, and that we purposed to enter Guiana, came
away in those canoas: one of them was a Cavallero, as the
Captain of the Arwacas after told us, another a Soldier, and
the third a Refiner.

Sir Walter Raleigh.

[1] Alligators.

THE MEN IN BUCKRAM

POINS. Welcome, Jack : where hast thou been?

FALSTAFF. A plague of all cowards, I say, and a vengeance too! marry, and amen! Give me a cup of sack, boy. Ere I lead this life long, I 'll sew nether socks and mend them and foot them too. A plague of all cowards! Give me a cup of sack, rogue. Is there no virtue extant? [*He drinks.*

PRINCE. Didst thou never see Titan kiss a dish of butter? pitiful-hearted Titan, that melted at the sweet tale of the sun's! if thou didst, then behold that compound.

FAL. You rogue, here's lime in this sack too : there is nothing but roguery to be found in villainous man : yet a coward is worse than a cup of sack with lime in it. A villainous coward! Go thy ways, old Jack ; die when thou wilt, if manhood, good manhood, be not forgot upon the face of the earth, then am I a shotten herring. There live not three good men unhanged in England ; and one of them is fat, and grows old : God help the while! a bad world, I say. I would I were a weaver ; I could sing psalms or anything. A plague of all cowards, I say still.

PRINCE. How now, wool-sack! what mutter you?

FAL. A king's son! If I do not beat thee out of thy kingdom with a dagger of lath, and drive all thy subjects afore thee like a flock of wild geese, I 'll never wear hair on my face more. You Prince of Wales!

PRINCE. Why, you whoreson round man, what's the matter?

FAL. Are not you a coward? answer me to that : and Poins there?

POINS. 'Zounds, ye fat paunch, an ye call me coward, by the Lord, I 'll stab thee.

FAL. I call thee coward! I 'll see thee damned ere I call thee coward : but I would give a thousand pound I could

Shake-
speare
1598

run as fast as thou canst. You are straight enough in the
shoulders, you care not who sees your back : call you that
backing of your friends? A plague upon such backing! give
me them that will face me. Give me a cup of sack : I am a
rogue, if I drunk to-day.

Shake-
speare
1598

PRINCE. O villain! thy lips are scarce wiped since thou
drunkest last.

FAL. All's one for that. [*He drinks.*] A plague of all
cowards, still say I.

PRINCE. What's the matter?

FAL. What's the matter! there be four of us here have
ta'en a thousand pound this day morning.

PRINCE. Where is it, Jack? where is it?

FAL. Where is it! taken from us it is : a hundred upon
poor four of us.

PRINCE. What, a hundred, man?

FAL. I am a rogue, if I were not at half-sword with a dozen
of them two hours together. I have 'scaped by miracle. I
am eight times thrust through the doublet, four through the
hose; my buckler cut through and through; my sword
hacked like a hand-saw—*ecce signum!* I never dealt better
since I was a man : all would not do. A plague of all
cowards! Let them speak : if they speak more or less than
truth, they are villains and the sons of darkness.

PRINCE. Speak, sirs; how was it?

GADSHILL. We four set upon some dozen——

FAL. Sixteen at least, my lord.

GADS. And bound them.

PETO. No, no, they were not bound.

FAL. You rogue, they were bound, every man of them; or
I am a Jew else, an Ebrew Jew.

GADS. As we were sharing, some six or seven fresh men
set upon us——

FAL. And unbound the rest, and then come in the other.

PRINCE. What, fought you with them all?

Shake-
speare
1598

FAL. All! I know not what you call all : but if I fought not with fifty of them, I am a bunch of radish : if there were not two or three and fifty upon poor old Jack, then am I no two-legged creature.

PRINCE. Pray God you have not murdered some of them.

FAL. Nay, that's past praying for : I have peppered two of them ; two I am sure I have paid, two rogues in buckram suits. I tell thee what, Hal, if I tell thee a lie, spit in my face, call me horse. Thou knowest my old ward ; here I lay, and thus I bore my point. Four rogues in buckram let drive at me——

PRINCE. What, four ? thou saidst but two even now.

FAL. Four, Hal : I told thee four.

POINS. Ay, ay, he said four.

FAL. These four came all a-front, and mainly thrust at me. I made me no more ado but took all their seven points in my target, thus.

PRINCE. Seven ? why, there were but four even now.

FAL. In buckram ?

POINS. Ay, four, in buckram suits.

FAL. Seven, by these hilts, or I am a villain else.

PRINCE. Prithee, let him alone ; we shall have more anon.

FAL. Dost thou hear me, Hal ?

PRINCE. Ay, and mark thee too, Jack.

FAL. Do so, for it is worth the listening to. These nine in buckram that I told thee of——

PRINCE. So, two more already.

FAL. Their points being broken——

POINS. Down fell their hose.

FAL. Began to give me ground : but I followed me close, came in foot and hand ; and with a thought seven of the eleven I paid.

PRINCE. O monstrous ! eleven buckram men grown out of two !

FAL. But, as the devil would have it, three misbegotten

knaves in Kendal green came at my back and let drive at
me; for it was so dark, Hal, that thou couldst not see thy
hand.

Shake-
speare
1598

PRINCE. These lies are like thy father that begets them;
gross as a mountain, open, palpable. Why, thou clay-brained
guts, thou knotty-pated fool, thou whoreson, obscene, greasy
tallow-catch——

FAL. What, art thou mad? art thou mad? is not the truth
the truth?

PRINCE. Why, how couldst thou know these men in Kendal
green, when it was so dark thou couldst not see thy hand?
come, tell us your reason: what sayest thou to this?

POINS. Come, your reason, Jack, your reason.

FAL. What, upon compulsion? 'Zounds, an I were at the
strappado, or all the racks in the world, I would not tell you
on compulsion. Give you a reason on compulsion! if reasons
were as plentiful as blackberries. I would give no man a
reason upon compulsion, I.

PRINCE. I'll be no longer guilty of this sin; this sanguine
coward, this bed-presser, this horseback breaker, this huge
hill of flesh,——

FAL. 'Sblood, you starveling, you elf-skin, you dried neat's
tongue, you bull's pizzle, you stock-fish! O for breath to
utter what is like thee! you tailor's-yard, you sheath, you
bow-case, you vile standing-tuck,——

PRINCE. Well, breathe awhile, and then to it again: and
when thou hast tired thyself in base comparisons, hear me
speak but this.

POINS. Mark, Jack.

PRINCE. We two saw you four set on four and bound them,
and were masters of their wealth. Mark now, how a plain tale
shall put you down. Then did we two set on you four; and,
with a word, out-faced you from your prize, and have it;
yea, and can show it you here in the house: and, Falstaff,
you carried your guts away as nimbly, with as quick dexterity,

Shake-
speare
1598
and roared for mercy and still run and roared, as ever I heard
bull-calf. What a slave art thou, to hack thy sword as thou
hast done, and then say it was in fight! What trick, what
device, what starting-hole, canst thou now find out to hide
thee from this open and apparent shame?

Poins. Come, let's hear, Jack; what trick hast thou now?

Fal. By the Lord, I knew ye as well as he that made ye.
Why, hear you, my masters : was it for me to kill the heir
apparent? should I turn upon the true prince? why, thou
knowest I am as valiant as Hercules: but beware instinct;
the lion will not touch the true prince. Instinct is a great
matter; I was now a coward on instinct. I shall think the
better of myself and thee during my life; I for a valiant
lion, and thou for a true prince. But, by the Lord, lads, I
am glad you have the money. Hostess, clap to the doors:
watch to-night, pray to-morrow. Gallants, lads, boys, hearts
of gold, all the titles of good fellowship come to you! What,
shall we be merry? shall we have a play extempore?

Prince. Content; and the argument shall be thy running
away.

Fal. Ah, no more of that, Hal, an thou lovest me!

William Shakespeare.

A PLOT AGAINST THE THRONE

Hayward
1599
SO, partly upon love to King Richard, and partly upon fear
lest King Henry would be as ready to invade as he was to
inveigh against the riches of religious houses : this Abbot [of
Westminster] was the first man that blew the coals, and put
fuel to the fire of this confederacy. And first he observed afar
off, then he searched more nearly and narrowly (and yet warely
too) how the minds of certain Noblemen were affected, or,
rather, infected against King Henry; tempering his speeches
in such sort, that, if matters sorted to his mind, he might

take them upon him; if his courses were crossed, he might
clearly decline them. At last, he invited to his house, upon
a day in Michaelmas term, those whom he had found to be
most sound for his purpose : the chief of whom were such as
in the Parliament before had in some sort been touched in
reputation, although by pardon and reconcilement the harm
did seem to be closed up. Their names were John Holland,
Duke of Exeter, of whom mention hath been made before ;
Thomas Holland, his brother's son, Duke of Surrey; Edward,
Duke of Aumerle ; John Montacute, Earl of Salisbury ;
Hugh Spencer, Earl of Gloucester; John, Bishop of Carlisle ;
Sir Thomas Blunt, and Magdalen, one of King Richard's
chapel, who, in all points, both of feature and favour, so
nearly resembled King Richard, that the Lords dissembled
afterwards that he was King Richard indeed.

These and some others were highly feasted by the Abbot ;
and after dinner they withdrew themselves into a secret
chamber to counsel. Here the Duke of Exeter, who was
most hotly bent either to restore or to revenge the cause of
his deposed brother, declared unto the rest the allegiance
that they had sworn unto King Richard ; the honours and
preferments whereunto they were by him advanced ; that,
therefore, they were bound, both in conscience by the one,
and in kindness by the other, to take his part against all
men ; that King Henry, contrary to both, had dispoiled him
of his royal dignity, and unjustly possessed himself thereof,
whilst they stood looking on, and showed neither the
obedience of subjects nor love of friends, as though they
were men who knew to do anything better than to defend,
and, if need were, to die for their lawful Prince and loving
Patron ; that King Henry, by violent invading or fraudulent
insinuating himself into the kingdom of his natural and
liege Prince, was but a tyrant and usurper, and such a one
as it was lawful for any man by any means to throw down,
without respect whether he were a good man or evil, for it

Hayward is lawful for no man, upon pretence and show of goodness, to
1599 draw sovereignty unto himself; that the laws and examples
of best governed commonwealths did not only permit this
action, but highly honoured it with statues and garlands,
and titles of nobility, and also rewarded it with all the
wealth of the suppressed tyrant; that this enterprise would
be very profitable, and almost necessary to the commonwealth, by extinguishing those wars which the Scots
menaced, the Frenchmen prepared, and the Welshmen had
already begun upon this occasion and quarrel; that he did
not distrust but it might be accomplished by open arms, but
he thought it more sure for them, and for the commonwealth
more safe, to put first in proof some secret policy; and to
that purpose he devised, that a solemn joust should be
challenged, to be kept at Oxford in Christmas holidays,
between him and twenty on his part, and the Earl of Salisbury and twenty on his part, to which King Henry should
be invited, and when he was most intentive in regarding
their military disport, he should suddenly be surprised by
men which without suspicion might at that time be assembled,
both for number and preparation sufficient for the exploit,
and thereby King Richard presently be restored, both to his
liberty, and to his estate.

This device was no sooner uttered, then allowed and ap-
plauded of the rest of the confederates: and so resolving
upon the enterprise, they took an oath upon the Evangelists,
the one to be true and secret to the other, even to the hour
and point of death; the Lords also made an indenture sexti-
partite, wherein they bound themselves to do their best
assay, for the death of one King and deliverance of the other;
this they sealed and subscribed, and delivered to every Lord
a counterpane of the same: and, further, they concluded
what forces should be gathered, by whom, how they should
be ordered and placed, and to whose trust the execution
should be committed.

When all things were thus contrived, and their hungry, Hayward
ambitious minds were well-filled with the vain winds of hope   1599
and desire, the Duke of Exeter came to the king at Windsor,
and desired him, for the love that he bare to the noble feats
of Chivalry, that he would vouchsafe to honour with his
presence the martial exercise, that was appointed between
him and the Earl of Salisbury, and to be the Judge of their
performances if any controversy should arise.

The King supposing that to be intended in deed which
was pretended in show, easily yielded to his request. The
Duke, supposing his purpose now half performed, departed to
his house, and so did the other confederates, where they
busily bestirred themselves, in raising men, and preparing
horse and armour for the accomplishment of this act.

When the Duchess of Exeter, King Henry's sister, perceived the drift of the device, and saw that the Duke was
upon his journey: alas! good lady, how was she distracted
in mind, with a sharp conflict of her conceits! One way she
was moved with nature towards her brother; another way
she was more strongly stirred, with love towards her Lord
and husband; and both ways she was divided in duty. ' And
what ' (said she) ' is this love then against nature ? or above it ?
shall I be undutiful to my Prince ? or is no duty comparable
to the duty of a wife ? heigh ho: in what perplexities
(wretched woman) am I plunged, to see my two dearest
friends in this case of extremity, that (it is doubtful which) but
certainly one must be ruined by the other !' Herewith, such
a shower of tears streamed down her cheeks, that it drowned
her speech, and stopped the passage of further complaint:
which, when the Duke espied, he stepped unto her, and
seizing softly upon her hand, used these words: ' What,
Bess ? is it kindness to me or kindred to your brother that
thus hath set your eyes on float ? Content yourself, woman,
for whatsoever the event shall be, it cannot be evil to you,
nor worse to me than now it is. For if my purpose prevail,

Hayward
1599

and my brother be restored again to his crown, both of us shall be sure never to decline; if it be prevented, and your brother continue still in his estate, no harm shall be done unto you, and I shall be then sure of that destruction which I do now continually dread; the fear whereof in expecting, is a greater torment than the pain in suffering.' When he had thus said, he kissed her, and so leaving her to the torture of a thousand thorny thoughts, he took his journey towards Oxford, with a great company, both of Archers and Horsemen. There he found all the rest of his complices, well armed and banded, except only the Duke of Aumerle. The King also hearing that both the Challengers and Defendants were in a readiness, determined the day following to ride to Oxford, according to his promise and appointment.

Now, the confederates much marvelled at the stay of the Duke of Aumerle; some only blamed his slackness, others began to suspect it; every man conjectured as he was diversly affected between confidence and fear: and in this confusion of opinions, they sent unto him in post, to know the certain truth. Before the messenger came to the Duke, he was departed from Westminster towards Oxford, not the direct way, but went first to see his Father the Duke of York, and carried with him his counterpane of the indenture of confederacy. As they sat at dinner, the Father espied it in his bosom, and demanded what it was? The Son humbly craved pardon, and said that it nothing touched him. ' By St. George' (quoth the Father) ' but I will see it,' and so whether upon a precedent jealousy, or some present cause of suspicion, he took it away from him by force. When he perceived the contents, he suddenly arose from the table, and with great fierceness both of countenance and speech, uttered to his Son these words:

' I see, traitor, that idleness hath made thee so wanton and mutinous, that thou playest with thy faith as children do with sticks: thou hast been once already faithless to King

Richard, and now again art false to King Henry, so that, like Hayward the fish Sepia, thou troublest all the waters wherein thou livest. 1599 Thou knowest that in open Parliament I became surety and pledge for thy allegiance, both in body and goods: and can neither thy duty nor my desert restrain thee from seeking my destruction? In faith, but I will rather help forward thine.' With that he commanded his horses to be made ready, and presently took his journey towards Windsor, where the King then lay.

The Duke of Aumerle had no time either to consult with his friends, or to consider with himself what was best to be done : but taking advice upon the sudden, he mounted likewise on horseback, and posted towards Windsor another way. It was no need to force him forward ; his youthful blood, and his sudden danger, were instead of two wings, to keep his horse in Pegasus pace: so that he came to Windsor, and was alighted at the castle, before his stiff aged Father could come near. Then he entered the gates, and caused them to be surely locked, and took the keys into his own hands, pretending some secret cause for which he would deliver them unto the King. When he came in presence, he kneeled down and humbly craved of the King mercy and forgiveness. The King demanded, for what offence? Then with a confused voice, and sad countenance, casting down his eyes as altogether abashed, partly with fear of his danger, and partly with shame of his discredit, he declared unto the King all the manner of the conspiracy. The King seemed neither rashly to believe, nor negligently to distrust the Duke's report ; neither stood it with policy to entertain the discovery with any hard and violent usage : therefore with gracious speeches he comforted the Duke, and ' If this be true,' said he, 'we pardon you : if it be feigned, at your extreme peril be it.'

By this time the Duke of York was rapping at the Castle gates, and being admitted to the King's presence, he delivered to him the indenture of confederacy, which he had

Hayward taken from his son. When the King had read it, and was
1599 thereby persuaded of the truth of the matter, he was not a
little disquieted in mind, complaining of the inconstant disposition of those men, whom neither cruelty (he said) could
make firm to King Richard, nor clemency to him; but upon
dislike of every present government, they were desirous of
any change. So being possessed with deeper thoughts than
to gaze upon games, he laid his journey aside, and determined to attend at Windsor what course his enemies would
take, and which way they would set forward: knowing right
well that in civil tumults, an advised patience, and opportunity well taken, are the only weapons of advantage; and
that it is a special point of wisdom to make benefit of the
enemy's folly. In the meantime he directed his letters to
the Earl of Northumberland his High Constable, and to the
Earl of Cumberland his High Marshal, and to others his
most assured friends, concerning these sudden and unexpected accidents.

The confederates all this time hearing nothing of the
Duke of Aumerle, and seeing no preparation for the King's
coming, were out of doubt that their treason was betrayed.
And now, considering that once before they had been pardoned, the guilt of this their rebellion excluded them from
all hope of further mercy: whereupon they became desperate, and so resolved to prosecute that by open arms wherein
their privy practices had failed. And first they apparelled
Magdalen (a man very like to King Richard both in stature
and countenance, and of years not disagreeable) in princely
attire; and gave forth that he was King Richard, and that
either by favour or negligence of his keepers, he was escaped
out of prison, and desired the faith and aid of his loving
subjects. Then they determined to dispatch messengers to
Charles, King of France, to desire his help and assistance
on the behalf of his son-in-law, if need should require.

The common people, which commonly are soon changeable,

Hayward
1599

and on the sudden as prone to pity as they were before
excessively cruel, most earnestly wished the enlargement of
King Richard, and earnestly wishing, did easily believe it;
in which imaginary conceit, being otherwise men of no deep
search, the presence of Magdalen most strongly confirmed
them. And so, either upon ignorance of truth, or delight
in trouble, they joined themselves in great troops to the
Lords, desiring nothing more than to be the means whereby
King Richard should be restored, as in a manner resuming
their first affections and humours towards him. Then the
Lords of this association, with great force, but with greater
fame, as the manner is of matters unknown, advanced
forward in battle array towards Windsor, against King
Henry, as against an enemy of the common state; having in
their company above forty thousand armed men. The
King, upon intelligence of their approach, secretly, with a
few horse, the next Sunday night after New Year's day,
departed from Windsor to the Tower of London, and the
same night, before it was day, the confederates came to the
Castle of Windsor; where, missing their expected prey,
they stood doubtful and divided in opinions which way to
bend their course. Some advised them with all speed to
follow the King to London, and not to leave him any leave
and liberty to unite an army against them; that winter was
no let but in idle and peaceable times; that in civil dissen-
sions nothing is more safe than speed, and greater advantage
always groweth by dispatching than deferring; that whilst
some were in fear, some in doubt, and some ignorant, the
City, yea, the realm, might easily be possessed; and that
many armies, whose fury at the first rush could not be resisted,
by delays did wear out and waste to nothing. Others, who
would seem to be considerate and wise, but in very deed
were no better than dastards, persuaded rather to set
King Richard first at liberty; for if their counterfeiting
should be discovered before they possessed themselves of

his person, the people undoubtedly would fall from them, to
the certain confusion of them all.   Hereupon they gave over
the pursuit, and retired to Colebrook, and there delayed
out the time of doing in deliberating, being neither courageously quick, nor considerately staid, but faintly and fear-
fully shrinking back; and when they once began to relent,
they decreased every day more and more both in power and
in hope.

King Henry, the next morning after he was come to the
Tower, sent to the Mayor of the City to put soldiers in arms
for his assistance, who presently presented unto him three
thousand archers, and three thousand bill men, besides those
that were appointed for defence of the City.   The King
spent upon him many good speeches, and liberally loaded
him with promises and thanks; and soon after he issued out
of London with twenty thousand tall men, and came to
Hounslow Heath, abiding there, and, as it were, daring his
enemies to join issue in the field: contemning their disorderly
multitude as a vain terror of names without forces.   But
the confederates, either for fear of the King's power or for
distrust of their own, or else lingering, perhaps, after some
succour out of France, refused the encounter; and doubtful
it is whether they showed greater courage in setting up the
danger, or cowardice in declining it when it was presented
unto them.

Sir John Hayward.

THE PASSAGE OF THE ALPS

ANNIBALL, being departed from Druentia, marched
for the most through the champion countries, and
came in peace and quietly to the foot of the Alps, for any
trouble from the peasants that there inhabited.   And albeit
he had some knowledge of the Alps before by report (which
useth to make things that are uncertain much more than

in deed and truth they are), yet seeing now near at hand the
height of those hills, and the snows, entermingled along
with the sky; the rude and misshapen houses set upon
rocks; the cattle, sheep, oxen, and horses, singed with cold;
the people with long shagged hair, and without any trimming,
both living and lifeless creatures, even parched stiff and
stark with frost; and all things else more strange and ill-
favoured than can be spoken: then began his soldiers to
fear afresh. So soon as they advanced forward, and began
to march up the first cliffs, there appeared over their heads
the mountain people, who had seized the hills: who, if they
had kept the secret and hidden valleys, and suddenly all
at once charged upon them, they would have made a foul
slaughter of them, and put them to flight. Then Anniball
commandeth the ensigns to stand still, and sent certain Gauls
afore, as espials; by whom he understood that there was no
passage that way: whereupon he pitched his camp amongst
those craggy and steep rough places upon as large a plain
and valley as he could find. Then by the same Gauls (who
much differed not in tongue and manners from the other,
and had entermingled themselves in talk with mountaineers)
he understood that they kept the passage but in the daytime, and slipt away in the night, every one to his own
harbour.

So at the break of day he mounted those steep hills,
as if he would openly in the daytime march through
the straits. Thus having spent the day in making semblance and shew of one thing, and intending another, he
encamped himself strongly where he had rested and stayed:
and so soon as he perceived that the mountain people were
departed from the steep hills and kept not so strait watch
and ward; after that he had made shew of fires, more than
for the number of those that remained behind; and left
with the Cavalry all the bag and baggage, with the
greatest part of the footmen: himself in person took unto

him the nimblest, most active, and valiant soldiers lightly appointed, and with all speed passed through the straits aforesaid, and encamped on the very hills which the enemies
before held and beset.   Then in the morning betime his camp
dislodged : and the army behind began to march and set
forward.   By which time the mountaineers, at the ordinary
signal given, came forth out of their castles and forts, and
met at the usual place of their accustomed guards ; but then
all at once they might see some of the enemies over their
heads, to have gained their own fortress, and others also
marching in the way.   Both which objects at one time presented to their eye, made them blank and to stand still in
a muse a good while.   But afterwards, when they saw
Anniball his army distressed in the straits, and in great
trouble and disorder among themselves in the march, by
reason especially the horses were so affrighted, supposing
that the least fear and terror (besides) that they could procure would be enough for their enemies' overthrow and
confusion, they crossed the rocks overthwart, and (as they
were accustomed and used to them) ran to and fro, up and
down through the blind and unhaunted byways.

But then, verily, the Carthaginians were much encumbered,
as well by their enemies as also by the disadvantage of
the place, and more ado there was among them (whiles every
one strived avie who should first escape the danger) than
with the enemy.   There was nothing that disordered and
troubled the army in the march so much as their own
horses, which (by reason of the dissonant and divers cries,
that the echoes between the woods and valleys redoubled)
were affrighted ; and also if any of them chanced to be
stricken, galled, or wounded, they kept such wincing and
flinging about them, that they overthrew and made great
havoc of men, and of all sorts of carriage.   Besides, the
press was so great, and the straits of both sides so steep
and craggy, that many a man was thrown down headlong

a mighty height: yea, and some of them armed: and the
sumpter horses and beasts for carriage, especially, tumbled
down amain with their load, as if a house or castle had
come down with a mischief.   Which, although it were
terrible to behold, yet Anniball for a while stood still, and
kept his own men together, for fear of increasing this
disorder and affright.   But after that he saw his army disbanded and marching in disarray, and that it was to no
purpose to lead his army safe through the straits, if he lost
the carriages : for fear hereof he ran down from the higher
ground, and albeit, with the violence of his charge, he
discomforted the enemy, yet he increased the trouble and
fear of his own people.

But that was soon appeased in a very moment, after
the ways and passages were once cleared, by reason of the
mountaineers that were fled; so that within a while the
whole host passed through, not only at ease and leisure,
but also in a manner without any noise at all.   This done,
he seized upon a castle, which was the chief strength
of that country, with other villages lying about it; and
for three days' space he victualled and maintained his
whole army with the cattle of his prisoners.   And for that
he was now neither molested with the mountaineers,
who were at the first discomfited, nor greatly encumbered
with the difficulties of the ways, in those three days he rid
a good deal of ground, and journeyed a great way into the
country; until at the length he came to another coast well
peopled (for such mountain and hilly quarters) where he
had like to have been overtaken, not by open force, but
even in his own professed cunning : first, by a subtle practice, and after by a secret ambush.   Certain ancient men,
the rulers and governors of the castles, repaired unto
Anniball as Orators, saying, that they having been
taught and made wise by the profitable example of other
men's harms, made choice rather to try the amity

than prove the force of the Carthaginians; and therefore were willing to do his commandment, and be at his devotion: requesting him to take at their hand victuals and guides for their journey, yea, and hostages also for better assurance of promises to be performed. Anniball neither overhastily and rashly believing them, nor yet churlishly distrusting and refusing their offer, lest being rejected and cast off, they might become open and professed enemies, gave them good language, and a courteous answer, received the hostages whom they gave, accepted victuals which they had brought with them to maintain his army by the way, and followed their guides, but so, as his army was not disarrayed in their march, as if he had been amongst his friends, and in a peaceable country.

First went in the vauntguard the elephants and the horsemen; himself marched after with the flower and strength of his footmen, looking all about him with an heedful eye. So soon as he was entered a narrow passage, which of the one side lay under a steep hill that commanded them aloft, the barbarous people rose out of their ambush from all parts at once, both before and behind, and charged upon him both afar off and near at hand; yea and rolled down mighty huge stones upon them as they marched. But the greatest number came behind upon their backs: against whom he turned and made head with the power of his footmen, and without all peradventure (if the tail both of his army had not been strong and well fortified) they must need have received in that lane and straits an exceeding great overthrow. And even then, as it was, they came to an extremity of danger, and in manner fell into a present mischief. For whiles Anniball made long stay, and doubted whether he should engage the regiment of footmen within the straits, for that he had not left any succours in the rear-guard to back the footmen, like as himself was a defence to the horsemen; the mountaineers came overthwart and flanked them; and breaking through

the files of the battle, beset the way, and crossed upon him.
So that Anniball took up his lodging for one night, without
his carriages and horsemen. The morrow after, whenas
the barbarous people ran between them more coldly than
before, he joined his forces together, and passed the strait,
not without great damage and loss; but with more hurt of
the sumpter horses than of men. After this, the mountaineers
(fewer in number, and in robbing wise rather than in warlike
sort) ran in heaps, one while upon the vaward, other while upon
the rearward, as any one of them could either get the vantage
of ground, or by going one while afore, and by staying another
while behind, win and catch any occasion and opportunity.

The elephants, as they were driven with great leisure,
because through these narrow straits they were ready
ever and anon to run on their noses : so what way soever
they went, they kept the army safe and sure from the
enemies; who being not used unto them, durst not once
come near. The ninth day he won the very tops of Alps,
through by-lanes and blind cranks : after he had wandered
many times out of the way, either through the deceitful-
ness of their guides, or for that, when they durst not trust
them, they adventured rashly themselves upon the valleys,
and guessed the way at adventure, and went by aim. Two
days abode he encamped upon the tops thereof, and the
soldiers wearied with travel and fight rested that time ;
certain also of the sumpter horses (which had slipt aside
from the rocks) by following the tracks of the army as it
marched, came to the camp. When they were thus overtoiled and wearied with these tedious travails, the snow that
fell (for now the star Vergilie was set and gone down out of
the horizon) increased their fear exceedingly. Now whenas at the break of day the ensigns were set forward, and
the army marched slowly through the thick and deep snow ;
and that their appeared in the countenance of them all
slothfulness and desperation : Anniball advanced before the

standards and commanded his soldiers to stay upon a certain high hill (from whence they had a goodly prospect and might see a great way all about them), and there shewed unto them Italy, and the goodly champain fields about the Po, which lie hard under the foot of the Alpine mountains: saying, that even then they mounted the walls, not only of Italy, but also of the City of Rome; as for all besides (saith he) will be plain and easy to be travelled: and after one or two battles at the most, ye shall have at your command the very Castle and head City of all Italy.

Then began the army to march forward; and as yet the enemies verily themselves adventured nothing at all but some petty robberies by stealth, as opportunity and occasion served. Howbeit they had much more difficult travelling down the hill than in the climbing and getting up; for that most of the avenues to the Alps from Italy side, as they be shorter, so they are more upright: for all the way in a manner was steep, narrow, and slippery, so as neither they could hold themselves from sliding, nor if any tripped and stumbled never so little, could they possibly (they staggered so) recover themselves and keep sure footing, but one fell upon another, as well horse as man. After this they came to a much narrower rock, with crags and rags so steep downright, that hardly a nimble soldier without his armour and baggage (do what he could to take hold with hands upon the twigs and plants that thereabout grew forth) was able to creep down. This place being before naturally of itself steep and pendant with a downfall, now was choked and dammed up with a new fall of earth, which left a bank behind it of a wonderful and monstrous height. There the horsemen stood still as if they had been come to their way's end; and when Anniball marvelled much what the matter might be that stayed them so as they marched not on, word was brought him that the rock was unaccessible and unpassable.

Whereupon he went himself in person to view the place, and then he saw indeed without all doubt that although he had fetched a compass about, yet he had gained nought thereby, but conducted his army to pass through wilds, and such places as before had never been beaten and trodden. And verily, that (of all other) was such, as it was impossible to pass through. For whereas there lay old snow untouched and not trodden on, and over it other snow newly fallen, of a small depth; in this soft and tender snow, and the same not very deep, their feet as they went easily took hold; but that snow, being once with the gait of so many people and beasts upon it fretted and thawed, they were fain to go upon the bare ice underneath, and in the slabbery snow-broth, as it relented and melted about their heels. There they had foul ado and much struggling, for that they could not tread sure upon the slippery ice; and again, going as they did (down hill), their feet sooner failed them; and when they had helped themselves once in getting up, either with hands or knees, if they chanced to fall again, when those their props and stays deceived them, there were no twigs nor roots about whereon a man might take hold and rest or stay himself, either by hand or foot. And, therefore, all that the poor garrons [1] and beasts could do was to tumble and wallow only upon the slippery and glassy ice, and the molten, slabbie snow. Otherwhiles, also, they perished as they went in the deep snow, whilst it was yet soft and tender; for when they were once slidden and fallen, with flinging out their heels, and beating with their hoofs more forcibly for to take hold, they brake the ice through, so as most of them, as if they had been caught fast and fettered, stuck still in the deep, hard-frozen, and congealed ice.

At last, whenas both man and beast were wearied and overtoiled, and all to no purpose, they encamped upon the top of a hill, having with very much ado cleansed the place

[1] Geldings.

Holland
1600

aforehand for that purpose : such a deal of snow there was to be digged, fayed,[1] and thrown out. This done, the soldiers were brought to break that rock, through which was their only way ; and against the time that it was to be hewed through, they felled and overthrew many huge trees that grew thereabout, and made a mighty heap and pile of wood : the wind served fitly for the time to kindle a fire, and then they set all a-burning. Now, when the rock was on fire and red-hot, they poured thereon strong vinegar for to calcine for to dissolve it. Whenas the rock was thus baked (as it were) with fire, they digged into it, and opened it with pickaxes, and made the descent gentle and easy by means of moderate windings and turnings : so as not only the horses and other beasts, but even the elephants, also, might be able to go down. Four days he spent about the levelling of this rock : and the beasts were almost pined and lost for hunger. For the hill tops for the most are bare of grass, and look what fog[2] and forage there was, the snow over-hilled it. The dales and lower grounds have some little banks lying to the sun, and rivers withal near unto the woods, yea, and places more meet and beseeming for men to inhabit. There were labouring beasts put out to grass and pasture, and the soldiers that were wearied with making the ways had three days allowed to rest in.

Philemon Holland.

THE MOST CHRISTIAN KING

Danett
1601

A MONG men famous for devotion, he sent into Cambria for one Friar Robert, whom he called the Holy Man, because of his holy life, and in whose honour the King that now is caused a church to be built at Plessis du Parc, in place

---

[1] Cleaned out.   [2] Green fodder.

of the chapel near to Plessis, at the bridge foot. This hermit Danett 1601
being twelve years of age entered into a rock, where he
remained till he was forty-three years old, or thereabout, to
wit, even till this present that the King sent for him by one
of the stewards of his house, whom the Prince of Tarente,
the King of Naples' son, accompanied thither. For the said
hermit would not depart thence, without permission both of
the Pope and of his Prince; which was great wisdom in so
simple a man. He builded in the place where he lived two
churches, and never ate, since the time he entered into this
strait kind of life, either fish, flesh, eggs, any kind of white-
meat, or of fat. I never saw in my time a man of so holy
life, nor by whose mouth the Holy Ghost seemed rather to
speak; for he never had been scholar, but was utterly un-
learned; true it is, that his Italian tongue caused somewhat
the greater admiration of him. This hermit passed through
Naples, being honoured and received, as if he had been a
great Legate sent from the See Apostolic, both by the King
and by his children; with whom he communed of the affairs
of the court, as if he had been a courtier all the days of his
life. From thence he went to Rome, where he was visited
by all the Cardinals, and had audience given him thrice of
the Pope, communing with him alone; and sitting each time
hard by him in a goodly chair three or four hours together,
which was great honour to so simple a person. His answers
were so wise that all men wondered at them; so far forth
that our Holy Father gave him leave to erect a new order,
called the Hermits of St. Francis. From thence he came
to the King, who honoured him as if he had been the Pope
himself, falling down before him, and desiring him to prolong his life; whereunto he answered as a wise man should.
I have often heard him talk with the King that now is, in
presence of all the nobility of the realm, and that within
these two months, and sure he seemed by his words to be
inspired with the Holy Ghost; otherwise he could never have

Danett
1601

communed of such matters as he did. He is yet living and may change either to better or worse; wherefore I will speak no further of him. Some mocked at his hermit's coming, whom they called the Holy Man; but they knew not the deep cogitations of this wise King, neither had seen the occasions that moved him to send for him.

The King lay in his Castle of Plessis, accompanied with few besides the archers of his Guard, and troubled with suspicions. Notwithstanding, he had given good order for this inconvenience, for he left none of those whom he suspected either in the town or country, but made his archers to cause them to depart, and to convey them away. No man debated any matter with him, unless it were of some great importance that concerned himself: he seemed rather a dead corpse than a living creature, for he was leaner than a man would believe: he apparelled himself sumptuously, yea, more sumptuously than in all his life before; for he wore no gown but of crimson satin, furred with good martens; he gave gifts to whom it pleased him without any suit; for no man durst move any suit to him, nor debate any matter with him. He punished faults sharply, to the end he might be feared, and not lose his authority, as himself told me. He changed officers, cassed[1] companies of men of arms, diminished pensions, or took them clean away; and told me but a few days before his death that he passed away the time in making and marring of men. To be short, he caused himself to be more spoken of within his realm than ever was any King, and all for fear lest men should think him dead. For, as I said, few saw him; but when they heard of his doings, all men stood in fear of him, so far forth, that they hardly believed him to be sick. Out of the realm he had men in all places, as, for example in England he had some to feed King Edward still with hope of his daughter's marriage, and he paid truly both him and his servants all that was due unto them. Out of Spain he received

[1] Broke, i.e. disbanded.

goodly words and fair promises of perfect friendship and amity, and great presents from all places. He made a good horse or a good mule to be bought for him whatsoever it cost ; but this he did not in this realm, but in some strange country, to persuade men that he was in health. Dogs he sent for round about, into Spain for a kind of Spanish grey-hound, called in French *Allans* ; into Britain for little beagles, grey-hounds, and spaniels, which he paid dear for; into Valence for little rugged dogs which he made to be bought above the owner's own price. Into Sicily he sent for good mules, especially to some officer of the country, for the which he paid double the value ; to Naples for horses, and for divers strange beasts into divers countries, as into Barbary for a kind of little lions, no greater than little foxes, which he called Adites ; into Denmark and Sweden for two kinds of strange beasts, one of the which were called Helles, being of shape like a hart, and of the greatness of a buff, with horns short and thick ; the other Rengiers, being of the big-ness and colour of a buck, save that their horns be much greater: for each of the which two beasts he gave to the merchants that sold them 4500 guildons. But when all these strange things were brought him he made no account of them, no, very seldom spake with those that brought them. To be short, he did so many such like strange things, that he was more feared now both of his neighbours and subjects than ever before, which was his only desire, for to that end did he all this. . . .

. He discoursed continually of some matter or other, and that very gravely, and his disease endured from Monday till Saturday night. Wherefore I will now make comparison between the troubles and sorrows he caused others to suffer, and those he suffered himself before his death, because I trust they have carried him into Paradise, and been part of his Purgatory. For notwithstanding that they were not so grievous, neither endured so long, as those which he caused

Danett
1601

divers others to suffer, yet because his vocation in this world
was higher than theirs, by means whereof he had never been
contraried, but so well obeyed, that he seemed a Prince able
to have governed all Europe: this little trouble that he
endured contrary to his accustomed nature was to him a
great torment. He hoped ever in this good hermit that
was at Plessis, whom he caused to come to him out of Cala-
bria, and continually sent to him: saying, that if it pleased
him he could prolong his life. For notwithstanding all these
commandments given to those whom he sent to the Dauphin,
his son, yet came his spirits again to him, in such sort that
he was in hope to recover; and if it had so happened, he
would easily have disparkled the assembly sent to this new
King. But because of the vain hope he had in this hermit,
a Doctor of Divinity and certain others thought good to advertise him that his only hope must be in the mercy of God;
and they devised that Master James Cothier, his Physician, in
whom he had reposed his whole confidence, and to whom he
gave monthly ten thousand crowns in hope he would prolong
his life, should be present when this speech should be used to
him. This was Master Oliver, his barber's device, to the end
he might wholly think upon his conscience, and leave all his
other imaginations conceived of this holy man, and of the said
Master James, his Physician. But even like as he advanced
the said Master Oliver and others too suddenly, without any
desert, to a higher estate than was fit for them; even so
they took upon them boldly to do such a message to so great
a Prince otherwise than became them, not using that reverence and humility that was to be used in such a case, and
such as they should have used, whom he had brought up of
a long time, and lately commanded out of his presence for
the suspicions conceived of them.

And again, like as unto two great personages whom he
had put to death in his time (to wit, the Duke of Nemours
and the Earl of Saint Paul: for one of the which he

repented him at his death, and for the other not), he had
sent a sharp message of death by commissioners appointed
thereunto; who briefly pronounced their sentence unto
them, and forthwith gave them confessors, and but a
very short space to dispose of their consciences: even so
the abovenamed signified his death unto him rudely and
in few words, saying: 'Sir, it is reason we do our duties,
hope no more in this holy man, nor any other thing, for
sure you are but dead; therefore think upon your conscience, for your hour is come'; and every one of them
said somewhat briefly to him to that effect. But he answered: 'I trust God will help me; and, peradventure, I am
not so sick as you suppose.' What a sharp corrosive was it
to him to hear these news and this cruel sentence! For never
man feared death more than he, nor sought so many ways
to avoid it as he did. Moreover, in all his lifetime he had
given commandment to all his servants, as well myself as
others, that when we should see him in danger of death, we
should only move him to confess himself and dispose of his
conscience, not sounding in his ear this dreadful word *Death*,
knowing that he should not be able patiently to hear that
cruel sentence; notwithstanding, he endured both that and
divers other punishments till the very hour of death more
patiently than ever I saw any man. To this son, whom he
called King, he sent many messages, and confessed himself
very devoutly, and said divers prayers answerable to the
Sacraments he received, which also himself demanded. He
spake as heartily as if he had not been sick, and talked of
all matters touching the King his son's estate; and among
other things gave commandment that the Lord of Cordes
should not depart from his son by the space of half a year
after his death; and further, that he should be entreated
to attempt nothing against Calais, nor elsewhere; saying,
that notwithstanding he had devised these enterprises for
the King's profit and the benefit of the realm: yet were they

Danett
1601

Dauett very dangerous, especially that of Calais, for fear of moving
1601   the Englishmen thereby to war.   Further, he willed especially that after his death the realm should rest in peace the
space of five or six years, a matter which he would never
yield unto during his life, though very needful; for notwithstanding it were great and large, yet was it in poor and
miserable estate, especially because of the passing to and fro
of the men of arms, who continually removed from one country
to another.   He gave order, also, that no quarrel should be
picked in Britaine, but that Duke Francis should be suffered
to live in quiet, and not be put in any doubt or fear of war,
neither yet any other neighbour bordering upon the realm, to
the end the King and the realm might rest in peace till the
King were of years to dispose thereof at his own pleasure.

Thus you see how indiscreetly his death was signified to
him, which I have rehearsed because I began to make a
comparison between those evils which he had caused divers
of his subjects to suffer and those himself suffered before his
death, to the end you may perceive that, notwithstanding
they were not so grievous nor so long (as I have said), yet
were they grievous to him considering his nature, which
demanded obedience, and had been better obeyed than any
Prince in his time; so that one half word contrarying his
mind was to him a grievous punishment.   Five or six days
before his death he had all men in suspicion, especially all
that were worthy of credit and authority, yea, he grew
jealous of his own son, and caused him to be straitly guarded,
neither did any man see him or speak with him but by his
commandment; at the length he began to stand in doubt
also of his daughter, and of his son-in-law, now Duke of
Bourbon, and would needs know what men entered into
Plessis with them, and in the end brake off an assembly that
the Duke of Bourbon, his son-in-law, held there by his commandment.   Moreover, at the same time that his said son-
in-law and the Earl of Dunois (returning from the convoy

of the embassage that came to Amboise to the marriage of
the King, his son, and the Queen) entered into the Castle of
Plessis with a great band of men : the King, who caused the
gates to be straitly kept, being in the gallery that looked
into the court of the said Castle, caused one of the Captains
of his Guard to come to him, whom they commanded to feel,
as he talked with the said Noblemen's servants, whether they
ware any brigandines under their cloaks, not making show
as though he came purposely for that intent. Hereby you
may perceive if he caused divers others to live in fear and
suspicion under him, whether he were paid now with the
like himself; for of whom could he be assured, mistrusting
his son, his daughter, and his son-in-law ? Wherefore thus
much I will say not only of him, but of all other Princes that
desire to be feared, that they never feel the revenge thereof
till their age, and then their penance is to fear all men.

What great grief think you was it to this poor King
to be troubled with these passions ? He had a Physician
called Master James Cothier, to whom he gave in five months
54,000 crowns, after the rate of 10,000 the month, and 4000
over, besides the Bishopric of Amiens for his nephew, and
other offices and lands for him and his friends. The said
Physician used him so roughly, that a man would not give
his servant so sharp language as he gave the King; and yet
the King so much feared him, that he durst not command
him out of his presence; for notwithstanding that he complained to divers of him, yet durst he not change him as he
did all his other servants, because this Physician once said
thus boldly to him : ' I know that one day you will command
me away as you do all your other servants, but you shall
not live eight days after,' binding it with a great oath.
Which words put the King in such fear, that ever after he
flattered him, and bestowed gifts upon him, which was a
marvellous Purgatory to him in this world, considering of
how many Noblemen and gentlemen he had been obeyed.

Danett
1601

Moreover, he had caused divers cruel prisons to be made; as, for example, cages, being eight feet square, and one foot more than a man's height, some of iron, and some of wood plated with iron both within and without, with horrible iron works. He that first devised them was the Bishop of Verdun, who incontinent was himself put into the first that was made, where he remained fourteen years. Many have cursed him for his device, and among others myself, for I lay in one of them, under the King that now reigneth, the space of eight months. He had also caused certain Almains to make terrible heavy irons to lay men in, among the which there was a fetter to put on their feet very hard to be opened, like to a carcan, with a weighty chain, and a great iron ball at the end thereof, heavy beyond all measure. These irons were called the King's Nets. Notwithstanding, I have seen divers gentlemen lie in them as prisoners, who came forth afterward with great honour, and were advanced by him to high estates: as, for example, a son of the Lord of Grutuze, in Flanders, taken prisoner in the wars, whom the King afterward richly married, and made one of his Chamber and Seneschal of Anjou, and gave him charge of a hundred lances; and, in like manner, the Lord of Piennes and the Lord of Vergy, taken prisoners also in the wars, who both had charge of men of arms under the King and other goodly offices, and were of the Privy Chamber either to him or his son. The like happened also to the Lord of Richbourg, the Constable's brother, and to one Roquebertin of the country of Cathelony, being likewise taken prisoners in the wars, whom he afterward highly advanced, with divers others of divers countries too long to rehearse.

But now to return to the matter. As in his time these divers and sundry cruel prisons were devised, even so he before his death lay in the like, yea, in much crueller prison than any of them, and was in greater fear than they that stood in fear of him, which I account as a great grace towards him, and as part of his Purgatory, and rehearse it only to show that every man, of what estate or condition soever he be, is punished either secretly or openly, especially those that punish others. Further, the King a little before his death enclosed his Castle of Plessis with a grate of iron bars, and at the four corners of the said Castle caused four strong watch-houses of iron to be built. The said grate was made directly over against the Castle wall round about the Castle, on the outer side of the ditch, which was very steep. He caused also to be masoned into the wall a great number of iron spears, each of them having divers heads set close together. Moreover, he appointed ten cross-bow-men to be continually in the said ditches, and to lie in the four iron houses built in the bottom of the said ditches, and gave them commandment to shoot at every man that approached near to the gate, before the gate opened. He knew well that this fortification was to no purpose against a great force or an army, but that he doubted not : his only fear was that certain Noblemen of his realm, having intelligence in the Castle, would attempt to enter it in the night, partly by love and partly by force, and take the government upon them, and make him live as a man bereft of his wits, and unworthy to rule. The Castle gate never opened before eight of the clock in the morning, neither was the drawbridge let down till that hour, and then entered his officers ; and the Captains of his Guard placed the ordinary warders, and appointed archers to the watch, both at the gate and within the court, as if it had been a frontier town straitly kept. Neither entered any man without the King's commandment but by the wicket, save the stewards of his house, and such like officers that went not to him. Is it possible, then, to hold a King (I mean using him like a Prince) in a straiter prison than he held himself? The cages wherein he held others were about eight feet square, and he, being so great a Prince, had but a little court in the Castle to walk

in, yea, and seldom came he into that; for usually he kept
himself in the gallery, from whence he never stirred but
when he went to mass, at which time he passed through the
chambers, and not through the court.

Think you that he was not in fear as well as others,
seeing he locked himself in after this sort, kept himself
thus close, stood in such fear of his children and nearest
kinsmen, and changed and removed his servants from day
to day, whom he had brought up and whose good estate
depended wholly upon him, in such sort that he durst
trust none of them, but bound himself in these strange
chains and bands? The place, I confess, was larger than
a common prison, so was his estate greater than a common prisoner's. But a man will say, peradventure, that
other Princes have been more suspicious than he, whereunto I agree; but none, sure, in our time, neither any so
wise as he, nor that had so good subjects as he had; and as
touching them, peradventure they were cruel tyrants, but
he never punished any without desert. All this above
written I have rehearsed, not so much to publish the suspicions of the King our Master, as partly to prove that the
patient enduring of these passions, being equal with those
he had caused others to endure, and of this sickness being
sharp and troublesome to him, and the which he feared
greatly before he fell into it, is to be accounted as a punishment God gave him in this world, to ease him in the world
to come; and partly to give an example to those that shall
come after him, to have some more compassion on their
people than he had, and to be less rigorous in punishing
than he was. Notwithstanding, for my part I am not able
to accuse him, neither saw I ever a better Prince; for though
himself pressed his subjects, yet would he suffer none other
so to do, friend or foe.

After all these fears, sorrows, and suspicions, God (according to His accustomed goodness) wrought a miracle upon

him, healing him both in soul and body : for He took him   Danett
out of this miserable world, being perfect of sense, under-   1601
standing, and memory, having received all his Sacraments
without all grief to man's judgment, and talking continually
even within a *Pater noster* while of his death; so that he
gave order for his funeral, and named those that should
accompany his body to the grave; saying ever, that he
trusted to die on no day but Saturday, and that our Lady,
in whom he had ever put his confidence, and always devoutly
served, had purchased him this grace ; and sure so it happened,
for he ended his life upon Saturday, the 30th of August, in
the year 1483, at eight of the clock at night, in the said
Castle of Plessis, where he fell sick the Monday before.   His
soul, I trust, is with God, and resteth in His blessed Realm
of Paradise.

Thomas Danett.

JULIUS CAESAR

HIS pleasures could never make him lose one minute   Florio
of an hour, nor turn one step from the occasions,   1603
that might any way further his advancement.   This passion
did so soveraignly oversway all others, and possessed his
mind with so uncontrolled an authority, that she carried him
whither she list.   Truly I am grieved, when in other things
I consider this man's greatness, and the wondrous parts
that were in him ; so great sufficiency in all manner of
knowledge and learning, as there is almost no science
wherein he hath not written.   He was so good an orator,
that divers have preferred his eloquence before Cicero's ;
and himself (in mine opinion) in that faculty thought
himself nothing short of him.   And his two *Anti-Catos* were
especially written to overbalance the eloquence which
Cicero had employed in his *Cato*.   And for all other matters ;

Florio
1603

was ever mind so vigilant, so active, and so patient of labour as his? And doubtless, it was also embellished with sundry rare seeds of virtue. I mean lively, natural, and not counterfeits. He was exceeding sober, and so homely in his feeding, that Oppius reporteth : how upon a time, through a certain Cook's negligence, his meat being dressed with a kind of medicinable Oil instead of Olive-oil, and so brought to the board, although he found it, yet he fed heartily of it, only because he would not shame his Host: another time he caused his Baker to be whipped, because he had served him with other than common household bread. Cato himself was wont to say of him, that he was the first sober man had addressed himself to the ruin of his country. And whereas the same Cato called him one day drunkard, it happened in this manner. Being both together in the Senate House, where Catiline's conspiracy was much spoken of, wherein Caesar was greatly suspected to have a hand ; a note was by a friend of his brought, and in very secret sort delivered him, which Cato perceiving, supposing it might be something that the Conspirators advertised him of, instantly summoned him to show it, which Caesar, to avoid a greater suspicion, refused not: it was by chance an amorous letter, which Servilia, Cato's sister, writ to him: Cato having read it, threw it at him, saying : ' Hold it again, thou drunkard.' I say it was rather a word of disdain and anger, than an express reproach of this vice, as often we nickname those that anger us with the first nicknames of reproaches that come into our mouth, though merely impertinent to those with whom we fall out. Considering that the vice wherewith Cato charged him hath near coherency unto that wherein he had surprised Caesar : for Venus and Bacchus (as the vulgar Proverb saith) agree well together, but with me Venus is much more blithe and gamesome, being accompanied with sobriety.

The examples of his mildness and clemency, toward such

Florio
1603

as had offended him, are infinite: I mean, besides those
he showed during the Civil Wars, which (as by his own
writings may plainly appear) he used to blandish and allure
his enemies, to make them fear his future domination and
victories the less. But if any shall say, those examples are
not of validity to witness his genuine and natural affability,
we may lawfully answer, that at least they show us a
wonderful confidence and greatness of courage to have been
in him. It hath often befallen him, to send whole armies
back again to his enemies, after he had vanquished them,
without deigning to bind them so much as with an oath, if
not to favour, at least not to bear arms against him. He
hath three or four times taken some of Pompey's chief
Captains prisoners, and as often set them at liberty again.
Pompey declared all such as would not follow and accompany
him in his wars, to be his enemies; and he caused those to
be proclaimed as friends, who either would not stir at all, or
not effectually arm themselves against him. To such of his
Captains as fled from him to procure other conditions, he
sent them their weapons, their horses, and all other furniture.
The Cities he had taken, by main force, he freed to follow
what faction they would, giving them no other garrison than
the memory of his clemency and mildness. In the day of
his great battle of Pharsalia, he expressly inhibited, that
unless they were driven to unavoidable extremity, no man
should lay hands upon any Roman citizen. In my judgment
these are very hazardous parts, and it is no wonder, if in
the Civil War's tumultuous broils we have now on foot those
that fight for the ancient laws and state of their country, as
he did, do not follow and imitate the example. They are
extraordinary means, and which only belongs to Caesar's
fortune, and to his admirable foresight, successfully to direct,
and happily to conduct them. When I consider the incomparable greatness and invaluable worth of his mind, I
excuse Victory, in that she could not well give him over, in

Florio
1603 this most unjust and unnatural cause. But to return to his clemency; we have divers genuine and lively examples, even in the time of his all-swaying government, when all things were reduced into his hands, and he needed no longer to dissemble. Caius Memmius had written certain detracting and railing Orations against him, which he at full and most sharply had answered; nevertheless, he shortly after helped to make him consul. Caius Calvus, who had composed divers most injurious Epigrams against him, having employed sundry of his friends to be reconciled to him again, Caesar descended to write first unto him. And our good Catullus, who under the name of Mumurra had so rudely and bitterly railed against him, at last coming to excuse himself, Caesar that very night made him to sup at his own table. Having been advertised how some were over lavish in railing against him, all he did was but in a publike oration to declare how he was advertised of it. His enemies he feared less than he hated them. Certain conspiracies and conventicles were made against his life, which being discovered unto him, he was contented by an edict to publish, how he was throughly informed of them, and never prosecuted the Authors. Touching the respect he ever bare unto his friends : Caius Oppius travelling with him, and falling very sick, having but one chamber, he resigned the same unto him, and himself was contented to lie all night abroad and upon the bare ground. Concerning his justice, he caused a servant of his, whom he exceedingly loved, to be executed, forsomuch as he had lain with the wife of a Roman Knight, although no man sued or complained of him. Never was man that showed more moderation in his victory, or more resolution in his adverse fortune. But all these noble inclinations, rich gifts, worthy qualities, were altered, smothered, and eclipsed by this furious passion of Ambition, by which he suffered himself to be so far misled, that it may be well affirmed she only ruled the Stern of all

his actions. Of a liberal man, she made him a common Florio 1603
thief, that so he might the better supply his profusion and
prodigality; and made him utter that vile and most injurious
speech: that if the wickedest and most pernicious men of
the world had for his service and furtherance been faithful
unto him, he would to the utmost of his power have
cherished and preferred them, as well as if they had been
the honestest. It so besotted, and as it were made him
drunk with so extreme vanity, that in the presence of all his
fellow-citizens he durst vaunt himself, to have made that
great and far-spread Roman Commonwealth a shapeless and
bodiless name; and pronounce that his Sentences or Answers
should thenceforward serve as Laws: and sitting to receive
the whole body of the Senate coming toward him, and suffer
himself to be adored: and in his presence divine honours
to be done him. To conclude, this only vice (in mine
opinion) lost and overthrew in him the fairest natural and
richest ingenuity that ever was, and hath made his memory
abhominable to all honest minds, insomuch as by the ruin
of his country, and subversion of the mightiest state and
most flourishing Commonwealth that ever the world shall
see, he went about to procure his glory.

John Florio.

TAMERLANE

NOW the Prince of Ciarcan had divided his forces into Knolles 1603
two parts, and given commandment to the first, that
as soon as they perceived the enemies to pursue the hundred
horse that so disorderly of purpose fled, they should receive
them, and so retire all together. He in the meantime with
the rest of his power stood close in a valley, near to a wood
side, unseen at all. Where having suffered two thousand of
the Enemies' Horse (the vantcurriers of the Turks' army) to

pass by him, he following them in the tail, charged them
home, the other which before retired now turning upon them
also; so that the Turks seeing themselves thus beset, and
hardly laid unto both before and behind, as men discouraged
fled; in which flight most of them were slain, and the rest
taken Prisoners. This was the first encounter betwixt the
Turks and the Parthians; all the Prisoners there taken were
by the Prince as a present sent to Tamerlane, and among the
rest the Bassa of Natolia who led these troops; of whom
Tamerlane earnestly demanded what caused Bajazet so little
to esteem of him, as to show so great contempt of his army,
which he should find strong enough to abate his pride.
Whereunto the Bassa answered, that his Lord was the Sun
upon Earth, which could not endure any equal; and that he
rather was astonished to see, how he from so far had enterprised so dangerous a journey, to hinder the fortune of his
lord, in whose favour the Heavens (as he said) did bend
themselves to further his greatness, and unto whom all the
world subjected itself; and that he committed great folly in
going about to resist the same. Unto which so proud a
speech Tamerlane replied, that he was sent from Heaven to
punish his rashness, and to teach him, that the proud are
hated of God, whose promise is to pluck down the mighty
and raise up the lowly. ' As for thyself' (said he) ' thou hast
already felt (although I pity thy mishap) what the valour of
my Parthian Horse is against thy Turkish; and thy Master I
have already caused to raise his siege of Constantinople and
to look to his own things here in Asia.' Furthermore,
Tamerlane changing his speech demanded, if his Master did
come resolved to bid him battle? ' Assure yourself' (said he)
' there is nothing he more desireth; and would to God I
might acknowledge your greatness in giving me leave to
assist my Lord at that battle.' ' Good leave have thou ' (said
Tamerlane); ' go thy ways and tell thy Lord that thou hast
seen me, and that he shall in the battle find me on horse-

back, where he shall see a green ensign displayed.' The Bassa, thanking him, swore that next unto his Lord he vowed unto him his service. And so returning, declared unto Bajazet how that he had seen Tamerlane, and truly reported unto him all that he had willed him to say; not forgetting over all, to publish his courtesy and bounty; who besides that he had frankly set him at liberty, had also given him a very fair horse well furnished, although he well knew he was to serve against himself. Whereunto Bajazet answered no more, but that he would shortly make trial of him, and that he well hoped before the march were ended, to make him acknowledge his own folly.

The next day the two Armies drew near together, and encamped within a league the one of the other; where all the night long you might have heard such noise of horses, as that it seemed the Heavens were full of voices, the air did so resound, and every man thought the night long, to come to the trial of his valour, and the gaining of his desires. The Scythians (a people no less greedy than needy) talked of nothing but the spoil; the proud Parthians, of their honour; and the poor Christians, of their deliverance, all to be gained by the next day's victory; every man during the night time speaking according to his own humour. All which Tamerlane walking this night up and down in his camp heard, and much rejoiced to see the hope that his soldiers had already in general conceived of the victory. Who after the second watch returning unto his pavilion, and there casting himself upon a carpet, had thought to have slept a while; but his cares not suffering him so to do, he then, as his manner was, called for a book, wherein was contained the lives of his Fathers and Ancestors, and of other valiant Worthies, the which he used ordinarily to read, as he then did; not as therewith vainly to deceive the time, but to make use thereof, by the imitation of that which was by them worthily done, and declining of such dangers as they by their rashness or oversight fell into. And afterwards having a little slumbered, he commanded Axalla to be sent for, who forthwith came unto him, with divers other great Lords and Captains, the chief Commanders of his Army; with whom after he had a while consulted of the order of the battle, he mounted on horseback himself, and sent every one of them to their own charges, to put the same in readiness. At which very instant he received news that the Enemy marched forward and came to take his ground for the battle; whose order of march Tamerlane was desirous to see, that so accordingly he might marshal his own. And having caused three thousand Horsemen to advance forward, with charge to begin the skirmish, himself followed after to lodge every part of his forces in such places as he had foreseen to be fittest for his advantage.

Now, seeing the Janizaries march in a square battle in the midst, and upon the two fronts two great squadrons of Horsemen, which seemed to be thirty thousand Horse, and another which advanced and covered the battalion of the Janizaries, he thought this their order to be very good, and hard to be broken; and thereupon turning himself to Axalla, who was near unto him, said: 'I had thought this day to have fought on foot, but I see that it behoveth me now to fight on horseback, to give courage unto my Soldiers, to open the great battalion of our Enemies. And my will is, that my men come forward unto me as soon as they may, for I will advance forward with an hundred thousand Footmen, fifty thousand upon each of my two wings, and in the midst of them forty thousand of my best Horsemen. My pleasure is, that after they have tried the force of these men, that they come unto my avantguard, of whom I will dispose, and fifty thousand Horse more in three bodies, whom thou shalt command; which I will assist with eighty thousand Horse, wherein shall be mine own Person, having an hundred thousand Footmen behind me, who shall march in two squadrons; and for my rearward I appoint forty thousand Horse and fifty thousand Footmen, who shall not march but to my aid.   And I will make choice of ten thousand of my best Horse, whom I will send into every place where I shall think needful within my army, for to impart my commands.'   Over the first forty thousand Horse the Prince Ciarcan commanded; over the foremost Footmen was the Lord Synopes, a Genoese, kinsman to Axalla, and his lieutenant over the Footmen, a captain of great estimation ; the Prince Axalla's own charge consisted of five squadrons of Horsemen. Bajazet his army, being also both fair and great, came bravely still on forward towards their enemies, who stirred not one whit from the place they had taken for the battle, except certain light Horsemen, Scythians, Parthians, and Muscovites, who sent out as loose men, hotly skirmished betwixt the two armies.   Now was Tamerlane by an espy advertised that Bajazet, having before given order for the disposing of his army, was on foot in the midst of thirty thousand Janizaries, his principal men of war and greatest strength, wherein he meant that day to fight, and in whom he had reposed his greatest hope.   His battle of Horse was very fair, amounting to the number of an hundred and forty thousand Horse, all old soldiers.   The Sultan of Egypt having also sent unto his aid thirty thousand Mamalukes, all very good Horsemen, with thirty thousand Foot.   So that his army, marching all in one front, in form of an half-moon (but not so well knit together as was Tamerlane's, whose squadrons directly followed one another), seemed almost as great as his ; and so with infinite numbers of most horrible outcries still advanced forward ; Tamerlane his soldiers all the while standing fast, with great silence.

There was not possible to be seen a more furious charge, than was by the Turks given upon the Prince of Ciarcan, who had commandment not to fight before the Enemy came unto him ; neither could have been chosen a fairer plain, and

where the skilful choice of the place was of less advantage
for the one or the other; but that Tamerlane had the river
on the left hand of his army serving him to some small
advantage. Now this young Prince of Ciarcan, with his forty
thousand Horse, was in this first encounter almost wholly
overthrown; yet having fought right valiantly, and entered
even into the midst of the Janizaries (where the Person of
Bajazet was), putting them in disorder, was himself there
slain. About which time Axalla set upon them with the
avantguard, but not with like danger; for having overthrown
one of the Enemy's wings, and cut it all to pieces, and his
Footmen coming to join with him, as they had been commanded, he faced the battalion of the Janizaries, who right
valiantly behaved themselves for the safety of their Prince.
This hard fight continued one hour, and yet you could not
have seen any scattered, but the one still resolutely fighting
against the other. You might there have seen the Horsemen
like mountains rush together, and infinite numbers of men
die, cry, lament, and threaten all at one instant. Tamerlane
had patience all this while to see the event of this so mortal
a fight; but perceiving his men at length to give ground, he
sent ten thousand of his Horse to join again with the ten
thousand appointed for the rearward, and commanded them
to assist him at such time as he should have need of them,
and at the very same time charged himself, and made them
to give him room, causing the Footmen to charge also, over
whom the Prince of Thanais commanded, who gave a furious
onset upon the battalion of the Janizaries, wherein was yet
the Person of Bajazet, who had sustained a great burden.

Now Bajazet had in his army a great number of mercenary
Tartars, called Destenses, with many thousands of other
soldiers taken up in the countries of the poor exiled
Mahometan Princes; in whose just quarrel, and the Greek
Emperor's, Tamerlane had chiefly undertaken that war; these
Tartarians and other soldiers, seeing some their friends, and

othersome their natural and loving Princes in the army of Tamerlane, stricken with the terror of disloyalty, and abhorring the cruelty of the proud Tyrant, in the heat of the battle revolted from Bajazet to their own Princes; which their revolt much weakened Bajazet's forces. Who nevertheless, with his own men of war, especially the Janizaries, and the help of the Christian soldiers brought to his aid from Servia and other places of Europe, with great courage maintained the fight; but the multitude, and not true valour, prevailed; for, as much as might be done by valiant and courageous men, was by the Janizaries and the rest performed both for the preservation of the Person of their Prince, and the gaining of the victory. But in the end, the Horsemen with whom Tamerlane himself was, giving a fresh charge, and his avantguard wholly knit again unto him, reinforcing the charge, he with much ado obtained the victory.

Bajazet himself wounded, and now mounted on horseback, thinking to have escaped by flight, fell into the hands of Axalla; unto whom he yielded himself, thinking it had been Tamerlane: who for a space knew him not, but took him for some other great commander of the Turks. Musa (surnamed Zelebi, or the Noble) one of Bajazet his sons, with divers others of Bajazet his great captains, were there taken also; and amongst the rest, George, the Despot of Servia, who notwithstanding this misfortune had that day gained unto himself the reputation of a great and worthy Captain; insomuch that Tamerlane, even in the very heat of the battle, marvelling to see him and the Servians, with the other Christians which he had brought to the aid of Bajazet, so valiantly to fight, said unto some of the Captains that were near unto him: 'See how courageously yonder religious fight;' supposing them by their strange attire to have been some of the Turks' superstitous votaries. But being now taken, and afterwards brought to Tamerlane, he was by him courteously welcomed; but yet withal reproved, for that he had fought for Bajazet against him, who was come in favour of the Christian Emperor, and the other poor oppressed princes, such as the Despot himself was. Who thereunto boldly answered, that indeed it was not according to his duty, but according to the prosperity of Bajazet, unto whom it seemed that all the World did bend, and that his own safety had caused him, though against his will, to take part with him. Whereupon Tamerlane held him excused; and so without more ado gave him leave at his own pleasure to depart.

Bajazet also himself being afterwards brought unto Tamerlane as a prisoner, and by him courteously entertained, never showed any token of submission at all, but according to his proud nature, without respect of his present state, presumptuously answered him unto whatsoever he demanded. Wherewith Tamerlane moved, told him, that it was now in his power to make him to lose his life. Whereunto he answered no more, but, ' Do it ' ; for that that loss should be his greatest happiness. Tamerlane afterwards demanding of him what made him so proud as to enterprise to bring into his subjection so noble a Prince as was the Greek Emperor, he answered : ' Even the same thing that hath moved thee to invade me, namely, the desire of glory and sovereignity.' ' But wherefore, then ' (said Tamerlane), ' dost thou use so great cruelty towards them thou hast overcome, without respect of age or sex ? ' ' That did I ' (said he) ' to give the greater terror unto my Enemies.' ' And what wouldst thou have done with me' (said Tamerlane) ' had it been my fortune to have fallen into thy hands, as thou art now in mine ? ' ' I would ' (said Bajazet) ' have enclosed thee in a cage of iron, and so in triumph have carried thee up and down my Kingdom.' ' Even so ' (said Tamerlane) ' shalt thou be served.' And so causing him to be taken out of his presence, turning unto his followers, said : ' Behold a proud and cruel man, he deserveth to be chastised accordingly, and to be made an example unto all the proud and cruel of the world, of the just wrath of

God against them. I acknowledge that God hath this day
delivered into my hands a great Enemy, to whom we must
therefore give thanks.' Which he performed the same day;
for the battle was won at four of the clock, and there was
yet five hours of daylight. The next day Tamerlane commanded the dead to be buried; where among the rest they
found the body of the Prince of Ciarcan, dead in the midst
of the Janizaries, where he lay enclosed with their dead
bodies, in token he died not unrevenged; whose untimely
death Tamerlane for all that greatly lamented, for he was his
Kinsman, and like enough one day to have done great service.
Whose dead body Tamerlane caused to be embalmed, and
with two thousand Horse (and divers of the Turks prisoners
chained and tied together) to be conveyed to Samercand,
until his coming thither. All the other dead bodies were,
with all honour that might be, buried at Sennas.

This great and bloody battle, fought in the year of our
Lord 1397, not far from the Mount Stella (where sometime
the great King Mithridates was by Pompey the Great in a
great battle overthrown), was fought from seven o'clock in
the morning, until four in the afternoon; Victory all that
while, as it were with doubtful wings, hovering over both
armies, as uncertain where to light; until at length the
fortune of Tamerlane prevailed. Whose wisdom, next unto
God, gave that day's victory unto his soldiers; for that the
politic tiring of the strong forces of Bajazet was the safeguard
of his own; whereas if he had gone unto the battle in one
front, assuredly the multitude finding such strong resistance
had put itself into confusion, whereas this successive manner
of aiding of his men made them all unto him profitable. The
number of them that were in this battle slain is of divers
diversely reported; the Turks themselves reporting, that Bajazet there lost the noble Mustapha, his son, with two hundred
thousand of his men, and Tamerlane not many fewer; and
some other speaking of a far less number, as that there should

Knolles
1603

be slain of the Turks about threescore thousand, and of Tamerlane's army not past twenty thousand. But leaving the certainty of the number unto the credit of the reporters, like enough it is, that the slaughter was exceeding great in so long a fight, betwixt two such armies as never before (as, I suppose) met in field together.

By this one day's event is plainly to be seen the uncertainty of worldly things, and what small assurance even the greatest have in them. Behold, Bajazet the Terror of the World, and, as he thought, superior to fortune, in an instant with his state in one battle overthrown into the bottom of misery and despair; and that at such time as he thought least, even in the midst of his greatest strength. It was three days (as they report) before he could be pacified, but as a desperate man still seeking after death, and calling for it; neither did Tamerlane, after he had once spoken with him, at all afterwards courteously use him, but as of a proud man caused small account to be made of him; and to manifest that he knew how to punish the haughty, made him to be shackled in fetters and chains of gold, and so to be shut up in an iron cage made like a grate, in such sort as that he might on every side be seen; and so carried him up and down as he passed through Asia, to be of his own people scorned and derided. And to his further disgrace, upon festival days used him for a footstool to tread upon when he mounted to horse, and at other times scornfully fed him like a dog with crumbs fallen from his table. A rare example of the uncertainty of worldly honour, that he unto whose ambitious mind Asia and Europe, two great parts of the world, were too little, should be now carried up and down cooped up in a little iron cage, like some perilous wild beast. All which Tamerlane did not so much for hatred to the man as to manifest the just judgment of God against the arrogant folly of the proud. It is reported that Tamerlane being requested by one of his noblemen that might be bold to speak unto him, to remit

some part of his severity against the person of so great a   Knolles
Prince, answered, that he did not use that rigor against him   1603
as a King, but rather did punish him as a proud ambitious
Tyrant, polluted with the blood of his own brother.

Richard Knolles.

TWO CHARACTERS

I

THE PATIENT MAN

THE patient man is made of a metal, not so hard as flex-   Hall
ible. His shoulders are large; fit for a load of in-   1608
juries: which he bears, not out of baseness and cowardliness,
because he dare not revenge; but out of Christian fortitude,
because he may not: he hath so conquered himself, that
wrongs cannot conquer him; and herein alone finds, that
victory consists in yielding. He is above nature, while he
seems below himself. The vilest creature knows how to turn
again; but, to command himself not to resist, being urged,
is more than heroical. His constructions are ever full of
charity and favour: either this wrong was not done, or not
with intent of wrong; or, if that, upon mis-information; or,
if none of these, rashness, though a fault, shall serve for an
excuse. Himself craves the offender's pardon, before his
confession; and a slight answer contents, where the offended
desires to forgive. He is God's best witness: and, when he
stands before the bar for truth, his tongue is calmly free, his
forehead firm; and, he, with erect and settled countenance,
hears his unjust sentence, and rejoices in it. The gaolers,
that attend him, are to him his pages of honour; his dun-
geon, the lower part of the vault of heaven; his rack or
wheel, the stairs of his ascent to glory: he challengeth his
executioners; and encounters the fiercest pains, with

strength of resolution; and, while he suffers, the beholders
pity him, the tormentors complain of weariness, and both
of them wonder. No anguish can master him; whether by
violence or by lingering. He accounts expectation no punishment; and can abide to have his hopes adjourned, till a
new day. Good laws serve for his protection, not for his
revenge; and his own power, to avoid indignities, not to
return them. His hopes are so strong, that they can insult
over the greatest discouragements; and his apprehensions
so deep, that, when he hath once fastened, he sooner leav-
eth his life than his hold. Neither time nor perverseness
can make him cast off his charitable endeavours, and despair
of prevailing; but, in spite of all crosses and all denials, he
redoubleth his beneficial offers of love. He trieth the sea,
after many shipwrecks; and beats still at that door, which
he never saw opened. Contrariety of events doth but exercise, not dismay him; and, when crosses afflict him, he
sees a divine hand invisibly striking with these sensible
scourges: against which he dares not rebel, not murmur.
Hence, all things befall him alike; and he goes with the
same mind to the shambles and to the fold. His recreations are calm and gentle; and not more full of relaxation
than void of fury. This man only can turn necessity into
virtue, and put evil to good use. He is the surest friend;
the latest and easiest enemy; the greatest conqueror; and
so much more happy than others, by how much he could
abide to be more miserable.

II

THE SLOTHFUL MAN

He is a religious man, and wears the time in his cloister;
and, as the cloak of his doing nothing, pleads contemplation: yet is he no whit the leaner for his thoughts;
no whit learneder. He takes no less care how to spend

time than others how to gain by the expense; and, when
business importunes him, is more troubled to forethink what
he must do than another to effect it. Summer is out of his
favour for nothing but long days, that make no haste to their
even. He loves still to have the sun witness of his rising;
and lies long, more for lothness to dress him than will to
sleep: and, after some stretching and yawning, calls for
dinner, unwashed; which having digested with a sleep in
his chair, he walks forth to the bench in the market-place,
and looks for companions: whomsoever he meets, he stays
with idle questions and lingering discourse: how the days
are lengthened; how kindly the weather is; how false the
clock; how forward the spring; and ends ever with 'What
shall we do?' It pleases him no less to hinder others than
not to work himself. When all the people are gone from
church, he is left sleeping in his seat alone. He enters
bonds; and forfeits them by forgetting the day: and asks
his neighbour, when his own field was fallowed, whether the
next piece of ground belong not to himself. His care is
either none or too late: when winter is come, after some
sharp visitations, he looks on his pile of wood, and asks how
much was cropped the last spring. Necessity drives him to
every action; and what he cannot avoid, he will yet defer.
Every change troubles him, although to the better; and his
dullness counterfeits a kind of contentment. When he is
warned on a jury, he would rather pay the mulct than
appear. All but that which nature will not permit, he
doth by a deputy: and counts it troublesome to do nothing;
but, to do anything, yet more. He is witty in nothing but
framing excuses to sit still; which, if the occasion yield not,
he coineth with ease. There is no work, that is not either
dangerous or thankless; and whereof he foresees not the
inconvenience and gainlessness, before he enters: which if
it be verified in event, his next idleness hath found a reason
to patronise it. He would rather freeze, than fetch wood:

Hall
1608

and chooses rather to steal, than work; to beg, than take
pains to steal; and, in many things, to want, than beg.   He
is so loath to leave his neighbour's fire, that he is fain to
walk home in the dark; and, if he be not looked to, wears
out the night in the chimney-corner; or, if not that, lies
down in his clothes to save two labours.   He eats and prays
himself asleep; and dreams of no other torment, but work.
This man is a standing pool; and cannot choose but gather
corruption : he is descried, amongst a thousand neighbours,
by a dry and nasty hand, that stills savours of the sheet;
a beard uncut, uncombed; an eye and an ear yellow with
their excretions ; a coat shaken on, ragged, unbrushed; by
linen and face striving whether shall excell in uncleanliness.
For body, he hath a swollen leg, a dusky and swinish eye, a
blown cheek, a drawling tongue, a heavy foot, and is nothing
but a colder earth moulded with standing water : to conclude, is a man in nothing, but in speech and shape.

Joseph Hall, Bishop of Norwich.

CHARACTER OF A GALLANT

Dekker
1609

FIRST, having diligently enquired out an Ordinary of
the largest reckoning, whither most of your courtly
gallants do resort, let it be your use to repair thither some
half hour after eleven ; for then you shall find most of your
fashionmongers planted in the room waiting for meat.   Ride
thither upon your galloway-nag, or your Spanish jennet, a
swift ambling pace, in your hose, and doublet (gilt rapier
and poniard bestowed in their places), and your French
lackey carrying your cloak, and running before you; or
rather in a coach, for that will both hide you from the
basilisk eyes of your creditors, and outrun a whole kennel
of bitter-mouthed sergeants.

Being arrived in the room, salute not any but those of

your acquaintance : walk up and down by the rest as scornfully and as carelessly as a gentleman-usher : select some
friend (having first thrown off your cloak) to walk up and
down the room with you, let him be suited, if you can, worse
by far than yourself, he will be a foil to you : and this will
be a means to publish your clothes better than Paul's, a
Tennis-court, or a Play-house : discourse as loud as you can,
no matter to what purpose if you but make a noise, and
laugh in fashion, and have a good sour face to promise
quarrelling, you shall be much observed.

If you be a soldier, talk how often you have been in
action : as the Portingale voyage, Cales voyage, the Island
voyage, besides some eight or nine employments in Ireland
and the Low Countries : then you may discourse how honourably your Grave used you ; observe that you call your Grave
Maurice, your Grave : How often you have drunk with Count
such a one, and such a Count, on your knees to your Grave's
health : and let it be your virtue to give place neither to Saint
Kynock, nor to any Dutchman whatsoever in the Seventeen
Provinces, for that soldier's complement[1] of drinking. And if
you perceive that the untravelled company about you take
this down well, ply them with more such stuff, as how you
have interpreted between the French King and a great
Lord of Barbary, when they have been drinking healths
together, and that will be an excellent occasion to publish
your languages, if you have them : if not, get some frag-
ments of French, or small parcels of Italian, to fling about
the table : but beware how you speak any Latin there : your
Ordinary most commonly hath no more to do with Latin
than a desperate town of garrison hath.

If you be a courtier, discourse of the obtaining of suits :
of your mistress's favours, etc. Make inquiry, if any gentleman at board have any suit, to get which he would use the
good means of a great man's interest with the King : and

[1] Accomplishment.

Dekker
1609 withal (if you have not so much grace left in you as to blush) that you are (thanks to your stars) in mighty credit, though in your own conscience you know, and are guilty to yourself, that you dare not (but only upon the privileges of handsome clothes) presume to peep into the presence. Demand if there be any gentleman (whom any there is acquainted with) that is troubled with two offices; or any vicar with two church-livings; which will politely insinuate, that your inquiry after them is because you have good means to obtain them; yea and rather than your tongue should not be heard in the room, but that you should sit (like an ass) with your finger in your mouth, and speak nothing: discourse how often this Lady hath sent her coach for you; and how often you have sweat in the tennis-court with that great Lord: for indeed the sweating together in France (I mean the society of tennis) is a great argument of most dear affection, even between noblemen and peasants.

If you be a poet, and come into the Ordinary (though it can be no great glory to be an Ordinary poet) order yourself thus. Observe no man, doff not cap to that gentleman to-day at dinner, to whom, not two nights since, you were beholden for a supper; but, after a turn or two in the room, take occasion (pulling out your gloves) to have some epigram, or satire, or sonnet fastened in one of them, that may (as it were vomitingly to you) offer itself to the Gentlemen; they will presently desire it: but, without much conjuration from them, and a pretty kind of counterfeit lothness in yourself, do not read it; and though it be none of your own, swear you made it. Marry, if you chance to get into your hands any witty thing of another man's, that is somewhat better. I would counsel you then, if demand be made who composed it, you may say: ' Faith, a learned gentlemen, a very worthy friend.' And this seeming to lay it on another man will be counted either modesty in you, or a sign that you are not ambitious of praise, or else that you dare not take it upon you for fear of the sharpness it carries with it. Besides, it will add much to your fame to let your tongue walk faster than your teeth, though you be never so hungry, and, rather than you should sit like a dumb coxcomb, to repeat by heart either some verses of your own or of any other man's, stretching even very good lines upon the rack of the censure : though it be against all law, honesty, or conscience, it may chance save you the price of your Ordinary, and beget you other suppliments. Marry, I would further intreat our poet to be in league with the Mistress of the Ordinary, because from her (upon condition that he will but rhyme Knights and young Gentlemen to her house, and maintain the table in good fooling) he may easily make up his mouth at her cost, gratis.

Thus much for particular men. But in general let all that are in *Ordinary*-pay, march after the sound of these directions. Before the meat come smoking to the board, our gallant must draw out his tobacco-box, the ladle for the cold snuff into the nostril, the tongs and prining-iron : all which artillery may be of gold or silver (if he can reach to the price of it), it will be a reasonable useful pawn at all times, when the current of his money falls out to run low. And here you must observe to know in what state tobacco is in town better than the merchants, and to discourse of the apothecaries where it is to be sold and to be able to speak of their wines, as readily as the apothecary himself reading the barbarous hand of a doctor : then let him show his several tricks in taking it, as the Whiff, the Ring, etc. For these are complements that gain Gentlemen no mean respect, and for which indeed they are more worthily noted, I ensure you, than for any skill that they have in learning.

When you are set down to dinner, you must eat as impudently as can be (for that is most gentleman-like) : when your Knight is upon his stewed mutton, be presently, though you be but a Captain, in the bosom of your goose : and when

Dekker your Justice of Peace is knuckle-deep in goose, you may,
1609   without disparagement to your blood, though you have a
Lady to your mother, fall very manfully to your woodcocks. . . .

After dinner, every man as his business leads him : some
to dice, . . . some to plays, some to take up friends in the
Court, some to take up money in the City, some to lend testers
in Paul's, others to borrow crowns upon the Exchange : and
thus, as the people is said to be a beast of many heads
(yet all those heads like Hydra's) ever growing, . . . so, in
an Ordinary, you shall find the variety of a whole Kingdom
in a few apes of the Kingdom.

You must not swear in your dicing : for that argues a
violent impatience to depart from your money, and in time
will betray a man's need. Take heed of it. No! whether
you be at primero or hazard, you shall sit as patiently
(though you lose a whole half-year's exhibition) as a disarmed
gentleman does when he's in the unmerciful fingers of
Serjeants. Marry, I will allow you to sweat privately, and
tear six or seven score pair[1] of cards, be the damnation of
some dozen or twenty bale of dice, and forswear play a
thousand times in an hour, but not swear. Dice yourself
into your shirt : and, if you have a beard that your friend
will lend but an angel upon, shave it off, and pawn that,
rather than to go home blind[2] to your lodging. Further, it
is to be remembered, he that is a great gamester may be
trusted for a quarter's board at all times, and apparel provided, if need be.

At your twelvepenny Ordinary, you may give any Justice
of Peace, or young Knight (if he sit but one degree towards
the equinoctial of the saltseller) leave to pay for the wine ;
and he shall not refuse it, though it be a week before the
receiving of his quarter's rent, which is a time albeit of good
hope, yet of present necessity.

                                        Thomas Dekker.

[1] Packs.   [2] Penniless.

THREE CHARACTERS

I

A WORTHY COMMANDER IN THE WARS

IS one that accounts learning the nourishment of military Overbury virtue, and lays that as his first foundation. He never 1616 bloudies his sword but in heat of battle; and had rather save one of his own soldiers than kill ten of his enemies. He accounts it an idle, vainglorious, and suspected bounty to be full of good words; his rewarding, therefore, of the deserver arrives so timely, that his liberality can never be said to be gouty-handed. He holds it next his creed, that no coward can be an honest man, and dare die in it. He doth not think his body yields a more spreading shadow after a victory than before; and when he looks upon his enemy's dead body, 'tis with a kind of noble heaviness, not insultation; he is so honourably merciful to women in surprisal, that only makes him an excellent courtier. He knows the hazard of battles, not the pomp of ceremonies, are soldiers' best theatres, and strives to gain reputation, not by the multitude, but by the greatness of his actions. He is the first in giving the charge, and the last in retiring his foot. Equal toil he endures with the common soldier: from his example they all take fire, as one torch lights many. He understands in war there is no mean to err twice; the first, and least fault being sufficient to ruin an army: faults, therefore, he pardons none; they that are presidents of disorder, or mutiny, repair it by being examples of his justice. Besiege him never so strictly, so long as the air is not cut from him, his heart faints not. He hath learned so well to make use of a victory, as to get it, and in pursuing his enemy like a whirlwind carries all afore him; being assured, if ever a man would benefit himself upon his foe, then is the time, when they have lost force, wisdom,

Overbury courage, and reputation. The goodness of his cause is the
1616 special motive to his valour; never is he known to slight the
weakest enemy that comes armed against him in the hand of
justice. Hasty and overmuch heat he accounts the step-
dame to all great actions, that will not suffer them to thrive :
if he cannot overcome his enemy by force, he does it by
time. If ever he shake hands with war, he can die more
calmly than most courtiers, for his continual dangers have
been, as it were, so many meditations of death ; he thinks
not out of his own calling when he accounts life a continual
warfare, and his prayers then best become him when armed
cap-à-pie. He utters them like the great Hebrew general,
on horseback. He casts a smiling contempt upon calumny,
it meets him as if glass should encounter adamant. He
thinks war is never to be given o'er, but on one of these
three conditions : an assured peace, absolute victory, or an
honest death. Lastly, when peace folds him up, his silver
head should lean near the golden sceptre, and die in his
prince's bosom.

II

A TINKER

Is a movable: for he hath no abiding place. By his
motion he gathers heat, thence his choleric nature. He
seems to be very devout, for his life is a continual pilgrimage, and sometimes in humility goes barefoot, thereon
making necessity a virtue. His house is as ancient as Tubal
Cain's, and so is [he] a runagate by antiquity : yet he proves
himself a gallant, for he carries all his wealth upon his back ;
or a philosopher, for he bears all his substance about him.
From his art was music first invented, and therefore is he
always furnished with a song : to which his hammer keeping
tune, proves that he was the first founder of the kettle-drum.
Note, that where the best ale is, there stands his music most

upon crotchets. The companion of his travels is some foul,
sunburnt quean, that since the terrible Statute recanted
gipsyism, and is turned pedleress. So marches he all over
England with his bag and baggage. His conversation is
unreprovable ; for he is ever mending. He observes truly
the statutes, and therefore he can rather steal than beg, in
which he is unremovably constant in spite of whips or
imprisonment : and a so strong enemy to idleness, that in
mending one hole he had rather make three than want
work, and when he hath done he throws the wallet of his
faults behind him. He embraceth naturally ancient custom,
conversing in open fields and lowly cottages. If he visit
cities or towns, 'tis but to deal upon the imperfections of our
weaker vessels. His tongue is very voluble, which with
canting proves him a linguist. He is entertained in every
place, but enters no further than the door, to avoid suspicion.
Some would take him to be a coward ; but believe it, he is a
lad of mettle, his valour is commonly three or four yards
long, fastened to a pike in the end for flying off. He is very
provident, for he will fight but with one at once, and then
also he had rather submit than be counted obstinate. To
conclude, if he 'scape Tyburn and Banbury he dies a beggar.

III

A FAIR AND HAPPY MILK-MAID

Is a country wench, that is so far from making herself
beautiful by art, that one look of hers is able to put all
face-physic out of countenance. She knows a fair look is
but a dumb orator to commend virtue, therefore minds it
not. All her excellencies stand in her so silently, as if they
had stolen upon her without her knowledge. The lining of
her apparel (which is herself) is far better than outsides of
tissue : for though she be not arrayed in the spoil of the

Overbury
1616

silk-worm, she is decked in innocency, a far better wearing. She doth not, with lying long abed, spoil both her complexion and conditions; nature hath taught her too immoderate sleep is rust to the soul : she rises, therefore, with chanticleer, her dame's cock, and at night makes the lamb her curfew.   In milking a cow, and straining the teats through her fingers, it seems that so sweet a milk-press makes the milk the whiter or sweeter; for never came almond glove or aromatic ointment on her palm to taint it. The golden ears of corn fall and kiss her feet when she reaps them, as if they wish to be bound and led prisoners by the same hand that felled them.   Her breath is her own which scents all the year long of June, like a new made haycock.   She makes her hand hard with labour, and her heart soft with pity : and when winter evenings fall early (sitting at her merry wheel) she sings a defiance to the giddy wheel of fortune.   She doth all things with so sweet a grace, it seems ignorance will not suffer her to do ill, being her mind is to do well.   She bestows her year's wages at next fair; and in choosing her garments, counts no bravery in the world like decency.   The garden and bee-hive are all her physic and chirurgery, and she lives the longer for it.   She dares go alone and unfold sheep in the night, and fears no manner of ill, because she means none : yet to say truth, she is never alone, for she is still accompanied with old songs, honest thoughts, and prayers, but short ones; yet they have their efficacy, in that they are not palled with ensuing idle cogitations.   Lastly, her dreams are so chaste that she dare tell them; only a Friday's dream is all her superstition : that she conceals for fear of anger.   Thus lives she, and all her care is she may die in the spring-time, to have store of flowers stuck upon her winding-sheet.

Sir Thomas Overbury.

THE DELIGHTFUL PASSAGE OF THE
PUPPET-PLAY

Shelton
1620

H ERE Tyrians and Trojans were all silent, I mean all
the spectators of the motion[1] had their ears hanged
upon the interpreter's mouth, that should declare the
wonders.   By and by there was a great sound of kettledrums and trumpets, and a volley of great-shot within the
motion, which passing away briefly, the boy began to raise
his voice and to say: 'This true history, which is here
represented to you, is taken word for word out of the French
Chronicles and the Spanish Romants, which are in every-
body's mouth, and sung by boys up and down the streets.
It treats of the liberty that Signor Don Gayferos gave to
Melisendra, his wife, that was imprisoned by the Moors in
Spain, in the city of Sansuenna, which was then so called, and
now Saragosa; and look you there how Don Gayferos is
playing at tables according to the song :

> "Now Don Gayferos at Tables doth play,
> Unmindful of Melisendra away."

And that personage that peeps out there with a crown on his
head and a sceptre in his hand is the Emperor Charlemaine,
the supposed father of the said Melisendra, who, grieved
with the sloth and neglect of his son-in-law, comes to chide
him : and mark with what vehemency and earnestness he
rates him, as if he meant to give him half-a-dozen cons[2] with
his sceptre.   Some authors there be that say he did, and
sound ones too; and after he had told him many things
concerning the danger of his reputation, if he did not free
his spouse, 'twas said he told him " I have said enough ;
look to it."   Look ye, Sir, again, how the Emperor turns his

---

[1] Puppet show.   [2] Raps.

back, and in what case he leaves Don Gayferos, who, all enraged, flings the tables and the tablemen from him, and hastily calls for his armour, and borrows his cousin-german Roldan his sword Durindana, who offers him his company in this difficult enterprise. But the valorous enraged knight would not accept it, saying, that he is sufficient to free his spouse, though she were put in the deep centre of the earth : and now he goes to arm himself for his journey.

'Now turn your eyes to yonder tower that appears, for you must suppose it is one of the towers of the Castle of Saragosa, which is now called the Aliaferia, and that lady that appears in the window, clad in a Moorish habit, is the peerless Melisendra, that many a time looks towards France, thinking on Paris and her spouse, the only comforts in her imprisonment. Behold, also, a strange accident now that happens, perhaps never the like seen ! See you not that Moor that comes fair and softly, with his finger in his mouth, behind Melisendra ? Look what a smack he gives her in the midst of her lips, and how suddenly she begins to spit and to wipe them with her white smock sleeve, and how she laments, and for very anguish despiteously roots up her fair hairs, as if they were to blame for this wickedness. Mark you, also, that grave Moor that stands in that open gallery, it is Marsilius, King of Sansuenna, who, when he saw the Moor's sauciness, although he were a kinsman and a great favourite of his, he commanded him straight to be apprehended, and to have two hundred stripes given him, and to be carried through the chief streets of the city with minstrels before and rods of justice behind. And look ye how the sentence is put in execution, before the fault be scarce committed; for your Moors use not (as we do) any legal proceeding.' 'Child, child' (cried Don Quixote aloud), 'on with your story in a direct line, and fall not into your crooks and your transversals, for to verify a thing I tell you there had need be a legal proceeding.' Then Master Peter, too, said from within : ' Boy, fall not you to your flourishes, but do as that gentleman commands you, which is the best course. Sing you your plain-song, and meddle not with the treble, lest the strings break.' ' I will, master' (said the boy), and proceeded, saying :

' He that you see there' (quoth he) ' on horseback, clad in a Gascoigne cloak, is Don Gayferos himself, to whom his wife (now revenged on the Moor for his boldness) shows herself from the battlements of the castle, taking him to be some passenger with whom she passed all the discourse mentioned in the Romant, that says :

> " Friend, if toward France you go,
> Ask if Gayferos be there or no. "

The rest I omit, for all prolixity is irksome ; 'tis sufficient that you see there how Don Gayferos discovers himself, and by Melisendra's jocund behaviour we may imagine she knows him, and the rather because now we see she lets herself down from a bay-window to ride away behind her good spouse ; but alas, unhappy creature, one of the skirts of her kirtle hath caught upon one of the iron bars of the window, and she hovers in the air without possibility of coming to the ground ; but see how pitiful heaven relieves her in her greatest necessity ! for Don Gayferos comes, and, without any care of her rich kirtle, lays hold of it, and forcibly brings her down with him, and at one hoist sets her astride upon his horse's crupper, and commands her to sit fast and clasp her arms about him that she fall not ; for Melisendra was not used to that kind of riding. Look you how the horse by its neighing shows that he is proud with the burden of his valiant master and fair mistress. Look how they turn their backs to the city, and merrily take their way toward Paris. Peace be with you, O peerless couple of true lovers ! Safely may you arrive at your desired country, without fortune's hindering your prosperous voyage ! May your friends and kindred see you enjoy the rest of your years (as many as Nestor's) peaceably!'

Here Master Peter cried out aloud again, saying : ' Plainness, good boy, do not you soar so high, this affectation is scurvy.' The interpreter answered nothing but went on saying : ' There wanted not some idle spectators that pry into everything, who saw the going down of Melisendra, and gave Marsilius notice of it, who straight commanded to sound an alarm ; and now behold how fast the city even sinks again with the noise of bells that sound in the high towers of the Mesquits.' [1]

' There you are out, boy ' (said Don Quixote), ' and Master Peter is very improper in his bells ; for amongst Moors you have no bells, but kettledrums and a kind of shawms that be like our waits ; so that your sounding of bells in Sansuenna is a most idle foppery.' ' Stand not upon trifles, Signor Don Quixote ' (said Master Peter), ' and so strictly upon everything, for we shall not know how to please you. Have you not a thousand comedies ordinarily represented as full of incongruities and absurdities, and yet they run their career happily, and are heard not only with applause, but great admiration also? On boy, say on, and so I fill my purse, let there be as many improprieties as motes in the sun.' ' You are in the right ' (quoth Don Quixote), and the boy proceeded :

' Look what a company of gallant knights go out of the city in pursuit of the Catholic lovers, how many trumpets sound, how many shawms play, how many drums and kettles make a noise. I fear me they will overtake them, and bring them back both bound to the same horse's tail, which would be a horrible spectacle.'

Don Quixote, seeing and hearing such a deal of Moorism, and such a coil, he thought fit to succour those that fled. So, standing up, with a loud voice, he cried out : ' I will never consent while I live that in my presence such an outrage as

[1] ' Moorish Churches.'

this be offered to so valiant and to so amorous a bold knight as Don Gayferos. Stay, you base scoundrels, do not you follow or persecute him : if you do you must first wage war with me.' So doing and speaking, he unsheathed his sword, and at one frisk he got to the motion, and with an unseen, posting fury he began to rain strokes upon the Puppetish Moorism, overthrowing some and beheading others, maiming this and cutting in pieces that ; and amongst many other blows he fetched one so downright that, had not Master Peter tumbled and squatted down, he had clipped his mazzard as easily as if it had been made of march-pane. Master Peter cried out, saying : ' Hold, Signor Don Quixote, hold ; and know that these you hurl down, destroy, and kill are not real Moors, but shapes made of pasteboard : look you, look you now (wretch that I am), he spoils all, and undoes me.' But, for all this, Don Quixote still multiplied his slashes, doubling and redoubling his blows as thick as hops.

And in a word, in less than two credos, he cast down the whole motion (all the tackling first cut to fitters, and all the puppets). King Marsilius was sore wounded, and the Emperor Charlemaine his head and crown were parted in two places ; the Senate and Auditors were all in a hurry ; and the ape got up to the top of the house, and so out of the window ; the Scholar was frighted ; the Page clean dastarded ; and even Sancho himself was in a terrible perplexity, for (as he swore after the storm was past) he never saw his master so outrageous.

The general ruin of the motion thus performed, Don Quixote began to be somewhat pacified, and said: ' Now would I have all those here at this instant before me that believe not how profitable knights-errant are to the world ; and had not I been now present what (I marvel) would have become of Signor Don Gayferos and the fair Melisendra ? I warrant, ere this, those dogs would have overtaken, and showed them some foul play : when all is done, long live knight-errantry above all things living in the world ! '

'Long live it, in God's name' (said Master Peter again, with a pitiful voice), 'and may I die since I live to be so unhappy as to say with King Don Rodrigo, yesterday I was Lord of all Spain, but to-day have not a battlement I can call mine. . . . It is not yet half an hour, scarce half a minute, that I was master of kings and emperors, had my stables, coffers, and bags full of horses and treasure ; but now I am desolate, dejected, and poor ; and, to add more affliction, without my ape, that before I can catch him again I am like to sweat for it, and all through the inconsiderate furies of this Sir Knight, who is said to protect the fatherless, to rectify wrongs, and to do other charitable works, but to me only this his generous intention hath been defective, I thank God for it.   In fine, it could be none but the Knight of the Sorrowful Countenance that discountenanced me and mine.'   Sancho grew compassionate to hear Master Peter's lamentation, and said : ' Weep not nor grieve, Master Peter, for thou breakest my heart; and let me tell thee that my master Don Quixote is so scrupulous and Catholical a Christian that if he fall into the reckoning that he hath done thee any wrong, he knows how, and will satisfy it with much advantage.' ' If' (said Master Peter) ' Don Quixote would but pay me for some part of the pieces that he hath spoiled I should be contented, and his worship might not be troubled in conscience ; for he that keeps that that is another man's against the owner's will, and restores it not, can hardly be saved.'

'That's true' (quoth Don Quixote), 'but hitherto, Master Peter, I know not whether I have detained ought of yours.' 'No? not?' said Master Peter : 'why these poor relics that lie upon the hard and barren earth, who scattered and annihilated them but the invincible force of that powerful arm ? and whose were those bodies but mine ? and with whom did I maintain myself but with them?'   'Well, I now' (said Don Quixote) 'verily believe what I have done often, that the enchanters that persecute me do nothing but put shapes, really as they are before my eyes, and by and by truck and change them at their pleasures. Verily, my masters, you that hear me, I tell you all that here passed seemed to me to be really so, and immediately that that Melisendra was Melisendra; Don Gayferos, Don Gayferos; and Marsilius, Marsilius; and Charlemaine, Charlemaine. And this was it that stirred up my choler; and, to accomplish my profession of knight-errant, my meaning was to succour those that fled, and to this good purpose I did all that you have seen: which, if it fell out unluckily, 'twas no fault of mine, but of my wicked persecutors; yet for all this error (though it proceeded from no malice of mine) I myself will condemn myself in the charge; let Master Peter see what he will have for the spoiled pieces, and I will pay it all in present current coin of Castile.'

Master Peter made him a lowleg, saying: 'I could expect no less from the unheard of christianity of the most valorous Don Quixote de la Mancha, the true succourer and bulwark of all those that be in need and necessity, or wandering vagamunds; and now let the Venter[1] and the Grand Sancho be arbitrators, and price-setters between your worship and me, and let them say what every torn piece was worth.' The Venter and Sancho both agreed; and by and by Master Peter reached up Marsilius, King of Saragosa, headless, and said: 'You see how impossible it is for this Prince to return to his first being, and therefore, saving your better judgments, I think fit to have for him two shillings and threepence.'

'On then,' quoth Don Quixote. 'Then for this' (quoth Master Peter) 'that is parted from head to foot' (taking the Emperor Charlemaine up), 'I think two shillings and sevenpence halfpenny is little enough.' 'Not very little,' quoth Sancho. 'Nor much,' said the Venter; 'but moderate the bargain, and let him have half-a-crown.' 'Let him have his full asking' (said Don Quixote); 'for, for such a mishap as

[1] Sp. *Ventero*=innkeeper.

this, we'll ne'er stand upon three halfpence more or less, and make an end quickly, Master Peter, for it is near supper-time, and I have certain suspicions that I shall eat.' 'For this puppet,' said Master Peter, 'without a nose and an eye wanting, of the fair Melisendra, I ask but in justice fourteenpence halfpenny.'

'Now the Devil's in it' (said Don Quixote), 'if Melisendra be not now in France, or upon the borders at least, with her husband, for the horse they rid on to my seeming rather flew than ran; and therefore sell me not a cat for a coney, presenting me here, Melisendra, noseless, when she, if the time require it, is wantonly solacing with her husband in France. God give each man his own, Master Peter, let us have plain dealing; and so proceed.' Master Peter, that saw Don Quixote in a wrong vein, and that he returned to his old theme, thought yet he should not escape him, and so replied: 'Indeed this should not be Melisendra, now I think on 't, but some one of the damsels that served her, so that fivepence for her will content me.'

Thus he went on pricing of other torn puppets, which the arbitrating judges moderated to the satisfaction of both parties, and the whole prices of all were twenty-one shillings and elevenpence, which, when Sancho had disbursed, Master Peter demanded, over and above, twelvepence for his labour to look for the ape. 'Give it him, Sancho' (said Don Quixote), 'not to catch his ape but a monkey,[1] and I would give five pounds for a reward to anybody that would certainly tell me that the Lady Melisendra and Don Gayferos were safely arrived in France among their own people.' 'None can better tell than my ape' (said Master Peter), 'though the Devil himself will scarce catch him; yet I imagine making much of him and hunger will force him to seek me to-night, and by morning we shall come together.'

[1] As we say 'to catch a fox.'

Well, to conclude, the storm of the motion passed and all Shelton 1620 supped merrily, and like good fellows, at Don Quixote's charge, who was liberal in extremity. Before day, the fellow with the lances and halberts was gone, and somewhat after the Scholar and the Page came to take leave of Don Quixote, the one to return homeward, and the other to prosecute his intended voyage, and, for a relief, Don Quixote gave him six shillings. Master Peter would have no more to do with him, for he knew him too well. So he got up before the sun, and, gathering the relics of the motion together, and his ape, he betook him to his adventures. The Venter, that knew not Don Quixote, wondered as much at his liberality as his madness. I conclude Sancho payed him honestly by his master's order, and, taking leave about eight of the clock, they left the vente,[1] and went on their way, where we must leave them.

Thomas Shelton.

THE PROVING OF ALIPIUS

A LIPIUS (having not forsaken that course of the world, Mathew 1620 which his parents had inculcated so often to him) went before me to Rome, that he might study the laws; where he was, with an incredible appetite, carried away to see the gladiators fight. For when first he was averse and did detest such spectacles as those, certain friends and fellows of his in study, meeting casually one day after dinner, and conducting him with a familiar kind of violence to the amphitheatre (at such time as those tragical and dismal pastimes were presented to the people), he of himself did vehemently resist and refuse to go; yet being forced, he said thus : ' If you drag my body thither, and place it there, shall you therefore be able to make me apply my mind, and open mine eyes

[1] Sp. *Venta*=inn.

to those spectacles? No; but I will be absent even while I am present; and so will I conquer both them and you.' Whereupon yet they were not the less desirous to lead him on, perhaps out of a kind of curiosity to know whether or no he could be as good as his word.

As soon as they were arrived and placed, that whole world was swelling and even boiling again with those most vast and unnatural entertainments. He, shutting the windows of his eyes, forbade his mind to mingle itself with that mischief; and I would to God he had also stopped his ears! For by occasion of a certain fatal blow which was given, and by a strong cry of the whole people, which rung so loud about him (being overcome by curiosity, and, as it were, resolved that whatsoever it were he would overcome that also, and despise it even after he had seen it), he opened his eyes, and was stricken with a deeper wound in his soul than the other was in his body; and he fell more miserably than the man whom he desired to behold. For upon that fall it was that the cry was made, which entered into his ears and opened his eyes, that there might be a way whereby he also should be wounded and defeated at the heart.

He was at that time a man rather of a bold than of a valiant mind; and so much the weaker he was, for that he presumed upon himself, who ought to have confided only in Thee. For as soon as he beheld that blood, he withal drunk down a kind of savageness of mind, and turned not his head aside, but fastened his sight upon it, and swallowed up the very Furies themselves, and knew not of it; and he was enamoured with the wickedness of those combats, and made drunk with a delight in blood. He was now no more the man that came thither, but he grew to be even one of that common people to which he went, and an entire companion of those that led him. What shall I say more? He beheld them, he cried out for company, he was inflamed with the pleasure of it; and he carried home from thence

such a measure of madness as provoked him to return, not
only now with them by whom he was formerly debauched,
but more earnestly than they, and so far as to be seducing
of others.   But yet even from thence Thou drewest him with
a most powerful and merciful hand, and Thou taughtest him
that he was to confide in Thee and not in himself.   But this
was done long after.

But this was laid up in his memory for his recovery afterward; as also when he studied at Carthage under me, and
walking at noon-day in the market-place (considering that
which he was to recite, according to the custom of scholars),
thou sufferedst him to be apprehended as a thief by the
officers of the place.   Nor didst Thou, as I think, permit it
for any other reason, O our God, but for that he, who was
afterward to prove so great a man, might early begin to
learn that one man was not easily to condemn another with
temerarious cruelty, of whose cause he was juridically to take
knowledge.   He was walking then alone before the tribunal,
with his tables and style in his hand; when behold, a certain
young scholar, who was indeed a thief, carrying secretly a
hatchet, did enter, without being observed by him, into
certain grates of lead which overlooked Silver Street, and he
began to cut the lead.   But the noise of the hatchet being
heard, the silversmiths who dwelt below began to mutter;
and sent forth to apprehend whom they should chance to
find.   And as soon as he overheard their talk he fled away,
leaving the instrument behind him, as fearing lest with it,
and by it, he might be taken.

But Alipius, who perceived him not as he went in, heard
him as he came out; and saw him speedily depart away.
And being desirous to understand the cause, went into the
place, and finding the hatchet, he paused a while and
wondered at it.   When behold! they that were sent found
him alone with the instrument in his hand, by the noise
whereof they were stirred up.   They stay him, they draw

him along; and having gathered together the next dwellers
of the market-place, they congratulated with themselves for
taking such a notorious thief; and from thence they were
carrying him towards the justice.

Hitherto he was in need to be instructed; but then, O
Lord, Thou didst instantly come to the succour of his innocency, whereof Thou only wert the witness. And when he
was to be led either to the prison or place of punishment,
there encountered them a certain architect who had the
chief care of public buildings. They were particularly glad
to meet him, who was often wont to have advertisement of
such things as were stolen out of the market-place; as if he
perhaps might know by whom this particular offence had
been committed. But this man had often seen Alipius in
the house of a certain senator whom he used to court, and
instantly knowing him, he took him by the hand and
separated him from that confusion of people. And inquir-
ing after the cause of that so great mischance, he understood
what had been done, and willed all them who were there,
in rage and tumult, to go along with him; and so they went
to the house of that young man who had committed the fact.
Now there was a boy standing at the door, and he was so
young as that (being without fear of doing his master any
hurt thereby) he disclosed the whole matter freely, for he
was a kind of a foot-boy that followed him to the market;
whom afterwards, as soon as Alipius remembered, he inti-
mated so much to the architect. And he showed the hatchet
to the boy, asking him whose it was, who instantly answered,
'Ours'; then, also, being examined, he confessed the rest.
And so was this crime removed from Alipius to that house;
and the multitude being confounded for having already begun
to triumph over this man (who futurely was to become a
dispenser of Thy word, and an examiner of many causes in
Thy Church), he departed with increase of experience and
knowledge.   *Sir Tobie Mathew.*

A WONDER FOR WISE MEN

THIS King (to speak of him in terms equal to his de- Bacon
serving) was one of the best sort of wonders: a 1622
wonder for wise men. He had parts (both in his virtues and
his fortune) not so fit for a commonplace as for observation.
Certainly he was religious, both in his affection and obser-
vance. But as he could see clear (for those times) through
superstition; so he would be blinded now and then by
human policy. He advanced church-men. He was tender
in the privilege of sanctuaries, though they wrought him much
mischief. He built and endowed many religious foundations,
besides his memorable hospital of the Savoy: and yet was
he a great alms-giver in secret; which showed that his
works in public were dedicated rather to God's glory than
his own. He professed always to love and seek peace; and
it was his usual preface in his treaties, that when Christ
came into the world peace was sung, and when He
went out of the world peace was bequeathed. And this
virtue could not proceed out of fear or softness, for he was
valiant and active; and therefore no doubt it was truly
Christian and moral. Yet he knew the way to peace was
not to seem to be desirous to avoid wars. Therefore would
he make offers and fames of wars, till he had mended the
conditions of peace. It was also much, that one that was
so great a lover of peace should be so happy in war. For
his arms, either in foreign or civil wars, were never infor-
tunate; neither did he know what a disaster meant. The
war of his coming in, and the rebellions of the Earl of
Lincoln and the Lord Audley, were ended by victory.
The wars of France and Scotland by peaces sought at his
hands. That of Brittaine by accident of the Duke's death.
The insurrection of the Lord Lovell, and that of Perkin at
Exeter and in Kent, by flight of the rebels before they

came to blows. So that his fortune of arms was still inviolate. The rather sure, for that in the quenching of the commotions of his subjects he ever went in person : sometimes reserving himself to back and second his lieutenants, but ever in action. And yet that was not merely forwardness, but partly distrust of others.

He did much maintain and countenance his laws; which (nevertheless) was no impediment to him to work his will. For it was so handled that neither prerogative nor profit went to diminution. And yet as he would sometimes strain up his laws to his prerogative, so would he also let down his prerogative to his Parliament. For mint and wars and martial discipline (things of absolute power) he would nevertheless bring to Parliament. Justice was well administered in his time, save where the King was party ; save also that the Council Table intermeddled too much with *meum* and *tuum*. For it was a very court of justice during his time ; especially in the beginning. But in that part both of justice and policy which is the durable part, and cut as it were in brass or marble, which is the making of good laws, he did excel. And with his justice he was also a merciful prince : as in whose time there were but three of the nobility that suffered; the Earl of Warwick ; the Lord Chamberlain ; and the Lord Audley : though the first two were instead of numbers in the dislike and obloquy of the people. But there were never so great rebellions expiated with so little blood drawn by the hand of justice, as the two rebellions of Blackheath and Exeter. As for the severity used upon those which were taken in Kent, it was but upon a scum of people. His pardons went ever both before and after his sword. But then he had withal a strange kind of interchanging of large and inexpected pardons with severe executions : which (his wisdom considered) could not be imputed to any inconstancy or inequality ; but either to some reason which we do not now know, or to a principle

he had set unto himself, that he would vary, and try both   Bacon
ways in turn. But the less blood he drew the more he   1622
took of treasure : and as some construed it, he was the more
sparing in the one that he might be the more pressing in
the other; for both would have been intolerable. Of nature
assuredly he coveted to accumulate treasure ; and was a
little poor in admiring riches. The people (into whom there
is infused for the preservation of monarchies a natural desire
to discharge their princes, though it be with the unjust
charge of their counsellors and ministers) did impute this
unto Cardinal Morton and Sir Reignold Bray; who as it
after appeared (as counsellors of ancient authority with him)
did so second his humours, as nevertheless they did temper
them. Whereas Empson and Dudley that followed, being
persons that had no reputation with him otherwise than by
the servile following of his bent, did not give way only (as
the first did) but shape him way to those extremities, for
which himself was touched with remorse at his death ; and
which his successor renounced, and sought to purge.

This excess of his had at that time many glosses and interpre-
tations. Some thought the continual rebellions wherewith
he had been vexed had made him grow to hate his people :
some thought it was done to pull down their stomachs and to
keep them low : some, for that he would leave his son a
golden fleece : some suspected he had some high design
upon foreign parts. But those perhaps shall come nearest
the truth that fetch not their reasons so far off ; but rather impute it to nature, age, peace, and a mind fixed upon no other
ambition or pursuit : whereunto I should add, that having
every day occasion to take notice of the necessities and
shifts for money of other great princes abroad, it did the
better by comparison set off to him the felicity of full coffers.
As to his expending of treasure, he never spared charge
which his affairs required : and in his buildings was magnificent ; but his rewards were very limited. So that his

liberality was rather upon his own state and memory than upon the deserts of others. He was of an high mind, and loved his own will and his own way; as one that revered himself, and would reign indeed. Had he been a private man he would have been termed proud: but in a wise prince, it was but keeping of distance; which indeed he did towards all; not admitting any near or full approach either to his power or to his secrets. For he was governed by none. His Queen (notwithstanding she had presented him with divers children; and with a crown also, though he would not acknowledge it) could do nothing with him. His mother he reverenced much, heard little. For any person agreeable to him for society (such as was Hastings to King Edward the Fourth, or Charles Brandon after to King Henry the Eighth), he had none; except we should account for such persons Foxe and Bray and Empson, because they were so much with him. But it was but as the instrument is much with the workman. He had nothing in him of vain-glory, but yet kept state and majesty to the height; being sensible that majesty maketh the people bow, but vain-glory boweth to them.

To his confederates abroad he was constant and just; but not open. But rather such was his inquiry and such his closeness, as they stood in the light towards him, and he stood in the dark to them; yet without strangeness, but with a semblance of mutual communication of affairs. As for little envies or emulations upon foreign princes (which are frequent with many Kings), he had never any; but went substantially to his own business. Certain it is, that though his reputation was great at home, yet it was greater abroad. For foreigners that could not see the passages of affairs, but made their judgments upon the issues of them, noted that he was ever in strife and ever aloft. It grew also from the airs which the princes and states abroad received from their ambassadors and agents here; which were attending the court in great number; whom he did not only content with courtesy, reward, and privateness; but (upon such conferences as passed with them) put them in admiration to find his universal insight into the affairs of the world: which though he did suck chiefly from themselves, yet that which he had gathered from them all seemed admirable to every one. So that they did write ever to their superiors in high terms concerning his wisdom and art of rule. Nay, when they were returned, they did commonly maintain intelligence with him; such a dexterity he had to impropriate to himself all foreign instruments.

He was careful and liberal to obtain good intelligence from all parts abroad; wherein he did not only use his interest in the liegers here, and his pensioners which he had both in the court of Rome and other the courts of Christendom, but the industry and vigilancy of his own ambassadors in foreign parts. For which purpose his instructions were ever extreme curious and articulate; and in them more articles touching inquisition than touching negotiation: requiring likewise from his ambassadors an answer, in particular distinct articles, respectively to his questions.

As for his secret spials which he did employ both at home and abroad, by them to discover what practices and conspiracies were against him; surely his case required it; he had such moles perpetually working and casting to undermine him. Neither can it be reprehended; for if spials be lawful against lawful enemies, much more against conspirators and traitors. But indeed to give them credence by oaths or curses, that cannot be well maintained; for those are too holy vestments for a disguise. Yet surely there was this further good in his employing of these flies [1] and familiars; that as the use of them was cause that many conspiracies were revealed, so the fame and suspicion of them kept (no doubt) many conspiracies from being attempted.

[1] Familiar and menial spirits.

Towards his Queen he was nothing uxorious; nor scarce indulgent; but companiable and respective, and without jealousy. Towards his children he was full of paternal affection, careful of their education, aspiring to their high advancement, regular to see that they should not want of any due honour and respect; but not greatly willing to cast any popular lustre upon them.

To his Council he did refer much, and sat oft in person; knowing it to be the way to assist his power and inform his judgment: in which respect also he was fairly patient of liberty both of advice and of vote, till himself were declared. He kept a strait hand on his nobility, and chose rather to advance clergymen and lawyers, which were more obsequious to him, but had less interest in the people; which made for his absoluteness, but not for his safety. Insomuch as I am persuaded it was one of the causes of his troublesome reign. For that his nobles, though they were loyal and obedient, yet did not co-operate with him, but let every man go his own way. He was not afraid of an able man, as Lewis the Eleventh was. But contrariwise he was served by the ablest men that then were to be found; without which his affairs could not have prospered as they did. For war, Bedford, Oxford, Surrey, Dawbeny, Brooke, Poynings. For other affairs, Morton, Foxe, Bray, the Prior of Lanthony, Warham, Urswick, Hussey, Frowick, and others. Neither did he care how cunning they were that he did employ: for he thought himself to have the master-reach. And as he chose well, so he held them up well. For it is a strange thing, that though he were a dark prince, and infinitely suspicious, and his times full of secret conspiracies and troubles; yet in twenty-four years' reign he never put down or discomposed Councillor or near servant, save only Stanley the Lord Chamberlain. As for the disposition of his subjects in general towards him, it stood thus with him; that of the three affections which naturally tie the hearts of the subjects

to their sovereign,—love, fear, and reverence—he had the
last in height; the second in good measure; and so little of
the first, as he was beholding to the other two.

He was a Prince, sad, serious, and full of thoughts and
secret observations; and full of notes and memorials of his
own hand, especially touching persons; as whom to employ,
whom to reward, whom to inquire of, whom to beware of,
what were the dependencies, what were the factions, and
the like; keeping (as it were) a journal of his thoughts.
There is to this day a merry tale : that his monkey (set on
as it was thought by one of his Chamber) tore his principal
note-book all to pieces, when by chance it lay forth : whereat the Court which liked not those pensive accounts was
almost tickled with sport.

He was indeed full of apprehensions and suspicions. But
as he did easily take them, so he did easily check them and
master them; whereby they were not dangerous, but
troubled himself more than others. It is true, his thoughts
were so many, as they could not well always stand together;
but that which did good one way, did hurt another. Neither
did he at some times weigh them aright in their proportions.
Certainly that rumour which did him so much mischief
(that the Duke of York should be saved and alive) was (at
the first) of his own nourishing, because he would have more
reason not to reign in the right of his wife. He was affable,
and both well and fair spoken; and would use strange
sweetness and blandishments of words, where he desired
to effect or persuade anything that he took to heart. He
was rather studious than learned; reading most books that
were of any worth, in the French tongue. Yet he understood the Latin, as appeareth in that Cardinal Hadrian and
others, who could very well have written French, did use to
write to him in Latin.

For his pleasures, there is no news of them. And yet by
his instructions to Marsin and Stile touching the Queen of

Naples, it seemeth he could interrogate well touching beauty. He did by pleasures as great princes do by banquets, come and look a little upon them, and turn away. For never prince was more wholly given to his affairs, nor in them more of himself: insomuch as in triumphs of jousts and tourneys and balls and masques (which they then called disguises) he was rather a princely and gentle spectator than seemed much to be delighted.

No doubt, in him as in all men (and most of all in Kings) his fortune wrought upon his nature, and his nature upon his fortune. He attained to the crown, not only from a private fortune, which might endow him with moderation; but also from the fortune of an exiled man, which had quickened in him all seeds of observation and industry. And his times being rather prosperous than calm, had raised his confidence by success, but almost marred his nature by troubles. His wisdom, by often evading from perils, was turned rather into a dexterity to deliver himself from dangers when they pressed him, than into a providence to prevent and remove them afar off. And even in nature, the sight of his mind was like some sights of eyes; rather strong at hand than to carry afar off. For his wit increased upon the occasion; and so much the more if the occasion were sharpened by danger. Again, whether it were the shortness of his foresight, or the strength of his will, or the dazzling of his suspicions, or what it was; certain it is that the perpetual troubles of his fortunes (there being no more matter out of which they grew) could not have been without some great defects and main errors in his nature, customs, and proceedings, which he had enough to do to save and help with a thousand little industries and watches. But those do best appear in the story itself. Yet take him with all his defects, if a man should compare him with the Kings his concurrents in France and Spain, he shall find him more politic than Lewis the Twelfth of France, and more entire and sincere than Ferdi-

nando of Spain.   But if you shall change Lewis the Twelfth   Bacon 1622
for Lewis the Eleventh, who lived a little before, then the
consort is more perfect.   For that Lewis the Eleventh, Ferdinando, and Henry may be esteemed for the *tres magi* of
Kings of those ages.   To conclude, if this King did no
greater matters, it was long of himself; for what he minded
he compassed.

He was a comely personage, a little above just stature,
well and straight limbed, but slender.   His countenance
was reverend, and a little like a churchman : and as it was
not strange or dark, so neither was it winning or pleasing,
but as the face of one well disposed.   But it was to the
disadvantage of the painter, for it was best when he spake.

His worth may bear a tale or two, that may put upon him
somewhat that may seem divine.   When the Lady Margaret
his mother had divers great suitors for marriage, she dreamed
one night that one in the likeness of a bishop in pontifical
habit did tender her Edmund, Earl of Richmond (the King's
father), for her husband.   Neither had she ever any child
but the King, though she had three husbands.   One day
when King Henry the Sixth (whose innocency gave him
holiness) was washing his hands at a great feast, and cast
his eye upon King Henry, then a young youth, he said :
'This is the lad that shall possess quietly that that we now
strive for.'   But that that was truly divine in him, was that
he had the fortune of a true Christian as well as of a great
King, in living exercised and dying repentant.   So as he had
an happy warfare in both conflicts, both of sin and the cross.

He was born at Pembroke Castle, and lieth buried at
Westminster, in one of the stateliest and daintiest monu-
ments of Europe, both for the chapel and for the sepulchre.
So that he dwelleth more richly dead, in the monument of his
tomb, than he did alive in Richmond or any of his palaces.
I could wish he did the like in this monument of his fame.

Francis Bacon, Viscount St. Alban.

STEPS IN HIS SICKNESS

MEDITATION I

Donne
1624

VARIABLE, and therefore miserable condition of man; this minute I was well, and am ill, this minute. I am surprised with a sudden change, and alteration to worse, and can impute it to no cause, nor call it by any name. We study health, and we deliberate upon our meats, and drink, and air, and exercises, and we hew, and we polish every stone that goes to that building; and so our health is a long and a regular work; but in a minute a cannon batters all; overthrows all; diminishes all: a sickness unprevented for all our diligence, unsuspected for all our curiosity; nay, undeserved, if we consider only disorder, summons us, destroys us in an instant. O miserable condition of man! which was not imprinted by God, who as He is immortal Himself, had put a coal, a beam of immortality into us, which we might have blown into a flame, but blew it out by our first sin; we beggared ourselves by hearkening after false riches, and infatuated ourselves by hearkening after false knowledge. So that now, we do not only die, but die upon the rack, die by the torment of sickness; nor that only, but are preafflicted, superafflicted with these jealousies and suspicions, and apprehensions of sickness, before we can call it a sickness: we are not sure we are ill; one hand asks the other by the pulse, and our eye asks our own urine how we do. O multiplied misery! we die, and cannot enjoy death, because we die in this torment of sickness; we are tormented with sickness, and cannot stay till the torment come, but preapprehensions and presages prophesy those torments, which induce that death before either come; and our dissolution is conceived in these first changes, quickened in the sickness itself, and born in death, which bears date from these first changes. Is this the honour which man hath by

being a little world, that he hath these earthquakes in him- Donne
self, sudden shakings, these lightnings, sudden flashes; 1624
these thunders, sudden noises; these eclipses, sudden effus-
cations, and darkening of his senses; these blazing stars,
sudden fiery exhalations; these rivers of blood, sudden red
waters? Is he a world to himself only therefore, that he
hath enough in himself, not only to destroy and execute
himself, but to presage that execution upon himself? to
assist the sickness, to antedate the sickness, to make the
sickness the more irremediable by sad apprehensions, and
as if he would make a fire the more vehement, by sprinkling
water upon the coals, so to wrap a hot fever in cold melancholy, lest the fever alone should not destroy fast enough
without this contribution, nor perfect the work (which is
destruction) except we joined an artificial sickness of our
own melancholy, to our natural, our unnatural fever? O
perplexed discomposition! O riddling distemper! O miserable condition of man!

MEDITATION II

THE heavens are not the less constant, because they move
continually, because they move continually one and the
same way. The earth is not the more constant, because
it lies still continually, because continually it changes and
melts in all the parts thereof. Man, who is the noblest
part of the earth, melts so away as if he were a statue, not
of earth, but of snow. We see his own envy melts him, he
grows lean with that; he will say, another's beauty melts
him; but he feels that a fever doth not melt him like snow,
but pour him out like lead, like iron, like brass melted in a
furnace; it doth not only melt him, but calcine him, reduce
him to atoms, and to ashes, not to water, but to lime. And
how quickly? Sooner than thou canst receive an answer,
sooner than thou canst conceive the question; earth is the

Donne
1624
centre of my body, heaven is the centre of my soul: these two are the natural places of these two; but those go not to these two in an equal pace: my body falls down without pushing, my soul does not go up without pulling: ascension is my soul's pace and measure, but precipitation my body's: and even angels, whose home is heaven, and who are winged too, yet had a ladder to go to heaven by steps. The sun which goes so many miles in a minute, the stars of the firmament which go so very many more, go not so fast, as my body to the earth. In the same instant that I feel the first attempt of the disease, I feel the victory; in the twinkling of an eye, I can scarce see; instantly the taste is insipid and fatuous; instantly the appetite is dull and desireless; instantly the knees are sinking and strengthless; and in an instant sleep, which is the picture, the copy of death, is taken away, that the original, death itself, may succeed, and that so I might have death to the life. It was part of Adam's punishment: *In the sweat of thy brows thou shalt eat thy bread* : it is multiplied to me, I have earned bread in the sweat of my brows, in the labour of my calling, and I have it; and I sweat again, and again, from the brow to the sole of the foot, but I eat no bread, I taste no sustenance: miserable distribution of mankind, where one-half lacks meat, and the other stomach.

MEDITATION III

We attribute but one privilege and advantage to man's body, above other moving creatures: that he is not as others, grovelling, but of an erect, of an upright form, naturally built, and disposed to the contemplation of heaven. Indeed it is a thankful form, and recompenses that soul, which gives it, with carrying that soul so many foot higher towards heaven. Other creatures look to the earth; and even that is no unfit object, no unfit contemplation for man;

for thither he must come; but because man is not to stay
there, as other creatures are, man in his natural form is
carried to the contemplation of that place, which is his
home, heaven. This is man's prerogative: but what state
hath he in this dignity? A fever can fillip him down, a
fever can depose him; a fever can bring that head, which
yesterday carried a crown of gold, five foot towards a crown
of glory, as low as his own foot, to-day. When God came
to breathe into man the breath of life, He found him flat
upon the ground; when He comes to withdraw that breath
from him again, He prepares him to it, by laying him flat
upon his bed. Scarce any prison so close, that affords not
the prisoner two or three steps. The anchorites that barked
themselves up in hollow trees, and immured themselves in
hollow walls; that perverse man, that barrelled himself in
a tub, all could stand, or sit, and enjoy some change of
posture. A sickbed is a grave, and all that the patient says
there is but a varying of his own epitaph. Every night's
bed is a type of the grave; at night we tell our servants at
what hour we will rise; here we cannot tell ourselves, at
what day, what week, what month. Here the head lies as
low as the foot; the head of the people, as low as they
whom those feet trod upon; and that hand that signed
pardons, is too weak to beg his own, if he might have it for
lifting up that hand: strange fetters to the feet, strange
manacles to the hands, when the feet and hands are bound
so much the faster, by how much the cords are slacker; so
much the less able to do their offices, by how much more
the sinews and ligaments are the looser. In the grave I may
speak through the stones, in the voice of my friends, in the
accents of those words, which their love may afford my
memory; here I am mine own ghost, and rather affright my
beholders, than instruct them; they conceive the worst of me
now, and yet fear worse; they give me for dead now, and
yet wonder how I do, when they wake at midnight, and ask

Donne
1624

how I do to-morrow. Miserable, and (though common to all) inhuman posture, where I must practise my lying in the grave, by lying still, and not practise my resurrection, by rising any more.

MEDITATION IV

It is too little to call man a little world : except God, man is a diminutive to nothing. Man consists of more pieces, more parts, than the world ; than the world doth, nay, than the world is. And if those pieces were extended and stretched out in man, as they are in the world, man would be the giant, and the world the dwarf, the world but the map, and the man the world. If all the veins in our bodies were extended to rivers, and all the sinews to veins of mines, and all the muscles, that lie upon one another, to hills, and all the bones to quarries of stones, and all the other pieces to the proportion of those which correspond to them in the world, the air would be too little for this orb of man to move in, the firmament would be but enough for this star; for, as the whole world has nothing, to which something in man doth not answer, so hath man many pieces, of which the whole world hath no representation. Enlarge this meditation upon this great world, man, so far, as to consider the immensity of the creatures this world produces : our creatures are our thoughts, creatures that are born giants; that reach from east to west, from earth to heaven, that do not only bestride all the sea and land, but span the sun and firmament at once ; my thoughts reach all, comprehend all. Inexplicable mystery : I their creator am in a close prison, in a sick bed, anywhere, and any one of my creatures, my thoughts, is with the sun, and beyond the sun, overtakes the sun, and overgoes the sun in one pace, one step, everywhere. And then as the other world produces serpents, and vipers, malignant and venomous

creatures, and worms, and caterpillars, that endeavour to Donne
devour that world produces them, and monsters compiled 1624
and complicated of diverse parents and kinds, so this world,
ourselves, produces all these in us, in producing diseases
and sicknesses of all those sorts: venomous and infectious
diseases, feeding and consuming diseases, and manifold and
entangled diseases made up of many several ones. And can
the other world name so many venomous, so many consuming,
so many monstrous creatures, as we can diseases of all those
kinds? O miserable abundance, O beggarly riches! How much
do we lack of having remedies for every disease, when as yet
we have not names for them? But we have a Hercules against
these giants, these monsters; that is, the physician: he
musters up all the forces of the other world to succour this;
all nature to relieve man. We have the physician, but we are
not the physician. Here we shrink in our proportion, sink
in our dignity, in respect of very mean creatures, who are
physicians to themselves. The hart that is pursued and
wounded, they say, knows an herb which, being eaten,
throws off the arrow: a strange kind of vomit. The dog
that pursues it, though he be subject to sickness, even pro-
verbially, knows his grass that recovers him. And it may
be true, that the drugger is as near to man as to other
creatures; it may be that obvious and present simples, easy
to be had, would cure him; but the apothecary is not so
near him, nor the physician so near him, as they two are to
other creatures; man hath not that innate instinct to apply
those natural medicines to his present danger as those inferior creatures have; he is not his own apothecary, his own
physician, as they are. Call back, therefore, thy meditations
again, and bring it down: What is become of man's great
extent and proportion, when himself shrinks himself, and
consumes himself to an handful of dust? What is become
of his soaring thoughts, his compassing thoughts, when himself brings himself to the ignorance, to the thoughtlessness

Donne
1624
of the grave? His diseases are his own, but the physician
not; he hath them at home, but he must send for the
physician.

John Donne, Dean of St. Paul's.

TWO PILGRIMS

I

THE DEATH OF JOHN DAVYS

Mitchel-
bourne
1625
HERE as I stood for Patane, about the 27th of
December, I met with a junk of the Japons, which
had been pirating along the coast of China and Camboia.
Their Pilot being dead, with ignorance and foul weather
they had cast away their ship on the sholds of the great
island Borneo; and to enter into the country of Borneo they
durst not: for the Japons are not suffered to land in any port
in India with weapons, being accounted a people so desperate
and daring, that they are feared in all places where they
come. These people, their ship being splitted, with their
shallops entered this junk, wherein I met them, which was
of Patane, and killed all the people save one old Pilot. This
junk was laden with rice, which when they had possessed
and furnished with such furniture, necessaries, and arms as
they saved out of their sunken ship, they shaped their
course for Japan; but the badness of their junk, contrary
winds, and unseasonableness of the year forced them to
leeward, which was the cause of mine unlucky meeting them.

After I had hailed them, and made them come to
leeward, sending my boat aboard them, I found them by
their men and furniture very unproportionable for such a
ship as they were in, which was a junk not above seventy
tons in burthen, and they were ninety men, and most of
them in too gallant a habit for sailors, and such an equality

of behaviour among them that they seemed all fellows; yet
one among them there was that they called Captain, but
gave him little respect.   I caused them to come to an
anchor, and upon further examination I found their lading
to be only rice, and for the most part spilt with wet, for
their ship was leak both under and above water.   Upon
questioning with them, I understood them to be men of war,
that had pillaged on the coast of China and Camboia, and, as
I said before, had cast away their ship on the sholds of Bornea.
Here we rode at anchor under a small island, near to the
Isle of Bintam, two days entertaining them with good usage,
not taking anything from them, thinking to have gathered
by their knowledge the place and passage of certain ships,
on the coast of China to have made my voyage.   But these
rogues, being desperate in winds and fortunes, being hopeless
in that paltry junk ever to return to their country, resolved
with themselves either to gain my ship or to lose their lives.
And upon mutual courtesies with gifts and feastings between
us, sometimes five-and-twenty or six-and-twenty of their
chiefest came aboard : whereof I would not suffer above six
to have weapons.   There was never the like number of our
men aboard their junk.   I willed Captain John Davis in the
morning to possess himself of their weapons, and to put the
company before mast, and to leave some guard on their
weapons, while they searched in the rice, doubting that by
searching and finding that which would dislike them they
might suddenly set upon my men, and put them to the
sword : as the sequel proved.

Captain Davis, being beguiled with their humble semblance, would not possess himself of their weapons, though
I sent twice of purpose from my ship to will him to do
it.   They passed all the day, my men searching in the
rice, and they looking on.   At the sun-setting, after
long search and nothing found, save a little storax and
benjamin, they seeing opportunity, and talking to the

rest of the company which were in my ship, being near to their junk, they resolved, at a watch-word between them, to set upon us resolutely in both ships. This being concluded, they suddenly killed and drove overboard all my men that were in their ship; and those which were aboard my ship sallied out of my cabin, where they were put, with such weapons as they had, finding certain targets in my cabin, and other things that they used as weapons. Myself being aloft on the deck, knowing what was likely to follow, leapt into the waist, where, with the boatswains, carpenter, and some few more, we kept them under the half-deck. At their first coming forth of the cabin, they met Captain Davis coming out of the gunroom, whom they pulled into the cabin, and giving him six or seven mortal wounds, they thrust him out of the cabin before them. His wounds were so mortal, that he died as soon as he came into the waist. They pressed so fiercely to come to us, as we receiving them on our pikes, they would gather on our pikes with their hands to reach us with their swords. It was near half an hour before we could stone them back into the cabin: in which time we had killed three or four of their leaders. After they were driven into the cabin, they fought with us at the least four hours before we could suppress them, often firing the cabin, burning the bedding, and much other stuff that was there. And had we not with two demy-culverins, from under the half-deck, beaten down the bulk-head and the pump of the ship, we could not have suppressed them from burning the ship. This ordnance being charged with cross-bars, bullets, and case-shot, and bent close to the bulk-head, so violently marred therewith boards and splinters, that it left but one of them standing of two-and-twenty. Their legs, arms, and bodies were so torn, as it was strange to see how the shot had massacred them. In all this conflict they never would desire their lives, though they were hopeless to escape, such was the desperateness of these Japonians.

Only one leapt overboard, which afterward swam to our ship again, and asked for grace ; we took him in, and asked him what was their purpose? He told us, that they meant to take our ship, and to cut all our throats. He would say no more, but desired that he might be cut in pieces.

II

AN ORDEAL BY FIRE

THE seven-and-twentieth, all night being very tempest-uous, fearful thunder and lightning, and abundance of rain, we had under our house, in a room for that purpose, some small store of steel betel-boxes, and such like; where also lay two men, appointed by Captain Bonner to watch the house, the boat being left behind them ashore. That night John Cocket (*alias* Tucker), a youth, who had long lived at Surat, and he also lodged there: about midnight came thieves to open the door, which one within perceiving, with crying out feared them away. Two hours after they returned, and one of them, putting in his arm, was struck at with a sword, but missed, fled away the second time; and they within made the door so fast as they could (which was but hurdles). About four in the morning, coming again, and opening the door, one went in, taking some brass betel-boxes, our men being all fast asleep; and in returning, rubbed against Tucker's legs, who, starting up, caught hold of him and cried: 'A thief, I have him;' which scarce pronounced, with a pitiful accent, cried out again: 'O! he is gone, and hath stabbed me with his creeze:' which was so suddenly done, as those who lay by him had not time to rescue him. There was at that time aloft the surgeon of the *Dragon*, etc., who presently ran down with a light, but too late; the villain having with a knife given him two wounds, one whereof to the heart, who, without speaking

Hore
1625

more words than 'Lord have mercy upon me,' presently died.

We in vain searched each bush and place about our house, and I went to call the Cowals (or waiters), who every night till this kept watch in a balley[1] within twenty paces of our house; missing whom, I went instantly to the Pongolo Cowalla's house, and calling him, asked him, where was the watch ? He said at the balley, which I denying, he affirmed to have charged one that night. Then I told him we had a man slain, and willed him to search narrowly if any suspicious person could be apprehended; he forthwith went and acquainted the King therewith, who presently came down with the Chief thereabouts, saw the dead body, and affirmed he would do what might be to find the murderer. Master Nichols charged the Cowals to be actors or authors hereof, and required to have them all sent for, and one after another to touch the corpse, whereto the King gave order. And when each one had taken him by the hand, and no cause to suspect any appeared, Master Nichols demanded if there were no more Cowals; it was answered, no more save one, who was sick, and kept his bed. Him the King commanded to be sent for, whose very looks and demeanour condemned him, in the opinion of all, to be the villain sought for. The King commanded to take the dead man by the hand, which with extreme quaking, and many distracted gestures and answers, he did, but would not hold it any time. Master Nichols urged this to be the man, and required justice. The King caused him to be bound, and professed in his conscience that was the man who killed him, but that he must be tried by their law also, whereto the fellow assented.

And while preparation was made thereto, we sent word to Captain Bonner, who came ashore to see the event hereof: presently after whose coming, a fire was made, and an iron pan with a gallon of oil set thereon, which leisurely boiled

[1] [?]

till it came to such a degree of heat, that a green leaf but Hore
dipped therein was sodden and shivered. The prisoner then 1625
called, and persisting in denial of the fact, was, in testimony
of his innocency, to take out of the said oil a small ball of
brass, little bigger than a musket-shot, with his naked hand ;
and that if any burning or scalding appeared thereon, he
was contented to die, which he addressed himself to perform.
Stripping up his sleeve above the elbow, and taking a kind
of protestation, desiring that as he was clear thereof, so he
might prosper in this act ; [he] dipped his hand to the wrist
in the burning oil, took out the ball, held it fast, and crying,
' Olla Basar,' or ' Great is the Lord,' tossed it up, caught it
again, and then cast it on the ground, showing his hand
unto all that would, which had no more sign of hurt than if
he had experimented the same in cold water—the devil, it
seems, being loth at that time to lose his credit. The
fellow was instantly released, and within an hour after
returned in his holiday apparel, and none so lusty as he,
though but a little before he had been sick, and so weak, as
he was fain to be brought upon men's shoulders to his trial.
And this was all the justice we could have for our murdered
man, though in all likelihood, and their judgments also, he
was the actor.

Purchas his Pilgrims.

SOME UNIVERSITY CHARACTERS

I.

AN OLD COLLEGE BUTLER

I S none of the worst Students in the house, for he keeps Earle
the set hours at his book more duly than any. His 1628
authority is great over men's good names, which he charges
many times with shrewd aspersions, which they hardly wipe

Earle
1628

off without payment. His Box and Counters prove him to be a man of reckoning; yet he is stricter in his accounts than a Usurer, and delivers not a farthing without writing. He doubles the pain of *Gallobelgicus*, for his books go out once a quarter, and they are much in the same nature, brief notes and sums of affairs, and are out of request as soon. His comings in are like a Tailor's, from the shreds of bread, the chippings, and remnants of the broken crust; excepting his vails[1] from the barrel, which poor folks buy for their hogs, but drink themselves. He divides a halfpenny loaf with more subtlety than Kekerman, and subdivides the *a primo ortum* so nicely, that a stomach of great capacity can hardly apprehend it. He is a very sober man, considering his manifold temptations of drink and strangers, and if he be overseen, 'tis within his own liberties, and no man ought to take exceptions. He is never so well pleased with his place as when a gentleman is beholding to him for showing him the Buttery, whom he greets with a cup of single beer and sliced manchet, and tells him 'tis the fashion of the College. He domineers over Freshmen when they first come to the Hatch, and puzzles them with strange language of Cues and Cees, and some broken Latin which he has learnt at his Bin. His faculty's extraordinary is the warming of a pair of Cards, and telling out a dozen of Counters for Post and Pair, and no man is more methodical in these businesses. Thus he spends his age, till the tap of it is run out, and then a fresh one is set abroach.

II

A DOWNRIGHT SCHOLAR

Is one that has much learning in the Ore, unwrought and untried, which time and experience fashions and refines. He is good metal in the inside, though rough and unscoured

---

[1] Profits.

without, and therefore hated of the Courtier, that is quite contrary. The time has got a vein of making him ridiculous, and men laugh at him by tradition, and no unlucky absurdity but is put upon his profession, and done like a scholar. But his fault is only this, that his mind is somewhat much taken up with his mind, and his thoughts not loaden with any carriage besides. He has not put on the quaint garb of the age, which is now become a man's Total. He has not humbled his meditations to the industry of Compliment, nor afflicted his brain in an elaborate leg. His body is not set upon nice Pins, to be turning and flexible for every motion, but his scrape is homely, and his nod worse. He cannot kiss his hand and cry Madam, nor talk idly enough to bear her company. His smacking of a Gentlewoman is somewhat too savoury, and he mistakes her nose for her lip. A very Woodcock would puzzle him in carving, and he wants the logick of a Capon. He has not the glib faculty of sliding over a tale, but his words come squeamishly out of his mouth, and the laughter commonly before the jest. He names this word College too often, and his discourse beats too much on the University. The perplexity of mannerliness will not let him feed, and he is sharp set at an argument when he should cut his meat. He is discarded for a gamester at all games but one-and-thirty, and at tables he reaches not beyond doublets. His fingers are not long and drawn out to handle a Fiddle, but his fist is clenched with the habit of disputing. He ascends a horse somewhat sinisterly, though not on the left side, and they both go jogging in grief together. He is exceedingly censured by the Inns a Court men for that heinous Vice, being out of fashion. He cannot speak to a Dog in his own Dialect, and understands Greek better than the language of a Falconer. He has been used to a dark room and dark Clothes, and his eyes dazzle at a Sattin Doublet. The Hermitage of his Study has made him somewhat uncouth in the world, and men make him worse by staring on him.

Earle
1628

Thus is he silly and ridiculous, and it continues with him for some quarter of a year, out of the University. But practise him a little in men, and brush him o'er with good company, and he shall outbalance those glisterers as much as a solid substance does a feather, or Gold Gold-lace.

III

A MERE YOUNG GENTLEMAN OF THE UNIVERSITY

Is one that comes there to wear a gown and to say hereafter he has been at the University. His Father sent him thither because he heard there were the best Fencing and Dancing Schools; from these he has his Education, from his Tutor the oversight. The first element of his Knowledge is to be shown the Colleges and initiated in a Tavern by the way, which hereafter he will learn of himself. The two marks of his Seniority is the bare Velvet of his gown and his proficiency at Tennis, where, when he can once play a Set, he is a Freshman no more. His Study has commonly handsome Shelves, his Books neat Silk strings, which he shows to his Father's man, and is loath to untie or take down for fear of misplacing. Upon foul days for recreation he retires thither, and looks over the pretty book his Tutor reads to him, which is commonly some short history, or a piece of *Euphormio*; for which his Tutor gives him Money to spend next day. His main loitering is at the Library, where he studies Arms and books of Honour, and turns a Gentleman-Critick in pedigrees. Of all things, he endures not to be mistaken for a Scholar, and hates a black suit though it be of Sattin. His companion is ordinarily some stale fellow, that has been notorious for an Ingle[1] to gold hatbands, whom he admires at first, afterward scorns. If he have spirit or wit, he may light of better company, and may learn some flashes of wit which may do

[1] A parasite.

him Knight's service in the Country hereafter. But he is
now gone to the Inns of Court, where he studies to forget
what he learned before, his acquaintance and the fashion.

IV

AN UNIVERSITY DUN

Is a Gentleman's follower cheaply purchased, for his own
money has hired him. He is an inferior Creditor of some
ten shillings or downwards, contracted for Horse-hire, or
perchance for drink, too weak to be put in Suit, and he
arrests your modesty. He is now very expensive of his time,
for he will wait upon your Stairs a whole Afternoon, and dance
attendance with more patience than a Gentleman-Usher. He
is a sore beleaguerer of Chambers, and assaults them sometimes with furious knocks; yet finds strong resistance commonly, and is kept out. He is a great complainer of Scholars'
loitering, for he is sure never to find them within, and yet
he is the chief cause many times that makes them study.
He grumbles at the ingratitude of men, that shun him for
his kindness, but indeed it is his own fault, for he is too great
an upbraider. No man puts them more to their brain than
he; and by shifting him off they learn to shift in the world.
Some choose their rooms a purpose to avoid his surprisals,
and think the best commodity in them his Prospect. He
is like a rejected acquaintance, hunts those that care not for
his company, and he knows it well enough, and yet will not
keep away. The sole place to supply him is the Buttery,
where he takes grievous use upon your Name, and he is one
much wrought with good Beer and Rhetorick. He is a man
of most unfortunate voyages, and no Gallant walks the street
to less purpose.

                              John Earle, Bishop of Salisbury.

AN UNEQUAL COMBAT

Digby
1629

FOR after Theagenes had embarked himself to follow on his intended journey, a favourable wind in a short time brought him to Alexandria; whither he sent a servant one day before him to provide him a convenient house near the Ambassador's, and other necessaries; and the next day came thither himself, and the first thing he did was to go kiss the hand of his kinsman Aristobulus, who received him with all the demonstration of joy and honour that might be, and caused him to stay supper with him; after which he sent his son Leodivius, with many of his servants and torches, to accompany him to his lodging, which was not far off. But the night had slided so insensibly away while they were in their pleasing conversation, it being the nature of long absence of dear friends to cause at their first encounter much greediness of enjoying each other, that when they came out of the house they found the streets quiet and no living creature stirring in them; and the moon, which was then near the full, shining out a clear light upon them, so that the coolness and solitude was the greatest sign that it was not noonday.

Wherefore they caused the lights and other servants to stay there, who then could serve but for vain magnificence, and Theagenes sent his servants to his lodging before, while he, and Leodivius, and another gentleman, that Leodivius took with him to accompany him, that he might not return all alone to his father's house, came softly after, sucking in the fresh air, and pleasing themselves in the coolness of the night which succeeded a hot day, it being then in the beginning of the summer: but as they were entertaining themselves in some gentle discourse, a rare voice, accompanied with a sweet instrument, called their ears to silent attention, while with their eyes they

sought to inform themselves where the person was that
sung, when they saw a gentlewoman in a loose and night
habit, that stood in an open window supported like a gallery
with bars of iron, with a lute in her hand, which with
excellent skill she made to keep time with her divine voice,
and that issued out of as fair a body, by what they could
judge at that light; only there seemed to sit so much sadness
upon her beautiful face, that one might judge she herself
took little pleasure in her own soul-ravishing harmony.

The three spectators remained attentive to this fair sight
and sweet music, Leodivius only knowing who she was,
who coming a little nearer towards the window, fifteen
men all armed, as the moon shining upon their bucklers
and coats of mail did make evident, rushed out upon him
with much violence, and with their drawn swords made
so many furious blows and thrusts at him, that if his better
genius had not defended him it had been impossible that
he could have outlived that minute; but he, nothing at all
dismayed, drew his sword, and struck the foremost of them
such a blow upon the head, that if it had not been armed
with a good cap of steel, certainly he should have received
no more cumber from that man; yet the weight of it was
such that it made the Egyptian run reeling backwards two
or three steps, and the blade, not able to sustain such a
force, broke in many pieces, so that nothing but the hilts
remained in Leodivius's hand; who seeing himself thus
disarmed, suddenly recollected his spirits, and using short
discourse within himself, resolved, as being his best, to run
to his father's house to call for assistance to bring off in
safety his kinsman and his other friend, whose false sword
served him in the same manner as Leodivius's had done,
as though they had conspired to betray their masters in
their greatest need. Here one might see differing effects
from like causes, for a like resolute valour without as-
tonishment that caused Leodivius to run discreetly away

for succour, caused him to stand still in the place where his sword broke, defending his enemies' blows with the piece that remained in his hand, as being ashamed to leave Theagenes in the midst of so many that strived to take his life from him: but he was soon out of danger by all their pressing beyond him, whom they saw disarmed, to come to Theagenes, who had interposed himself between Leodivius and them that followed him, of which the master of all these bravos was one, so that the rest seeing him engaged in a fierce battle, they all came to assist him. Theagenes then found himself in great perplexity, for having retired to a narrow place of the street, that he might keep his assailants all in front before him, the overhanging pentises took away the light of the moon, and his enemies having at the top of their bucklers artificial lanterns whose light was cast only forwards by their being made with an iron plate on that side towards the holders, so that their bodies remained in darkness, had not only the advantage of seeing him when he could not see them, but also dazzled and offended his eyes with the many near lights, which made him mistake those objects that dimly he discerned. The number of his enemies, and the disparity of the weapons, might have given him just cause to seek the saving of his life rather by the swiftness of his legs than by an obstinate defence; but he, that did not value it at so high a rate as to think that it could warrant such an action, resolved rather to die in the midst of his enemies, than to do anything that might be interpreted to proceed from fear: with which resolution he made good the place he stood in, and whensoever any of them were too bold in coming near him, he entertained them with such rude welcomes, that they had little encouragement to make a second return.

After Theagenes had remained some time thus beating down their swords and wounding many of them, and showing wonderful effects of a settled and not transported valour,

and that their beginning to slack their fury in pressing upon
him gave a little freedom to his thoughts, all his spirits being
before united in his heart and hands, he considered how it
must certainly be some mistake that made him to be thus
treated by men that he knew not, and to whom he was sure
he in his particular could have given no offence, being but
that day arrived at Alexandria from very remote parts;
wherefore he spoke to them in the best manner he could, to
make himself understood in a tongue that he was not well
master of, and asked what moved them to use him so dis-
courteously that was a stranger there, and was not guilty of
having injured any of them ; to which words of his, one that
seemed to be of the best quality among them, by a cassock
embroidered with gold which he wore over his jack of mail,
answered him with much fury in this manner: Villain,
thou liest, thou hast done me wrong which cannot be satisfied
with less than thy life ; and by thy example let the rest of
thy lascivious countrymen learn to shun those gentlewomen
where other men have interest, as they would do houses
infected with the plague, or the thunder that executeth
God's vengeance.'   These words put all patience out of
Theagenes's breast, so that now he dispensed his blows
rather with fury than art ; but his hand was so exercised
in the perfectest rules of true art, that without his endeavours or taking notice, it never failed of making exactly
regulated motions, which had such force imparted to them
by a just anger, that few of them were made in vain.

But at length his enemies, that had bought with much
of their blood the knowledge of his power and strength,
attempted to do that behind him, which they durst not to his
face ; for some of them running down a little lane that was
near the place where they fought, made a circuit and came to
assault Theagenes behind, which he perceived by a blow upon
his shoulders : but it seemed that the fearful giver of it was
so apprehensive lest Theagenes should turn about, that his

Digby
1629

quaking hand laid it on so softly that it did him no hurt, but served to warn him of the danger he was in. He then perceiving himself thus beset on every side, summoned all his spirits to serve him at this his so great necessity, and choosing to cut his way through the thickest of them, that so it might appear that he wrought his own liberty in despite of their strongest oppositions, did make a quick thrust at him that was nearest before him, which entering within his weapons before he was aware that he had occasion to ward it, Theagenes accompanied it with the whole weight of his body, running on so violently, as the other's jack not giving way, and his sword not yielding, he bore him down, and running over him made him serve for a bridge to cross the kennel. He being thus acquit of their beseiging him, began to retire himself with a settled pace towards the Ambassador's house, but in such a manner, that though his feet carried him one way his face looked another, and his hands sent forwards many bloody messages of his angry spirit ; but one of them pressed so eagerly and unwarily upon him, that as he lifted up his sword to make a blow at Theagenes, he avoided it with a gentle motion of his body, and gave him such a strong reverse upon the head, that finding it disarmed, for he had lost his iron cap with much stirring in the scuffle, it divided it in two parts, and his brains flew into his neighbour's face ; upon whom Theagenes turned, having thus rid himself of his fiercest enemy, and stepping in with his left leg, made himself master of his sword, and with his own did run him into the belly under his jack, so that he fell down, witnessing with a deep groan that his life was at her last minute. The other Egyptians by that knew him to be their master, for whose quarrel only they all fought, so that they left Theagenes, and all of them attended to succour their wounded lord ; but all too late, for without ever speaking, he gave up his ghost in their arms ; while by this means Theagenes, who received but little hurt, had time to walk leisurely to the Ambassador's house, from whence, upon the alarm that Leodivius gave, many were coming to his rescue with such arms as, hastily, they could recover; the cause of whose coming so late, for he met them half way, was, that it was long before Leodivius, though he knocked and called aloud, could get the gates open; for all in the house were gone to take their rest.

Digby
1629

Sir Kenelm Digby.

THREE CHARACTERS

I

A MISTRESS

IS the fairest treasure the avarice of Love can covet; and the only white at which he shoots his arrows, nor while his aim is noble can he ever hit upon repentance. She is chaste, for the devil enters the Idol and gives the Oracle, when wantonness possesseth beauty and wit maintains it lawful. She is as fair as Nature intended her, helped perhaps to a more pleasing grace by the sweetness of education, not by the sleight of Art. She is young, for a woman past the delicacy of her spring may well move by virtue to respect, never by beauty to affection. She is innocent even from the knowledge of sin, for vice is too strong to be wrestled with, and gives her frailty the foil. She is not proud, though the amorous youth interpret her modesty to that fence ; but in her virtue wears so much Majesty lust dares not rebel, nor though masqued, under the pretence of love, capitulate with her. She entertains not every parley offered, although the Articles pretended to her advantage ; advice and her own fears restrain her, and woman never owed ruin to too much caution. She glories not in the plurality of servants, a multitude of adorers heaven can only challenge, and it is impiety in her weakness to desire superstition from many. She is deaf to the whispers of love, and even on the marriage

Habing-
ton
1635

hour can break off, without the least suspicion of scandal, to
the former liberty of her carriage. She avoids a too near
conversation with man, and, like the Parthian, overcomes by
flight. Her language is not copious but apposite, and she
had rather suffer the reproach of being dull company, than
have the title of Witty with that of Bold and Wanton. In
her carriage she is sober, and thinks her youth expresseth
life enough without the giddy motion, fashion of late hath
taken up. She danceth to the best applause but doats not
on the vanity of it, nor licenseth an irregular meeting to
vaunt the levity of her skill. She sings, but not perpetually,
for she knows, silence in woman is the most persuading
oratory. She never arrived to so much familiarity with man
as to know the diminutive of his name, and call him by it;
and she can show a competent favour: without yielding her
hand to his grip. She never understood the language of a
kiss, but at salutation, nor dares the Courtier use so much of
his practised impudence as to offer the rape of it from her:
because chastity hath writ it unlawful, and her behaviour
proclaims it unwelcome. She is never sad, and yet not
jiggish; her conscience is clear from guilt, and that secures
her from sorrow. She is not passionately in love with poetry,
because it softens the heart too much to love; but she likes
the harmony in the Composition; and the brave examples of
virtue celebrated by it she proposeth to her imitation.
She is not vain in the history of her gay kindred or acquaintance; since virtue is often tenant to a cottage, and familiarity
with greatness (if worth be not transcendant above the title)
is but a glorious servitude, fools only are willing to suffer.
She is not ambitious to be praised, and yet values death
beneath infamy. And I'll conclude (though the next synod
of Ladies condemn this character as an heresy brought
by a Precisian) that only she who hath as great a share in
virtue as in beauty, deserves a noble love to serve her, and a
free Poesic to speak her.

II

A WIFE

Is the sweetest part in the harmony of our being. To the love of which, as the charms of Nature inchant us, so the law of grace by special privilege invites us. Without her, Man, if piety not restrain him, is the creator of sin; or, if an innated cold render him not only the business of the present age, the murderer of posterity. She is so religious that every day crowns her a martyr, and her zeal neither rebellious nor uncivil. She is so true a friend, her Husband may to her communicate even his ambitions, and if success crown not expectation, remain nevertheless uncondemned. She is colleague with him in the Empire of prosperity; and a safe retiring place when adversity exiles him from the World. She is so chaste, she never understood the language lust speaks in, nor with a smile applauds it, although there appear wit in the Metaphore. She is fair only to win on his affections, nor would she be Mistress of the most eloquent beauty, if there were danger, that might persuade the passionate auditory to the least irregular thought. She is noble by a long descent, but her memory is so evil a herald, she never boasts the story of her Ancestors. She is so moderately rich, that the defect of portion doth neither bring penury to his estate, nor the superfluity license her to Riot. She is liberal, and yet owes not ruin to vanity, but knows Charity to be the soul of goodness, and Virtue without reward often prone to be her own destroyer. She is much at home, and when she visits 'tis for mutual commerce, not for intelligence. She can go to Court and return no passionate doater on bravery; and when she hath seen the gay things muster up themselves there she considers them as Cobwebs the Spider vanity hath spun. She is so general in her acquaintance, that she is familiar with all whom fame speaks virtuous; but thinks there can be no friendship but with one; and there-

Habing-
ton
1635

fore had she neither friend nor private servant. She so squares her passion to her Husband's fortunes, that in the Country she lives without a froward Melancholy, in the Town without a fantastic Pride. She is so temperate she never read the modern policy of glorious forfeits; since she finds Nature is no Epicure if Art provoke her not by curiosity. She is inquisitive only of new ways to please him, and her wit sails by no other compass than that of his direction. She looks upon him as Conjurors upon the Circle, beyond which there is nothing but Death and Hell; and in him she believes paradise circumscrib'd. His virtues are her wonder and imitation; and his errors, her credulity thinks no more fraility than makes him descend to the title of Man. In a word, she so lives that she may die; and leave no cloud upon her Memory, but have her character nobly mentioned: while the bad Wife is flattered into infamy, and buys pleasure at too dear a rate if she only pays for it Repentance.

III

A FRIEND

Is a man. For the free and open discovery of thoughts to woman cannot pass without an over licentious familiarity, or a justly occasioned suspicion; and friendship can neither stand with vice or infamy. He is virtuous, for Love begot in sin is a mishapen monster, and seldom outlives his birth. He is noble, and inherits the virtues of all his progenitors; though happily unskilful to blazon his paternal coat; so little should nobility serve for story, but when it encourageth to action. He is so valiant, Fear could never be listened to when she whispered danger; and yet fights not unless religion confirms the quarrel lawful. He submits his actions to the government of virtue, not to the wild decrees of popular opinion; and when his conscience is fully satisfied, he cares not how mistake and ignorance interpret him. He

hath so much fortitude he can forgive an injury; and when
he hath overthrown his opposer, not insult upon his weakness.   He is an absolute governor, no destroyer, of his
passions, which he employs to the noble increase of virtue.
He is wise, for who hopes to reap a harvest from the sands
may expect the perfect offices of friendship from a fool.
He hath by a liberal education been softened to civility; for
that rugged honesty some rude men possess, is an undigested
Chaos; which may contain the seeds of goodness, but it
wants form and order.

Habing-
ton
1635

He is no flatterer; but when he finds his friend any way
imperfect, he freely but gently informs him; nor yet shall
some few errors cancel the bond of friendship; because he
remembers no endeavours can raise man above his frailty.
He is as slow to enter into that title, as he is to forsake it;
a monstrous vice must disobliege, because an extraordinary
virtue did first unite; and when he parts, he doth it without
a duel.   He is neither effeminate, nor a common courtier;
the first is so passionate a doater upon himself, he cannot
spare love enough to be justly named friendship: the latter
hath his love so diffusive among the beauties, that man is
not considerable.   He is not accustomed to any sordid way
of gain, for who is any way mechanick will sell his friend
upon more profitable terms.   He is bountiful, and thinks no
treasure of fortune equal to the preservation of him he loves;
yet not so lavish as to buy friendship and perhaps afterward
find himself overseen in the purchase.   He is not exceptious,
for jealousy proceeds from weakness, and his virtues quit
him from suspicions.   He freely gives advice, but so little
peremptory is his opinion that he ingeniously submits it to
an abler judgment.   He is open in expression of his thoughts
and easeth his melancholy by enlarging it; and no Sanctuary
preserves so safely, as he his friend afflicted.   He makes use
of no engines of his friendship to extort a secret; but if
committed to his charge his heart receives it, and that and

it come both to light together. In life he is the most amiable object to the soul, in death the most deplorable.

William Habington.

A BOUT WITH THE ADVERSARY

HAVING declared how gracious the Lord hath been toward me, and that people he sent me to, I shall next show how the murderer Satan, visibly appearing to a wicked man, stirred him up to stab me, and how mercifully I was delivered therefrom. I was spending a day in family humiliation, and was come to the mid-day, when one comes to the gate and knocks. Now I had given order beforehand that if any knocked at the gate that day, none should open but myself. When I opened, I saw two men standing without; the one whereof (being a rich man) was chief constable of that paroch, the other was a tenant of his. Their errand was to shew me that the tenant had a bairn to be baptized (for I baptized none till first I conferred with the father, and exhorted and instructed him as need required). When I had spoken what I thought necessary, and was ready to turn into my house, the constable, dismissing the other, told me he had something to say to me in private. I looking upon him, saw his eyes like the eyes of a cat in the night, did presently conceive that he had a mischief in his heart; yet I resolved not to refuse what he desired, but I keeped a watchful eye upon him, and stayed at some distance; and being near to the door of the church, I went in and invited him to follow me. As soon as he entered within the doors, he fell a trembling, and I a wondering. His trembling continuing and growing without any speech, I approached to him and invited him to a seat, wherein he could hardly sit. The great trembling was like to throw him out of the seat; I laid my arm about him, and asked him what ailed him; but for a time he could speak none.

At last his shaking ceased, and he began to speak, telling me that for a long time the Devil had appeared to him : first, at Glasgow he bought a horse from him, receiving a sixpence in earnest, and that in the end he offered to him a great purse full of silver to be his, making no mention of the horse ; he said that he blessed himself, and so the buyer with the silver and gold that was poured out upon the table vanished. But some days thereafter he appeared to him at his own house, naming him by his name, and said to him, 'Ye are mine, for I arled [1] you with a sixpence, which yet ye have.' Then said he, 'I asked his name, and he answered, "They call me Nickel Downus"' (I supposed that he repeated evil, that he should have said Nihil Damus). Being thus molested with these and many other apparitions of the Devil, he said he left Scotland ; but being come to Ireland, he did often likewise appear to him : 'And now of late he still commands me to kill and slay ; and often,' says he, 'my whinger hath been drawn and kept under my cloak to obey his commands, but still something holds my hand that I cannot strike.' But then I asked him whom he was bidden kill ? He answered : 'Any that comes in my way ; but

> " The better they be,
> The better service to me,
> Or else I shall kill thee."'

When he uttered these words, he fell again a trembling, and was stopped in his speaking, looking lamentably at me, designing me to be the person he aimed at ; then he fell a crying and lamenting.

I showed him the horribleness of his ignorance and drunkenness ; he made many promises of reformation, which were not well keeped ; for within a fortnight he went to an ale-house to crave the price of his malt, and, sitting there long at drink, as he was going homeward, the Devil appeared to him, and challenged him for opening to me

[1] Hanselled.

what had passed betwixt them secretly, and followed him to the house, pulling his cap off his head and his band from about his neck, saying to him: 'On Hallow-night I shall have thee, soul and body, in despite of the minister and of all that will do for thee.' The man being exceedingly terrified, sent presently for me, and told me, as is here formerly set down, being driven to his bed by this terror. When I came, his wife told me with what amazement he entered the house bare-headed, and his band rent, saying he had hardly escaped. He entreated me, for Christ's sake, to be with him that night wherein Satan had threatened to carry him away. I instructed him the best I could, and praying with him, promised to be with him that night, providing he would fly to Christ for refuge, and not to me, who was but a weak and wretched creature. I intended to have spent the day before that night wherein I was to be with him, as I had done that day when he first came to me, and thought to have killed me; but when the day came I had no mind of my resolution till it was near night, and being in great doubt what to do, I went to my chamber in great heaviness. I durst not break or slight my promise, and how durst I go, being so unprepared for so pitched a conflict?

Being thus humbled before the Lord, I was encouraged to go, trusting to His gracious goodness, who is the preserver of men against the wiles and violences of Satan; and so coming about daylight going, I called to one man of that village who was under the reputation of a godly man, and an elder of the congregation. To him I imparted the whole matter, desiring him to convene the people of that village, and tell them no more but that I would stay that night in the house of the sick man with them. I began with prayer, and thereafter expounded the doctrine of Christ's tentations, closing with a prayer, and singing of a psalm; and after that did the like on another passage of Scripture; and after that another, still intermixing prayer and singing, till toward the morning.

All this time my chair being close by the sick man's bedside, Blair
when I uttered anything which he did not understand, with 1636
his hand he laid hold on my arm, requesting me to say that
better. I hearkened to him, and laboured to do so. In the
morning he took great courage to himself, defying Satan and
all his works.

Thereafter he recovered, behaving himself better, and was
charitable to the poor; but I was never satisfied with him,
he continuing still ignorant. In the end he sickened, and
therein seemed very penitent. The last time I saw him, I
asked at him : whether Satan had ever appeared to him after
that night wherein I continued with him ? He answered,
'Never,' taking the Lord witness thereof; and shortly
thereafter died.

Rev. Robert Blair.

A STRATAGEM

HIS Majesty being earnestly importuned by his Scottish Monson
subjects to have the assistance of some of his ships 1636
to redress the spoils committed by the pirates on their coast,
out of care to them, and honour to himself, he dispatched
Sir William Monson and Sir Francis Howard in great haste
upon that service, commanding such victuals and other things
as they stood in need of to be sent after them.

They departed from Margate Road the 14th May, and
arrived at Leith in Scotland on the 23d of the same ; thence
he immediately went to Edinburgh, and presented himself
to the Lords of that Realm, acquainting them with the cause
of his coming, and the charge he had from his Majesty to
defend that coast from pirates ; and therefore desired to be
informed by their Lordships concerning their strength, their
number, and their place of abode. He desired to be furnished
with able pilots; for his Majesty's ships were of greater
burden and value than usually had been employed on those

Monson
1636

coasts; and besides, that the navigation to the northward of that place was not frequented by our nation, and therefore unknown to us. It pleased their Lordships to recommend the care thereof to the Trinity House of Leith, expressly commanding them to appoint the ablest pilots that could be chosen amongst them. This command of theirs was accordingly obeyed, and their pilots repaired aboard the next morning. Sir William immediately set sail, leaving instructions for his victuals to follow him to the Island of Orkney; which the Lords of Scotland took into their provident care, and performed it accordingly.

The first of June Sir William arrived at Sinclair Castle, the house of the Earl of Caithness, the utmost promontory of Great Britain. Here he found neither the number nor the danger of pirates so terrible as report made them; from twenty they were vanished to two, and both of them men of base condition; the one of them not long before my boatswain's mate in the narrow seas; the other of as mean quality and rank, and first made a seaman by Sir William. Neither can this man be properly called a pirate; for being amongst them, and misliking their damnable courses, he, with three others, left their society, and in an English barque they had taken, stole from them, and put himself into the hands of the Earl of Caithness, where I found both him and the bark, which I brought away with me. The day before I came to Caithness I was disappointed of meeting the boatswain's mate, the pirate, Clarke by name, who had been ashore with the Earl and friendly entertained, because his house and tenants lay open to his spoil. That day there arrived a Scottish barque from the Frith, which gave an account of Sir William's coming to Leith with an intent to pursue such pirates as he could hear of. This news made Clarke quit that coast and fly into the island, where he refreshed himself amongst the fishermen.

But Sir William being now out of hope of him, and out of

doubt of any others thereabout, stayed not at Caithness, but Monson
the same night passed to the Island of Orkney, where he 1636
found more civil, kind, and friendly usage, than could be
expected from such kind of creatures in show.   Here he left
Sir Francis Howard for guard of the coast and prosecuted
his intention against Clarke, not sparing any place to seek
him in where there was a possibility to find him.   After
some time spent at sea, he put into the Island of Shetland,
and from thence to those of Hebrides, where he designed
Sir Francis Howard should meet him.   The brutishness and
uncivility of those people of the Hebrides exceeds the savages
of America ; and it may be well said of them that education
is a second nature ; for there cannot be greater difference
betwixt day and night than betwixt the conversation of
those of Orkney and those of the Hebrides.

Being out of hopes of meeting with Clarke, Sir William
directed his course for Broad Haven in Ireland, a harbour
frequented by pirates, in respect of the security thereof, and
the remoteness, few knowing it, and the relief such people
find by a gentleman there dwelling, who spared not his own
daughters to bid them welcome.   The danger Sir William
ran into was great, and worse to think, that two ships of His
Majesty's of that consequence should be hazarded on so
slender an occasion, as the pursuit of so few petit[1] pirates.
Betwixt those islands and Ireland he met with so great a
storm and ground-seas, that it were fit only for a poet to
describe.   Of four vessels he had in company, one was
swallowed up in the seas ; the other three were separated,
and saw one another no more till they met in England.
When the seas had spent their fury the storm began to
abate, and the 28th he arrived at Broad Haven, a place
unknown to any one in his ship but the pirate he had taken
from the Earl of Caithness, as you have heard, of whom he
made use to execute this stratagem.

<hr>

[1] Petty.

Being now come to the well-head of all pirates, and desirous to be fully informed of the condition of those people of Broad Haven, as soon as he came to an anchor he made choice of such persons of his company as formerly had been pirates, to give the less suspicion of his purpose. These men he sent in his boat to the gentlemen of that place, and took upon him to be a pirate, and the name of Captain Manwaring. The man he trusted in this service extolled the wealth he had on board him; his royal disposition and liberality to those that showed him courtesy. This hope of wealth and reward set their hearts on fire. He used the commendations and names of sundry pirates, their acquaintance; and feigned messages to the women from their sweethearts, who he made believe had sent them tokens, which he had on board for them. The silly women conceived so great a joy at it, that it took away all suspicion of deceit. The gentleman of that place, like a wily fox, absented himself, and left his wife and hackney daughters to entertain the new welcome guests, till he beheld the coast clear. And when he saw his time, he returned; and to make his credit and reputation seem the greater with Captain Manwaring, expressed the favours he had done to sundry pirates, though it was to his eminent peril, which he did not esteem, if he might do Captain Manwaring any service. So much he was devoted to his person when he heard the report of his wealth; and to endear him the more he promised to send two gentlemen of trust the next morning on board him, to give him the better assurance of his fidelity; and in the meantime, because he should not be unfurnished of victuals, he directed him to send his men ashore armed, and in a warlike manner, that it might appear their cattle were taken by violence, which he would appoint in a place with their ears slit, to be distinguished from other beasts.

The messenger being fully satisfied, and having executed

his stratagem, returned aboard that night. At the dawning of the day the play began, for that was the hour appointed for the wolf to seek his prey; and Captain Chester, with fifty armed men, in a disorderly manner, like pirates, went on shore, and acted so much as was agreed on; and the cattle being killed, he was, in a secret manner, invited to the house of the gentleman; but at his entreaty was to make it appear publicly that he came not by invitation, but of his own accord. Here he was welcomed and friendly entertained by the daughters, whose desire was to hear of their sweethearts and to receive their tokens; but all in general coveted to see Captain Manwaring, who they confidently believed would enrich them all. The gentleman, Mr. Cormack by name, was punctual in all his undertaking, and the two ambassadors he promised came aboard and delivered a friendly (though in a rude manner, like their country) message of their love, and assurance of their service to Captain Manwaring. Their message ended, Sir William wished them to observe and consider whether they thought that ship and company to be pirates? for they could well judge of pirates because of their familiarity and acquaintance with them? It was a folly to dissemble any longer; for though they would, yet they could not betray Sir William's design; and therefore in as rough and rude a manner as they delivered their message, he told them how they had transgressed, and the next thing they were to expect was death; and commanded them to be put in irons, in dark and several places, being careful to permit neither boat nor man to go ashore until his own landing.

The time approached Sir William promised to visit them; and for his greater honour they had drawn down four or five hundred people to attend on the shore side: which he perceiving, and seeming to be jealous of their number, pretended to be shy of going ashore, for fear of treachery. But if oaths, vows, or any kind of protestations would serve him

Monson
1636
he had them; and when they saw him thus convinced of their sincerity, and that he put himself upon them, three of their principal men run up to the arm-pits in water, striving who should have the credit to carry him ashore. One of these three was an Englishman, a late tradesman in London, and attended the arrival of pirates. The second had been a schoolmaster, and a man attended like another Apollo amongst these rude people. The third a merchant of Galloway, but his chiefest trade was to buy and sell with pirates. These three gallants, like gentleman-ushers, conducted Sir William to Mr. Cormack's house, and the meaner sort followed with acclamations of joy. At his landing happy was he to whom he would lend his ear. Falling into discourse, one told him they knew his friends, and though his name had not discovered it, yet his face did shew him to be a Manwaring. In short, they made him believe he might command them and their country, and that no man was ever so welcome as Captain Manwaring.

Entering into the house of Mr. Cormack, his three hackney daughters rose to entertain him, and conducted him to the hall newly strewed with rushes, as the richest decking their abilities or the meanness of the place could afford. In the corner was a harper, who played merrily, to make his welcome the greater. After some discourse, and several questions asked by the three daughters concerning their acquaintance and friends; but above all, being desirous to handle the tokens promised, and laughing and jeering at their two messengers aboard, who they did not suspect were detained prisoners, but drinking and frolicking in the ship, as the use was upon the arrival of pirates. After these passages the women offered to dance, one chose Sir William, which he excused, but gave free liberty for the rest of his company. The Englishman was so pleasant and merry that he seemed to have new life infused into him: he told Sir William the

heavens did foresee he was born to serve him and to relieve
him; he shewed him a pass, procured upon false pretences
from the Sheriff of that county, authorising him to travel
from place to place to make inquisition of his goods, which
he falsely pretended he was robbed of at sea; he laughed at
the cheat he had put upon the Sheriff in getting his pass,
and urged the advantage that might be made of it in sending to and fro in the country without suspicion. He
proffered Sir William the service of ten mariners of his
acquaintance, that lay lurking thereabouts, expecting the
coming in of men-of-war, which sea-faring men he had
power to command. His antic behaviour was enough to
to put the melancholiest man in good humour; sometimes
he played the part of a commanding Sheriff; then he acted
his own, with many witty passages how he deceived the
Sheriff. Sir William embraced his offer of ten mariners, with
a promise of reward, and caused him to write effectually for
them, as may appear by this that follows :—

' Honest brother Dick, and the rest, we are all made men;
for valiant Captain Manwaring, and all his gallant crew are
arrived in this place. Make haste; for he flourisheth in
wealth, and is most kind to all men. Farewell; and once
again make haste.'

This letter being writ and the pass enclosed in it, Sir
William took it into his own hand, offering to hire a messenger to carry it; but night drawing on, which required his
return on board, and having drawn from the country all the
secret he desired, he caused the harp to cease playing and
commanded silence, because he was to speak. He told
them that hitherto they had played their part, and he had
no part in the comedy ; but though his was last, and might
be termed the epilogue, yet it would prove more tragical

Monson
1636

than theirs. He put them out of doubt that he was no pirate, but a scourge to such, and was sent from His Majesty to discover, suppress, and punish them and their abettors, whom His Majesty did not think worthy the name of subjects; he told them that he had received sufficient information of the protection given to pirates in that harbour, and by Cormack; and that he could find no better expedient to confirm what had been told him, than by taking upon him the habit of a pirate, and one of their associates; and that they had made themselves guilty in the law, without further accusations: and now there remained nothing but to proceed to their execution, by virtue of his commission; and to that purpose, he had brought a gallows ready framed, which he caused to be set up, meaning to begin the mournful dance with the two men they thought had been merry dancing aboard the ship. He told the Englishman, he should be the next, because his offence did surpass the rest, being an Englishman, who should be a pattern of good life to those people we have sought to reduce to civility, since we first possessed that country; and seeing man naturally is rather up to follow evil example than good, he should be hanged for example. He told the schoolmaster he was a fit tutor for the children of the devil, and that he had apt scholars to follow his damnable instructions; and that as the members are governed by the head, the way to make his members sound was to shorten him by the head, and therefore willed him to admonish his scholars from the top of the gallows, which should be a pulpit prepared for him. He asked the merchant, whether he imagined there could be thieves if there were no receivers? And as the contriver and plotter of evil is worse than he that executes it, so is the abettor and a receiver to be condemned before the thief. He told him that pirates could no more live by their occupation were it not for buyers, than a poor labourer work without wages; that the offence in a merchant was more heinous than in another man, because his trade must be Monson
1636 maintained and upheld by peace; his time he told him was not long, and wished him to make his account with God, that he might be found a good merchant and factor to him though he had been a malefactor to the law.

Here was seen the mutability of the world; their mirth was turned into mourning, and their dancing into lamenting, each bewailing and repenting, as is the custom of offenders. The night calling Sir William away he appointed their guard to a boat, and left the carpenter ashore to finish the gallows, which was done by morning, and the prisoners ready to receive their doom; but being sued to by the whole country, with a promise never to connive again at pirates, after four and twenty hours fright in irons, he pardoned them. The Englishman was banished, not only from the coast, but from the sea-side throughout Ireland; and a copy of his pass sent to the Sheriff, with advice to be more cautious for the future in granting his safe conduct.

Sir William Monson.

A COVENANTING ARMY

OUR ready obedience being perceived, behold our un- Baillie
1639 happy party makes a new onset. They persuade the King to proclaim, in our borders, towards the former pro- clamation of our treason, and the offer of pardon, and their master's lands, to these who would desert us. This was done at Duns with a strong convoy of English horse. The like was intended at Kelso; but there Monro, Fleming, and Erskine, presenting themselves in battle array, did make Holland, with some thousand foot and horse, with their show alone, to retire in haste in a shameful disorder. It is thought Holland's commission was to cut off all he met in opposition

Baillie to him; but his soldiers that day were a great deal more
1639 nimble in their legs nor arms, except their cavaliers, whose
right arms were no less weary in whipping, than their heels
in jadding[1] their horses. We are informed that to repair
that disgrace Holland was commanded to return with far
more forces to execute his former commission: whereupon
our General raises his camp from Dunglass, advertises his
troops at Kelso to march towards him; both of them that
night meet together at Duns, and there they set down on
the head of that fair Law.[2] We found that advantage was
made of our obedience, and a course yet again, without
respect to promises, to be taken for our wreck. So we
returned to our former resolution of present fighting, and
sent posts athort all the country to haste on our friends for
that end. . . .

This our march did much affray the English camp; Duns
Law was in their sight within six or seven miles, for they lay
in pavilions some two miles above Berwick, on the other side
of Tweed, in a fair plain along the river. The King
himself, beholding us through a prospect,[3] did conjecture us
to be sixteen or eighteen thousand men; we were indeed
above twelve thousand; but at once we were above
twenty. We might have doubled that number, but we had
none there from the one full half of Scotland; not a
man beyond Tay; few from Lothian, Fife, Edinburgh,
March, for they were waiting on the ships, or employed in
carriages; the South behoved to observe the Border about
Carlisle; and the West the Irish shore: albeit that was
needless, for all that were either in the ships, or on the
South border, or might be spared from Ireland, were called
quickly to the royal standard; and when all were together,
their number was thought did not exceed in horse and foot,
English, Scots, Irish, sixteen thousand men, and these not of
the stoutest; for it was constantly reported that one night a

---

[1] Goading.   [2] Hill.   [3] Glass.

false alarm being in our camp, when our drums began to beat
and our matches on the hill to shine through the darkness,
there arose such a fray[1] in the English camp that very
many did betake them to their heels, expecting from us a
present invasion; yea, had not our wise and valorous Prince,
with his General Arundel, done diligence to encourage, and
to find out the groundless vanity of the fray, there had been
a greater flight than with honour could have been gotten
stayed.

It would have done you good to have cast your eyes athort
our brave and rich Hill, as oft as I did, with great contentment and joy, for I (quoth the wren) was there among the
rest, being chosen preacher by the gentlemen of our shire,
who came late with my Lord of Eglinton. I furnished to
half a dozen of good fellows muskets and pikes, and to my
boy, a broadsword. I carried myself, as the fashion was, a
sword, and a couple of Dutch pistols at my saddle; but I
promise, for the offence of no man, except a robber in the
way; for it was our part alone to pray and preach for the
encouragement of our countrymen, which I did to my power
most cheerfully. Our Hill was garnished on the top towards
the south and east with our mounted cannon, well near to
the number of forty, great and small. Our regiments lay on
the sides of the hill, almost round about: the place was not
a mile in circle, a pretty round rising in a declivity, without
steepness, to the height of a bowshot; on the top somewhat
plain; about a quarter of mile in length, and as much in
breadth, as I remember, capable of tents for forty thousand
men. The Crowners[2] lay in canvas lodges, high and wide;
their Captains about them in lesser ones; the soldiers about
all in huts of timber covered with divott or straw. Our
Crowners for the most part were noblemen: Rothes,
Lindsay, Sinclair, had among them two full regiments at
least from Fife; Balcarras, a horse troop; Loudoun, Mont-

[1] Panic.   [2] Commandants of Counties: here used for Colonels.

gomerie, Erskine, Boyd, Fleming, Kirkcudbright, Yester, Dalhousie, Eglinton, Cassillis, and others, either with whole or half regiments. Montrose's regiment was above fifteen hundred men in the Castle of Edinburgh: himself was expected. . . . Argyll was sent for to the treaty of peace; for without him none would mint[1] to treat: he came and set up his tent on the Hill, but few of his people with him. It was thought meet that he and his should lie about Stirling, in the heart of the country, to be always ready in subsidies for unexpected accidents; to be a terror to our neutralists, or but masked friends; to make all, without din, march forward, lest his uncanny trewsmen[2] should light on to call them up in their rear; always to have an eye what either the North, or the ships, or the West, or our staill[3] host should mister[4] of help. It was thought the country of England was more afraid for the barbariety of his Highlanders than of any other terror: those of the English that came to visit our camp did gaze much with admiration upon those souple fellows, with their plaids, targes, and dorlachs.[5] There were some companies of them under Captain Buchanan, and others in Erskine's regiment. Our Captains [were], for the most part, barons or gentlemen of good note; our Lieutenants, almost all soldiers who had served over sea in good charges; every company had, flying at the Captain's tent door, a brave new colour, stamped with the Scottish Arms, and this ditton, FOR CHRIST'S CROWN AND COVENANT, in golden letters. Our General had a brave royal tent; but it was not set up; his constant guard was some hundreds of our lawyers, musketeers, under Durie and Hope's command, all the way standing in good arms, with cocked matches, before his gate, well apparelled. He lay at the foot of the Hill in the Castle, with Baillie, his serjeant-major, or lieutenant-general. That place was destinate for Almond, in whose wisdom and valour

---

[1] Try.   [2] Men in trews.   [3] Campaigning.
        [4] Need.   [5] Daggers: also wallets.

we had but too much confidence; yet in the time of our
most need, the grievousness of his gravel, or the pretence of
it, made him go to France to be cut : always when he came
there it was found that he needed not incision, so he passed
to his charge in Holland where to us he was as dead in all
our dangers.

The councils of war were keeped daily in the Castle; the
ecclesiastic meetings in Rothes's large tent. The General,
with Baillie, came nightly for the setting of the [watch] on
their horses. Our soldiers were all lusty and full of courage;
the most of them stout young ploughmen; great cheerfulness in the face of all : the only difficulty was to get them
dollars or two the man for their voyage from home, and the
time they entered in pay; for among our yeomen, money at
any time, let be then, used to be very scarce ; but once
having entered on the common pay, their sixpence-a-day,
they were galliard. None of our gentlemen was anything
worse of lying some weeks together in their cloak and boots
on the ground, or standing all night in arms in the greatest
storm. Whiles,[1] through storm of weather and neglect of the
commissaries, our bread would be too long in coming, which
made some of the Eastland soldiers half-mutinous ; but at
once order being taken for our victuals from Edinburgh,
East Lothian, and the country about us, we were answered
better than we could have been at home. Our meanest
soldiers were always served in wheat-bread, and a groat
would have gotten them a lamb-leg, which was a dainty world
to the most of them. There had been an extraordinary crop
in that country the former year, beside abundance which
still was stolen away to the English camp for great prices;
we would have feared no inlake[2] for little money in some
months to come. March and Tevidale are the best mixed
and most plentiful shires both for grass and corn, for fleshes
and bread, in all our land. We were much obliged to the

[1] Sometimes.   [2] Necessity.

Baillie
1639

town of Edinburgh for money; Harry Rollock, by his sermons, moved them to shake out their purses; the garners of non-covenanters, especially of James Maxwell and my Lord Winton, gave us plenty of wheat. One of our ordinances was to seize on the rents of non-covenanters, for we thought it but reasonable, fra[1] they sided with those who put our lifes and our lands for ever to seal,[2] for the defence of our church and country, to employ for that cause (wherein their enteresse was as great as ours, if they would be Scottish men) a part of their rent for one year; but for all that, few of them did incur any loss by that our decreit,[3] for the peace prevented the execution.

Our soldiers grew in experience of arms, in courage, in favour daily; every one encouraged another; the sight of the nobles and their beloved pastors daily raised their hearts; the good sermons and prayers, morning and even, under the roof of heaven, to which their drums did call them for bells; the remonstrances very frequent of the goodness of their cause, of their conduct hitherto by a hand clearly divine; also Lesley his skill and fortune made them all so resolute for battle as could be wished. We were afraid that emulation among our nobles might have done harm when they should be met in the fields; but such was the wisdom and authority of that old, little, crooked soldier that all, with an incredible submission, from the beginning to the end, gave over themselves to be guided by him as if he had been Great Solyman. Certainly the obedience of our nobles to that man's advice was as great as their forbears wont to be to their King's commands: yet that was the man's understanding of our Scots humours, that gave out, not only to the nobles, but to very mean gentlemen, his directions in a very homely and simple form, as if they had been but the advices of their neighbour and companion; for, as he rightly observed, a difference would be used in commanding soldiers of fortune

---

[1] Seeing that.   [2] Sale (?)   [3] Sentence.

and of soldier volunteers, of which kind the most part of our camp did stand. He keeped daily in the Castle of Duns an honourable table for the nobles and strangers with himself, for gentleman waiters thereafter, at a long side table. I had the honour, by accident, one day to be his chaplain at table, on his left hand; the fare was as became a General in time of war: not so curious by far as Arundel's to our nobles; but you know that the English sumptuosity, both in war and peace, is despised by all their neighbours. It seems our General's table was on his own charge; for, so far as yet I know, neither he, nor any noble or gentlemen of considerable rent, got anything for their charge. Well I know that Eglinton, our Crowner, entertained all the gentlemen of note that were with him at his own table, all the time of our abode; and his son, Montgomerie, keeped with him very oft the chief officers of his regiments: for this was a voyage wherein we were glad to bestow our lives, let be our estates.

Had you lent your ear in the morning, or especially at even, and heard in the tents the sound of some singing psalms, some praying, and some reading scripture, you would have been refreshed: true, there was swearing, and cursing, and brawling in some quarters, whereat we were grieved; but we hoped, if our camp had been a little settled, to have gotten some way for these misorders; for all of any fashion did regrait, and all did promise to contribute their best endeavours for helping all abuses. For myself, I never found my mind in better temper than it was all that time fra [1] I came from home, till my head was again homeward; for I was as a man who had taken my leave from the world, and was resolved to die in that service without return. I found the favour of God shining upon me, and a sweet, meek, humble, yet strong and vehement spirit leading me all along; but I was no sooner on my way westward, after the conclusion of peace, than my old security returned.

Rev. Principal Baillie.

[1] After.

CAREY'S RAID

CAREY'S RAID

Carey
1639

WHEN I was warden of the East March, I had to do but with the opposite March, which Sir Robert Car had; but here I had to do with the East, Middle, and West Marches of Scotland. I had very good justice with Sir Robert Car, and the Laird of Fenhest, that had charge over the east part of the Middle March; but the west part, which was Liddisdale and the West March, kept me a great while in cumber. The first thing they did was the taking of Hartwesell, and carrying away of prisoners and all their goods. I sent to seek for justice for so great a wrong. The opposite officer sent me word: it was not in his power, for that they were all fugitives, and not answerable to the King's laws. I acquainted the King of Scots with his answer. He signified to me that it was true, and that if I could take my own revenge without hurting his honest subjects, he would be glad of it. I took no long time to resolve what to do, but sent some two hundred horse to the place where the principal outliers lived, and took and brought away all the goods they had. The outlaws themselves were in strongholds, and could no way be got hold of. But one of the chief of them, being of more courage than the rest, got to horse and came pricking after them, crying out and asking: What he was that durst avow that mighty work? One of the company came to him with a spear and ran him through the body, leaving his spear broke in him, of which wound he died. The goods were divided to poor men from whom they were taken before.

This act so irritated the outlaws that they vowed cruel revenge; and that before the next winter was ended they would leave the whole country waste, that there should be none to resist them. His name was Sim of the Cat-hill that was killed (an Armstrong), and it was a Ridley of Hartwesell

that killed him. They presently took a resolution to be revenged on that town. Thither they came, and set many
houses of the town on fire, and took away all their goods ;
and as they were running up and down the streets with
lights in their hands to set more houses on fire, there was
one other of the Ridleys that was in a strong stone house
that made a shot out amongst them, and it was his good hap
to kill an Armstrong, one of the sons of the chiefest outlaw.
The death of this young man wrought so deep an impression
amongst them, as many vows were made, that before the
end of next winter, they would lay the whole Border waste.
This (the murder) was done about the end of May. The
chief of all these outlaws was old Sim of Whittram. He
had five or six sons, as able men as the Borders had. This
old man and his sons had not so few as two hundred at their
commands, that were ever ready to ride with them to all
actions at their beck.

The high parts of the March towards Scotland were put
in a mighty fear, and the chief of them, for themselves and
the rest, petitioned to me, and did assure me, that unless I
did take some course with them by the end of that summer,
there was none of the inhabitants durst, or would, stay in
their dwellings the next winter, but they would fly the
country, and leave their houses and lands to the fury of the
outlaws. Upon this complaint I called the gentlemen of
the country together, and acquainted them with the misery
that the highest parts of the March towards Scotland were
likely to endure, if there were not timely prevention to avoid
it, and desired them to give me their best advice what
course were fit to be taken. They all shewed themselves
willing to give me their best counsels, and most of them
were of opinion, that I was not well advised to refuse the
hundred horse that my Lord Euers had ; and that now my
best way was speedily to acquaint the Queen and Council
with the necessity of having more soldiers, and that there

Carey **could** not be less than a hundred horse sent down for the
1639 defence of the country, besides the forty that I had already
in pay, and that there was nothing but force of soldiers
could keep them in awe: and to let the Council plainly
understand that the March, of themselves, were not able
to subsist, whenever the winter and long nights came in,
unless present cure and remedy were provided for them.

I desired them to advise better of it, and to see if they
could find out any other means to prevent their mischievous
intentions, without putting the Queen or country to any
further charge. They all resolved there was no second means.
Then I told them my intention what I meant to do, which
was: ' That myself, with my two deputies, and the forty horse
that I was allowed, would, with what speed we could, make
ourselves ready to go up to the wastes, and there we would
entrench ourselves, and lie as near as we could to the outlaws; and, if there were any brave spirits among them that
would go with us, they should be very welcome, and fare
and lie as well as myself: and I did not doubt before the
summer ended to do something that should abate the pride
of these outlaws.' Those that were unwilling to hazard
themselves liked not this motion. They said, that in so
doing, I might keep the country in quiet the time I lay
there; but, when the winter approached, I could stay there
no longer, and that was the thieves' time to do all their
mischief. But there were divers young gentlemen that
offered to go with me, some with three, some with four
horses, and to stay with me so long as I would there continue.
I took a list of all those that offered to go with me, and
found that, with myself, my officers, the gentlemen, and our
servants, we should be about two hundred good men and
horse; a competent number, as I thought, for such a service.

The day and place was appointed for our meeting in the
wastes, and, by the help of the foot[1] of Liddisdale and

---

[1] Garrisons.

Risdale, we had soon built a pretty fort, and within it we had all cabins made to lie in, and every one brought beds or mattresses to lie on. There we stayed from the midst of June till almost the end of August. We were between fifty or sixty gentlemen, besides their servants, and my horsemen; so that we were not so few as two hundred horse. We wanted no provision for ourselves nor our horses, for the country people were well paid for anything they brought us; so that we had a good market every day before our fort, to buy what we lacked.

The chief outlaws, at our coming, fled their houses where they dwelt, and betook themselves to a large and great forest (with all their goods), which was called the Tarras. It was of that strength, and so surrounded with bogs and marsh grounds, and thick bushes and shrubs, as they feared not the force nor power of England nor Scotland so long as they were there. They sent me word that I was like the first puff of a haggis, hottest at the first, and bade me stay there as long as the weather would give me leave. They would stay in the Tarras-wood till I was weary of lying in the waste; and when I had had my time, and they no whit the worse, they would play their parts, which should keep me waking the next winter. Those gentleman of the country that came not with me were of the same mind; for they knew (or thought at least) that my force was not sufficient to withstand the fury of the outlaws.

The time I stayed at the fort I was not idle, but cast, by all means I could, how to take them in the great strength they were in. I found a means to send a hundred and fifty horsemen into Scotland (conveyed by a muffled[1] man, not known to any of the company) thirty miles within Scotland; and the business was so carried that none in the country took any alarm at this passage. They were quietly brought to the backside of the Tarras, to Scotland-ward. There they divided

[1] Disguised.

themselves into three parts, and took up three passages which the outlaws made themselves secure of, if from England side they should at any time be put at. They had their scouts on the tops of hills on the English side, to give them warning if at any time any power of men should come to surprise them. The three ambushes were safely laid without being discovered, and, about four o'clock in the morning, there were three hundred horse and a thousand foot that came directly to the place where the scouts lay. They gave the alarm; our men broke down as fast as they could into the wood. The outlaws thought themselves safe, assuring themselves at any time to escape; but they were so strongly set upon on the English side as they were forced to leave their goods and to betake themselves to their passages towards Scotland. There was presently five taken of the principal of them. The rest, seeing themselves, as they thought, betrayed, retired into the thick woods and bogs that our men durst not follow them for fear of losing themselves. The principal of the five that were taken were two of the eldest sons of Sim of Whittram. These five they brought to me to the fort, and a number of goods, both of sheep and kine, which satisfied most part of the country that they had stolen them from.

The five that were taken were of great worth and value amongst them: insomuch, that for their liberty, I should have what conditions I should demand or desire. First, all English prisoners were set at liberty. Then had I themselves, and most part of the gentlemen of the Scottish side so strictly bound in bonds, to enter to me, in fifteen days warning, any offender, that they durst not, for their lives, break any covenant that I made with them; and so, upon these conditions, I set them at liberty, and was never after troubled with these kind of people. Thus God blessed me in bringing this great trouble to so quiet an end. We broke up our fort, and every man retired to his own house.

After God had put an end to this troublesome business I rested in quiet the rest of the summer, and the next winter after; and had leisure, by little and little, to purge the March of inbred thieves : and God so blessed me, that I failed not in any of my undertakings, but did effect what I went for, which did so astonish all the malefactors as they were afraid to offend; so that the March rested very quiet from the invasion of the foreign, and from the petty stealths of the thieves that lived amongst ourselves.

Robert Carey, Earl of Monmouth.

A NIGHT'S ADVENTURES

THE night was somewhat dark and dusky, and the hour eleven, and having gone through two or three streets, and seeing himself all alone, and that he had nobody with whom to talk and converse, Don Juan resolved with himself to return home, and putting it in execution, passing through a street which had a walking place built upon pillars of marble, he might hear from a certain door that some did whist unto him with a soft and low voice.

The darkness of the night, which was made the more by means of that close walk, would not let him guess and conjecture whence that whisting directly came. Whereupon he stood still a while, attentively listening whence it should come; and whilst he was thus busied, he might see a door half-way open itself. He drew near thereunto, and might hear a low voice which spake thus : ' Is it Fabio ? ' Don Juan answered : ' Yes.' ' Then take this ' (replied they within), ' and have a care to have it safely kept, and return hither presently again, for it much importeth us.' Don Juan puts forth his hand and felt a bulk, he knew not what, and, thinking to take it with one of his hands, he found

that he had need to use both, and they had scarce put it
into his hands but they shut the door upon him and left
him.   And he went his way and found himself in the street
with his hands full, but knew not what burthen he bare.
But within a little while after he heard a babe begin to cry,
which it should seem had been but newly born.   Whereat
Don Juan remained amazed and suspensive, not knowing
what he should do, or what course to take in this strange
case.   For to return back to the door, and call there unto
them, he considered with himself that he might run some
danger for the babe's sake, having personated another man
to whom it was intended, and in leaving it there at the door,
the babe might have its life hazarded.   And to carry it
home to his own house, he had not any one there that could
give it the teat and those other helps that were needful,
nor did he know in all the city anybody whither he might
carry it.   But sithence that they had said unto him that he
should see it safe and return again presently, he determined
to carry it to his own house, and to leave it in the power
and custody of a woman that served them, and to return
forthwith to see whether or no they had any further need
of his service, since that he plainly perceived that they had
taken him for another, and that it was a mere mistake in
giving the babe unto him.

In conclusion, without making any further discourses, he
came home with it to his house, whenas Don Antonio was
not there.   He entered into one of the rooms next at hand,
and called his woman-servant unto him, and caused her to
unswathe the babe, and found it to be one of the fairest
creatures that ever they had seen.   The clothes wherein it
was lapt told that it came of rich and noble parents.   When
the woman had unswathed and opened it, they saw that it
was a man child.   Then said Don Juan to his woman: ' We
must needs get one to give this child suck ; but first of all, I
would have you take away these rich mantles, and lay them

aside in some safe place, and to put and wrap it in others
more mean and humble. And without making it known
that I brought it hither, you shall carry it to the house of
some one midwife or other, for such kind of women are
never commonly unprovided of necessary remedy in such
like necessities; you shall take money along with you,
wherewith she may remain satisfied and contented, and you
shall give it such parents as you yourself shall think fit, for
the better covering of the truth of my bringing it hither.'
His woman made answer. all should be done as he had
ordered it.

This business was no sooner put into so good a way, but
that Don Juan with all the haste he could returned to see
whether they would whist once more unto him; but a
little before that he came to the said house where they had
called unto him, he might hear a great clashing of swords,
as if many had been together by the ears slashing one
another. He stood listening a while, but could not hear any
one word pass between them. This hammering of iron was
in the dark, save only that by the light of those sparks
which the stones, wounded by their swords, raised, he had a
glimpse that there were many that had set upon one, and
he was confirmed in this truth by hearing that one say: 'O
traitors, though ye be many and I but a single man, yet
shall not your overmatching me in number make you prevail
in your purpose.' Which Don Juan hearing and seeing,
transported by his valiant heart, at two leaps he made into
the side of him that was assaulted, and taking his sword in
one hand and his buckler which he brought along with him
in the other, he said unto him that defended himself, in the
Italian tongue, that he might not be known to be a Spaniard:
'Fear you nothing, sir, for such succour is now come to you
as shall not fail you till his life fail. Bestir yourself, and set
yourself roundly to them; for traitors, though they be many,
are able to do but little.' To these words replied one of the

Mabbe
1640
adverse part : ' Thou liest in thy throat, for here is no traitor; but for the recovering of a man's lost honour it is lawful to take this or any other advantage whatsoever.'

There passed no more words between them, because the haste which they made to offend and wound their enemies would not give them leave to talk, who were (to Don Juan seeming) some six of them. They did press so hard upon his companion, that at two home-thrusts which they made at him at once full in his breast, they laid him flat on the ground. Don Juan thought that they had killed him, and with strange nimbleness and valour he bestirred him, and set upon them all, whom he made to give ground by the force of a shower which he rained down upon them of blows and thrusts. But all his diligence had not been able for to offend them and defend himself, if good fortune had not offered him her aid, by causing the neighbours thereabouts in that street to open their windows and come forth with lights, and to call out aloud to the Justice. Which they of the contrary part perceiving forsook the street, and turning their backs went their way.

Now, by this time, he that was fallen had got up again, for those stoccados and thrusts that were made at him lighted on a privy coat which he had, that was as hard and impenetrable as if it had been a rock of diamonds. Don Juan in this fray had let fall his hat, and seeking for it, instead of his own, lighted by chance on another, which he clapped on his head without looking whether it were his own or no. His fellow that was fallen came unto him and said : 'Sir, whosoever you be, I confess that I am indebted to you for my life, the which, with all that my estate besides can reach unto, I will spend in your service. Let me intreat you to do me a favour to tell me who you are, and what is your name, to the end that I may know to whom I owe so much, that I may manifest my thankfulness.' Whereunto replied Don Juan : ' I will not (sir), seeing myself now dis-

interested, be discourteous with you. To comply, therefore, Mabbe 1640
with your desire, and to fulfil your pleasure, I shall only tell
that I am a gentleman, a Spaniard, and a student in this
University ; if the knowing of my name may any whit import
you, I shall tell it you. But if, happily, you shall be pleased
in any other thing to make use of my service, I would then
(sir) have you know that my name is Don Juan de Gamboa.'
'You have done me a great favour herein,' replied he that
was fallen. 'But I (Señor Don Juan de Gamboa) will not
tell you who I am, nor my name, because I am willing you
should rather know it from another than myself, and I will
take care that both shall be made known unto you.'   Don
Juan had but a little before asked of him whether or
no he had not received some hurt, because he saw that they
had given him two great stoccados ; whereunto he answered,
that the goodness of his privy coat, next under God, had
defended him, but that yet, notwithstanding, his enemies
had made an end of him, if he had not stuck so close unto
him.

By this time there came towards them a company of
people more in number than those they had before to do
withal ; whereupon Don Juan said : 'If these be those our
enemies, stand (sir) upon your guard, and behave yourself
like yourself.'   'I believe' (replied the other) 'that they are
not enemies, but friends, which make towards us.'   And it
was so indeed ; for they that came were in all eight persons,
who compassed him round that was fallen, and whispered
some few words in his ear, but they were so soft and so
secret, that Don Juan could not hear them.   The party
defended turned presently aside from them to Don Juan,
and said unto him : 'Had not these my friends come in
unto me, I would by no means (Señor Don Juan) have
left you till you had finished this your well-begun work
by setting me in some place of safety.   But now, with
all the indearingness that I can, I shall intreat you that you

Mabbe
1640

will leave me, for it much importeth me that you yield to my request.' Having said this, he put his hand to his head, and found that he was without a hat, and, turning himself to those that came to him, he spake unto them to give him a hat, for his own was in fighting fallen from him. He had scarce spoke the word but that Don Juan put that which he had found upon his head. He that fell felt it with his hand, and, returning it to Don Juan, said unto him: 'That hat is none of mine. As you love me (Don Juan), take it, and carry it away with you as a trophy of this skirmish, and keep it well, for I believe it is known.'

They gave him another hat, and Don Juan, for to comply with that which he had intreated of him, interchanging some other but short compliments, he left him, not knowing who he was, and came home to his own house, without offering to go to that door where they had given him the babe, because he perceived that all the whole street was up, being awakened out of their sleep, and in a kind of tumult and uproar by reason of this quarrel.

James Mabbe (Don Diego Puede-Ser).

TWO FAVOURITES

I

LEICESTER

Naunton
1641

IT will be out of doubt, that my Lord of Leicester was one of the first whom she [Elizabeth] made Master of the Horse. He was the youngest son then living of the Duke of Northumberland, beheaded *primo Mariæ*; and his father was that Dudley which our histories couple with Empson; and both so much infamed for the Caterpillars of the Commonwealth during the reign of Henry the Seventh. He being of a noble extract, was executed the first year of Henry the

Eight: but not thereby [made] so extinct but that he left a Naunton plentiful estate, and such a son, who, as the vulgar speaks 1641 it, could live without the teat. For out of the ashes of his father's infamy he rose to be a Duke, and as high as subjection could permit or sovereignty endure ; and though he could not find out any appellation to assume the Crown in his own person, yet he projected, and very nearly effected it for his son Gilbert, by inter-marriage with the Lady Jane Grey, and so by that way to bring it about into his loins. Observations, which, though they lie behind us, and seem impertinent to the text, yet are they not much extravagant: for they must lead, and show us how the after-passages were brought about with the dependances, and on the hinges of a collateral workmanship.

And truly, it may amaze a well-settled judgment to look back into those times, and to consider how this Duke could attain to such a pitch of greatness; his father dying in ignominy and at the gallows, his estate confiscate, and that for peeling and polling, by the clamour and crucifige of the people. But when we better think upon it, we find that he was given up but as a sacrifice to please the people, not for any offence committed against the person of the King; so that upon the matter he was a martyr of the Prerogative, and the King in honour could do no less than give back to his son the privileges of his blood, with the acquirings of his father's profession : for he was a lawyer, and of the King's Councils at Law, before he became *ex interioribus consiliis*, where, besides the licking of his own fingers, he got the King a mass of riches, and that not with the hazard, but the loss of his fame and life for the King's father's sake. Certain it is that his son was left rich in purse and brain, which are good foundations, and full to ambition ; and it may be supposed, he was on all occasions well heard of the King, as a person of mark and compassion in his eye. But I find not that he did put up for advancement during Henry the Eight's

Naunton
1641

time, although a vast aspirer and provident storer. It seems he thought the King's reign was given to the falling sickness: but espying his time fitting, and the sovereignty in the hands of a pupil Prince, he thought he might as well then put up for it as the best. For having then possession of blood, and a purse, with a head-piece of a vast extent, he soon got honour, and no sooner there, but he began to side it with the best, even with the Protector, and in conclusion got his and his brother's heads; still aspiring, till he expired, in the loss of his own. So that posterity may by reading the father and grandfather make judgment of the son; for we shall find that this Robert (whose original we have now traced, the better to present him) was inheritor of the genius and craft of his father. . . .

We take him now as he was admitted into the Court, and the Queen's favour, where he was not to seek to play his part well, and dexterously. But his play was chiefly at the fore-game; not that he was a learner at the latter, but he loved not the after-wit, for they report (and I think not untruly) that he was seldom behind hand with his gamesters, and that they always went away with the loss. He was a very goodly person, and singular well-featured, and all his youth well-favoured, and of a sweet aspect, but high-fore-headed, which, as I should take it, was of discommenda-tion: but towards his latter end (which, with old men, was but a middle age) he grew high-coloured and red-faced. So that the Queen in this, had much of her father, for (ex-cepting some of her kindred, and some few that had hand-some wits in crooked bodies) she always took personage in the way of her election; for the people hath it to this day in proverb, King Harry loved a man. [He] being thus in her grace, she called to mind the sufferings of his ancestors, both in her father's and sister's reigns, and restored his and his brother's blood, creating Ambrose, the elder, Earl of Warwick, and himself Earl of Leicester, etc. And he was *ex primitiis*,

or of her first choice; for he rested not there, but long en-
joyed her favour: and therewith much that he listed, till
Time and Emulation (the companions of great ones) had resolved on his period, and to cover him at his setting in a
cloud at Cornbury: not by so violent a death, and by the
fatal sentence of judicature, as that of his father and grandfather was, but, as it is suggested, by that poison which he
had prepared for others, wherein they report him a rare
artist. I am not bound to give credit to all vulgar relations,
or to the libels of the times, which are commonly forced, and
falsified suitable to the moods and humours of men in passion
and discontent. But that which leads me to think him no
good man is, amongst others of known truth, that [matter]
of my Lord of Essex death in Ireland, and the marriage of his
Lady yet living: which I forbear to press, in regard that he
is long since dead, and others living whom it may concern.

To take him in the observations of his letters and writings
(which should best set him off), for such as fell into my hands,
I never yet saw a style or phrase more seeming religious,
and fuller of the streams of devotion; and were they not
sincere, I doubt much of his well-being; and I may fear he
was too well seen in the aphorisms and principles of
Nicholas the Florentine, and in the reaches of Caesar Borgia.
Hitherto I have touched him in his courtship; I conclude
him in his lance. He was sent Governor by the Queen to
the United States of Holland; where we read not of his
wonders; for they say that he had more of Mercury than of
Mars; and that his device might have been, without prejudice to the Great Caesar, *Veni, vidi, redii.*

II

RALEIGH

SIR WALTER RAWLEIGH was one, that (it seems) fortune had
picked out of purpose, of whom to make an example,

or to use as her tennis-ball, thereby to shew what she
could do; for she tossed him up of nothing, and to and
fro to greatness, and from thence down to little more
than to that wherein she found him, (a bare gentleman).
Not that he was less, for he was well descended, and of good
alliance, but poor in his beginnings: and for my Lord of
Oxford's jest of him (the Jack, and an upstart), we all know
it savours more of emulation and his humour than of truth;
and it is a certain note of the times, that the Queen in her
choice never took into her favour a mere new man or a
mechanic, as Comines observes of Lewis the Eleventh of
France, who did serve himself with persons of unknown
parents; such as was Oliver the Barber, whom he created Earl
of Dunoyes, and made him *ex secretis consiliis*, and alone in
his favour and familiarity.

His approaches to the University and Inns of Court
were the grounds of his improvement; but they were rather
excursions than sieges or settings down, for he stayed not
long in a place; and being the youngest brother, and the
house diminished in patrimony, he foresaw his own destiny:
that he was first to roll (through want and disability to subsist otherways) before he could come to a repose, and, as the
stone doth by long lying, gather moss. He first exposed
himself to the land service of Ireland, a militia which then
did not yield him food and raiment, (for it was ever very
poor): nor had he patience to stay there, though shortly after
he came thither again under the command of my Lord Grey,
but with his own colours flying in the field, having in his
interim cast a new chance, both in the Low-Countries, and
in a voyage to sea. And if ever man drew virtue out of
necessity, it was he: therewith was he the great example of
industry; and though he might then have taken that of the
Merchant to himself, *Per mare, per terras, currit mercator ad
Indos*, he might also have said, and truly with the Philosopher, *Omnia mea mecum porto*. For it was a long time before

he could brag of more than he carried at his back; and when Naunton
he got on the winning side, it was his commendations, that 1641
he took pains for it, and underwent many various adventures
for his after-perfection, and before he came into the publike
note of the world. And that it may appear how he came
up (*per ardua*) *Per varios casus, per tot discrimina rerum*, not
pulled up by chance, or by any gentle admittance of Fortune,
I will briefly describe his native parts, and those of his own
acquiring, which were the hopes of his rising.

He had in the outward man a good presence, in a handsome and well compacted person, a strong natural wit, and
a better judgment, with a bold and plausible tongue, whereby he could set out his parts to the best advantage ; and to
these he had the adjuncts of some general learning, which
by diligence he enforced to a great augmentation, and perfection. For he was an indefatigable reader, whether by sea
or land, and none of the least observers both of men and
the times. And I am confident, that among the second
causes of his growth, that variance between him, and my
Lord Grey, in his descent into Ireland, was a principal ; for
it drew them both over the Council Table, there to plead
their cause. Where what advantage he had in the cause I
know not, but he had much better in the telling of his tale ;
and so much, that the Queen and the Lords took no slight
mark of the man and his parts ; for from thence he came to
be known, and to have access to the Queen and the Lords :
and then we are not to doubt how such a man would comply,
and learn the way of progression. And whether Leicester
had then cast in a good word for him to the Queen, which
would have done no harm, I do not determine. But true it
is, he had gotten the Queen's ear at a trice, and she began
to be taken with his elocution, and loved to hear his reasons
to her demands : and the truth is, she took him for a kind
of Oracle, which nettled them all. Yea, those that he relied
on began to take his sudden favour as an alarum, and to be

Naunton sensible of their own supplantation, and to project his, which
1641 made him shortly after sing, *Fortune my Foe*, etc. So that,
finding his favour declining, and falling into a recess, he
undertook a new peregrination, to leave that *terra in-
firma* of the Court for that of the Wars, and by declining
himself, and by absence, to expel his and the passion of his
enemies: which in Court was a strange device of recovery,
but that he knew there was some ill office done him, that
he durst not attempt to mind any other ways, than by going
aside; thereby to teach envy a new way of forgetfulness,
and not so much as to think of him.

Howsoever, he had it always in mind never to forget himself;
and his device took so well, that at his return he came in (as
rams do, by going backward) with the greater strength, and
so continued to her last, great in her grace and Captain of the
Guard, where I must leave him; but with this observation:
that though he gained much at the Court, yet he took it not
out of the Exchequer, or merely out of the Queen's purse, but
by his wit, and the help of the Prerogative. For the Queen
was never profuse in the delivering out of her treasure, but
payed many, and most of her servants part in money and
the rest with grace, which, as the case stood, was taken for
good payment, leaving the arrear of recompence due to
their merit to her great successor, who paid them all with
advantage.

Sir Robert Naunton.

DISCOVERIES

I

DE SHAKESPEARE NOSTRAT.

Jonson   I REMEMBER the players have often mentioned it as
1641   an honour to Shakespeare, that in his writing (whatsoever he penned) he never blotted out a line. My

answer hath been: 'Would he had blotted a thousand,' which they thought a malevolent speech. I had not told posterity this, but for their ignorance, who chose that circumstance to commend their friend by, wherein he most faulted; and to justify mine own candour: for I loved the man, and do honour his memory, on this side idolatry, as much as any. He was, indeed, honest, and of an open and free nature; had an excellent phantasy, brave notions, and gentle expressions; wherein he flowed with that facility that sometimes it was necessary he should be stopped: *Sufflaminandus erat*, as Augustus said of Haterius. His wit was in his own power, would the rule of it had been so too. Many times he fell into those things, could not escape laughter: as when he said in the person of Caesar, one speaking to him, 'Caesar, thou dost me wrong.' He replied, 'Caesar did never wrong but with just cause,' and such like, which were ridiculous. But he redeemed his vices with his virtues. There was ever more in him to be praised than to be pardoned.

II

DOMINUS VERULAMIUS

I HAVE known many excellent men that would speak suddenly, to the admiration of their hearers; who upon study and premeditation have been forsaken by their own wits, and no way answered their fame: their eloquence was greater than their reading; and the things they uttered, better than those they knew: their fortune deserved better of them than their care. For men of present spirits, and of greater wits than study, do please more in the things they invent than in those they bring. And I have heard some of them compelled to speak, out of necessity, that have so infinitely exceeded themselves, as it was better both for them and their auditory that they were so surprised, not prepared. Nor was it safe then to cross them, for their adversary, their anger made them more eloquent. Yet these men I could not but love and admire, that they returned to their studies. They left not diligence (as many do) when their rashness prospered; for diligence is a great aid, even to an indifferent wit; when we are not contented with the examples of our own age, but would know the face of the former. Indeed, the more we confer with, the more we profit by, if the persons be chosen.

One, though he be excellent, and the chief, is not to be imitated alone: for no imitator ever grew up to his author; likeness is always on this side truth. Yet there happened in my time one noble speaker, who was full of gravity in his speaking. His language (where he could spare or pass by a jest) was nobly censorious. No man ever spake more neatly, more pressly, more weightily, or suffered less emptiness, less idleness, in what he uttered. No member of his speech, but consisted of his own graces. His hearers could not cough, or look aside from him, without loss. He commanded where he spoke; and had his judges angry and pleased at his devotion. No man had their affections more in his power. The fear of every man that heard him was, lest he should make an end.

Cicero is said to be the only wit that the people of Rome had equalled to their empire. *Ingenium par imperio.* We have had many, and in their several ages (to take in but the former *seculum*) Sir Thomas More, the elder Wyatt, Henry Earl of Surrey, Chaloner, Smith, Elyot, Bishop Gardiner, were for their times admirable; and the more because they began eloquence with us. Sir Nicholas Bacon was singular, and almost alone, in the beginning of Queen Elizabeth's time. Sir Philip Sidney, and Mr. Hooker (in different matters) grew great masters of wit and language, and in whom all vigour of invention and strength of judgment met. The Earl of Essex, noble and high: and Sir Walter Raleigh, not to be contemned, either for judgment or style. Sir Henry Savile, grave, and truly lettered; Sir Edwin Sandys, excellent in both; Lord Egerton, the Chancellor, a grave and great orator, and best when he was provoked. But his learned and able (though unfortunate) successor is he who hath filled up all numbers, and performed that in our tongue, which may be compared, or preferred, either to insolent Greece or haughty Rome. In short, within his view, and about his times, were all the wits born, that could honour a language or help study. Now things daily fall, wits grow downward, and eloquence grows backward: so that he may be named, and stand as the mark and ἀκμὴ of our language.

I have ever observed it to have been the office of a wise patriot, among the greatest affairs of the state, to take care of the commonwealth of learning. For schools, they are the seminaries of state, and nothing is worthier the study of a statesman than that part of the republic which we call the advancement of letters. Witness the case of Julius Caesar, who, in the heat of the Civil War, writ his books of Analogy, and dedicated them to Tully. This made the late Lord St. Alban entitle his work *Novum Organum*, which though by the most of superficial men, who cannot get beyond the title of nominals, it is not penetrated nor understood, it really openeth all defects of learning whatsoever, and is a book *Qui longum noto scriptore proroget aevum.*

My conceit of his person was never increased toward him by his place, or honours: but I have and do reverence him, for the greatness that was only proper to himself, in that he seemed to me, ever by his work, one of the greatest men, and most worthy of admiration, that had been in many ages. In his adversity I ever prayed that God would give him strength; for greatness he could not want. Neither could I condole in a word or syllable for him, as knowing no accident could do harm to virtue, but rather help to make it manifest.

III

THE TRUE ARTIFICER

Jonson
1641
It cannot but come to pass, that these men who cunningly seek to do more than enough may sometimes happen on something that is good and great; but very seldom: and when it comes, it doth not recompense the rest of their ill. For their jests, and their sentences (which they only and ambitiously seek for) stick out, and are more eminent, because all is sordid and vile about them; as lights are more discerned in a thick darkness than a faint shadow. Now because they speak all they can (however unfitly) they are thought to have the greater copy:[1] where the learned use ever election and a mean; they look back to what they intended at first, and make all an evened and proportioned body. The true artificer will not run away from nature, as he were afraid of her; or depart from life and the likeness of truth; but speak to the capacity of his hearers. And though his language differ from the vulgar somewhat, it shall not fly from all humanity, with the Tamer-lanes and Tamer-chams of the late age, which had nothing in them but the scenical strutting, and furious vociferation, to warrant them to the ignorant gapers. He knows it is his only art, so to carry it as none but artificers perceive it. In the meantime, perhaps, he is called barren, dull, a poor writer, and by what contumelious word can come in their cheeks, by these men, who without labour, judgment, knowledge, and almost sense, are received or preferred before him. He gratulates them, and their fortune. Another age, or juster men, will acknowledge the virtues of his studies, his wisdom in dividing, his subtlety in arguing, with what strength he doth inspire his readers, with what sweetness he strokes them; in inveighing, what sharpness; in jest what urbanity he uses:

[1] Abundance.

how he doth weigh in men's affections : how invade and break   Jonson
in upon them; and makes their minds like the things he writes.   1641
Then in his elocution to behold what word is proper, which
hath ornaments, which height, what is beautifully translated,
where figures are fit, which gentle, which strong, to show the
composition manly : and how he hath avoided faint, obscure,
obscene, sordid, humble, improper, or effeminate phrase;
which is not only praised of the most, but commended (which
is worse) especially for that it is naught.

Ben Jonson.

SIR FRANCIS DRAKE

FRANCIS DRAKE was born nigh South Tavistock in   Fuller
Devonshire, and brought up in Kent; God dividing   1642
the honour betwixt two counties, that the one might have
his birth, and the other his education.   His father, being a
minister, fled into Kent for fear of the Six Articles, wherein
the sting of popery still remained in England, though the
teeth thereof were knocked out, and the Pope's supremacy
abolished.   Coming into Kent, he bound his son Francis
apprentice to the master of a small bark, which traded into
France and Zealand, where he underwent a hard service;
and pains with patience in his youth did knit the joints of
his soul, and made them more solid and compacted.   His
master dying unmarried, in reward of his industry, bequeathed
his bark unto him for a legacy.

For some time he continued his master's profession.   But
the narrow seas were a prison for so large a spirit, born for
greater undertakings.   He soon grew weary of his bark,
which would scarce go alone, but as it crept along by the
shore; wherefore, selling it, he unfortunately, in 1567,
ventured most of his estate with Captain John Hawkins
into the West Indies, whose goods were taken by the

Spaniards at St. John de Ulva, and he himself scarce
escaped with life. The King of Spain being so tender in
those parts, that the least touch doth wound him, and so
jealous of the West Indies, his wife, that willingly he would
have none look upon her, and therefore used them with the
greater severity.

Drake was persuaded by the minister of his ship that he
might lawfully recover in value of the King of Spain, and
repair his losses upon him anywhere else. The case was
clear in sea-divinity, and few are such infidels as not to
believe doctrines which make for their own profit. Whereupon Drake, though a poor private man, hereafter undertook
to revenge himself on so mighty a monarch; who, as not
contented that the sun riseth and setteth in his dominions,
may seem to desire to make all his own where he shineth.
And now let us see how a dwarf, standing on the mount of
God's providence, may prove an overmatch for a giant.

After two or three several voyages to gain intelligence in
the West Indies, and some prizes taken, at last he effectually
set forward from Plymouth with two ships, the one of
seventy, the other twenty-five tons, and seventy-three men
and boys in both. He made with all speed and secrecy to
Nombre de Dios, as loth to put the town to too much charge,
which he knew they would willingly bestow, in providing
beforehand for his entertainment; which city was then the
granary of the West Indies, wherein the golden harvest
brought from Panama was hoarded up till it could be conveyed into Spain. They came hard aboard the shore, and
lay quiet all night, intending to attempt the town in the
dawning of the day.

But he was forced to alter his resolution, and assault it
sooner; for he heard his men muttering amongst themselves
of the strength and greatness of the town. and when men's
heads are once fly-blown with buzzes of suspicion, the vermin
multiply instantly, and one jealously begets another. Where-

fore he raised them from their nests before they had hatched
their fears, and, to put away those conceits, he persuaded
them it was day-dawning when the moon rose, and instantly
set on the town, and won it, being unwalled. In the
market-place the Spaniards saluted them with a volley of
shot ; Drake returned their greeting with a flight of arrows,
the best and ancient English compliment, which drove their
enemies away. Here Drake received a dangerous wound,
though he valiantly concealed it a long time, knowing if his
heart stooped, his men's would fall, and loth to leave off the
action, wherein if so bright an opportunity once setteth it
seldom riseth again. But at length his men forced him to
return to his ship, that his wound might be dressed, and this
unhappy accident defeated the whole design. Thus victory
sometimes slips through their fingers, who have caught it in
their hands.

But his valour would not let him give over the project as
long as there was either life or warmth in it. And therefore having received intelligence from the negroes, called
Symerons,[1] of many mules' lading of gold and silver, which
was to be brought from Panama, he, leaving competent
numbers to man his ships, went on land with the rest, and
bestowed himself in the woods by the way as they were to
pass, and so intercepted and carried away an infinite mass
of gold. As for the silver, which was not portable over
the mountains, they digged holes in the ground and hid it
therein.

There want not those who love to beat down the price of
every honourable action, though they themselves never mean
to be chapmen. These cry up Drake's fortune herein, to
cry down his valour : as if this his performance were nothing,
wherein a golden opportunity ran his head, with his long
forelock, into Drake's hands beyond expectation. But
certainly his resolution and unconquerable patience deserved

---

[1] Cimaroon Indians

Fuller much praise, to adventure on such a design, which had in it
1642 just no more probability than what was enough to keep it
from being impossible : yet I admire not so much at all the
treasure he took, as at the rich and deep mine of God's
providence.

Having now full freighted himself with wealth, and burnt
at the House of Crosses above two hundred thousand pounds
worth of Spanish merchandise, he returned with honour and
safety into England, and some years after undertook that his
famous voyage about the world, most accurately described by
our English authors : and yet a word or two thereof will not be
amiss.   Setting forward from Plymouth, he bore up for Cape
Verd, where, near to the island of St. Jago, he took prisoner
Nuno da Silva, an experienced Spanish pilot, whose direction
he used in the coasts of Brazil and Magellan Straits, and afterwards safely landed him at Guatulco in New Spain.   Hence
they took their course to the Island of Brava, and hereabouts
they met with those tempestuous winds, whose only praise is
that they continue not an hour, in which time they change
all the points of the compass.   Here they had great plenty of
rain, poured, not as in other places, as it were out of sieves,
but as out of spouts, so that a butt of water falls down in a
place : which, notwithstanding, is but a courteous injury in
that hot climate far from land, and where otherwise fresh
water cannot be provided.   Then, cutting the line, they saw
the face of that heaven which earth hideth from us, but
therein only three stars of the first greatness ; the rest few
and small compared to our hemisphere, as if God, on purpose,
had set up the best and biggest candles in that room wherein
his civilest guests are entertained.

Sailing the south of Brazil, he afterwards passed the
Magellan Straits, and then entered *Mare Pacificum*, [and] came
to the southernmost land at the height of $55\frac{1}{2}°$ latitude; thence
directing his course northward, he pillaged many Spanish
towns, and took rich prizes of high value in the kingdoms of

Chili, Peru, and New Spain. Then bending eastwards, he Fuller
coasted China and the Moluccas, where, by the King of 1642
Terrenate, a true gentleman pagan, he was most honourably
entertained. The King told them they and he were all of
one religion in this respect, that they believed not in gods
made of stocks and stones as did the Portuguese. He furnished them also with all necessaries that they wanted.

On the 9th of January following (1579), his ship, having
a large wind and a smooth sea, ran aground on a dangerous
shoal, and struck twice on it, knocking twice at the door of
death, which no doubt had opened the third time. Here
they stuck from eight o'clock at night till four the next
afternoon, having ground too much, and yet too little to
land on, and water too much, and yet too little to sail in.
Had God, who, as the wise man saith (Prov. xxx. 4),
' holdeth the winds in His fist,' but opened His little finger,
and let out the smallest blast, they had undoubtedly been
cast away, but there blew not any wind all the while. Then
they conceiving aright that the best way to lighten the ship
was first to ease it of the burden of their sins by true
repentance, humbled themselves by fasting under the hand
of God. Afterwards they received the communion, dining
on Christ in the sacrament, expecting no other than to sup
with Him in heaven. Then they cast out of their ship six
great pieces of ordnance, threw overboard as much wealth as
would break the heart of a miser to think on it, with much
sugar, and packs of spices, making a caudle of the sea round
about. Then they betook themselves to their prayers, the
best lever at such a dead lift indeed, and it pleased God that
the wind, formerly their mortal enemy, became their
friend, which, changing from the starboard to the larboard
of the ship, and rising by degrees, cleared them off to the
sea again, for which they returned unfeigned thanks to
Almighty God.

By the Cape of Good Hope and west of Africa he returned

Fuller   safe into England, and landed at Plymouth, being almost the
1642   first of those that made a thorough light through the world,
having in his whole voyage, though a curious searcher after
the time, lost one day through the variation of several
climates. He feasted the Queen in his ship at Dartford, who
knighted him for his service : yet it grieved him not a little,
that some prime courtiers refused the gold he offered them,
as gotten by piracy. Some of them would have been loth to
have been told that they had *aurum tholosanum* in their own
purses. Some think that they did it to show that their
envious pride was above their covetousness, who of set
purpose did blur the fair copy of his **performance**, because
they would not take pains to write after it.

I pass by his next West Indian voyage (1585), wherein he
took the cities of St. Jago, St. Domingo, Carthagena, and St.
Augustine in Florida: as also his service performed in 1588,
wherein he, with many others, helped to the waning of that
half-moon [1] which sought to govern all the motion of our sea.
I haste to his last voyage in 1595.

Queen Elizabeth, perceiving that the only way to make
the Spaniard a cripple for ever was to cut his sinews of war
in the West Indies, furnished Sir Francis Drake and Sir
John Hawkins with six of her own ships, besides twenty-one
ships and barks of their own providing, containing in all
2500 men and boys, for some service on America. But,
alas! this voyage was marred before begun. For so great
preparations being too big for a cover, the King of Spain
knew of it, and sent a caraval of adviso to the West Indies;
so that they had intelligence three weeks before the fleet
set forth of England, either to fortify or remove their treasure; whereas in other of Drake's voyages not two of his
own men knew whither he went; and managing such a
design is like carrying a mine in war: if it hath any vent,
all is spoiled. Besides, Drake and Hawkins, being in joint

1 The Armada.

Fuller
1642

commission, hindered each other. The latter took himself to be inferior rather in success than skill; and the action was unlike to prosper, when neither would follow, and both could not handsomely go abreast. It vexed old Hawkins that his counsel was not followed, in present sailing to America, but that they spent time in vain in assaulting the Canaries; and the grief that his advice was slighted, say some, was the cause of his death. Others impute it to the sorrow he took for the taking of his bark called the *Francis*, which five Spanish frigates had intercepted. But when the same heart hath two mortal wounds given it together, it is hard to say which of them killeth.

Drake continued his course for Port Rico, and, riding within the road, a shot from the castle entered the steerage of the ship, took away the stool from under him as he sat at supper, wounded Sir Nicholas Clifford and Brute Brown to death. 'Ah, dear Brute,' said Drake, 'I could grieve for thee, but now is no time for me to let down my spirits.' And indeed a soldier's most proper bemoaning a friend's death in war is in revenging it. And sure, as if grief had made the English furious, they soon after fired five Spanish ships of two hundred tons apiece, in despite of the castle.

America is not unfitly resembled to an hour-glass, which hath a narrow neck of land (suppose it the hole where the sand passeth) betwixt the parts thereof, Mexico and Peru. Now, the English had a design to march by land over this isthmus from Port Rico to Panama, where the Spanish treasure was laid up. Sir Thomas Baskervile, general of the land forces, undertook the service with seven hundred and fifty armed men. They marched through deep ways, the Spaniards much annoying them with shot out of the woods. One fort in the passage they assaulted in vain, and heard two others were built to stop them, besides Panama itself. They had so much of this breakfast, they thought they should surfeit of a dinner and supper of the same. No hope of

Fuller conquest, except with cloying the jaws of death, and thrust-
1642 ing men on the mouth of the cannon. Wherefore, fearing to
find the proverb true, that gold may be bought too dear, they
returned to their ships. Drake afterwards fired Nombre de
Dios, and many other petty towns, whose treasure the
Spaniards had conveyed away, burning the empty casks, when
their precious liquor was run out before, and then prepared
for their returning home.

Great was the difference betwixt the Indian cities now from
what they were when Drake first haunted these coasts. At
first the Spaniards here were safe and secure, counting their
treasure sufficient to defend itself, the remoteness thereof
being the greatest, almost only, resistance, and the fetching
of it more than the fighting for it. Whilst the King of Spain
guarded the head and heart of his dominions in Europe, he
left his long legs in America open to blows, till, finding them
to smart, being beaten black and blue by the English, he
learned to arm them at last, fortifying the most important of
them to make them impregnable.

Now began Sir Francis his discontent to feed upon him.
He conceived that expectation, a merciless usurer, comput-
ing each day since his departure, exacted an interest and
return of honour and profit proportionable to his great preparations, and transcending his former achievements. He
saw that all the good which he had done in this voyage consisted in the evil he had done to the Spaniards afar off,
whereof he could present but small visible fruits in England.
These apprehensions accompanying, if not causing, the disease of the flux wrought his sudden death. And sickness
did not so much untie his clothes, as sorrow did rend at once
the robe of his mortality asunder. He lived by the sea, died
on it, and was buried in it. Thus an extempore performance,
scarce heard to be begun before we hear it is ended, comes
off with better applause, or miscarries with less disgrace, than
a long-studied and openly-premeditated action. Besides, we

see how great spirits, having mounted to the highest pitch of Fuller performance, afterwards strain and break their credits in 1642 striving to go beyond it.   Lastly, God oftentimes leaves the brightest men in an eclipse, to show that they do but borrow their lustre from His reflection.

We will not justify all the actions of any man, though of a tamer profession than a sea-captain, in whom civility is often counted preciseness.   For the main, we say that this our captain was a religious man towards God and His houses, generally sparing churches where he came, chaste in his life, just in his dealings, true of his word, and merciful to those that were under him, hating nothing so much as idleness. And therefore, lest his soul should rust in peace at spare hours, he brought fresh water to Plymouth.   Careful he was for posterity, though men of his profession have as well an ebb of riot as a float of fortune, and providently raised a worshipful family of his kindred.   In a word, should those that speak against him fast till they fetch their bread where he did his, they would have a good stomach to eat it.

Rev. Thomas Fuller.

THE TRUE GENTLEMAN

WE will consider him in his birth, breeding, and behaviour.

1. *He is extracted from ancient and worshipful parentage.* When a pepin is planted on a pepin stock : the fruit growing thence is called a renate, a most delicious apple, as both by sire and dam well descended.   Thus his blood must needs be well purified who is gently born on both sides.

2. *If his birth be not, at least his qualities are generous.* What if he cannot with the Hevenninghams of Suffolk count five-and-twenty knights of his family, or tell sixteen knights

successively with the Tilneys of Norfolk, or with the Naun-
tons show where their ancestors had seven hundred pounds a
year before or at the Conquest : yet he hath endeavoured by
his own deserts to ennoble himself.   Thus valour makes him
son to Caesar ; learning entitles him kinsman to Tully ; and
piety reports him nephew to godly Constantine.   It graceth
a gentleman of low descent and high desert, when he will
own the meanness of his parentage.   How ridiculous is it
when many men brag that their families are more ancient
than the moon, which all know are later than the star which
some seventy years since shined in Cassiopea !   But if he be
generously born, see how his parents breed him.

3. *He is not in his youth possessed with the great hopes of his
possession.*   No flatterer reads constantly in his ears a survey
of the lands he is to inherit.   This hath made many boys'
thoughts swell so great, they could never be kept in compass
afterwards.   Only his parents acquaint him that he is the
next undoubted heir to correction, if misbehaving himself;
and he finds no more favour from his schoolmaster than his
schoolmaster finds diligence in him, whose rod respects
persons no more than bullets are partial in a battle.

4. *At the University he is so studious as if he intended learning
for his profession.*   He knows well that cunning is no burthen
to carry, as paying neither porterage by land, nor poundage
by sea.   Yea, though to have land be a good first, yet to
have learning is the surest second, which may stand to it
when the other may chance to be taken away.

5. *At the Inns of Court he applies himself to learn the laws of
the kingdom.*   Object not, why should a gentleman learn law,
who, if he needeth it, may have it for his money, and if he
have never so much of his own, he must but give it away?
For what a shame it is for a man of quality to be ignorant of
Solon in our Athens, of Lycurgus in our Sparta !   Besides,
law will help him to keep his own, and bestead his neighbours.   Say not that there be enough who make this their

set practice : for so there are also many masters of defence
by their profession ; and shall private men therefore learn no
skill at their weapons ?

As for the hospitality, the apparel, the travelling, the
company, the recreations, the marriage of gentlemen, they
are described in several of the following chapters. A word
or two of his behaviour in the country.

6. *He is courteous and affable to his neighbours.* As the
sword of the best-tempered metal is most flexible, so the
truly generous are most pliant and courteous in their behaviour to their inferiors.

7. *He delights to see himself and his servants well mounted* :
therefore he loveth good horsemanship. Let never any
foreign Rabshakeh send that brave to our Jerusalem, offering
'to lend her two thousand horses, if she be able for her part
to set riders upon them.' We know how Darius got the
Persian empire from the rest of his fellow peers, by the first
neighing of his generous steed. It were no harm if in some
needless suits of intricate precedency betwixt equal gentlemen, the priority were adjudged to him who keeps a stable
of most serviceable horses.

8. *He furnisheth and prepareth himself in peace against time
of war;* lest it be too late to learn when his skill is to be
used. He approves himself courageous when brought to the
trial, as well remembering the custom which is used at the
creation of knights of the bath, wherein the king's master-
cook cometh forth, and presenteth his great knife to the
new-made knights, admonishing them to be faithful and
valiant, otherwise he threatens them that that very knife is
prepared to cut off their spurs.

9. *If the commission of the peace finds him out, he faithfully
discharges it.* I say, finds him out, for a public office is a
guest which receives the best usage from them who never
invited it. And though he declined the place, the country
knew to prize his worth, who would be ignorant of his own.

Fuller
1642

He compounds many petty differences betwixt his neighbours, which are easier ended in his own porch than in
Westminster Hall; for many people think if once they have
fetched a warrant from a justice, they have given earnest to
follow the suit, though otherwise the matter be so mean
that the next night's sleep would have bound both parties
to the peace, and made them as good friends as ever
before. Yet,

10. *He connives not at the smothering of punishable faults.*
He hates that practice, as common as dangerous amongst
country people, who, having received again the goods which
were stolen from them, partly out of foolish pity, and partly
out of covetousness to save charges in prosecuting the law,
let the thief escape unpunished. Thus whilst private losses
are repaired, the wounds to the commonwealth, in the breach
of the laws, are left uncured; and thus petty larceners are
encouraged into felons, and afterwards are hanged for
pounds, because never whipped for pence, who, if they had
felt the chord, had never been brought to the halter.

11. *If chosen a member of Parliament, he is willing to do his
country service.* If he be no rhetorician to raise affections
(yea, Mercury was a greater speaker than Jupiter himself),
he counts it great wisdom to be the good manager of yea and
nay. The slow pace of his judgment is recompensed by the
swift following of his affections, when his judgment is once
soundly informed. And here we leave him in consultation,
wishing him, with the rest of his honourable society, all
happy success.

Rev. Thomas Fuller.

A VISION OF ENGLAND

Milton
1644

NOW once again by all concurrence of signs, and by
the general instinct of holy and devout men, as they
daily and solemnly express their thoughts, God is decreeing

to begin some new and great period in His Church, even
to the reforming of reformation itself; what does He then
but reveal Himself to His servants, and as His manner is, first
to His Englishmen? I say, as His manner is, first to us,
though we mark not the method of His counsels, and are
unworthy. Behold now this vast city, a city of refuge, the
mansion-house of liberty, encompassed and surrounded with
His protection ; the shop of war hath not there more anvils
and hammers working, to fashion out the plates and
instruments of armed justice in defence of beleaguered truth,
than there be pens and heads there, sitting by their studious
lamps, musing, searching, revolving new notions and ideas
wherewith to present, as with their homage and their fealty,
the approaching reformation : others as fast reading, trying
all things, assenting to the force of reason and convincement.
What could a man require more from a nation so pliant
and so prone to seek after knowledge ? What wants there
to such a towardly and pregnant soil, but wise and faithful
labourers, to make a knowing people, a nation of prophets,
of sages, and of worthies? We reckon more than five
months yet to harvest; there need not be five weeks, had
we but eyes to lift up, the fields are white already. Where
there is much desire to learn, there of necessity will be
much arguing, much writing, many opinions ; for opinion in
good men is but knowledge in the making. Under these
fantastic terrors of sect and schism, we wrong the earnest
and zealous thirst after knowledge and understanding, which
God hath stirred up in this city. What some lament of, we
rather should rejoice at, should rather praise this pious
forwardness among men, to reassume the ill-deputed care
of their religion into their own hands again. A little
generous prudence, a little forbearance of one another, and
some grain of charity might win all these diligences to join
and unite into one general and brotherly search after truth ;
could we but forego this prelatical tradition of crowding free

consciences and Christian liberties into canons and precepts of men. I doubt not, if some great and worthy stranger should come among us, wise to discern the mould and temper of a people, and how to govern it, observing the high hopes and aims, the diligent alacrity of our extended thoughts and reasonings in the pursuance of truth and freedom, but that he would cry out as Pyrrhus did, admiring the Roman docility and courage : ' If such were my Epirots, I would not despair the greatest design that could be attempted to make a church or kingdom happy.'

Yet these are the men cried out against for schismatics and sectaries, as if, while the temple of the Lord was building, some cutting, some squaring the marble, others hewing the cedars, there should be a sort of irrational men, who could not consider there must be many schisms and many dissections made in the quarry and in the timber ere the house of God can be built. And when every stone is laid artfully together, it cannot be united into a continuity, it can but be contiguous in this world : neither can every piece of the building be of one form; nay, rather the perfection consists in this, that out of many moderate varieties and brotherly dissimilitudes that are not vastly disproportional, arises the goodly and the graceful symmetry that commends the whole pile and structure.

Let us therefore be more considerate builders, more wise in spiritual architecture, when great reformation is expected. For now the time seems come, wherein Moses, the great prophet, may sit in heaven rejoicing to see that memorable and glorious wish of his fulfilled, when not only our seventy elders, but all the Lord's people, are become prophets. No marvel then though some men, and some good men too, perhaps, but young in goodness, as Joshua then was, envy them. They fret, and out of their own weakness are in agony, lest these divisions and subdivisions will undo us. The adversary again applauds, and waits the hour : when they have branched themselves out, saith he, small enough into parties and partitions, then will be our time. Fool! he sees not the firm root, out of which we all grow, though into branches; nor will beware, until he see our small divided maniples cutting through at every angle of his ill-united and unwieldy brigade. And that we are to hope better of all these supposed sects and schisms, and that we shall not need that solicitude, honest, perhaps, though over-timorous, of them that vex in this behalf, but shall laugh in the end at those malicious applauders of our differences, I have these reasons to persuade me.

First, when a city shall be as it were besieged and blocked about, her navigable river infested, inroads and incursions round, defiance and battle oft rumoured to be marching up, even to her walls and suburb trenches; that then the people, or the greater part, more than at other times, wholly taken up with the study of highest and most important matters to be reformed, should be disputing, reasoning, reading, inventing, discoursing, even to a rarity and admiration, things not before discoursed or written of, argues first a singular good will, contentedness, and confidence in your prudent foresight and safe government, Lords and Commons; and from thence derives itself to a gallant bravery and well-grounded contempt of their enemies, as if there were no small number of as great spirits among us, as his was who, when Rome was nigh besieged by Hannibal, being in the city, bought that piece of ground at no cheap rate whereon Hannibal himself encamped his own regiment.

Next, it is a lively and cheerful presage of our happy success and victory. For as in a body when the blood is fresh, the spirits pure and vigorous, not only to vital, but to rational faculties, and those in the acutest and the pertest operations of wit and subtlety, it argues in what good plight and constitution the body is; so when the cheerfulness of the people is so sprightly up, as that it has not only where-

Milton
1644

with to guard well its own freedom and safety, but to spare,
and to bestow upon the solidest and sublimest points of
controversy and new invention, it betokens us not degener-
ated, nor drooping to a fatal decay, by casting off the old
and wrinkled skin of corruption to outlive these pangs, and
wax young again, entering the glorious ways of truth and
prosperous virtue, destined to become great and honourable
in these latter ages. Methinks I see in my mind a noble
and puissant nation rousing herself like a strong man after
sleep, and shaking her invincible locks : methinks I see her
as an eagle mewing her mighty youth, and kindling her
undazzled eyes at the full midday beam ; purging and
unscaling her long-abused sight at the fountain itself of
heavenly radiance ; while the whole noise of timorous and
flocking birds, with those also that love the twilight, flutter
about, amazed at what she means, and in their envious
gabble would prognosticate a year of sects and schisms.

John Milton.

A KING OF FRANCE

Howel
1645

FRANCE, as all Christendom besides (for there was then
a truce twixt Spain and the Hollander), was in a profound peace, and had continued so twenty years together,
when Henry the Fourth fell upon some great martial design,
the bottom whereof is not known to this day ; and being
rich (for he had heap'd up in the Bastile a mount of gold
that was as high as a lance), he levy'd a huge army of 40,000
men, whence came the song, *The King of France with Forty
Thousand Men* ; and upon a sudden he put this army in
perfect equipage, and some say he invited our Prince Henry
to come unto him to be a sharer in his exploits. But going
one afternoon to the Bastile, to see his treasure and am-
munition, his coach stopp'd suddenly, by reason of some

colliers' and other carts that were in that narrow street;
whereupon one Ravillac, a Lay-Jesuit (who had a whole twelve-
month watch'd an opportunity to do the act), put his foot
boldly upon one of the wheels of the coach, and with a long
knife stretch'd himself over their shoulders who were in the
boot of the coach, and reach'd the King at the end, and
stabb'd him right in the left side to the heart, and pulling
out the fatal steel, he doubled his thrust; the King with a
ruthful voice cry'd out, '*Je suis blessé*' (I am hurt), and suddenly the blood issued out at his mouth. The regicide villain
was apprehended, and command given that no violence should
be offer'd him, that he might be reserved for the Law, and
some exquisite torture.

The Queen grew half distracted hereupon, who had been
crown'd Queen of France the day before in great triumph;
but a few days after she had something to countervail, if not
to overmatch, her sorrow: for according to Saint Lewis's law
she was made Queen-Regent of France during the King's
minority, who was then but about ten years of age.

Many consultations were held how to punish Ravillac,
and there was some Italian Physicians that undertook to
prescribe a torment that should last a constant torment for
three days; but he scap'd only with this. His body was
pull'd between four horses, that one might hear his bones
crack, and after the dislocation, they were set again, and
so he was carry'd in a cart, standing half naked, with a
torch in that hand which had committed the murder: and
in the place where the act was done, it was cut off, and
a gauntlet of hot oil was clap'd upon the stump, to stanch
the blood, whereat he gave a doleful shrick. Then was he
brought upon a stage, where a new pair of boots was provided for him, half filled with boiling oil, then his body was
pincer'd, and hot oil pour'd into the holes. In all the extremity of this torture he scarce shew'd any sense of pain;
but when the gauntlet was clap'd upon his arm to stanch

Howel
1645
the flux at that time of reeking blood, gave a shriek only. He bore up against all these torments about three hours before he died : all the confession that could be drawn from him was, *That he thought he had done God good Service to take away that King which would have embroiled all Christendom in an endless War.*

A fatal thing it was, that France should have three of her Kings come to such violent deaths in so short a revolution of time. Henry the Second, running at tilt with Monsieur Montgomery, was kill'd by a splinter of a lance that pierc'd his eye ; Henry the Third, not long after, was kill'd by a young Friar, who, in lieu of a letter which he pretended to have for him, pull'd out of his long sleeve a knife, and thrust him into the bottom of the belly . . . and so dispatch'd him ; but that regicide was hack'd to pieces in the place by the Nobles. The same destiny attended this King by Ravillac, which is become now a common name of reproach and infamy in France.

Never was King so much lamented as this ; there are a world not only of his pictures, but statues up and down France, and there's scarce a market-town but hath him erected in the market-place or over some gate, not upon sign-posts, as our Henry the Eight ; and by a publick Act of Parliament which was confirm'd in the Consistory at Rome, he was entitled Henry the Great, and so plac'd in the Temple of Immortality. A notable Prince he was, and of an admirable temper of body and mind. He had a graceful facetious way to gain both love and awe ; he would be never transported beyond himself with choler, but he would pass by anything with some reparty, some witty strain, wherein he was excellent. I will instance in a few which were told me from a good hand.

One day he was charg'd by the Duke of Bouillon to have changed his religion, he answer'd : 'No, cousin, I have chang'd no Religion, but an Opinion' ; and the Cardinal of

Perron being by, he enjoin'd him to write a treatise for his vindication. The Cardinal was long about the work, and when the King ask'd from time to time where his book was, he would still answer him: 'That he expected some manuscripts from Rome before he could finish it.' It happen'd, that one day the King took the Cardinal along with him to look on his workmen, and new-buildings at the Louvre; and passing by one corner which had been a long time begun, but left unfinish'd, the King ask'd the Chief Mason why that corner was not all this while perfected? 'Sir, it is because I want some choice stones.' 'No, no,' said the King, looking upon the Cardinal, 'it is because thou wantest manuscripts from Rome.' . . . Another time, when at the siege of Amiens, he having sent for the Count of Soissons (who had 100,000 franks a year pension from the Crown) to assist him in those wars, and that the Count excus'd himself by reason of his years and poverty, having exhausted himself in the former wars, and all that he could do now was to pray for his Majesty, which he would do heartily. This answer being brought to the King, he reply'd: 'Will my cousin, the Count of Soissons, do nothing else but pray for me? Tell him that Prayer without Fasting is not available; therefore I will make my cousin fast also from his pension of 100,000 per An.'

He was once troubled with a fit of the gout; and the Spanish Ambassador coming then to visit him, and saying he was sorry to see his Majesty so lame; he answer'd: 'As lame as I am, if there were occasion, your Master the King of Spain should no sooner have his foot in the stirrup but he should find me on horseback.'

By these few you may guess at the genius of this sprightfull Prince: I could make many more instances, but then I should exceed the bounds of a letter. When I am in Spain you shall hear further from me; and if you can think on anything wherein I may serve you, believe it, Sir, that any

Howel
1645

Howel   Employment from you, shall be welcome to—your most
1645   obliged Servant,

James Howel.

LUTHER AT WORMS

Bell   ON Tuesday in the Passion week, (said Luther), I was
1646   cited by the herald to appear at the Diet; he brought
with him a safe-conduct from the Emperor and many other
Princes, but the safe-conduct was soon broken, even the next
day (Wednesday), at Worms, where I was condemned, and
my books burned. Now, when I came to Erfurt, I received
intelligence that I was cast and condemned at Worms, yea,
and that in all cities and places thereabout it was published
and spread abroad; insomuch that the herald asked me
whether I meant to go to Worms or no? Although I was
somewhat astonished at the news, yet I answered the herald,
and said: 'Although in Worms there were as many devils as
there are tiles on the houses, yet, God willing, I will go
thither.'

When I came to Oppenheim, in the Palatinate, not far
from Worms, Bucer came unto me, and dissuaded me from
entering into the town; for, said he, Sglapion, the Emperor's
confessor, had been with him, and had entreated him to
warn me not to go thither, for I should be burned; but
rather that I should go to a gentleman there near at hand,
Francis Von Sickingen, and remain with him, who willingly
would receive and entertain me. This plot the wicked
wretches (said Luther) had devised against me, to the end I
should not appear; for if I had contracted the time, and stayed
away three days, then my safe-conduct had been expired, and
then they would have locked the town-gates, and without
hearing I should have been condemned and made away.
But I went on in all simplicity, and when I saw the city, I

Bell
1646

wrote presently to Spalatine, and gave him notice of my
coming, and desired to know where I should be lodged.
Then they all wondered at my coming, which was so far from
their expectation; for they verily thought I would have
stayed away, as scared through their threatenings. There
were two worthy gentlemen (John Von Hirschfeld and St.
John Schott), who received me by the Prince Elector's command, and brought me to their lodging.

No Prince came unto me, but only Earls and gentlemen,
who earnestly looked upon me, and who had exhibited four
hundred articles to his Imperial Majesty against those of the
spirituality, and desired a redress and a removing of those
their grievances, otherwise they themselves should be constrained to remedy the same; from all which grievances they
are now delivered through the Gospel, which I (God be
praised) have brought again to light. The Pope at that time
wrote to the Emperor, that he should not perform the safe-
conduct; for which end all the Bishops also pressed the
Emperor; but the Princes and States of the Empire would
not consent thereunto : for they alleged that a great tumult
thereupon would arise. I received of them a great deal of
courtesy, insomuch that the Papists were more afraid of me
than I was of them. For the Landgrave of Hesse (being
then but a young Prince) desired that I might be heard,
and he said openly unto me, 'Sir, is your cause just and
upright, then I beseech God to assist you.' Now being in
Worms, I wrote to Sglapion, and desired him to make a step
unto me, but he would not. Then being called, I appeared
in the Senate House before the Council and State of the
whole Empire, where the Emperor and the Princes Electors
in person were assembled.

Then Dr. Eck (the Bishop of Trier's fiscal) began, and
said unto me : 'Martin, thou art called hither to give answer
whether thou acknowledgest these writings to be thy books
or no ?' (The books lay on a table which he showed unto

me.) I answered and said : ' I believe they be mine.' But Hierome Schurfe presently thereupon said : ' Let the titles of them be read.' Now when the same were read, then I said : ' Yea, they are mine.' Then he said : ' Will you revoke them ?' I answered and said : ' Most gracious Lord and Emperor, some of my books are books of controversies, wherein I touch my adversaries : some, on the contrary, are books of doctrine ; the same I neither can nor will revoke. But if in case I have in my books of controversies been too violent against any man, then I am content therein to be better directed, and for that end I desire respite of time.' Then they gave me one day and one night. The next day I was cited by the Bishops and others, who were appointed to deal with me touching my revocation. Then I said: 'God's Word is not my word, therefore I know not how to give it away ; but in whatsoever is therein, besides the same, I will show obedience.' Then Marquis Joachim said unto me : ' Sir Martin, so far as I understand, you are content to be instructed, excepting only what may concern the Holy Writ.' I said, ' Yea ' ; then they pressed me to refer the cause to His Imperial Majesty. I said I durst not presume so to do. Then they said : ' Do you not think that we are also Christians, who with all care and diligence would finish and end such causes ? You ought to put so much trust and confidence in us, that we would conclude uprightly.' To that I answered and said : ' I dare not trust you so far, that you should conclude against yourselves, who even now have cast and condemned me, being under safe-conduct ; yet, nevertheless, that ye may see what I will do, I will yield up into your hands my safe-conduct, and do with me what ye please.' Then all the Princes said : ' Truly, he offereth enough, if not too much.' Afterwards they said : ' Yield unto us yet in some articles.' I said : ' In God's name, such articles as concern not the Holy Scriptures I will not stand against.' Presently hereupon, two Bishops went to the Emperor, and showed

him that I had revoked. Then the Emperor sent another Bell
Bishop unto me, to know if I had referred the cause to him, 1646
and to the Empire; I said, I had neither done it, nor intended so to do.

In this sort, (said Luther), did I alone resist so many,
insomuch that my Doctor, and divers others of my friends,
were much offended and vexed by reason of my constancy;
yea, some of them said, if I had referred the articles to
their consideration, they would have yielded, and given way
to those articles which in the council at Costnitz had been
condemned. Then came Cocleus upon me, and said: ' Sir
Martin, if you will yield up your safe-conduct, then I will
enter into dispute with you.' I, for my part, (said Luther),
in my simplicity, would have accepted thereof. But Hier-
onimus Schurfe earnestly entreated me not to do the same,
and in derision and scorn answered Cocleus and said: ' O
brave offer, if a man were so foolish as to entertain it !'

Then came a Doctor unto me, belonging to the Marquis of
Baden, essaying, with a strain of high-carried words, to move
me, admonished me, and said: ' Truly, Sir Martin, you are
bound to do much, and to yield for the sake of fraternal
love, and to the end that peace and tranquillity among the
people may be preserved, lest tumults and insurrections
should be occasioned and raised. Besides, it were also
greatly befitting you to show obedience to the Imperial
Majesty, and diligently to beware of causing offences in the
world; therefore I would advise you to revoke.' Whereupon (said Luther), I said : ' For the sake of brotherly love
and amity I could and would do much, so far as it were not
against the faith and honour of Christ.' When all these had
made their vain assaults, then the Chancellor of Trier said
unto me : ' Martin Luther, you are disobedient to the Imperial
Majesty; therefore you have leave and licence to depart
again with your safe-conduct.' In this sort I again departed
from Worms with a great deal of gentleness and courtesy, to

Bell
1646
the wondering of the whole Christian world, insomuch that the Papists wished they had left me at home.

Captain Henry Bell.

A PRIVATE BRAWL

Herbert
1648
I HAD not been long in London, when a violent burning fever seized upon me, which brought me almost to my death, though at last I did by slow degrees recover my health. Being thus upon my amendment, the Lord Lisle, afterwards Earl of Leicester, sent me word that Sir John Ayres intended to kill me in my bed, and wished me keep a guard upon my chamber and person. The same advertisement was confirmed by Lucy, Countess of Bedford, and the Lady Hoby shortly after. Hereupon I thought fit to entreat Sir William Herbert, now Lord Powis, to go to Sir John Ayres, and tell him that I marvelled much at the information given me by these great persons, and that I could not imagine any sufficient ground hereof; howbeit, if he had anything to say to me in a fair and noble way, I would give him the meeting as soon as I had got strength enough to stand upon my legs. Sir William hereupon brought me so ambiguous and doubtful an answer from him, that whatsoever he meant, he would not declare yet his intention, which was really, as I found afterwards, to kill me any way that he could. . . . Finding no means thus to surprise me, he sent me a letter to this effect : that he desired to meet me somewhere, and that it might so fall out as I might return quietly again. To this I replied, that if he desired to fight with me upon equal terms, I should upon assurance of the field and fair play give him meeting when he did any way specify the cause, and that I did not think fit to come to him upon any other terms, having been sufficiently informed of his plots to assassinate me.

After this, finding he could take no advantage against me, then, in a treacherous way, he resolved to assassinate me in this manner: hearing I was to come to Whitehall on horseback, with two lackeys only, he attended my coming back in a place called Scotland Yard, at the hither end of Whitehall, as you come to it from the Strand, hiding himself here with four men armed on purpose to kill me.

I took horse at Whitehall Gate, and passing by that place, he being armed with a sword and dagger, without giving me so much as the least warning, ran at me furiously, but instead of me, wounded my horse in the brisket, as far as his sword could enter for the bone. My horse hereupon starting aside, he ran him again in the shoulder, which, though it made the horse more timorous, yet gave me time to draw my sword. His men thereupon encompassed me, and wounded my horse in three places more ; this made my horse kick and fling in that manner, as his men durst not come near me ; which advantage I took to strike at Sir John Ayres with all my force, but he warded the blow both with his sword and dagger ; instead of doing him harm, I broke my sword within a foot of the hilt. Hereupon some passenger that knew me, and observing my horse bleeding in so many places, and so many men assaulting me, and my sword broken, cried to me several times, ' Ride away, ride away ;' but I, scorning a base flight upon what terms soever, instead thereof, alighted as well as I could from my horse.

I had no sooner put one foot upon the ground, but Sir John Ayres, pursuing me, made at my horse again, which the horse perceiving, pressed on me on the side I alighted, in that manner that he threw me down, so that I remained flat upon the ground, only one foot hanging in the stirrup, with that piece of a sword in my right hand. Sir John Ayres hereupon ran about the horse, and was thrusting his sword into me, when I, finding myself in this danger, did with both my arms reaching at his legs, pull them towards me, till he

Herbert fell down backwards on his head. One of my footmen
1648 hereupon, who was a little Shropshire boy, freed my foot
out of the stirrup; the other, which was a great fellow,
having run away as soon as he saw the first assault. This
gave me time to get upon my legs, and to put myself in the
best posture I could with that poor remnant of a weapon.

Sir John Ayres by this time likewise was got up, standing
betwixt me and some part of Whitehall, with two men on
each side of him, and his brother behind him, with at least
twenty or thirty persons of his friends, or attendants of the
Earl of Suffolk. Observing thus a body of men standing in
opposition against me, though to speak truly I saw no swords
drawn but by Sir John Ayres and his men, I ran violently
against Sir John Ayres; but he knowing my sword had no
point, held his sword and dagger over his head, as believing
I could strike rather than thrust; which I no sooner perceived but I put a home thrust to the middle of his breast,
that I threw him down with so much force, that his head
fell first to the ground, and his heels upwards. His men
hereupon assaulted me; when one, Mr. Mansel, a Glamorgan-
shire gentleman, finding so many set against me alone, closed
with one of them; a Scotch gentleman, also closing with
another, took him off also. All I could well do to those two
which remained was to ward their thrusts, which I did
with that resolution, that I got ground upon them.

Sir John Ayres was now got up a third time, when I,
making towards him with the intention to close, thinking
that there was otherwise no safety for me, put by a thrust of
his with my left hand, and so coming within him, received a
stab with his dagger on my right side, which ran down my
ribs as far as my hip, which I feeling, did with my right
elbow force his hand, together with the hilt of the dagger,
so near the upper part of my right side, that I made him
leave hold. The dagger now sticking in me, Sir Henry Cary,
afterwards Lord of Falkland, and Lord Deputy of Ireland,

finding the dagger thus in my body, snatched it out. This while I, being closed with Sir John Ayres, hurt him on the head, and threw him down a third time, when, kneeling on the ground, and bestriding him, I struck at him as hard as I could with my piece of a sword, and wounded him in four several places, and did almost cut off his left hand. His two men this while struck at me; but it pleased God even miraculously to defend me; for when I lifted up my sword to strike at Sir John Ayres, I bore off their blows half a dozen times. His friends, now finding him in this danger, took him by the head and shoulders, and drew him from betwixt my legs, and carried him along with them through Whitehall, at the stairs whereof he took boat. Sir Herbert Croft (as he told me afterwards) met him upon the water, vomiting all the way, which I believe was caused by the violence of the first thrust I gave him. His servants, brother, and friends being now retired also, I remained master of the place and his weapons; having first wrested his dagger from him, and afterwards struck his sword out of his hand.

This being done, I retired to a friend's house in the Strand, where I sent for a surgeon, who, searching my wound on the right side, and finding it not to be mortal, cured me in the space of some ten days, during which time I received many noble visits and messages from some of the best in the kingdom. Being now fully recovered of my hurts, I desired Sir Robert Harley to go to Sir John Ayres, and tell him, that though I thought he had not so much honour left in him that I could be any way ambitious to get it, yet that I desired to see him in the field with his sword in his hand. The answer that he sent me was, that . . . he would kill me with a musket out of a window.

Lord Herbert of Cherbury.

Herbert
1648

FLODDEN FIELD

Drum-
mond
1649

WHILEST the King stayed at Linlithgow, attending the gathering of his army, now ready to set forward, and full of cares and perplexity, in the Church of St. Michael [he] heard evensong (as then it was called). While he was at his devotion, an ancient man came in, his amber coloured locks hanging down upon his shoulders, his forehead high and inclining to baldness, his garment of azure colour somewhat long-girded about him with a towel or table napkin, of a comely and reverend aspect. Having enquired for the King, he intruded himself into the prease, passing thorow till he came to him; with a clownish simplicity, leaning over the Canon's seat where the King sat: 'Sir,' (said he), 'I am sent hither to intreat you for this time to delay your expedition, and to proceed no farther in your intended journey: for if you do, ye shall not prosper in your enterprise, nor any of your followers. I am farther charged to warn you, if ye be so refractory as to go forward, not to use the acquaintance, company, or counsel of women, as ye tender your honour, life, and estate.' After this warning he withdrew himself back again into the prease; when service was ended, the King enquired earnestly for him, but he could nowhere be found, neither could any of the standers by (of whom diverse did narrowly observe him, meaning afterwards to have discoursed further with him) feel or perceive how, when, or where he passed from them: having as it were vanished in their hands.

After his army had mustered in the Borough-moor of Edinburgh (a field then spacious and delightful by the shades of many stately and aged oaks), about the midst of the night there is a Proclamation heard at the Market Cross of the town, summoning a great many Burgesses, Gentlemen, Barons, Noblemen to appear within forty days before the

tribunal of one Plot-cock ;[1] the Provost of the town in his
timber gallery having heard his own name cited, cried out
that he declined that Judicatory, and appealed to the mercy
of God Almighty.

Nothing was the King moved with those advertisements,
thinking them scenic pieces acted by those who hated the
French and favoured the English faction; being so boldly
and to the life personated that they appalled and stroke
with fear ordinary and vulgar judgments, as tragi-comedies
of Spirits. The Earl of Angus dissuaded him from that expedition, and many of the most reverend Churchmen, but
the Angel which most conjured him was Margaret, his Queen,
who at that time was with child : her tears and prayers
shook the strongest beams of his resolutions. She had acquainted him with the visions and affrightments of her
sleep; that her chains and armlets appeared to be turned into
pearls; she had seen him fall from a great precipice; she
had lost one of her eyes. When he had answered these
were but dreams, arising from the many thoughts and cares
of the day : ' But it is no dream' (saith she) 'that ye have but
one son, and him a weakling ; if otherwise than well happen
unto you, what a lamentable day will that be, when ye
shall leave behind you, to so tender and weak a successor,
under the government of a woman, for inheritance, a miserable and bloody war ? It is no dream that ye are to fight a
mighty people, now turned insolent by their riches at home
and power abroad : that your Nobility are indigent ye know,
and may be bribed to leave you in your greatest danger. What
a folly, what a blindness is it to make this war yours, and to
quench the fire in your neighbour's house of France, to kindle
and burn up your own in Scotland ! Ye have no such
reason to assist the French, as ye have to keep your promises
to England, and enjoy a peace at home. Though the
English should make a conquest of France, will they take

_____
[1] The Devil.

your Crown, or disinherit their own race? This is even as the
left hand would cut off the right! Should the letters of the
Queen of France, (a woman twice married (the first half in
adultery, the last almost incest) whom ye did never nor
shall ever see) prove more powerful with you, than the cries
of your little son, and mine, than the tears, complaints,
curses of the orphans and widows which ye are to make?
If ye will go, suffer me to accompany you; it may be my
countrymen prove more kind towards me than they will to
you; and for my sake yield unto a peace. I hear the Queen
my sister will be with the army in her husband's absence;
if we shall meet, who knows what God by our means may
bring to pass?'

The king answered all her complaints with a speedy march
which he made over the Tweed : not staying till the whole
forces came to him, which were arising and prepared.
The twenty-two of August coming into England, he encamped near the Water of Twisel in Northumberland, where
at Twisel-haugh he made an Act, that if any man were slain
or hurt to death by the English, during the time of his
abode in England, his heirs should have his ward, relief and
marriage. Norham, Wark, Foord, Eatel, are taken and cast
down. Amidst this hostility the Lady Foord (a noble captive)
was brought in a pity-pleading manner, with her daughter (a
maid of excellent beauty) to the camp. Not without the
Earl of Surrey's direction, as many supposed, for they have a
vigorous Prince and his son (though natural, by the gifts of
nature and education above many lawful) to try the magic of
their eloquence and beauty upon. The King delighting in
their company, not only hearkeneth to the discourse of the
mother, but giveth way to her counsel : which was, if she
should be dismissed, to send him true and certain intelligence
of what the English would attempt, taking her way to their
camp; but in effect proved the winning of time to the Earl
of Surrey, and the losing of occasion to him. Her few days'

stay bred in him a kind of carelessness, sloth, procrastination and delay, a neglect and as it were a forgetfulness of his army and business: eighteen days' tarrying in England, in a territory not very fertile, had consumed much provision, the soldiers began to want necessaries, a number in the night by blind paths returned to their own country. In a short time only the Noblemen and their Vassals attended the King. These request him not to spend more time on that barren soil, but to turn their forces against Berwick, which town was of more importance than all the hamlets and poor villages of Northumberland, neither was it impregnable or difficult to be taken, the town and castle being no ways provided and furnished to endure a siege. The Courtiers move the King to continue the beleaguering of Berwick till their coming back: which would be an easy conquest, Northumberland once forraged,[1] in absence of the bravest of the English then in France.

Whilest the army languished, and the King spent time at Foord, the Earl of Surrey directeth an Herald to his camp, requiring him either to leave off the invasion of his master's country and turn back, giving satisfaction for wrongs committed, or that he would appoint a day and place wherein all differences might be ended by the sword. This challenge being advised in Council, most voices were that they should return home, and not with so small number as remained endanger the state of the whole kingdom, enough being already achieved for fame, and too much for their friendship with France; why should a few soldiers, and these already tired out by forcing of strengths, throwing down castles, be hazarded against such multitudes of the English, supplied lately, and increased with fresh auxiliaries? Thomas Howard, Admiral, a son of the Earl of Surrey, having newly brought with him to Newcastle, out of the army lying in France, five thousand men and one thousand tall seamen. If they should

_____
[1] Forayed.

Drum-
mond
1649

return home, the English army could not but disband, and
not conveniently this year be gathered again, consisting of
men levied from far and distant places. Again, if they should
be engaged to come to a battle ; their own country, being
fields to them well known, would prove more commodious
and secure to fight upon than English ground, besides the
opportunity of furnishing and providing the camp with all
necessaries at less charges. The French Embassador and
others of his faction remonstrate to the King, what a shameful retreat he would make, if at the desire of the enemy he
returned, and without the hazard of a battle, being so near
unto him ; that by fighting in England, he kept his own
country unforraged ; and consumed the provision of his
enemy which at last would weaken his forces. That for
contentment to both armies, Islay, a Scottish Herald, should
return with Rouge-Cross, the English, and condescend upon
a day, promising them the meantime tarrying and abode till
the righteousness of the cause were decided in a battle.

The set and appointed day by the Heralds, in which the
two armies should have joined, being come, and the English
not appearing, nor any from them, the Nobility again resort
to the King ; show how by the flight of the enemy matters
were prolonged from one day to another : the English forces
daily increasing, whilest the Scottish wear away and waxed
fewer ; that flight should be opposed to flight ; the day
designed by the Heralds not being kept, it would be no
reproach to them to turn home without battle, or if retiring,
to fight upon their own ground. If this counsel pleased him
not, but that he would there give them battle, the next was
to study all advantages for victory, either by stratagem, or
the odds and furtherance of the place of fight ; where the
Cheviot Hills decline towards the plainer fields arising behind
them with high tops with best ordnance should be fortified ;
the Water of Till running deep and foordless upon the right
hand, and but passable at the Bridge, the first companies of

the enemy being passed, before they could be relieved and
succoured by their followers, the Bridge by the artillery should
be beaten down, and the army charged when they began to
pass the water.

The King, impatient of counsel, answered : though their
number encreased to as many more as they were, he with
that remainder of his army would fight them. That advantages
were to be imbraced according to the occasion of the
fight without tedious deliberation : if any man was afraid he
might, if he pleased, return home. A strange resolution in a
Prince, who imagined every man in his army to have the
same strength, courage, boldness, and resolution with himself!
This answer astonished the Nobility, and since they
could not persuade him to a fair retreat, but that he will fight,
and that without the advantage of the Bridge, being inferior
in number to the English (for they were reckoned by the
scouts six and twenty thousand), they fortify themselves according
to the commodity of the hill where they lay encamped
with a resolution not to suffer the King to hazard
his person in the battle. If victory should incline to them,
their gains were but small and glory less, extending but
over some few of the Nobility, and a small parcel of the
body of the State of England, a number of yeomen and
pressed horsemen, the flower of the Kingdom being in
France. But if they were overthrown, their loss would prove
uncomparable, yea, unspeakable, a martial young King either
killed, taken, or put to flight ; wherefore they think it fitting,
not necessary, the King be pleased, with so many as either
chance or election might separate with him, to be a spectator
of the fortune of the day. To this the King replied, he
neither wanted ability to discharge the part of a Soldier, nor
wisdom to command as a General, and to outlive so many
valiant countrymen would be more terrible to him than
death itself. When forced to give way for his personal
presence in the field, they appoint some to be arrayed in

Drum-
mond
1649

like furniture of arms and a like guard as the King.
Shadows to personate him in sundry quarters of the field,
that the enemy should not set one man as their chief mark
to invade, from whose death the victory and conclusion of
the war might depend : and if the King should fall, the
army should not lose courage, nor be brought to believe he
were lost, so long as they saw a General with his coignoscance
and guard present and near them to be a witness of their
valour and achievements, as not long before at the battle of
Fornou in Italy had been practised by the French to their
King Charles the Eight.

By this time the Earl of Surrey, with the power of the
North of England, was come within three miles of the place
where the Scottish army was encamped ; and, perceiving he
could not but with great disadvantage fight them, he sendeth
an Herald requiring the King to come forth of his strength
to some indifferent ground, where he would be ready to encounter him.   The King being forward to condescend to
this request, the Lords cried out : it was madness to accept of
opportunity of fighting from his enemies, and to set all at a
main chance according to their appointment, it being their
advantage to prolong time, and trifle with him, in whose
camp there was already scarcity of victuals, which ere long
might put him to such a stand, that he should not know
well what to do.   Neither was it likely he could be furnished from the inner parts of the country, by reason of the
cumbersome ways for carriage to pass, after the falling of so
great and continued rains, and the softening of the ground.
That by sitting still, and committing nothing to fortune, he
might have his enemy at his pleasure ; if they dared assail
him, at their perils be it.   He lacked nothing but patience
to be victorious.

The Scots keeping their trenches, the Earl essayeth to
draw them out, and the ninth of September removing his
camp, marcheth towards the same Hill of Flodden where they

lay encamped; his vanguard with the cannon passeth the Water of Till at Twisel Bridge, the rearward going over at Myln-foord. King James seeing them pass the waters, imagineth they meant to win a hill between his camp and them. To prevent which (setting fire to the cabanes raised of boughs of trees and reeds) he removeth to another hill, before the English could observe his motion, the smoke darkening the air between the two armies. Whilest the Scottish army was removing, the English advance to the foot of Flodden Hill, by which they have double advantage : the Scottish ordinance could not much annoy them, they marching upwards and under the level thereof; again, by their shot they might easily gall their enemies as they came downwards upon them.

The fatal hour of the battle approaching, the English draw up in good order six and twenty thousand men (some write thirty) in two battles, any of which was equal in number to the whole Scottish army. Thomas Lord Howard, Admiral, had the vant-guard, of which Sir Edmond Howard, his brother, led one of the wings, and Sir Marmaduke Constable the other; the Lords Dacres and Clifford, with Sir Edward Stanley, kept the rear: the Earl of Surrey, with Latymer Scroop [and] Sir Stephen Bull, kept the main battle. The Scots by their fewness of number not being able to order many battaillons, marshal themselves in four, three of which should enter in fight and the fourth attend for supply. The King kept the middle or main; Alexander Gordon, Earl of Huntley, had the right wing of the van; the Earls of Crawford and Montrose led the other, and some have recorded the Lord Hume. The third army was guided by Matthew, Earl of Lennox, and the Earl of Argyle, where was Mackenney and Macklean, with the fierceness of the Highlanders. Adam Hepburn, Earl of Bothwell, with his friends and the flower of the Gentry of Lothian, kept off for sudden dispatches and chances of the battle.

The Earl of Huntley, making down the hill where they
encamped near the foot of Branx Town, encountereth that
wing of the English host which was led by Sir Edmond
Howard, which, after a furious and long fight he put to flight,
and so eagerly pursued the advantage, that Sir Edmond had
either been killed or taken, if he had not been rescued by
Bastard Hieron and the Lord Dacres. The battaillon which
the Earls Lennox and Argyle led (being Highlandmen) encouraged with this first glance of victory, loosing their ranks,
abandoning all order (for ought that the French Ambassador,
La Motte, by signs, threatenings, clamours, could do to them),
break furiously upon the enemy, and invade him in the face,
of whom they are not only valiantly received, but by Sir
Edward Stanley's traversing the hill enclosed, cut down at
their backs, and [laid] prostrate. The middle ward which
the King led, with which now the Earl of Bothwel with the
power of Lothian was joined, fought it out courageously,
body against body, and sword to sword. Numbers upon
either side falling, till darkness, and the black shadows of
the night, forced as it were by consent of both a retreat:
neither of them understanding the fortune of the day, and
unto whom victory appertained.

Many brave Scots did here fall, esteemed to above five
thousand, of the noblest and worthiest families of the kingdom : who chose rather to die than outlive their friends
and compatriots. The King's natural son, Alexander Arch-
Bishop of St. Andrews, the Bishop of the Isles, the Abbots
of Inchjefray and Kill-Winny; the Earls of Crawford, Morton,
Argyle, Lennox, Arrel, Cathness, Bothwel, Athol ; the Lords
Elphinstoun, Aerskin, Forbes, Ross, Lovet, Saintclare, Maxwell, with his three brothers, Simple, Borthicke; numbers
of Gentlemen, Balgowny, Blacka-Towre, Borchard, Sir
Alexander Seatoun, Mackenny, with Macklean, George,
Master of Angus, and Sir William Dowglas of Glenbervy,
with some two hundred Gentlemen of their name and Vassals

were here slain. The English left few less upon the place, but most part of them being of the common sort of soldiers, and men of no great mark, compared with so many Nobles killed and a King lost, the number was not esteemed nor the loss thought anything of. . . .

This fight began September 9, about four of the clock after noon, and continued three hours, the year 1513. About the dawning of the next morning the Lord Dacres, with his horse troops, taking a view of the field, and seeing the brazen ordnance of the Scots not transported, with most part of the fallen bodies not rifled, sendeth speedy advertisement to the Howards and the pensive army ; inviting all to the setting up of trophies, spoil, and transporting of their great ordnance to Berwick, amongst which were seven culverins of like size and making, called the Seven Sisters.

Divers diversely report of the fortune of the King ; we without affirming anything for certain, shall only set down what Fame hath published : a false witness often of human accidents, and which many times by malignant brains is forged, and by more malignant ears received and believed. The English hold that he was killed in this battle ; the Scots, that many in like arms with the like guards were killed, every one of which was held for the King. Amongst others, Alexander Lord Elphinstoun, his favourite, who had married Elizabeth Barley, one of the Dames of Honour of Queen Margaret. He was a man not unlike to the King in face and stature, and representing him in arms in the field, with the valiantest and most courageous of the army fought it out, and acting heroically his part, as a King was killed, heaps of slaughtered bodies environing his. In the search where the fight was, the number, tallness, furniture of the dead bodies being observed, their faces and wounds viewed, his body, as if it breathed yet majesty, was amidst the others selected, acknowledged for his Master's, brought to Berwick and embalmed. That it was not the body of the King, the girdle of iron which he ever wore, and then was not found about him, gave some, though not certain, testimony.

Some have recorded that, the fortune of the day inclining to the English, four tall men mounted upon lusty horses, wearing upon the points of their lances, for coignoscances, streamers of straw, mounting the King on a sorrel hackney, conveyed him far from the place of fight, and that he was seen beyond the Tweed, between Kelso and Dunce. After which what became of him was uncertain. Many hold he was killed in the Castle of Hume, either by the intelligence between the English and the Lord Hume's kindred, or out of fear (for they were at the slaughter of the King's father and the most violent in that fight), or of hopes of great fortunes, which would follow innovations and the confusion of the State, being men who lived best in a troubled Commonwealth and upon the Borders. One Carr a follower of the Lord Hume's, that same night the battle was fought, thrust the Abbot of Kelso out of his Abbacy: which he never durst attempt the King being alive. Another, David Carbreath, in the time of John the Governor, vaunted that however John wronged the Humes, he was one of six who had abated the insolence of King James, and brought him to know he was a Mortal. To these is added, that the Governor John, not long hereafter, cut off the heads of the Lord Hume and his brother without any known great cause.

The common people (ever more addicted to superstition than verity) believed he was living, and had passed over the seas, and according to his promise visited the Holy Sepulchre in Palestine. There, for his other offences and the bearing of arms against his father, in prayers and penance he spent the remainder of his tedious days.

William Drummond of Hawthornden.

BIBLIOGRAPHY

A Character of Irishmen

From the version of *Polychronicon Ranulphi Higden Monachi Cestrensis* (Bk. I. c. 34), edited for the Master of the Rolls by Churchill Babington (1865), after a manuscript in St. John's College Library, Cambridge, only a few years later in date than Trevisa's translation (1387).

The Court of the Great Chan

Chapter 22 of *The Voiage and travaile of Sir John Maundeville, Kt. . . . Which treateth of the Way to Hierusalem; and of Marvayles of Inde, With other Ilands and countryes.* 'Now (1725) published entire from an original MS. in the Cotton Library.'

The Battle of St. Albans

No. 239 of *The Paston Letters*, as reprinted by Mr. James Gairdner (London 1875). It first appeared in Vol. xx. of the *Archaeologia* (p. 519 *et seq.*), to which it was communicated in 1822 by Mr. Bayley, Keeper of the Records in the Tower. For the *Letters* themselves, two volumes were printed for the first time in 1787, from autographs in the possession of their editor, Mr. Fenn, of East Dereham ; two more appeared in 1789 ; a fifth, left ready at Fenn's death, was published by Mr. Serjeant Frere in 1823. The MSS. of the first two, presented to George III., have disappeared, as have those of the two next: only the fifth remaining in MS. to attest the authenticity of the letters.

The Dolorous Shirt

From the Second Book of *The Volume entituled and Named* The Recuyell of the Hystoryes of Troye, *composed and drawen oute of dyverce bookes of Latyn into Frensshe by the right venerable persone and worshipful man* Raoul le Feure *preest and chapelayn unto the right noble, glorious, and myghty prynce, in his tyme, Phelip, duc of Bourgoyne, etc.* 1464., *And translated and drawn out of Frensshinto Englisshe by* William Caxton, *Mercer of the Cyte of London*' (1471). Our text is that of the Kelmscott edition (1893).

How the Monk saw Heaven

Chapters lv. and lvi., with part of Chapter lvii., of *The Revelation of the Monk of Evesham* : written (Mr. Arber thinks) not later than 1196 ; abridged, under date of that year, in Roger de Wendover's *Flowers of History* ; and printed (*c.* 1482) by William de Machlinia, to whom, as responsible for the existing text, its authorship is here, for convenience's sake, assigned. Our text is that of Mr. Arber's reprint (1869) from the unique copy in the British Museum. The full title is *A meruelous reuelacion that was schewyd of almighty god by Sent Nycholas to a monk of Euyshamme yn the dayes of kyng Richard the fyrst And the yere of owre lorde, MCLXXXXVI.*

THE ADVENTURE OF THE CHARIOT

Book XIX., Chapters 3, 4, and 5, of *Le Morte Darthur*, recreated by Sir Thomas Malory from 'certain books of French,' and printed by William Caxton at London, in 1485. Our text is that of Sir Edward Strachey's edition (1861) : itself the result of a collation of the Southey-Upcott edition (1817) with the *editio princeps.*

A MOURNING REMEMBRANCE

Selected from *A Mornynge Remembrance*, the funeral sermon 'compyled by the Reverent Fader in God, Johan Fisher, Bysshop of Rochester,' in honour of Margaret, Countess of Richmond, mother of Henry VII., and delivered in 1505. Printed by Wynkyn de Worde in 1509, and reprinted in 1708 by Thomas Baker, whose text is ours.

A PAGEANT

Number 953 of *The Paston Letters* (Gairdner, 1875) addressed (17th January 1506) by William Makefyrr to Darcy and Alyngton.

THE KILLING OF LORD HASTINGS

From *The History of King Richard the Third (unfinished), written by* Master Thomas More *then one of the undersherriffs of London: about the yeare of our Lorde*, 1513. First printed in the Chronicles of Hardyng (1543) and Hall (1550) ; included in the folio edition of the *Works* of Sir Thomas More (1557) ; and reprinted *verbatim* (1883) by Dr. Lumby, whose text we follow.

WAT TYLER'S ENDING

From Vol. I. Chapter ccclxxxiv. of Sir John Froissart's *Cronycles of Englande, Fraunse, Spayne, Portugall, Scotlande, Bretaine, Flaunders, and other places adioynynge* : 'Translated out of French into our maternall Englisshe tongue, by John Bouchier, knyghte, Lord Berners : At the commandement of our most hyghe redouted soveraygne lorde Kynge Henry the VIII., Kynge of Englande, Fraunce, and Irelande, defender of the faith : and of the church of Englande and also of Irelande in earth the supreme heade.' Our text is modernised from that of the edition, in two volumes quarto, of 1812 : itself a reprint of the *editio princeps* produced by Pynson in 1523-1525.

THE CONQUEST OF BRITAIN

From the version by John Tiptoft, Earl of Worcester, of Caesar's *Commentaryes* (1530) : 'Newly translated owte of laten in to Englyshe as much as concernyth thys realm of England sometyme callyd Bretayne : which is the eldest hystoryes of all other that can be found that ever wrote of thys realm of England.' It has never been reprinted. Our text is that of the copy in the King's Library.

THE IMAGE OF DETRACTION

Excerpted from Book III. Chapter xxix. of *The Boke named The Governor devised by* Sir Thomas Elyot, Knyght (London 1531). Our text is that of Mr. H. H. S. Croft's edition of 1880.

THE CROWNING OF ANN BOLEYN.

Addressed the 25th day of June, 1533, to Archdeacon Hawkyns ; included among the Harleian MSS. ; here reprinted from *The Remains of Thomas Cranmer, D.D.*, collected and arranged (London, 1833) by the Rev. Henry Jenkyns, M.A.

A ROMAN VICTORY

The Seventeenth Chapter of the Sixth Book of *The History and Croniklis of Scotland*, translated (1530-33) from the *Scotorum Historiae* (1528) of Hector Boece by John Bellenden, Archdean of Moray and Canon of Ross, and printed at Edinburgh (*c.* 1536), by 'Thomas Davidson, a Northlande man, born on the Water of Dee,' presently (1540) Royal Printer. Our text is modernised from that of the edition prepared by Lord Dundrennan, for W. & C. Tait, and printed by them at Edinburgh in 1821.

SEEING THE WIND

Excerpted from *Toxophilus* (1545) : the text being edited from that of Mr. Arber's reprint (1868).

A CHARACTER OF LONDON

Excerpted from *A Notable Sermon of ye reverende father*, MAISTER HUGH LATIMER, *which he preached in ye Shrouds at paules churche in London on the xviii daye of Januarye. The yere of oure Lorde M.D, XLVIII :* in which year it was also published in the shape of a small black-letter quarto.

RALPH HYTHLODAYE

From *a Fruteful and pleasaunt Worke of the beste state of a publique Weale, and of the newe Yle called Utopia : written in Latine, by* Syr Thomas More, *knyght, and translated into Englyshe by* Raphe Robinson, *Citizein and Goldsmith of London.* Printed at London in 1551. Our text is that of Mr. Arber's reprint (1869) of the second edition (1556).

WOLSEY'S ARREST

From *The Life of Thomas Wolsey Cardinal Archbishop of York*, written (*c.* 1557) by George Cavendish, and printed, more or less incorrectly, in 1641. Our text is based on the edition issued from the Kelmscott Press in 1893, which is presented as a verbal and literal reproduction of the author's manuscript.

TWO BISHOPS

From John Foxe's *Actes and Monuments of these Latter and Perillous Dayes Touching Matters of the Church :* 'Wherein are comprehended and described the Great Persecutions and Horrible Troubles that have been wrought and practised by the Romishe Prelates, speciallye in this Realme of England and Scotlande from the year of Our Lorde a thousande unto the tyme nowe present. Gathered together and collected according to the true copies and wrytinges certificatorie as wel of the parties themselves that suffered, as also out of the Bishops Registers, which war the doers therof, by John Foxe.' 'Imprinted (1563) at London, by John Day, dwelling over Aldersgate. Cum privilegio Regie Magistatis.' Our text is that of the Townsend-Cattley edition of 1837-1842.

388   BIBLIOGRAPHY

A Pretty Thieft

From Book IV., Chapters 19 and 20 of *The Golden Asse*, translated from the Latin of Apuleius by William Adlington. The first edition appeared in 1566; there were half-a-dozen in some seventy years; the present text is that of the edition of 1639.

An Old Man's Misadventure

From *A Caveat or Warning for Common Cursitors, vulgarly called Vagabonds*, written by Thomas Harman Esquire and printed (for William Griffith) at London, 1566-7. No copy of this first edition is known to exist: our text is modernised from the reprint, by Dr. Furnivall and Mr. Edward Viles, of the third (1667) after collation with the second and fourth of 1567 and 1573.

An Escape

From *The Cronicles of Scotland*, by Robert Lindsay of Pitscottie. Our text is that of the edition prepared by [Sir] John Graham Dalyell, from the existing manuscripts, and published at Edinburgh, in two volumes, in 1814.

The Killing of David Beaton

From the First Book (1494-1558) of the *History of the Reformatioun of Religioun within the Realme of Scotland: Conteanyng the Maner and by What Persons the Light of Christis Evangell Hath Been Manifested unto this Realme, after that Horrible and Universall Defectioun from the Trewth which Iles Cume by the Meanes of that Romane Antichrist.* Written in 1566 —(so the late David Laing opined)—by John Knox. Printed at London, in 1586-87, by Vautrollier, and seized by order ere the impression was complete : at London in 1644, with many interpolations and falsifications, by David Buchanan ; and correctly at Edinburgh in 1732 under the supervision of the Rev. Matthew Crawfurd. Our text is modernised from the edition prepared by the late David Laing for the Bannatyne Club (Edinburgh, 1846), from a manuscript of 1566, written (it is held) at Knox's dictation and annotated and corrected in Knox's own hand. The passage is given under date of Knox's death.

A Scot Abroad

From the *Autobiography and Diary*, 1556-1601, of the Rev. James Melvill (1556-1614), 'Minister of Kilrenny in Fife, and Professor of Theology in the University of St. Andrews:' first printed at Edinburgh, for the Wodrow Society, in 1842, under the care of Robert Pitcairn, F.S.A. Scot. The original of the sketch was the author's uncle, Andrew Melville (1545-1622), some time Principal of the Universities of Glasgow and St. Andrews, and finally Professor of Theology at Sedan. He returning to Edinburgh, from a student's round in France and Switzerland, 'a lyttle befor Lambes,' in 1574, the story of his *Wanderjahre* is included under that heading by the diarist.

Agincourt

From *The Chronicles of England, Scotland, and Ireland:* 'First Collected and Published (1577) by Raphaell Hollinshed, William Harrison, and Others :

Now newlie augmented and continued (with manifold matters of singular note and worthie memorie) to the year 1586, by John Hooker *alias* Vowell, Gent, and others.' Save for the proper names, whose spelling is Hollinshed's own, our text is modernised from that of the edition of 1807 (London): printed, the Publishers declare, 'with the utmost Fidelity, from the best preceding Edition' with the Author's own Orthography, and with his Marginal Notes.'

THE YOUNG ALEXANDER

THE BANISHING OF CORIOLANUS

From the *Lives of the Noble Grecians and Romans. . . . Translated out of Plutarch's Greek into French by James Amiot. . . . and out of French into Englishe by Sir Thomas North, London,* 1579. Our text is that of the folio of 1657.

ENGLAND

Excerpted from *Euphues Glasse for Europe*, a chapter in, or appendix to, *Euphues and his England.* Our text is that of Mr. Arber's reprint (1868) from the *editio princeps* of 1580.

HOW WE CAME TO THE TOWN OF HOCHELAGA

From *A Short and Briefe Narration of the two Navigations and Discoveries of the North-weast partes called Newe France: First translated out of French into Italian by that famous learned man Gio. Bapt. Ramulius, and now turned into English by John Florio:* 'Worthy the Reading of all Venturers, Travellers, and Discoverers. Anno Domini 1580.'

A CORONATION

Excerpted from *The most solemne and magnificent coronation of Pheodor Ivanovich, Emperour of Russia, etc., the tenth of June, in the yeere* 1584: Seene and observed by Master Jerom Horsey, gentleman and servant to her Majesty, a man of great travell and long experience in those parts : wherewith is also joyned the course of his journey overland from Mosco to Emden.' Included by Richard Hakluyt in the first volume of his very famous *Principall Navigations, Voiages, and Discoueries of the English Nation,* London, 1599-1600. Our text is that of the edition of 1809-1811.

A FALSE WITCH

Book VII., Chapter i., of *The Discovery of Witchcraft; wherein the leud dealing of Witches and Witchmongers is notably detected, the Knaverie of Conjurers, the impiety of Inchantors, the folly of Soothsayers. . . .* London, 1584. Our text is that of Dr. Nicholson's reprint (1886).

THE FIRST LANDING IN VIRGINIA

From *The First Voyage made to the Coasts of America with two barks, wherein were Captaines M. Philip Amadas, and M. Arthur Barlowe, who discovered part of the country now called Virginia, Anno* 1584: 'Written by one of the said Captaines, and sent to Sir Walter Ralegh, Knight, at whose charge and direction the said Voyage was set forth.' First printed in Hakluyt's third volume (London, 1600). Our text is that of the reprint of 1809-11.

AN AFFAIR OF HONOUR

From Chapter vi. of *The Life of the Renowned Sir Philip Sidney*. . . . 'Written by Sir Fulke Grevile, Lord Brook, a Servant to Queen Elizabeth, and his Companion and Friend.' Printed after the text of the *editio princeps* (1652) but set here in the year of Sidney's death.

THE LAST FIGHT OF 'THE REVENGE'

From *A Report of the Truth of the fight about the Isles of Azores this last summer, betwixt* The Revenge, *One of Her Maiestie's Shippes and an Armada of the King of Spain :* Written some few weeks after the event by Sir Walter Raleigh and published the same year (1591) by William Ponsonby. Our text is based on that of Mr. Arber's reprint (1871).

GLORIANA

From the *Memoirs of His Own Life* : written some time before 1607, when the author died, by Sir James Melville, of Halhill, and for the first time accurately printed for the Bannatyne Club (Edinburgh 1827) from what is held to be the Author's own manuscript.

JOHN DAVYS THE NAVIGATOR

Excerpted from *The last Voyage of the worshipfull M. Thomas Candish, Esquire, intended for the South Sea, the Philippines and the coast of China, with 3 tall ships and two barks* : 'Written by M. John Jane, a man of good observation, imployed in the same and many other voyages.' Cavendish set out on this most disastrous expedition in 1591 ; but this story of Davys's part in it, the work of his supercargo, could not have been written till after 1593, under which date it is here presented. It first appeared in Hakluyt's fourth volume, and is here reprinted from the edition of 1809-1811. Authorities (it is to be noted) spell the Navigator's name with a *y* to distinguish him from a contemporary seaman, John Davis of Limehouse.

THE DIVINE ARETINE

From *The Unfortunate Traveller, or the Life of Jack Wilton,* 1594. Our text is modernised from the edition ' printed and issued by Charles Whittingham & Co., at the Chiswick Press, MDCCCXCII.'

DISCOVERING GUIANA

From *The Discouerie of the Large, Rich, and Beautiful Empire of Guiana, with a Relation of the Great and Golden City of Manoa (which the Spaniards call El Dorado) And the provinces of Emeria, Arromaia, Amapaia, and other countries with their riuers adioyning: Performed in the yeare* 1595 *by Sir W. Ralegh, Knight, Captaine of Her Maiestie's Guard, Ld. Warden of the Stanneries, and her Highnesse Lieutenant Generall of the Countie of Cornewall.'* Our text is that of the *editio princeps* : ' Imprinted at London by Robert Robinson, 1596.'

THE MEN IN BUCKRAM

From Act ii., Scene 4, of *The History of Henry the Fourth; With the Battell at Shrewsburie, between the King and Lord Henry Percy, surnamed Henrie Hotspur of the North; with the Humoures conceits of Sir John Falstaffe.* 'At London, printed by P. S. for Andrew Wise, dwelling in Paules Churchyard at the sign of the Angell.' Our text is that presented by Mr. Aldis Wright in Vol. iv. of *The Works of William Shakespeare* (London, 1891), itself a revised version of that of the First Folio (1623).

A PLOT AGAINST THE THRONE

From *The First Part of the Life and Raigne of Henrie IIII, extending to the end of the first yeare of his Raigne.* Written by Sir John Hayward; published in 1599; and reprinted in 1642, which edition is here followed.

THE PASSAGE OF THE ALPS

From Book XXI. of Philemon Holland's translation of Livy's *Romane Historie*, London, 1600. Our text is that of the *editio princeps*.

JULIUS CAESAR

Excerpted from 'The Historie of Spurina,' Book II. Chapter 33, of the *Essaies Written in French by Michael Lord of Montaigne*: 'Done into English according to the Last French Edition, by John Florio, Reader of the Italian Tongue unto the Soveraigne Maiestie of Anna, Queen of England, Scotland, France, and Ireland, etc., and one of the gentlemen of her Royale Priuie Chamber.' Printed in 1603. Our text is that of the edition of 1632.

THE MOST CHRISTIAN KING

From Book VI., Chapters 8 and 12, of *The Historie of Philip de Commines, Knight, Lord of Argenton.* Translated by Thomas Danett, London, 1601.

TAMERLANE

Excerpted from *The Generall Historie of the Turkes from the first beginning of that Nation to the rising of the Othoman Familie . . .* by Richard Knolles, London, 1603. Our text is that of the Sixth Edition, London, 1689.

TWO CHARACTERS

No. VI. of the 'Characterisms of Virtues,' and No. VIII. of the 'Characterisms of Vices,' contained in the *Characters of Virtues and Vices. In Two Books* (1608). Written by Joseph Hall, D.D., successively Bishop of Exeter and Norwich. Our text is that of the edition of Hall's *Works*, in Ten Volumes, prepared by Josiah Pratt, and published at London in 1808.

A COMPLETE GALLANT

From Chapter V. of *The Gull's Hornbook*, written by Thomas Dekker, and 'Imprinted at London for R.S., 1609.' Our text is that of Mr. Saintsbury's reprint in *Elizabethan and Jacobean Pamphlets* ('Pocket Library'), 1892.

THREE CHARACTERS

Selected from the set of 'Characters,' or 'Wittie Descriptions of the Properties of Sundry Persons,' issued (1616) with the Ninth Impression of Sir Thomas Overbury's 'poem,' *A Wife*. The first edition of that work, dated 1614, appeared a few months after Overbury's death in the September of 1613; to the second, also of 1614, there were added 'many wittie characters'—twenty-one, to speak by the card—'written by himself and other learned Gentlemen, his friends'; still more were included in subsequent editions, till in the ninth, the original of Dr. Rimbault's (1856), from which our text is modernised, the list is full eighty strong. Overbury's part in the work is, therefore, impossible to determine. But the authorship of our second excerpt, 'A Tinker' (Sixth Edition, 1615), with that of two others, 'An Apparitor' and 'An Almanack Maker,' was claimed by one J. Cocke.

THE PROVING OF ALIPIU

Book VI., Chapters 8 and 9, of *The Confessiones of the Incomparable Doctour, S. Augustine :* Translated by Sir Tobie Mathew, and printed at London in 1620.

A WONDER FOR WISE MEN

From *The Historie of the Raigne of King Henry the Seventh :* 'Written (1621) by the Right Honourable Francis Lord Verulam, Viscount St. Alban,' and 'Printed' (at London) 'by W. Staresby, for Matthew Lownes and William Barret, 1622.' Our text is that set forth in the Sixth Volume of Spedding's edition of the *Works of Francis Bacon* (London, 1858).

STEPS IN HIS SICKNESS

Meditations, I., II., III., and IV., in *Devotions upon Emergent Occasions, and Several Steps in my Sickness, Digested into* (1) *Meditations upon our Human Conditions ;* (2) *Expostulations and Debatements with God ;* (3) *Prayers upon the several occasions to Him :* by John Donne, Dean of St. Paul's : London, 1624. Our text is that of Dean Alford's edition, London, 1839.

TWO PILGRIMS

I. From *The Second Voyage of John Davis with Sir Edward Michelbourne, Knight, into the East Indies, in the* Tigre, *a ship of two hundred and forty tonnes, with a pinnace called the* Tigre's Whelpe. Printed (1625) in Part I., Book 3, of *Purchas his Pilgrims.* II. From William Hore's *Discourse of his Voyage in the* Dragon *and Expedition from Surat to Achen.* Printed in Part I., Book 5, of the same collection. These adventures, dated severally 1605, and 1619, are grouped under a common date, which is that of the publication of Purchas his book.

SOME UNIVERSITY CHARACTERS.

From the first edition, 1628, of *Microcosmographie, or, A Peece of the World Discovered in Essayes and Characters :* Attributed (1624) to John Earle, M.A., Fellow of Merton College, Oxford, afterwards Dean of Westminster, 1660, Bishop of Worcester, 1662, and Bishop of Salisbury, 1663. Our text is that of Mr. Arber's reprint (1862).

BIBLIOGRAPHY 393

An Unequal Combat

From *The Private Memoirs of Sir Kenelm Digby: Gentleman of the Bedchamber to King Charles the First:* Written by Himself. The MS., which Digby entitled *Loose Fantasies*, was first edited in 1827 by Sir Harris Nicholas. The characters are pseudonymous: Theagenes being Sir Kenelm himself, while Leodivius is probably the son of the Countess of Bristol by her first husband, Sir John Dive, and Alexandria is certainly Madrid. The passage is quoted under date of 1629, at which year the record ceases.

Three Characters

From the Second Edition (1635) of William Habington's *Castara.* Our text is that of Mr. Arber's reprint (1870) of the edition of 1640.

A Bout with the Adversary

From the *Memoirs* of the Rev. Robert Blair (1593-1666), printed—not in their integrity—in 1754, and republished by the Wodrow Society in 1848. The passage is quoted by Sharpe, pp. 114-116, in his edition of Law's *Memorials* (Edinburgh, 1818).

A Stratagem

From Book III. of *Naval Tracts*, written by Sir William Monson (1569-1636), first published in Churchill's *Voyages and Travels.* Our text is that of the Third Edition (lii. 225-228): 'Printed by assignment from Messrs. Churchill for Henry Lintot and John Osborn, at the Golden Bull in Paternoster Row,' London, 1745. The extract is printed under date of Monson's death.

A Covenanting Army

From Vol. I. of the *Letters and Journals* of Robert Baillie (1602-1661), Principal (1661) of the University of Glasgow. Edited by David Laing for the Bannatyne Club, and printed at Edinburgh for Robert Ogle in 1841.

'Carey's Raid'

From the *Memoirs of Robert Carey, Earl of Monmouth* (1559-1639), *written by Himself.* Published (1759) at London, 'from the original MS.,' with a Preface and Notes by the Earl of Orrery and Corke. Reprinted for Archibald Constable and John Murray at Edinburgh in 1808, with annotations by Walter Scott, who remarks that in his time the feat of arms depicted in our excerpt was still remembered in Liddisdale as 'Carey's Raid.' The extract is given under date of Carey's death.

A Night's Adventures

From Book II., 'The Lady Cornelia,' one of the *Exemplarie Novells*, of Miguel de Cervantes Saavedra: 'Turned into English by Don Diego Puede-Ser.' London, 1640.

Two Favourites

From the *Fragmenta Regalia* of Sir Robert Naunton (*d.* 1635) Knight, 'One of His Majesty's most Honourable Privy Council, and Master of the Court of Wards and Liveries.' Written (Mr. Arber thinks) about 1630, and first printed in 1641, under which date it is here presented. Our text is edited from that of Mr. Arber's reprint (1870) of the edition of 1653.

Discoveries

Selected and arranged from Ben Jonson's *Timber, or Discoveries made upon Men and Matter, As they have Flowed out of his Daily Readings; or Had their Reflux to His Peculiar Notion of the Times.* 'Written,' says Gifford, 'for the most part subsequently to 1630,' and first printed in the folio of 1641. Our text is that presented in the Ninth Volume of Gifford's edition, London, 1816.

Sir Francis Drake—The True Gentleman

From Thomas Fuller's *Holy and Profane State*, 1642. Reprinted from Pickering's edition, 1846.

A Vision of England

From *Areopagitica: A Speech for the Liberty of Unlicensed Printing. To the Parliament of England*: London, 1644.

A King of France

Excerpted from Book I., Section 1, Letter xviii., of the *Epistolae Ho-Elianae, Familiar Letters, Domestic and Foreign*, of 'James Howell, Esq.; One of the Clerks of his late Majesty's most Honourable Privy Council.' The letter, which is addressed 'To Sir James Crofts, from Paris,' is dated 12 May 1620 ; but, whether written then or not, it was published as late as 1645, under which year it is here presented. Our text is revised from that of Mr. Jacobs's reprint of 1891-3.

Luther at Worms

From the *Familiar Discourses of Dr. Martin Luther at his Table*: Translated from the High German (1646) by Captain Henry Bell. The text is that of the edition of 1791.

A Private Brawl

From the *Autobiography* written by Edward Lord Herbert of Cherbury (1582-3-1648), somewhere after 1642, and printed at Strawberry Hill by Horace Walpole in 1764. Given under date of Herbert's death, from Mr. Sidney Lee's edition, 1886.

THE BATTLE OF FLODDEN

From *The History of Scotland from the year 1423 until the year 1542. Containing the Lives and Reigns of James the I., the II., the III., the IV., the V. With several Memorials of State during the Reigns of James VI. and Charles I.* By William Drummond of Hawthornden. Published in 1656, with a Prefatory Introduction by Mr. Hall of Gray's Inn. 'Printed by Henry Hills for Rich. Tomlins and himself, and are to be sold at their house near Py-Corner.' The passage is given under date of Drummond's death.

Edinburgh : T. and A. CONSTABLE
Printers to Her Majesty

A LIST OF NEW BOOKS
AND ANNOUNCEMENTS OF
METHUEN AND COMPANY
PUBLISHERS : LONDON
36 ESSEX STREET
W.C.

CONTENTS

APRIL 1894

MESSRS. METHUEN'S
SPRING ANNOUNCEMENTS

——————◆——————

Gale. CRICKET SONGS. By NORMAN GALE. *Crown 8vo.*
Linen. 2s. 6d.
Also an edition, limited to 125 copies, on hand-made paper. *Demy*
8vo. 10s. 6d. *net.*
Also a small edition, of 15 copies only, on Japanese paper. *Demy*
8vo. 21s. *net.*

Mr. Gale's rural poems have made him widely popular, and this volume of spirited
verse will win him a new reputation among the lovers of our national game.

Flinders Petrie. THE HISTORY OF EGYPT, FROM THE
EARLIEST TIMES TO THE HYKSOS. By W. M. FLINDERS PETRIE,
Professor of Egyptology at University College. *Fully Illustrated.*
Crown 8vo. 6s.

This volume is the first of a History of Egypt in six volumes, intended both for
students and for general reading and reference, and will present a complete
record of what is now known, both of dated monuments and of events, from the
prehistoric age down to modern times. For the earlier periods every trace of the
various kings will be noticed, and all historical questions will be fully discussed.
The special features will be—

(1) The illustrations, largely photographic, or from *fac-simile* drawings; and, so
far as practicable, of new material not yet published. As yet, there is no
illustrated history of Egypt;

(2) The references given to the source of each statement and monument, making
this a key to the literature of the subject;

(3) The lists of all the known monuments of each king;

(4) The incorporation of current research down to the present time.

The volumes will cover the following periods ;—

I. Prehistoric to Hyksos times. By Prof. Flinders Petrie.
II. xviiith to xxth Dynasties. (The Same).
III. xxist to xxxth Dynasties. (The Same).
IV. The Ptolemaic Rule.
V. The Roman Rule.
VI. The Muhammedan Rule. By Stanley Lane Poole.

The volumes will be issued separately. The first will be ready in the autumn, the
Muhammedan volume early next year, and others at intervals of half a year.

Ottley. LANCELOT ANDREWES, Bishop of Winchester. A Biography. By R. L. OTTLEY, Principal of Pusey House, Oxford, and Fellow of Magdalen. *With Portrait. Crown 8vo. Buckram.* 5*s.*

This life of the saintly bishop and theologian, of whom no adequate biography exists, will have much value for English Churchmen. It is issued uniform with Mr. Lock's 'Life of Keble,' and written as it is by so distinguished a scholar as Mr. Ottley, it is as likely to become as popular.

Gladstone. THE SPEECHES AND PUBLIC ADDRESSES OF THE RT. HON. W. E. GLADSTONE, M.P. With Notes. Edited by A. W. HUTTON, M.A. (Librarian of the Gladstone Library), and H. J. COHEN, M.A. With Portraits. *8vo. Vol. IX.* 12*s. 6d.*

Messrs. METHUEN beg to announce that they are about to issue, in ten volumes 8vo, an authorised collection of Mr. Gladstone's Speeches, the work being undertaken with his sanction and under his superintendence. Notes and Introductions will be added.

In view of the interest in the Home Rule Question, it is proposed to issue Vols. IX. and X., which will include the speeches of the last seven or eight years, immediately, and then to proceed with the earlier volumes. Volume X. is already published.

Robbins. THE EARLY LIFE OF WILLIAM EWART GLADSTONE. By A. F. ROBBINS. *Crown 8vo.* 6*s.*

A full account of the early part of Mr. Gladstone's extraordinary career, based on much research, and containing a good deal of new matter, especially with regard to his school and college days.

Henley and Whibley. A BOOK OF ENGLISH PROSE. Collected by W. E. HENLEY and CHARLES WHIBLEY. *Crown 8vo.* Also small limited editions on Dutch and Japanese paper. 21*s.* and 42*s. net.*

A companion book to Mr. Henley's well-known 'Lyra Heroica.' It is believed that no such collection of splendid prose has ever been brought within the compass of one volume. Each piece, whether containing a character-sketch or incident, is complete in itself. The book will be finely printed and bound.

Beeching. SERMONS TO SCHOOLBOYS. Sermons by H. C. BEECHING, M.A., Rector of Yattendon, Berks. *Crown 8vo.* 2*s. 6d.*

Six sermons preached before the boys of Bradfield College.

Parkyn. CHARLES DARWIN: a Lecture delivered at Christ's College, Cambridge, by E. A. PARKYN, M.A. *Crown 8vo.* 1*s.*

A short account of the work and influence of Darwin.

Waldstein. JOHN RUSKIN : a Study. By CHARLES WALD-
STEIN, M.A., Fellow of King's College, Cambridge. *Post 8vo.* 5*s.*
Also a small edition on hand-made paper. *Demy 8vo.* 15*s. net.*

This is a frank and fair appreciation of Mr. Ruskin's work and influence—literary
and social—by an able critic, who has enough admiration to make him sympathetic, and enough discernment to make him impartial.

Sterne. TRISTRAM SHANDY. By LAWRENCE STERNE.
With an Introduction by CHARLES WHIBLEY, and a Portrait.
2 vols. Crown 8vo. 7*s.*

Congreve. THE COMEDIES OF WILLIAM CONGREVE.
Edited, with an Introduction, by G. S. STREET, and a Portrait.
Crown 8vo. 3*s. 6d.*

The above important editions of two English classics are finely printed by Messrs.
Constable, and handsomely bound. Each is carefully edited with scholarly
f introductions—biographical and critical. They are issued in two editions—
The ordinary edition on laid paper, bound in buckram, 3*s. 6d.* a volume.
The library edition (limited in number) on hand-made paper, bound in half parch-
ment, 7*s. 6d.* a volume, net.

UNIVERSITY EXTENSION SERIES

NEW VOLUME. Crown 8vo. 2*s. 6d.*

THE EARTH. An Introduction to Physiography. By EVAN
SMALL, M.A.

Methuen's Commercial Series

NEW VOLUMES.

THE ECONOMICS OF COMMERCE. By H. de B. GIBBINS,
M.A. 1*s. 6d.*

A PRIMER OF BUSINESS. By S. JACKSON, M.A. 1*s. 6d.*

COMMERCIAL ARITHMETIC. By F. G. TAYLOR, M.A.

SOCIAL QUESTIONS OF TO-DAY

NEW VOLUMES. Crown 8vo. 2*s. 6d.*

WOMEN'S WORK. By LADY DILKE, MISS BULLEY, and
MISS ABRAHAM.

TRUSTS, POOLS AND CORNERS : As affecting Commerce and Industry. By J. STEPHEN JEANS, M.R.I., F.S.S.

THE FACTORY SYSTEM. By R. COOKE TAYLOR.

THE STATE AND ITS CHILDREN. By GERTRUDE TUCKWELL.

Classical Translations

NEW VOLUMES.

Crown 8vo. Finely printed and bound in blue buckram.

LUCIAN—Six Dialogues (Nigrinus, Icaro-Menippus, The Cock, The Ship, The Parasite, The Love of Falsehood). Translated by S. T. IRWIN, M.A., Assistant Master at Clifton; late Scholar of Lincoln College, Oxford.

SOPHOCLES—Electra and Ajax. Translated by E. D. A. MORSHEAD, M.A., late Scholar of New College, Oxford ; Assistant Master at Winchester.

TACITUS—Agricola and Germania. Translated by R. B. TOWNSHEND, late Scholar of Trinity College, Cambridge.

CICERO—Select Orations (Pro Milone, Pro Murena, Philippic II., In Catilinam). Translated by H. E. D. BLAKISTON, M.A., Fellow and Tutor of Trinity College, Oxford.

Fiction

E. F. Benson. THE RUBICON. By E. F. BENSON, Author of 'Dodo.' *2 vols. Crown 8vo. 21s.*

The announcement of a new novel of society by the author of the brilliantly successful 'Dodo' will excite great interest, and it is believed that 'The Rubicon' will prove to have as much fascination as its predecessor.

Stanley Weyman. UNDER THE RED ROBE. By STANLEY WEYMAN, Author of 'A Gentleman of France,' etc. With 12 Illustrations by R. CATON WOODVILLE. *2 vols. Crown 8vo. 21s.*

Mr. Weyman's fine historical tales have placed him in the front rank of novelists, and this stirring story of Richelieu and the Huguenots will not lessen his reputation.

Mrs. Oliphant. THE PRODIGALS. By Mrs. OLIPHANT.
2 vols. Crown 8vo. 21s.

It is hardly necessary to say much about a new story from Mrs. Oliphant's graceful pen. The present one is a charming and pathetic study.

Baring Gould. THE QUEEN OF LOVE. By S. BARING GOULD, Author of 'Mehalah,' 'Cheap Jack Zita,' etc. *3 vols. Crown 8vo. 31s. 6d.*

A story of the Cheshire salt region—a new district for the exercise of Mr. Baring Gould's original and powerful gifts.

Gilbert Parker. THE TRANSLATION OF A SAVAGE. By GILBERT PARKER, Author of 'Pierre and His People,' 'Mrs. Falchion,' etc. *Crown 8vo. 5s.*

A story with a powerful and pathetic motive by a writer who has rapidly made his way to the front.

Richard Pryce. WINIFRED MOUNT. By RICHARD PRYCE, Author of 'Miss Maxwell's Affections,' 'Time and the Woman,' etc. *2 vols. Crown 8vo. 21s.*

A story of society by Mr. Pryce, whose clever pen has the lightness and ease of Octave Feuillet.

Constance Smith. A CUMBERER OF THE GROUND. By CONSTANCE SMITH, Author of 'The Riddle of Lawrence Haviland.' *3 vols. Crown 8vo. 31s. 6d.*

Carew. JIM B.: a Story. By F. S. CAREW. *Cr. 8vo. 2s. 6d.*

Standish O'Grady. THE COMING OF CURCULAIN. By STANDISH O'GRADY, Author of 'Finn and His Companions,' 'The Story of Ireland,' etc. *Crown 8vo. 2s. 6d.*

Curculain is one of the great legendary heroes of the Irish, and the adventures of his early life are told by Mr. O'Grady in his brilliant and fascinating manner.

NEW AND CHEAPER EDITIONS

Marie Corelli. BARABBAS: A DREAM OF THE WORLD'S TRAGEDY. By MARIE CORELLI, Author of 'A Romance of Two Worlds,' 'Vendetta,' etc. *Eighth Edition. Crown 8vo. 6s.*

A cheaper edition of a book which aroused in some quarters more violent hostility than any book of recent years. By most secular critics the authoress was accused of bad taste, bad art, and gross blasphemy; but in curious contrast, most of the religious papers acknowledged the reverence of treatment and the dignity of conception which characterised the book. Of this cheaper issue the fourth, fifth and sixth editions were sold on publication.

Baring Gould. CHEAP JACK ZITA. By S. BARING GOULD.
Crown 8vo. 6s.
A cheap edition of a story which has been recognised as Mr. Baring Gould's most
original effort since 'Mehalah.'

Fenn. THE STAR GAZERS. By G. MANVILLE FENN.
Crown 8vo. 3s. 6d.
An exciting story with many sensations, and a complex plot.

Esmè Stuart. A WOMAN OF FORTY. By ESMÈ STUART.
Crown 8vo. 3s. 6d.
Pathetic in motive, with an admirably worked out plot, and without overmuch
analysis of character, the book has won much praise and many readers.

Educational

Davis. TACITI GERMANIA. Edited with Notes and
Introduction. By R. F. DAVIS, M.A., Editor of the 'Agricola.'
Small crown 8vo.

Freese. THE CAPTIVI OF PLAUTUS. Abridged and Edited
for the use of Schools, with Introduction and Notes, by J. H.
FREESE, M.A. *Fcap.* 1s. 6d.

Stedman. GREEK TESTAMENT SELECTIONS. Edited
by A. M. M. STEDMAN, M.A. *Third and Revised Edition.*
Fcap. 8vo. 2s. 6d.

Stedman. STEPS TO FRENCH. By A. M. M. STEDMAN.
M.A. *18mo.*
An attempt to supply a very easy and very short book of French Lessons.

Stedman. A VOCABULARY OF LATIN IDIOMS AND
PHRASES. *Fcap. 8vo.*

Malden. ENGLISH RECORDS: A COMPANION TO ENGLISH
HISTORY. By H. E. MALDEN, M.A. *Crown 8vo.*

PRIMARY CLASSICS
A series of Classical Readers, Edited for Lower Forms with Introductions, Notes, Maps, and Vocabularies.

Herodotus. THE PERSIAN WARS. Edited by A. G. LIDDELL,
M.A., Assistant Master at Nottingham High School. *18mo.* 1s. 6d.

Livy. THE KINGS OF ROME. Edited by A. M. M.
STEDMAN, M.A. *18mo. Illustrated.* 1s. 6d.

Caesar. THE HELVETIAN WAR. Edited by A. M. M.
STEDMAN, M.A. *18mo.* 1s.

𝔑𝔢𝔴 𝔞𝔫𝔡 𝔕𝔢𝔠𝔢𝔫𝔱 𝔅𝔬𝔬𝔨𝔰

Poetry

Rudyard Kipling. BARRACK-ROOM BALLADS; And Other Verses. By RUDYARD KIPLING. *Seventh Edition. Crown 8vo. 6s.*

A Special Presentation Edition, bound in white buckram, with extra gilt ornament. *7s. 6d.*

'Mr. Kipling's verse is strong, vivid, full of character. . . . Unmistakable genius rings in every line.'—*Times.*

'The disreputable lingo of Cockayne is henceforth justified before the world; for a man of genius has taken it in hand, and has shown, beyond all cavilling, that in its way it also is a medium for literature. You are grateful, and you say to yourself, half in envy and half in admiration: "Here is a *book*; here, or one is a Dutchman, is one of the books of the year."'—*National Observer.*

'"Barrack-Room Ballads" contains some of the best work that Mr. Kipling has ever done, which is saying a good deal. "Fuzzy-Wuzzy," "Gunga Din," and "Tommy," are, in our opinion, altogether superior to anything of the kind that English literature has hitherto produced.'—*Athenæum.*

'These ballads are as wonderful in their descriptive power as they are vigorous in their dramatic force. There are few ballads in the English language more stirring than "The Ballad of East and West," worthy to stand by the Border ballads of Scott.'—*Spectator.*

'The ballads teem with imagination, they palpitate with emotion. We read them with laughter and tears; the metres throb in our pulses, the cunningly ordered words tingle with life; and if this be not poetry, what is?'—*Pall Mall Gazette.*

Henley. LYRA HEROICA: An Anthology selected from the best English Verse of the 16th, 17th, 18th, and 19th Centuries. By WILLIAM ERNEST HENLEY, Author of 'A Book of Verse,' 'Views and Reviews,' etc. *Crown 8vo. Stamped gilt buckram, gilt top, edges uncut. 6s.*

Mr. Henley has brought to the task of selection an instinct alike for poetry and for chivalry which seems to us quite wonderfully, and even unerringly, right.'—*Guardian.*

Tomson. A SUMMER NIGHT, AND OTHER POEMS. By GRAHAM R. TOMSON. With Frontispiece by A. TOMSON. *Fcap. 8vo. 3s. 6d.*

An edition on hand-made paper, limited to 50 copies. *10s. 6d. net.*

'Mrs. Tomson holds perhaps the very highest rank among poetesses of English birth. This selection will help her reputation.'—*Black and White.*

Ibsen. BRAND. A Drama by HENRIK IBSEN. Translated by WILLIAM WILSON. *Crown 8vo. Second Edition. 3s. 6d.*

'The greatest world-poem of the nineteenth century next to "Faust." "Brand" will have an astonishing interest for Englishmen. It is in the same set with "Agamemnon," with "Lear," with the literature that we now instinctively regard as high and holy.'—*Daily Chronicle.*

"Q." GREEN BAYS : Verses and Parodies.   By "Q.," Author
of 'Dead Man's Rock' etc.   *Second Edition.*   *Fcap. 8vo.*   3s. 6d.

'The verses display a rare and versatile gift of parody, great command of metre, and
a very pretty turn of humour.'—*Times.*

"A. G." VERSES TO ORDER. By "A. G." *Cr. 8vo.* 2s. 6d.
net.

A small volume of verse by a writer whose initials are well known to Oxford men
'A capital specimen of light academic poetry. These verses are very bright and
engaging, easy and sufficiently witty.'—*St. James's Gazette.*

Hosken. VERSES BY THE WAY. By J. D. HOSKEN.
Printed on laid paper, and bound in buckram, gilt top. 5s.
A small edition on hand-made paper. *Price 12s. 6d. net.*

A Volume of Lyrics and Sonnets by J. D. Hosken, the Postman Poet, of Helston,
Cornwall, whose interesting career is now more or less well known to the literary
public. Q, the Author of 'The Splendid Spur,' etc., writes a critical and
biographical introduction.

Scott. THE MAGIC HOUSE AND OTHER VERSES. By
DUNCAN C. SCOTT. *Extra Post 8vo, bound in buckram.* 5s.

Langbridge. BALLADS OF THE BRAVE : Poems of Chivalry,
Enterprise, Courage, and Constancy, from the Earliest Times to the
Present Day. Edited, with Notes, by Rev. F. LANGBRIDGE.
Crown 8vo. *Buckram 3s. 6d.* School Edition, 2s. 6d. Also in three
parts, *Price 1s. each.*

'A very happy conception happily carried out. These "Ballads of the Brave" are
intended to suit the real tastes of boys, and will suit the taste of the great majority.'
—*Spectator.*   'The book is full of splendid things.'—*World.*

General Literature

Collingwood. JOHN RUSKIN : His Life and Work. By
W. G. COLLINGWOOD, M.A., late Scholar of University College,
Oxford, Author of the 'Art Teaching of John Ruskin,' Editor of
Mr. Ruskin's Poems. 2 *vols.* 8vo. 32s. *Second Edition.*

This important work is written by Mr. Collingwood, who has been for some years
Mr. Ruskin's private secretary, and who has had unique advantages in obtaining
materials for this book from Mr. Ruskin himself and from his friends. It contains
a large amount of new matter, and of letters which have never been published,
and is, in fact, a full and authoritative biography of Mr. Ruskin. The book
contains numerous portraits of Mr. Ruskin, including a coloured one from a

A 2

water-colour portrait by himself, and also 13 sketches, never before published, by Mr. Ruskin and Mr. Arthur Severn. A bibliography is added.

'No more magnificent volumes have been published for a long time. . . .'—*Times.*

'This most lovingly written and most profoundly interesting book.'—*Daily News.*

'It is long since we have had a biography with such varied delights of substance and of form. Such a book is a pleasure for the day, and a joy for ever.'—*Daily Chronicle.*

'Mr. Ruskin could not well have been more fortunate in his biographer.'—*Globe.*

'A noble monument of a noble subject. One of the most beautiful books about one of the noblest lives of our century.'—*Glasgow Herald.*

Gladstone. THE SPEECHES AND PUBLIC ADDRESSES OF THE RT. HON. W. E. GLADSTONE, M.P. With Notes and Introductions. Edited by A. W. HUTTON, M.A. (Librarian of the Gladstone Library), and H. J. COHEN, M.A. With Portraits. 8vo. *Vol. X.* 12s. 6d.

Russell. THE LIFE OF ADMIRAL LORD COLLING-WOOD. By W. CLARK RUSSELL, Author of 'The Wreck of the Grosvenor.' With Illustrations by F. BRANGWYN. 8vo. 15s.

'A really good book.'—*Saturday Review.*

'A most excellent and wholesome book, which we should like to see in the hands of every boy in the country.'—*St. James's Gazette.*

Clark. THE COLLEGES OF OXFORD: Their History and their Traditions. By Members of the University. Edited by A. CLARK, M.A., Fellow and Tutor of Lincoln College. 8vo. 12s. 6d.

'Whether the reader approaches the book as a patriotic member of a college, as an antiquary, or as a student of the organic growth of college foundation, it will amply reward his attention.'—*Times.*

'A delightful book, learned and lively.'—*Academy.*

'A work which will certainly be appealed to for many years as the standard book on the Colleges of Oxford.'—*Athenæum.*

Wells. OXFORD AND OXFORD LIFE. By Members of the University. Edited by J. WELLS, M.A., Fellow and Tutor of Wadham College. Crown 8vo. 3s. 6d.

This work contains an account of life at Oxford—intellectual, social, and religious—a careful estimate of necessary expenses, a review of recent changes, a statement of the present position of the University, and chapters on Women's Education, aids to study, and University Extension.

'We congratulate Mr. Wells on the production of a readable and intelligent account of Oxford as it is at the present time, written by persons who are, with hardly an exception, possessed of a close acquaintance with the system and life of the University.'—*Athenæum.*

Perrens. THE HISTORY OF FLORENCE FROM THE TIME OF THE MEDICIS TO THE FALL OF THE REPUBLIC. By F. T. PERRENS. Translated by HANNAH LYNCH. In three volumes. *Vol. I. 8vo. 12s. 6d.*

This is a translation from the French of the best history of Florence in existence. This volume covers a period of profound interest—political and literary—and is written with great vivacity.

This is a standard book by an honest and intelligent historian, who has deserved well of his countrymen, and of all who are interested in Italian history.'—*Manchester Guardian.*

Browning. GUELPHS AND GHIBELLINES: A Short History of Mediæval Italy, A.D. 1250-1409. By OSCAR BROWNING, Fellow and Tutor of King's College, Cambridge. *Second Edition. Crown 8vo. 5s.*

'A very able book.'—*Westminster Gazette.*
'A vivid picture of mediæval Italy.'—*Standard.*

O'Grady. THE STORY OF IRELAND. By STANDISH O'GRADY, Author of ' Finn and his Companions.' *Cr. 8vo. 2s. 6d.*

'Novel and very fascinating history. Wonderfully alluring.'—*Cork Examiner.*
'Most delightful, most stimulating. Its racy humour, its original imaginings, its perfectly unique history, make it one of the freshest, breeziest volumes.'—*Methodist Times.*
'A survey at once graphic, acute, and quaintly written.'—*Times.*

Dixon. ENGLISH POETRY FROM BLAKE TO BROWNING. By W. M. DIXON, M.A. *Crown 8vo. 3s. 6d.*

A Popular Account of the Poetry of the Century.
'Scholarly in conception, and full of sound and suggestive criticism.'—*Times.*
'The book is remarkable for freshness of thought expressed in graceful language.'—*Manchester Examiner.*

Bowden. THE EXAMPLE OF BUDDHA: Being Quotations from Buddhist Literature for each Day in the Year. Compiled by E. M. BOWDEN. With Preface by Sir EDWIN ARNOLD. *Third Edition. 16mo. 2s. 6d.*

Ditchfield. OUR ENGLISH VILLAGES: Their Story and their Antiquities. By P. H. DITCHFIELD, M.A., F.R.H.S., Rector of Barkham, Berks. *Post 8vo. 2s. 6d.* Illustrated.

'An extremely amusing and interesting little book, which should find a place in every parochial library.'—*Guardian.*

Ditchfield. OLD ENGLISH SPORTS. By P. H. DITCH-
FIELD, M.A. *Crown 8vo.* 2s. 6d. Illustrated.
'A charming account of old English Sports.'—*Morning Post.*

Massee. A MONOGRAPH OF THE MYXOGASTRES. By
GEORGE MASSEE. With 12 Coloured Plates. *Royal 8vo.* 18s. *net.*
'A work much in advance of any book in the language treating of this group of
organisms. It is indispensable to every student of the Mxyogastres. The
coloured plates deserve high praise for their accuracy and execution.'—*Nature.*

Bushill. PROFIT SHARING AND THE LABOUR QUES-
TION. By T. W. BUSHILL, a Profit Sharing Employer. With an
Introduction by SEDLEY TAYLOR, Author of ' Profit Sharing between
Capital and Labour.' *Crown 8vo.* 2s. 6d.

John Beever. PRACTICAL FLY-FISHING, Founded on
Nature, by JOHN BEEVER, late of the Thwaite House, Coniston. A
New Edition, with a Memoir of the Author by W. G. COLLINGWOOD,
M.A., Author of 'The Life and Work of John Ruskin,' etc. Also
additional Notes and a chapter on Char-Fishing, by A. and A. R.
SEVERN. With a specially designed title-page. *Crown 8vo.* 3s. 6d.
A little book on Fly-Fishing by an old friend of Mr. Ruskin. It has been out of
print for some time, and being still much in request, is now issued with a Memoir
of the Author by W. G. Collingwood.

Theology

Driver. SERMONS ON SUBJECTS CONNECTED WITH
THE OLD TESTAMENT. By S. R. DRIVER, D.D., Canon of
Christ Church, Regius Professor of Hebrew in the University of
Oxford. *Crown 8vo.* 6s.
'A welcome companion to the author's famous 'Introduction.' No man can read these
discourses without feeling that Dr. Driver is fully alive to the deeper teaching of
the Old Testament.'—*Guardian.*

Cheyne. FOUNDERS OF OLD TESTAMENT CRITICISM:
Biographical, Descriptive, and Critical Studies. By T. K. CHEYNE,
D.D., Oriel Professor of the Interpretation of Holy Scripture at
Oxford. *Large crown 8vo.* 7s. 6d.
This important book is a historical sketch of O.T. Criticism in the form of biographi-
cal studies from the days of Eithhorn to those of Driver and Robertson Smith.
It is the only book of its kind in English.
'The volume is one of great interest and value. It displays all the author's well-
known ability and learning, and its opportune publication has laid all students ot
theology, and specially of Bible criticism, under weighty obligation.'—*Scotsman.*
'A very learned and instructive work.'—*Times*

Prior. CAMBRIDGE SERMONS. Edited by C. H. PRIOR, M.A., Fellow and Tutor of Pembroke College. *Crown 8vo.* 6s.

A volume of sermons preached before the University of Cambridge by various preachers, including the Archbishop of Canterbury and Bishop Westcott.
'A representative collection. Bishop Westcott's is a noble sermon.'—*Guardian.*
'Full of thoughtfulness and dignity.'—*Record.*

Burne. PARSON AND PEASANT: Chapters of their Natural History. By J. B. BURNE, M.A. *Cr. 8vo.* 5s.

'"Parson and Peasant" is a book not only to be interested in, but to learn something from—a book which may prove a help to many a clergyman, and broaden the hearts and ripen the charity of laymen.'—*Derby Mercury.*

Cunningham. THE PATH TOWARDS KNOWLEDGE: Essays on Questions of the Day. By W. CUNNINGHAM, D.D., Fellow of Trinity College, Cambridge, Professor of Economics at King's College, London. *Crown 8vo.* 4s. 6d.

Essays on Marriage and Population, Socialism, Money, Education, Positivism, etc.

James. CURIOSITIES OF CHRISTIAN HISTORY PRIOR TO THE REFORMATION. By CROAKE JAMES, Author of 'Curiosities of Law and Lawyers.' *Crown 8vo.* 7s. 6d.

'This volume contains a great deal of quaint and curious matter, affording some "particulars of the interesting persons, episodes, and events from the Christian's point of view during the first fourteen centuries." Wherever we dip into his pages we find something worth dipping into.'—*John Bull.*

Lock. THE LIFE OF JOHN KEBLE. By WALTER LOCK, M.A. With Portrait from a painting by GEORGE RICHMOND, R.A. *Crown 8vo. Buckram 5s. Sixth Edition.*

'A fine portrait of one of the most saintly characters of our age, and a valuable contribution to the history of that Oxford Movement.'—*Times.*

Kaufmann. CHARLES KINGSLEY. By M. KAUFMANN, M.A. *Crown 8vo. Buckram. 5s.*

A biography of Kingsley, especially dealing with his achievements in social reform.
'The author has certainly gone about his work with conscientiousness and industry.'—*Sheffield Daily Telegraph.*

Oliphant. THOMAS CHALMERS: A Biography. By Mrs. OLIPHANT. With Portrait. *Crown 8vo. Buckram, 5s.*

'A well-executed biography, worthy of its author and of the remarkable man who is its subject. Mrs. Oliphant relates lucidly and dramatically the important part which Chalmers played in the memorable secession.'—*Times.*

Leaders of Religion

Edited by H. C. BEECHING, M.A. *With Portrait, crown 8vo.* 2s. 6d.

A series of short biographies of the most prominent leaders of religious life and thought.

The following are ready—

2/6

CARDINAL NEWMAN. By R. H. HUTTON.

'Few who read this book will fail to be struck by the wonderful insight it displays into the nature of the Cardinal's genius and the spirit of his life.'—WILFRID WARD, in the *Tablet*.

'Full of knowledge, excellent in method, and intelligent in criticism. We regard it as wholly admirable.'—*Academy*.

JOHN WESLEY. By J. H. OVERTON, M.A.

'It is well done: the story is clearly told, proportion is duly observed, and there is no lack either of discrimination or of sympathy.'—*Manchester Guardian*.

BISHOP WILBERFORCE. By G. W. DANIEL, M.A.

CHARLES SIMEON. By H. C. G. MOULE, M.A.

CARDINAL MANNING. By A. W. HUTTON, M.A.

Other volumes will be announced in due course.

WORKS BY S. BARING GOULD.

OLD COUNTRY LIFE. With Sixty-seven Illustrations by W. PARKINSON, F. D. BEDFORD, and F. MASEY. *Large Crown 8vo, cloth super extra, top edge gilt*, 10s. 6d. *Fourth and Cheaper Edition.* 6s.

' "Old Country Life," as healthy wholesome reading, full of breezy life and movement, full of quaint stories vigorously told, will not be excelled by any book to be published throughout the year. Sound, hearty, and English to the core.'—*World*.

HISTORIC ODDITIES AND STRANGE EVENTS. *Third Edition. Crown 8vo.* 6s.

'A collection of exciting and entertaining chapters. The whole volume is delightful reading.'—*Times*.

FREAKS OF FANATICISM. *Third Edition. Crown 8vo.* 6s.

'Mr. Baring Gould has a keen eye for colour and effect, and the subjects he has chosen give ample scope to his descriptive and analytic faculties. A perfectly fascinating book.'—*Scottish Leader*.

SONGS OF THE WEST: Traditional Ballads and Songs of the West of England, with their Traditional Melodies. Collected by S. BARING GOULD, M.A., and H. FLEETWOOD SHEPPARD, M.A. Arranged for Voice and Piano. In 4 Parts (containing 25 Songs each), *Parts I., II., III.*, 3s. *each. Part IV.*, 5s. *In one Vol., roan*, 15s.

'A rich and varied collection of humour, pathos, grace, and poetic fancy.'—*Saturday Review.*

YORKSHIRE ODDITIES AND STRANGE EVENTS. *Fourth Edition. Crown 8vo. 6s.*

STRANGE SURVIVALS AND SUPERSTITIONS. With Illustrations. By S. BARING GOULD. *Crown 8vo. Second Edition.* 6s.

A book on such subjects as Foundations, Gables, Holes, Gallows, Raising the Hat, Old Ballads, etc. etc. It traces in a most interesting manner their origin and history.
'We have read Mr. Baring Gould's book from beginning to end. It is full of quaint and various information, and there is not a dull page in it.'—*Notes and Queries.*

THE TRAGEDY OF THE CAESARS: The Emperors of the Julian and Claudian Lines. With numerous Illustrations from Busts, Gems, Cameos, etc. By S. BARING GOULD, Author of 'Mehalah,' etc. *Second Edition.* 2 vols. *Royal 8vo.* 30s.

' A most splendid and fascinating book on a subject of undying interest. The great feature of the book is the use the author has made of the existing portraits of the Caesars, and the admirable critical subtlety he has exhibited in dealing with this line of research. It is brilliantly written, and the illustrations are supplied on a scale of profuse magnificence.'—*Daily Chronicle.*
' The volumes will in no sense disappoint the general reader. Indeed, in their way, there is nothing in any sense so good in English. . . . Mr. Baring Gould has presented his narrative in such a way as not to make one dull page.'—*Athenæum.*

MR. BARING GOULD'S NOVELS.

' To say that a book is by the author of " Mehalah " is to imply that it contains a story cast on strong lines, containing dramatic possibilities, vivid and sympathetic descriptions of Nature, and a wealth of ingenious imagery.'—*Speaker.*
' That whatever Mr. Baring Gould writes is well worth reading, is a conclusion that may be very generally accepted. His views of life are fresh and vigorous, his language pointed and characteristic, the incidents of which he makes use are striking and original, his characters are life-like, and though somewhat exceptional people, are drawn and coloured with artistic force. Add to this that his descriptions of scenes and scenery are painted with the loving eyes and skilled hands of a master of his art, that he is always fresh and never dull, and under such conditions it is no wonder that readers have gained confidence both in his power of amusing and satisfying them, and that year by year his popularity widens.'—*Court Circular.*

IN THE ROAR OF THE SEA : A Tale of the Cornish Coast.
New Edition. 6s.

MRS. CURGENVEN OF CURGENVEN. *Third Edition.* 6s.
A powerful and characteristic story of Devon life. The 'Graphic' speaks of it as *a
novel of vigorous humour and sustained power*; the 'Sussex Daily News' says
that *the swing of the narrative is splendid*; and the 'Speaker' mentions its
bright imaginative power.

CHEAP JACK ZITA. By S. BARING GOULD. *Crown 8vo.* 6s.
A Romance of the Ely Fen District in 1815.
'A powerful drama of human passion.'—*Westminster Gazette.*
'A story worthy the author.'—*National Observer.*

ARMINELL : A Social Romance. *New Edition. Crown 8vo.*
3s. 6d.

URITH : A Story of Dartmoor. *Third Edition. Crown 8vo.* 3s.6d.
'The author is at his best.'—*Times.*
'He has nearly reached the high water-mark of " Mehalah." '—*National Observer.*

MARGERY OF QUETHER, and other Stories. *Crown 8vo.*
3s. 6d.

JACQUETTA, and other Stories. *Crown 8vo.* 3s. 6d.

Fiction

SIX SHILLING NOVELS

Corelli. BARABBAS : A DREAM OF THE WORLD'S
TRAGEDY. By MARIE CORELLI, Author of 'A Romance of Two
Worlds,' 'Vendetta,' etc. *Eighth Edition Crown 8vo.* 6s.
Miss Corelli's new romance has been received with much disapprobation by the
secular papers, and with warm welcome by the religious papers. By the former
she has been accused of blasphemy and bad taste; 'a gory nightmare'; 'a hideous
travesty'; 'grotesque vulgarisation'; 'unworthy of criticism'; 'vulgar redun-
dancy'; 'sickening details'—these are some of the secular flowers of speech.
On the other hand, the 'Guardian' praises 'the dignity of its conceptions, the
reserve round the Central Figure, the fine imagery of the scene and circumstance,
so much that is elevating and devout'; the 'Illustrated Church News' styles the
book 'reverent and artistic, broad based on the rock of our common nature, and
appealing to what is best in it '; the 'Christian World' says it is written 'by one
who has more than conventional reverence, who has tried to tell the story that it
may be read again with open and attentive eyes'; the 'Church of England
Pulpit' welcomes 'a book which teems with faith without any appearance of
irreverence.'

Benson. DODO: A DETAIL OF THE DAY. By E. F.
BENSON. *Crown 8vo. Thirteenth Edition.* 6s.

A story of society by a new writer, full of interest and power, which has attracted
by its brilliance universal attention. The best critics were cordial in their
praise. The 'Guardian spoke of 'Dodo,' as *unusually clever and interesting*;
the 'Spectator called it *a delightfully witty sketch of society*; the 'Speaker'
said the dialogue was *a perpetual feast of epigram and paradox*; the
'Athenæum' spoke of the author as *a writer of quite exceptional ability*,
the 'Academy' praised his *amazing cleverness*; the 'World' said the book was
brilliantly written; and half-a-dozen papers declared there was *not a dull page
in the book*.

Norris. HIS GRACE. By W. E. NORRIS, Author of
'Mademoiselle de Mersac.' *Third Edition. Crown 8vo.* 6s.

An edition in one volume of a novel which in its two volume form quickly ran through
two editions.

'The characters are delineated by the author with his characteristic skill and
vivacity, and the story is told with that ease of manners and Thackerayan insight which give strength of flavour to Mr. Norris's novels. No one can depict
the Englishwoman of the better classes with more subtlety. —*Glasgow Herald*.

'Mr. Norris has drawn a really fine character in the Duke of Hurstbourne, at once
unconventional and very true to the conventionalities of life, weak and strong in
a breath, capable of inane follies and heroic decisions, yet not so definitely por-
trayed as to relieve a reader of the necessity of study on his own behalf'—
Athenæum.

Parker. MRS. FALCHION. By GILBERT PARKER, Author of
'Pierre and His People.' *New Edition in one volume.* 6s.

Mr. Parker's second book has received a warm welcome. The 'Athenæum called
it *a splendid study of character*; the 'Pall Mall Gazette' spoke of the writing as
but little behind anything that has been done by any writer of our time; the
'St. James'' called it *a very striking and admirable novel*; and the 'Westminster Gazette' applied to it the epithet of *distinguished*.

Parker. PIERRE AND HIS PEOPLE. By GILBERT
PARKER. *Crown 8vo. Buckram.* 6s.

'Stories happily conceived and finely executed. There is strength and genius in Mr.
Parker's style.'—*Daily Telegraph*.

Anthony Hope. A CHANGE OF AIR: A Novel. By
ANTHONY HOPE, Author of 'Mr. Witt's Widow,' etc. 1 vol.
Crown 8vo. 6s.

A bright story by Mr. Hope, who has, the *Athenæum* says, 'a decided outlook and
individuality of his own.'

'A graceful, vivacious comedy, true to human nature. The characters are traced
with a masterly hand.'—*Times*.

Pryce. TIME AND THE WOMAN. By RICHARD PRYCE, Author of 'Miss Maxwell's Affections,' 'The Quiet Mrs. Fleming,' etc. New and Cheaper Edition. *Crown 8vo.* 6s.

'Mr. Pryce's work recalls the style of Octave Feuillet, by its clearness, conciseness, its literary reserve.'—*Athenæum.*

Gray. ELSA. A Novel. By E. M'QUEEN GRAY. *Crown 8vo.* 6s.

'A charming novel. The characters are not only powerful sketches, but minutely and carefully finished portraits.'—*Guardian.*

Marriott Watson. DIOGENES OF LONDON and other Sketches. By H. B. MARRIOTT WATSON, Author of 'The Web of the Spider.' *Crown 8vo. Buckram.* 6s.

By all those who delight in the uses of words, who rate the exercise of prose above the exercise of verse, who rejoice in all proofs of its delicacy and its strength, who believe that English prose is chief among the moulds of thought, by these Mr. Marriott Watson's book will be welcomed.'—*National Observer.*

Gilchrist. THE STONE DRAGON. By MURRAY GILCHRIST *Crown 8vo. Buckram.* 6s.

A volume of stories of power so weird and original as to ensure them a ready welcome. 'The author's faults are atoned for by certain positive and admirable merits. The romances have not their counterpart in modern literature, and to read them is a unique experience.'—*National Observer.*

THREE-AND-SIXPENNY NOVELS

Norris. A DEPLORABLE AFFAIR. By W. E. NORRIS, Author of 'His Grace.' *Crown 8vo.* 3s. 6d.

'What with its interesting story, its graceful manner, and its perpetual good humour, the book is as enjoyable as any that has come from its author's pen.'—*Scotsman.*

Pearce. JACO TRELOAR. By J. H. PEARCE, Author of 'Esther Pentreath.' *New Edition. Crown 8vo.* 3s. 6d.

A tragic story of Cornish life by a writer of remarkable power, whose first novel has been highly praised by Mr. Gladstone.

The 'Spectator' speaks of Mr. Pearce as *a writer of exceptional power*; the 'Daily Telegraph' calls it *powerful and picturesque*; the 'Birmingham Post' asserts that it is *a novel of high quality.*

Esmè Stuart. A WOMAN OF FORTY. By ESMÈ STUART, Author of 'Muriel's Marriage,' 'Virginié's Husband,' etc. *New Edition. Crown 8vo. 3s. 6d.*

'The story is well written, and some of the scenes show great dramatic power.'— *Daily Chronicle.*

Fenn. THE STAR GAZERS. By G. MANVILLE FENN, Author of 'Eli's Children,' etc. *New Edition. Cr. 8vo. 3s. 6d.*

'A stirring romance.'—*Western Morning News.*

'Told with all the dramatic power for which Mr. Fenn is conspicuous.'—*Bradford Observer.*

Dickinson. A VICAR'S WIFE. By EVELYN DICKINSON. *Crown 8vo. 3s. 6d.*

Prowse. THE POISON OF ASPS. By R. ORTON PROWSE. *Crown 8vo. 3s. 6d.*

Lynn Linton. THE TRUE HISTORY OF JOSHUA DAVIDSON, Christian and Communist. By E. LYNN LINTON. Eleventh Edition. *Post 8vo. 1s.*

Methuen's Novel Series

A series of copyright Novels, by well-known Authors, bound in red buckram, at the price of three shillings and sixpence. The first volumes are :— **3/6**

1. JACQUETTA. By S. BARING GOULD, Author of 'Mehalah, etc.
2. ARMINELL : A Social Romance. By S. BARING GOULD Author of 'Mehalah,' etc.
3. MARGERY OF QUETHER. By S. BARING GOULD.
4. URITH. By S. BARING GOULD.
5. DERRICK VAUGHAN, NOVELIST. With Portrait of Author. By EDNA LYALL, Author of 'Donovan,' etc.
6. JACK'S FATHER. By W. E. NORRIS.

Other Volumes will be announced in due course.

HALF-CROWN NOVELS
A Series of Novels by popular Authors, tastefully bound in cloth.   2/6

1 THE PLAN OF CAMPAIGN. By F. MABEL ROBINSON.
2. DISENCHANTMENT. By F. MABEL ROBINSON.
3. MR. BUTLER'S WARD. By F. MABEL ROBINSON.
4. HOVENDEN, V.C. By F. MABEL ROBINSON.
5. ELI'S CHILDREN. By G. MANVILLE FENN.
6. A DOUBLE KNOT. By G. MANVILLE FENN.
7. DISARMED. By M. BETHAM EDWARDS.
8. A LOST ILLUSION. By LESLIE KEITH.
9. A MARRIAGE AT SEA. By W. CLARK RUSSELL.
10. IN TENT AND BUNGALOW. By the Author of 'Indian Idylls.'
11. MY STEWARDSHIP. By E. M'QUEEN GRAY.
12. A REVEREND GENTLEMAN. By J. M. COBBAN.
13. THE STORY OF CHRIS. By ROWLAND GREY.

Other volumes will be announced in due course.

Books for Boys and Girls

Baring Gould. THE ICELANDER'S SWORD. By S. BARING GOULD, Author of 'Mehalah,' etc. With Twenty-nine Illustrations by J. MOYR SMITH. *Crown 8vo. 6s.*

A stirring story of Iceland, written for boys by the author of ' In the Roar of the Sea.

Cuthell. TWO LITTLE CHILDREN AND CHING. By EDITH E. CUTHELL. Profusely Illustrated. *Crown 8vo. Cloth, gilt edges. 6s.*

Another story, with a dog hero, by the author of the very popular 'Only a Guard-Room Dog.'

Blake. TODDLEBEN'S HERO. By M. M. BLAKE, Author of 'The Siege of Norwich Castle.' With 36 Illustrations. *Crown 8vo. 5s.*

A story of military life for children.

Cuthell. ONLY A GUARD-ROOM DOG. By Mrs. CUTHELL. With 16 Illustrations by W. PARKINSON. *Square Crown 8vo.* 6*s.*

'This is a charming story. Tangle was but a little mongrel Skye terrier, but he had a big heart in his little body, and played a hero's part more than once. The book can be warmly recommended.'—*Standard.*

Collingwood. THE DOCTOR OF THE JULIET. By HARRY COLLINGWOOD, Author of 'The Pirate Island,' etc. Illustrated by GORDON BROWNE. *Crown 8vo.* 6*s.*

'"The Doctor of the Juliet," well illustrated by Gordon Browne, is one of Harry Collingwood's best efforts.'—*Morning Post.*

Clark Russell. MASTER ROCKAFELLAR'S VOYAGE. By W. CLARK RUSSELL, Author of 'The Wreck of the Grosvenor,' etc. Illustrated by GORDON BROWNE. *Crown 8vo.* 3*s.* 6*d.*

'Mr. Clark Russell's story of "Master Rockafellar's Voyage" will be among the favourites of the Christmas books. There is a rattle and "go" all through it, and its illustrations are charming in themselves, and very much above the average in the way in which they are produced.'—*Guardian.*

Manville Fenn. SYD BELTON : Or, The Boy who would not go to Sea. By G. MANVILLE FENN, Author of 'In the King's Name,' etc. Illustrated by GORDON BROWNE. *Crown 8vo.* 3*s.* 6*d.*

Who among the young story-reading public will not rejoice at the sight of the old combination, so often proved admirable—a story by Manville Fenn, illustrated by Gordon Browne? The story, too, is one of the good old sort, full of life and vigour, breeziness and fun.'—*Journal of Education.*

The Peacock Library

A Series of Books for Girls by well-known Authors, handsomely bound in blue and silver, and well illustrated. Crown 8vo.

3/6

1. A PINCH OF EXPERIENCE. By L. B. WALFORD.
2. THE RED GRANGE. By Mrs. MOLESWORTH.
3. THE SECRET OF MADAME DE MONLUC. By the Author of 'Mdle Mori.'
4. DUMPS. By Mrs. PARR, Author of 'Adam and Eve.'
5. OUT OF THE FASHION. By L. T. MEADE.
6. A GIRL OF THE PEOPLE. By L. T. MEADE.
7. HEPSY GIPSY. By L. T. MEADE.
8. THE HONOURABLE MISS. By L. T. MEADE.
9. MY LAND OF BEULAH. By Mrs. LEITH ADAMS.

University Extension Series

A series of books on historical, literary, and scientific subjects, suitable for extension students and home reading circles. Each volume is complete in itself, and the subjects are treated by competent writers in a broad and philosophic spirit.

Edited by J. E. SYMES, M.A.,

Principal of University College, Nottingham.

Crown 8vo.   Price (with some exceptions) 2s. 6d.

The following volumes are ready :—

THE INDUSTRIAL HISTORY OF ENGLAND. By H. DE B. GIBBINS, M.A., late Scholar of Wadham College, Oxon., Cobden Prizeman. *Third Edition.* With Maps and Plans. 3s.

'A compact and clear story of our industrial development. A study of this concise but luminous book cannot fail to give the reader a clear insight into the principal phenomena of our industrial history. The editor and publishers are to be congratulated on this first volume of their venture, and we shall look with expectant interest for the succeeding volumes of the series.'—*University Extension Journal.*

A HISTORY OF ENGLISH POLITICAL ECONOMY. By L. L. PRICE, M.A., Fellow of Oriel College, Oxon.

PROBLEMS OF POVERTY: An Inquiry into the Industrial Conditions of the Poor. By J. A. HOBSON, M.A.

VICTORIAN POETS. By A. SHARP.

THE FRENCH REVOLUTION. By J. E. SYMES, M.A.

PSYCHOLOGY. By F. S. GRANGER, M.A., Lecturer in Philosophy at University College, Nottingham.

THE EVOLUTION OF PLANT LIFE: Lower Forms. By G. MASSEE, Kew Gardens. With Illustrations.

AIR AND WATER. Professor V. B. LEWES, M.A. Illustrated.

THE CHEMISTRY OF LIFE AND HEALTH. By C. W. KIMMINS, M.A. Camb. Illustrated.

THE MECHANICS OF DAILY LIFE. By V. P. SELLS, M.A. Illustrated.

ENGLISH SOCIAL REFORMERS. H. DE B. GIBBINS, M.A.

ENGLISH TRADE AND FINANCE IN THE SEVEN-
TEENTH CENTURY. By W. A. S. HEWINS, B.A.

THE CHEMISTRY OF FIRE. The Elementary Principles of
Chemistry. By M. M. PATTISON MUIR, M.A. Illustrated.

An exposition of the Elementary Principles of Chemistry.

A TEXT-BOOK OF AGRICULTURAL BOTANY. By M. C.
POTTER, M.A., F.L.S. Illustrated. 3s. 6d.

THE VAULT OF HEAVEN. A Popular Introduction to
Astronomy. By R. A. GREGORY. With numerous Illustrations.
Crown 8vo.

METEOROLOGY. The Elements of Weather and Climate.
By H. N. DICKSON, F.R.S.E., F.R. Met. Soc. Illustrated.

A MANUAL OF ELECTRICAL SCIENCE. By GEORGE
J. BURCH, M.A. With numerous Illustrations. 3s.

Social Questions of To-day

Edited by H. DE B. GIBBINS, M.A.

Crown 8vo. 2s. 6d.

2/6

A series of volumes upon those topics of social, economic,
and industrial interest that are at the present moment foremost in the public mind. Each volume of the series is written by an
author who is an acknowledged authority upon the subject with which
he deals.

The following Volumes of the Series are ready :—

TRADE UNIONISM—NEW AND OLD. By G. HOWELL,
M.P., Author of 'The Conflicts of Capital and Labour.' *Second
Edition.*

THE CO-OPERATIVE MOVEMENT TO-DAY. By G. J.
HOLYOAKE, Author of 'The History of Co-operation.'

MUTUAL THRIFT. By Rev. J. FROME WILKINSON, M.A., Author of 'The Friendly Society Movement.'

PROBLEMS OF POVERTY : An Inquiry into the Industrial Conditions of the Poor. By J. A. HOBSON, M.A.

THE COMMERCE OF NATIONS. By C. F. BASTABLE, M.A., Professor of Economics at Trinity College, Dublin.

THE ALIEN INVASION. By W. H. WILKINS, B.A., Secretary to the Society for Preventing the Immigration of Destitute Aliens.

THE RURAL EXODUS. By P. ANDERSON GRAHAM.

LAND NATIONALIZATION. By HAROLD COX, B.A.

A SHORTER WORKING DAY. By H. DE B. GIBBINS and R. A. HADFIELD, of the Hecla Works, Sheffield.

BACK TO THE LAND : An Inquiry into the Cure for Rural Depopulation. By H. E. MOORE.

Methuen's Commercial Series

BRITISH COMMERCE AND COLONIES FROM ELIZABETH TO VICTORIA. By H. DE B. GIBBINS, M.A., Author of 'The Industrial History of England,' etc., etc. *2s.*

A MANUAL OF FRENCH COMMERCIAL CORRESPONDENCE. By S. E. BALLY, Modern Language Master at the Manchester Grammar School. *2s.*

COMMERCIAL GEOGRAPHY, with special reference to Trade Routes, New Markets, and Manufacturing Districts. By L. D. LYDE, M.A., of The Academy, Glasgow. *2s.*

COMMERCIAL EXAMINATION PAPERS. By H. DE B. GIBBINS, M.A. *1s. 6d.*

THE ECONOMICS OF COMMERCE. By H. DE B. GIBBINS, M.A. *1s. 6d.*

Edinburgh : T. and A. CONSTABLE, Printers to Her Majesty.

www.ingramcontent.com/pod-product-compliance
Lightning Source LLC
Chambersburg PA
CBHW030951110726
47900CB00004B/1221